THE RELUCTANT BRIDE
WAS WAITING. . . .

The bridegroom approached—not as one who cele-
brates his good fortune, but sullenly, tragically
drunk.

Old Belllounds leaped off the porch. His gray hair
stood up like a lion's mane. His strides were like a
giant's. With a lunge he met his reeling son, swinging a huge fist into the glowering face. Jack fell
limply to the ground.

"Lay there, yau damned prodigal!" the old man
roared, terrible in his rage. "You disgrace me—an'
you disgrace the girl who's been a daughter to me!
. . . If you ever have another weddin' day, it'll not be
me who sets it!"

Books by Zane Grey

Amber's Mirage and Other
   Stories
Arizona Ames
The Arizona Clan
Black Mesa
The Border Legion
Boulder Dam
The Call of the Canyon
Captives of the Desert
Code of the West
Deerstalker
Desert Gold
The Desert of Wheat
Drift Fence
The Dude Ranger
Fighting Caravans
Forlorn River
The Fugitive Trail
The Hash Knife Outfit
The Heritage of the Desert
Horse Heaven Hill
Knights of the Range
The Light of Western Stars
Lone Star Ranger
Lost Pueblo
The Lost Wagon Train
Majesty's Rancho
Man of the Forest
The Maverick Queen
Raiders of the Spanish Peaks

The Rainbow Trail
The Ranger and Other Stories
Riders of the Purple Sage
Robbers' Roost
Rogue River Feud
The Secret of Quaking Asp
   Cabin and Other Stories
Shadow on the Trail
The Shepherd of Guadeloupe
Stairs of Sand
Sunset Pass
Tappan's Burro
30,000 on the Hoof
Thunder Mountain
The Thundering Herd
To the Last Man
The Trail Driver
Twin Sombreros
Under the Tonto Rim
The U.P. Trail
Valley of Wild Horses
The Vanishing American
Wanderer of the Wasteland
West of the Pecos
Western Union
Wilderness Trek
Wildfire
Wild Horse Mesa
Wyoming

Published by POCKET BOOKS

ZANE GREY

THE MYSTERIOUS RIDER

PUBLISHED BY POCKET BOOKS NEW YORK

POCKET BOOKS, a division of Simon & Schuster, Inc.
1230 Avenue of the Americas, New York, N.Y. 10020

Copyright 1921 by Zane Grey; copyright renewed 1948
by Lina Elise Grey

Published by arrangement with Harper & Row, Publishers, Inc.

ISBN: 0-671-63169-1

First Pocket Books printing March, 1969

15   14   13   12   11   10

POCKET and colophon are registered trademarks
of Simon & Schuster, Inc.

Printed in the U.S.A.

THE MYSTERIOUS RIDER

A SEPTEMBER SUN, losing some of its heat if not its brilliance, was dropping low in the west over the black Colorado range. Purple haze began to thicken in the timbered notches. Gray foothills, round and billowy, rolled down from the higher country. They were smooth, sweeping, with long velvety slopes and isolated patches of aspens that blazed in autumn gold. Splotches of red vine colored the soft gray of sage. Old White Slides, a mountain scarred by avalanche, towered with bleak rocky peak above the valley, sheltering it from the north.

A girl rode along the slope, with gaze on the sweep and range and color of the mountain fastness that was her home. She followed an old trail which led to a bluff overlooking an arm of the valley. Once it had been a familiar lookout for her, but she had not visited the place of late. It was associated with serious hours of her life. Here seven years before, when she was twelve, she had made a hard choice to please her guardian—the old rancher whom she loved and called father, who had indeed been a father to her. That choice had been to go to school in Denver. Four years she had lived away from her beloved gray hills and black mountains. Only once since her return had she climbed to this height, and that occasion, too, was memorable as an unhappy hour. It had been three years ago. Today girlish ordeals and griefs seemed back in the past: she was a woman at nineteen and face to face with the first great problem in her life.

The trail came up back of the bluff, through a clump of aspens with white trunks and yellow fluttering leaves, and led across a level bench of luxuriant grass and wild flowers to the rocky edge.

She dismounted and threw the bridle. Her mustang, used

to being petted, rubbed his sleek, dark head against her and evidently expected like demonstration in return, but as none was forthcoming he bent his nose to the grass and began grazing. The girl's eyes were intent upon some waving, slender, white-and-blue flowers. They smiled up wanly, like pale stars, out of the long grass that had a tinge of gold.

"Columbines," she mused, wistfully, as she plucked several of the flowers and held them up to gaze wonderingly at them, as if to see in them some revelation of the mystery that shrouded her birth and her name. Then she stood with dreamy gaze upon the distant ranges.

"Columbine! . . . So they named me—those miners who found me—a baby—lost in the woods—asleep among the columbines." She spoke aloud, as if the sound of her voice might convince her.

So much of the mystery of her had been revealed that day by the man she had always called father. Vaguely she had always been conscious of some mystery, something strange about her childhood, some relation never explained.

"No name but Columbine," she whispered, sadly, and now she understood a strange longing of her heart.

Scarcely an hour back, as she ran down the wide porch of White Slides ranch-house, she had encountered the man who had taken care of her all her life. He had looked upon her as kindly and fatherly as of old, yet with a difference. She seemed to see him as old Bill Belllounds, pioneer and rancher, of huge frame and broad face, hard and scarred and grizzled, with big eyes of blue fire.

"Collie," the old man had said, "I reckon hyar's news. A letter from Jack. . . . He's comin' home."

Belllounds had waved the letter. His huge hand trembled as he reached to put it on her shoulder. The hardness of him seemed strangely softened. Jack was his son. Buster Jack, the range had always called him, with other terms, less kind, that never got to the ears of his father. Jack had been sent away three years ago, just before Columbine's return from school. Therefore she had not seen him for over seven years. But she remembered him well—a big, rangy boy, handsome and wild, who had made her childhood almost unendurable.

"Yes—my son—Jack—he's comin' home," said Belllounds,

with a break in his voice. "An', Collie—now I must tell you somethin'."

"Yes, dad," she had replied, with strong clasp of the heavy hand on her shoulder.

"Thet's just it, lass. I ain't your dad. I've tried to be a dad to you an' I've loved you as my own. But you're not flesh an' blood of mine. An' now I must tell you."

The brief story followed. Seventeen years ago miners working a claim of Belllounds's in the mountains above Middle Park had found a child asleep in the columbines along the trail. Near that point Indians, probably Arapahoes coming across the mountains to attack the Utes, had captured or killed the occupants of a prairie-schooner. There was no other clue. The miners took the child to their camp, fed and cared for it, and, after the manner of their kind, named it Columbine. Then they brought it to Belllounds.

"Collie," said the old rancher, "it needn't never have been told, an' wouldn't but fer one reason. I'm gettin' old. I reckon I'd never split my property between you an' Jack. So I mean you an' him to marry. You always steadied Jack. With a wife like you'll be—wal, mebbe Jack'll—"

"Dad!" burst out Columbine. "Marry Jack! . . . Why, I—I don't even remember him!"

"Haw! Haw!" laughed Belllounds. "Wal, you dog-gone soon will. Jack's in Kremmlin', an' he'll be hyar tonight or tomorrow."

"But—I—I don't l-love him," faltered Columbine.

The old man lost his mirth; the strong-lined face resumed its hard cast; the big eyes smoldered. Her appealing objection had wounded him. She was reminded of how sensitive the old man had always been to any reflection cast upon his son.

"Wal, thet's onlucky," he replied, gruffly. "Mebbe you'll change. I reckon no girl could help a boy much, onless she cared for him. Anyway, you an' Jack will marry."

He had stalked away and Columbine had ridden her mustang far up the valley slope where she could be alone. Standing on the verge of the bluff, she suddenly became aware that the quiet and solitude of her lonely resting-place had been disrupted. Cattle were bawling below her and along the slope of Old White Slides and on the grassy uplands above. She had forgotten that the cattle were being driven down into the lowlands for the fall round-up. A great red-and-white-spotted herd was milling in the park just beneath her. Calves and yearlings were making the dust fly along the mountain slope; wild old steers were crashing in the sage, holding level, unwilling to be driven down; cows were running and lowing for their lost ones. Melodious and clear rose the clarion calls of the cowboys. The cattle knew those calls and only the wild steers kept up-grade.

Columbine also knew each call and to which cowboy it belonged. They sang and yelled and swore, but it was all music to her. Here and there along the slope, where the aspen groves clustered, a horse would flash across an open space; the dust would fly, and a cowboy would peal out a lusty yell that rang along the slope and echoed under the bluff and lingered long after the daring rider had vanished in the steep thickets.

"I wonder which is Wils," murmured Columbine, as she watched and listened, vaguely conscious of a little difference, a strange check in her remembrance of this particular cowboy. She felt the change, yet did not understand. One after one she recognized the riders on the slopes below, but Wilson Moore was not among them. He must be above her, then, and she turned to gaze across the grassy bluff, up the long, yellow slope, to where the gleaming aspens half hid a red bluff of mountain, towering aloft. Then from far to her left, high up a scrubby ridge of the slope, rang down a voice that thrilled her: *"Go—aloong—you—ooooo."* Red cattle dashed pell-mell down the slope, raising the dust, tearing the brush, rolling rocks, and letting out hoarse bawls.

"Whoop-ee!" High-pitched and pealing came a clearer yell.

Columbine saw a white mustang flash out on top of the ridge, silhouetted against the blue, with mane and tail flying. His gait on that edge of steep slope proved his rider to be a reckless cowboy for whom no heights or depths had terrors. She would have recognized him from the way he rode, if she had not known the slim, erect figure. The cowboy saw her instantly. He pulled the mustang, about to plunge down the slope, and lifted him, rearing and wheeling. Then Columbine waved her hand. The cowboy spurred his horse along the crest of the ridge, disappeared behind the grove of aspens, and came in sight again around to the right, where on the grassy bench he slowed to a walk in descent to the bluff.

The girl watched him come, conscious of an unfamiliar sense of uncertainty in this meeting, and of the fact that she was seeing him differently from any other time in the years he had been a playmate, a friend, almost like a brother. He had ridden for Belllounds for years, and was a cowboy because he loved cattle well and horses better, and above all a life in the open. Unlike most cowboys, he had been to school; he had a family in Denver that objected to his wild range life, and often importuned him to come home; he seemed aloof sometimes and not readily understood.

While many thoughts whirled through Columbine's mind she watched the cowboy ride slowly down to her, and she became more concerned with a sudden restraint. How was Wilson going to take the news of this forced change about to come in her life? That thought leaped up. It gave her a strange pang. But she and he were only good friends. As to that, she reflected, of late they had not been the friends and comrades they formerly were. In the thrilling uncertainty of this meeting she had forgotten his distant manner and the absence of little attentions she had missed.

By this time the cowboy had reached the level, and with the lazy grace of his kind slipped out of the saddle. He was tall, slim, round-limbed, with the small hips of a rider, and square, though not broad, shoulders. He stood straight like an Indian. His eyes were hazel, his features regular, his face bronzed. All men of the open had still, lean, strong faces, but added to this in him was a steadiness of expression, a restraint that seemed to hide sadness.

"Howdy, Columbine!" he said. "What are you doing up here? You might get run over."

"Hello, Wils!" she replied, slowly. "Oh, I guess I can keep out of the way."

"Some bad steers in that bunch. If any of them run over here Pronto will leave you to walk home. That mustang hates cattle. And he's only half broke, you know."

"I forgot you were driving today," she replied, and looked away from him. There was a moment's pause—long, it seemed to her.

"What'd you come for?" he asked, curiously.

"I wanted to gather columbines. See." She held out the nodding flowers toward him. "Take one. . . . Do you like them?"

"Yes. I like columbine," he replied, taking one of them. His keen hazel eyes softened, darkened. "Colorado's flower."

"Columbine! . . . It is my name."

"Well, could you have a better? It sure suits you."

"Why?" she asked, and she looked at him again.

"You're slender—graceful. You sort of hold your head high and proud. Your skin is white. Your eyes are blue. Not bluebell blue, but columbine blue—and they turn purple when you're angry."

"Compliments! Wilson, this is new kind of talk for you," she said.

"You're different today."

"Yes, I am." She looked across the valley toward the westering sun, and the slight flush faded from her cheeks. "I have no right to hold my head proud. No one knows who I am—where I came from."

"As if that made any difference!" he exclaimed.

"Belllounds is not my dad. I have no dad. I was a waif. They found me in the woods—a baby—lost among the flowers. Columbine Belllounds I've always been. But that is not my name. No one can tell what my name really is."

"I knew your story years ago, Columbine," he replied, earnestly. "Everybody knows. Old Bill ought to have told you long before this. But he loves you. So does—everybody. You must not let this knowledge sadden you. . . . I'm sorry you've never known a mother or a sister. Why, I could tell you of many orphans who—whose stories were different."

"You don't understand. I've been happy. I've not longed for any—any one except a mother. It's only—"

"What don't I understand?"

"I've not told you all."

"No? Well, go on," he said, slowly.

Meaning of the hesitation and the restraint that had obstructed her thought now flashed over Columbine. It lay in what Wilson Moore might think of her prospective marriage to Jack Belllounds. Still she could not guess why that should make her feel strangely uncertain of the ground she stood on or how it could cause a constraint she had to fight herself to hide. Moreover, to her annoyance, she found that she was evading his direct request for the news she had withheld.

"Jack Belllounds is coming home tonight or tomorrow," she said. Then, waiting for her companion to reply, she kept an unseeing gaze upon the scanty pines fringing Old White Slides. But no reply appeared to be forthcoming from Moore. His silence compelled her to turn to him. The cowboy's face had subtly altered; it was darker with a tinge of red under the bronze; and his lower lip was released from his teeth, even as she looked. He had his eyes intent upon the lasso he was coiling. Suddenly he faced her and the dark fire of his eyes gave her a shock.

"I've been expecting that shorthorn back for months," he said, bluntly.

"You—never—liked Jack?" queried Columbine, slowly. That was not what she wanted to say, but the thought spoke itself.

"I should smile I never did."

"Ever since you and he fought—long ago—all over—"

His sharp gesture made the coiled lasso loosen.

"Ever since I licked him good—don't forget that," interrupted Wilson. The red had faded from the bronze.

"Yes, you licked him," mused Columbine. "I remember that. And Jack's hated you ever since."

"There's been no love lost."

"But, Wils, you never before talked this way—spoke out so—against Jack," she protested.

"Well, I'm not the kind to talk behind a fellow's back. But I'm not mealy-mouthed, either, and—and—"

He did not complete the sentence and his meaning was enigmatic. Altogether Moore seemed not like himself. The fact disturbed Columbine. Always she had confided in him. Here was a most complex situation—she burned to tell him, yet somehow feared to—she felt an incomprehensible satisfaction in his bitter reference to Jack—she seemed to realize that she valued Wilson's friendship more than she had known, and now for some strange reason it was slipping from her.

"We—we were such good friends—pards," said Columbine, hurriedly and irrelevantly.

"Who?" He stared at her.

"Why, you—and me."

"Oh!" His tone softened, but there was still disapproval in his glance. "What of that?"

"Something has happened to make me think I've missed you—lately—that's all."

"Ahuh!" His tone held finality and bitterness, but he would not commit himself. Columbine sensed a pride in him that seemed the cause of his aloofness.

"Wilson, why have you been different lately?" she asked, plaintively.

"What's the good to tell you now?" he queried, in reply.

That gave her a blank sense of actual loss. She had lived in dreams and he in realities. Right now she could not dispel her dream—see and understand all that he seemed to. She felt like a child, then, growing old swiftly. The strange past longing for a mother surged up in her like a strong tide. Some one to lean on, some one who loved her, some one to help her in this hour when fatality knocked at the door of her youth—how she needed that!

"It might be bad for me—to tell me, but tell me, anyhow," she said, finally, answering as some one older than she had been an hour ago—to something feminine that leaped up. She did not understand this impulse, but it was in her.

"No!" declared Moore, with dark red staining his face. He slapped the lasso against his saddle, and tied it with clumsy hands. He did not look at her. His tone expressed anger and amaze.

"Dad says I must marry Jack," she said, with a sudden return to her natural simplicity.

"I heard him tell that months ago," snapped Moore.

"You did! Was that—why?" she whispered.

"It was," he answered, ringingly.

"But that was no reason for you to be—be—to stay away from me," she declared, with rising spirit.

He laughed shortly.

"Wils, didn't you like me any more after dad said that?" she queried.

"Columbine, a girl nineteen years and about to—to get married—ought not to be a fool," he replied, with sarcasm.

"I'm not a fool," she rejoined, hotly.

"You ask fool questions."

"Well, you *didn't* like me afterward or you'd never have mistreated me."

"If you say I mistreated you—you say what's untrue," he replied, just as hotly.

They had never been so near a quarrel before. Columbine experienced a sensation new to her—a commingling of fear, heat, and pang, it seemed, all in one throb. Wilson was hurting her. A quiver ran all over her, along her veins, swelling and tingling.

"You mean I lie?" she flashed.

"Yes, I do—if—"

But before he could conclude she slapped his face. It grew pale then, while she began to tremble.

"Oh—I didn't intend that. Forgive me," she faltered.

He rubbed his cheek. The hurt had not been great, so far as the blow was concerned. But his eyes were dark with pain and anger.

"Oh, don't distress yourself," he burst out. "You slapped me before—once, years ago—for kissing you. I—I apologize for saying you lied. You're only out of your head. So am I."

That poured oil upon the troubled waters. The cowboy appeared to be hesitating between sudden flight and the risk of staying longer.

"Maybe that's it," replied Columbine, with a half-laugh. She was not far from tears and fury with herself. "Let us make up—be friends again."

Moore squared around aggressively. He seemed to fortify himself against something in her. She felt that. But his face grew harder and older than she had ever seen it.

"Columbine, do *you* know where Jack Belllounds has been

for these three years?" he asked, deliberately, entirely ignoring her overtures of friendship.

"No. Somebody said Denver. Some one else said Kansas City. I never asked dad, because I knew Jack had been sent away. I've supposed he was working—making a man of himself."

"Well, I hope to Heaven—for your sake—what you suppose comes true," returned Moore, with exceeding bitterness.

"Do *you* know where he has been?" asked Columbine. Some strange feeling prompted that. There was a mystery here. Wilson's agitation seemed strange and deep.

"Yes, I do." The cowboy bit that out through closing teeth, as if locking them against an almost overmastering temptation.

Columbine lost her curiosity. She was woman enough to realize that there might well be facts which would only make her situation harder.

"Wilson," she began, hurriedly, "I owe all I am to dad. He has cared for me—sent me to school. He has been so good to me. I've loved him always. It would be a shabby return for all his protection and love if—if I refused—"

"Old Bill is the best man ever," interrupted Moore, as if to repudiate any hint of disloyalty to his employer. "Everybody in Middle Park and all over owes Bill something. He's sure good. There never was anything wrong with him except his crazy blindness about his son. Buster Jack—the—the—"

Columbine put a hand over Moore's lips.

"The man I must marry," she said, solemnly.

"You must—you will?" he demanded.

"Of course. What else could I do? I never thought of refusing."

"Columbine!" Wilson's cry was so poignant, his gesture so violent, his dark eyes so piercing that Columbine sustained a shock that held her trembling and mute. "How can you love Jack Belllounds? You were twelve years old when you saw him last. How can you love him?"

"I don't," replied Columbine.

"Then how could you marry him?"

"I owe dad obedience. It's his hope that I can steady Jack."

"Steady Jack!" exclaimed Moore, passionately. "Why, you girl—you white-faced flower! *You* with your innocence and sweetness steady that damned pup! My Heavens! He was a gambler and a drunkard. He—"

"Hush!" implored Columbine.

"He cheated at cards," declared the cowboy, with a scorn that placed that vice as utterly base.

"But Jack was only a wild boy," replied Columbine, trying with brave words to champion the son of the man she loved as her father. "He has been sent away to work. He'll have outgrown that wildness. He'll come home a man."

"Bah!" cried Moore, harshly.

Columbine felt a sinking within her. Where was her strength? She, who could walk and ride so many miles, to become sick with an inward quaking! It was childish. She struggled to hide her weakness from him.

"It's not like you to be this way," she said. "You used to be generous. Am I to blame? Did I choose my life?"

Moore looked quickly away from her, and standing with a hand on his horse, he was silent for a moment. The squaring of his shoulders bore testimony to his thought. Presently he swung up into the saddle. The mustang snorted and champed the bit and tossed his head, ready to bolt.

"Forget my temper," begged the cowboy, looking down upon Columbine. "I take it all back. I'm sorry. Don't let a word of mine worry you. I was only jealous."

"Jealous!" exclaimed Columbine, wonderingly.

"Yes. That makes a fellow see red and green. Bad medicine! You never felt it."

"What were you jealous of?" asked Columbine.

The cowboy had himself in hand now and he regarded her with a grim amusement.

"Well, Columbine, it's like a story," he replied. "I'm the fellow disowned by his family—a wanderer of the wilds—no good—and no prospects. . . . Now our friend Jack, he's handsome and rich. He has a doting old dad. Cattle, horses—ranches! He wins the girl. See!"

Spurring his mustang, the cowboy rode away. At the edge of the slope he turned in the saddle. "I've got to drive in this bunch of cattle. It's late. You hurry home." Then he was gone. The stones cracked and rolled down under the side of the bluff.

Columbine stood where he had left her; dubious, yet with the blood still hot in her cheeks.

"Jealous? . . . He wins the girl?" she murmured in repetition to herself. "What ever could he have meant? He didn't mean—he didn't—"

The simple, logical interpretation of Wilson's words opened Columbine's mind to a disturbing possibility of which she had never dreamed. That he might love her! If he did, why had he not said so? Jealous, maybe, but he did not love her! The next throb of thought was like a knock at a door of her heart—a door never yet opened, inside which seemed a mystery of feeling, of hope, despair, unknown longing, and clamorous voices. The woman just born in her, instinctive and self-preservative, shut that door before she had more than a glimpse inside. But then she felt her heart swell with its nameless burdens.

Pronto was grazing near at hand. She caught him and mounted. It struck her then that her hands were numb with cold. The wind had ceased fluttering the aspens, but the yellow leaves were falling, rustling. Out on the brow of the slope she faced home and the west.

A glorious Colorado sunset had just reached the wonderful height of its color and transformation. The sage slopes below her seemed rosy velvet; the golden aspens on the farther reaches were on fire at the tips; the foothills rolled clear and mellow and rich in the light; the gulf of distance on to the great black range was veiled in mountain purple; and the dim peaks beyond the range stood up, sunset-flushed and grand. The narrow belt of blue sky between crags and clouds was like a river full of fleecy sails and wisps of silver. Above towered a pall of dark cloud, full of the shades of approaching night.

"Oh, beautiful!" breathed the girl, with all her worship of nature. That wild world of sunset grandeur and loneliness and beauty was hers. Over there, under a peak of the black range, was the place where she had been found, a baby, lost in the forest. She belonged to that, and so it belonged to her. Strength came to her from the glory of light on the hills.

Pronto shot up his ears and checked his trot.

"What is it, boy?" called Columbine. The trail was getting dark. Shadows were creeping up the slope as she rode down to meet them. The mustang had keen sight and scent. She reined him to a halt.

All was silent. The valley had begun to shade on the far side and the rose and gold seemed fading from the nearer. Below, on the level floor of the valley, lay the rambling old ranch-house, with the cabins nestling around, and the corrals leading out to the soft hay-fields, misty and gray in the twilight. A single light gleamed. It was like a beacon.

The air was cold with a nip of frost. From far on the other side of the ridge she had descended came the bawls of the last stragging cattle of the round-up. But surely Pronto had not shot up his ears for them. As if in answer a wild sound pealed down the slope, making the mustang jump. Columbine had heard it before.

"Pronto, it's only a wolf," she soothed him.

The peal was loud, rather harsh at first, then softened to a mourn, wild, lonely, haunting. A pack of coyotes barked in angry answer, a sharp, staccato, yelping chorus, the more piercing notes biting on the cold night air. These mountain mourns and yelps were music to Columbine. She rode on down the trail in the gathering darkness, less afraid of the night and its wild denizens than of what awaited her at White Slides Ranch.

2

DARKNESS SETTLED DOWN like a black mantle over the valley. Columbine rather hoped to find Wilson waiting to take care of her horse, as used to be his habit, but she was disappointed. No light showed from the cabin in which the cowboys lived; he had not yet come in from the round-up. She unsaddled, and turned Pronto loose in the pasture.

The windows of the long, low ranch-house were bright squares in the blackness, sending cheerful rays afar. Columbine wondered in trepidation if Jack Belllounds had come home. It required effort of will to approach the house. Yet since she must meet him, the sooner the ordeal was over the better. Nevertheless she tiptoed past the bright windows, and went all the length of the long porch, and turned around and went back, and then hesitated, fighting a slow drag of her spirit, an oppression upon her heart. The door was crude and heavy. It opened hard.

Columbine entered a big room lighted by a lamp on the upper table and by blazing logs in a huge stone fireplace. This was the living-room, rather gloomy in the corners, and bare, but comfortable, for all simple needs. The logs were new and the chinks between them filled with clay, still white, showing that the house was of recent build.

The rancher, Belllounds, sat in his easy-chair before the fire, his big, horny hands extended to the warmth. He was in his shirt-sleeves, a gray, bold-faced man, of over sixty years, still muscular and rugged.

At Columbine's entrance he raised his drooping head, and so removed the suggestion of sadness in his posture.

"Wal, lass, hyar you are," was his greeting. "Jake has been hollerin' thet chuck was ready. Now we can eat."

"Dad—did—did your son come?" asked Columbine.

"No. I got word jest at sundown. One of Baker's cow-punchers from up the valley. He rode up from Kremmlin' an' stopped to say Jack was celebratin' his arrival by too much red liquor. Reckon he won't be home tonight. Mebbe to-morrow."

Belllounds spoke in an even, heavy tone, without any apparent feeling. Always he was mercilessly frank and never spared the truth. But Columbine, who knew him well, felt how this news flayed him. Resentment stirred in her toward the wayward son, but she knew better than to voice it.

"Natural like, I reckon, fer Jack to feel gay on gettin' home. I ain't holdin' thet ag'in' him. These last three years must have been gallin' to thet boy."

Columbine stretched her hands to the blaze.

"It's cold, dad," she averred. "I didn't dress warmly, so I nearly froze. Autumn is here and there's frost in the air. Oh, the hills were all gold and red—the aspen leaves were falling. I love autumn, but it means winter is so near."

"Wal, wal, time flies," sighed the old man. "Where'd you ride?"

"Up the west slope to the bluff. It's far. I don't go there often."

"Meet any of the boys? I sent the outfit to drive stock down from the mountain. I've lost a good many head lately. They're eatin' some weed thet poisons them. They swell up an' die. Wuss this year than ever before."

"Why, that is serious, dad! Poor things! That's worse than eating loco. . . . Yes, I met Wilson Moore driving down the slope."

"Ahuh! Wal, let's eat."

They took seats at the table which the cook, Jake, was loading with steaming victuals. Supper appeared to be a rather sumptuous one this evening, in honor of the expected guest, who had not come. Columbine helped the old man to his favorite dishes, stealing furtive glances at his lined and shadowed face. She sensed a subtle change in him since the afternoon, but could not see any sign of it in his look or demeanor. His appetite was as hearty as ever.

"So you met Wils. Is he still makin' up to you?" asked Belllounds, presently.

"No, he isn't. I don't see that he ever did—that—dad," she replied.

"You're a kid in mind an' a woman in body. Thet cow-puncher has been lovesick over you since you were a little girl. It's what kept him hyar ridin' fer me."

"Dad, I don't believe it," said Columbine, feeling the blood at her temples. "You always imagined such things about Wilson, and the other boys as well."

"Ahuh! I'm an old fool about wimmen, hey? Mebbe I was years ago. But I can see now. . . . Didn't Wils always get ory-eyed when any of the other boys shined up to you?"

"I can't remember that he did," replied Columbine. She felt a desire to laugh, yet the subject was anything but amusing to her.

"Wal, you've always been innocent-like. Thank the Lord you never leaned to tricks of most pretty lasses, makin' eyes at all the men. Anyway, a matter of three months ago I told Wils to keep away from you—thet you were not fer any poor cowpuncher."

"You never liked him. Why? Was it fair, taking him as boys come?"

"Wal, I reckon it wasn't," replied Belllounds, and as he looked up his broad face changed to ruddy color. "Thet boy's the best rider an' roper I've had in years. He ain't the bronco-bustin' kind. He never drank. He was honest an' will-in'. He saves his money. He's good at handlin' stock. Thet boy will be a rich rancher some day."

"Strange, then, you never liked him," murmured Columbine. She felt ashamed of the good it did her to hear Wilson praised.

"No, it ain't strange. I have my own reasons," replied Belllounds, gruffly, as he resumed eating.

Columbine believed she could guess the cause of the old rancher's unreasonable antipathy for this cowboy. Not improbably it was because Wilson had always been superior in every way to Jack Belllounds. The boys had been natural rivals in everything pertaining to life on the range. What Bill Bell-

lounds admired most in men was paramount in Wilson and
lacking in his own son.

"Will you put Jack in charge of your ranches, now?" asked
Columbine.

"Not much. I reckon I'll try him hyar at White Slides as
foreman. An' if he runs the outfit, then I'll see."

"Dad, he'll never run the White Slides outfit," asserted
Columbine.

"Wal, it is a hard bunch, I'll agree. But I reckon the boys
will stay, exceptin', mebbe, Wils. An' it'll be jest as well
fer him to leave."

"It's not good business to send away your best cowboy.
I've heard you complain lately of lack of men."

"I sure do need men," replied Belllounds, seriously. "Stock
gettin' more'n we can handle. I sent word over the range to
Meeker, hopin' to get some men there. What I need most
jest now is a fellar who knows dogs an' who'll hunt down the
wolves an' lions an' bears thet're livin' off my cattle."

"Dad, you need a whole outfit to handle the packs of
hounds you've got. Such an assortment of them! There must
be a hundred. Only yesterday some man brought a lot of
mangy, long-eared canines. It's funny. Why, dad, you're the
laughing-stock of the range!"

"Yes, an' the range'll be thankin' me when I rid it of all
these varmints," declared Belllounds. "Lass, I swore I'd buy
every dog fetched to me, until I had enough to kill off the
coyotes an' lofers an' lions. I'll do it, too. But I need a hunter."

"Why not put Wilson Moore in charge of the hounds?
He's a hunter."

"Wal, lass, thet might be a good idee," replied the rancher,
nodding his grizzled head. "Say, you're sort of wantin' me to
keep Wils on."

"Yes, dad."

"Why? Do you like him so much?"

"I like him—of course. He has been almost a brother to
me."

"Ahuh! Wal, are you sure you don't like him more'n you
ought—considerin' what's in the wind?"

"Yes, I'm sure I don't," replied Columbine, with tingling cheeks.

"Wal, I'm glad of thet. Reckon it'll be no great matter whether Wils stays or leaves. If he wants to I'll give him a job with the hounds."

That evening Columbine went to her room early. It was a cozy little blanketed nest which she had arranged and furnished herself. There was a little square window cut through the logs and through which many a night the snow had blown in upon her bed. She loved her little isolated refuge. This night it was cold, the first time this autumn, and the lighted lamp, though brightening the room, did not make it appreciably warmer. There was a stone fireplace, but as she had neglected to bring in wood she could not start a fire. So she undressed, blew out the lamp, and went to bed.

Columbine was soon warm, and the darkness of her little room seemed good to her. Sleep she felt never would come that night. She wanted to think; she could not help but think; and she tried to halt the whirl of her mind. Wilson Moore occupied the foremost place in her varying thoughts—a fact quite remarkable and unaccountable. She tried to change it. In vain! Wilson persisted—on his white mustang flying across the ridgetop—coming to her as never before—with his anger and disapproval—his strange, poignant cry, "Columbine!" that haunted her—with his bitter smile and his resignation and his mocking talk of jealousy. He persisted and grew with the old rancher's frank praise.

"I must not think of him," she whispered. "Why, I'll be— be married soon. . . . Married!"

That word transformed her thought, and where she had thrilled she now felt cold. She revolved the fact in mind.

"It's true, I'll be married, because I ought—I must," she said, half aloud. "Because I can't help myself. I ought to want to—for dad's sake. . . . But I don't—I don't."

She longed above all things to be good, loyal, loving, helpful, to show her gratitude for the home and the affection that had been bestowed upon a nameless waif. Bill Belllounds had not been under any obligation to succor a strange, lost child. He had done it because he was big, noble. Many splendid deeds had been laid at the old rancher's door. She was not of an ungrateful nature. She meant to pay. But the significance of the price began to dawn upon her.

"It will change my whole life," she whispered, aghast.

But how? Columbine pondered. She must go over the details of that change. No mother had ever taught her. The few women that had been in the Belllounds home from time to time had not been sympathetic or had not stayed long enough to help her much. Even her school life in Denver had left her still a child as regarded the serious problems of women.

"If I'm his wife," she went on, "I'll have to be with him— I'll have to give up this little room—I'll never be free—alone —happy, any more."

That was the first detail she enumerated. It was also the last. Realization came with a sickening little shudder. And that moment gave birth to the nucleus of an unconscious revolt.

The coyotes were howling. Wild, sharp, sweet notes! They soothed her troubled, aching head, lulled her toward sleep, reminded her of the gold-and-purple sunset, and the slopes of sage, the lonely heights, and the beauty that would never change. On the morrow, she drowsily thought, she would persuade Wilson not to kill all the coyotes; to leave a few, because she loved them.

Bill Belllounds had settled in Middle Park in 1860. It was wild country, a home of the Ute Indians, and a natural paradise for elk, deer, antelope, buffalo. The mountain ranges harbored bear. These ranges sheltered the rolling valley land which some explorer had named Middle Park in earlier days.

Much of this inclosed table-land was prairie, where long grass and wild flowers grew luxuriantly. Belllounds was a cattleman, and he saw the possibilities there. To which end he sought the friendship of Piah, chief of the Utes. This noble red man was well disposed toward the white settlers, and his tribe, during those troublous times, kept peace with these invaders of their mountain home.

In 1868 Belllounds was instrumental in persuading the Utes
to relinquish Middle Park. The slopes of the hills were heavily
timbered; gold and silver had been found in the mountains.
It was a country that attracted prospectors, cattlemen, lum-
bermen. The summer season was not long enough to grow
grain, and the nights too frosty for corn; otherwise Middle
Park would have increased rapidly in population.

In the years that succeeded the departure of the Utes Bill
Belllounds developed several cattle-ranches and acquired others. White Slides Ranch lay some twenty-old miles from Middle Park, being a winding arm of the main valley land. Its
development was a matter of later years, and Belllounds
lived there because the country was wilder. The rancher, as
he advanced in years, seemed to want to keep the loneliness
that had been his in earlier days. At the time of the return of
his son to White Slides Belllounds was rich in cattle and
land, but he avowed frankly that he had not saved any money, and probably never would. His hand was always open
to every man and he never remembered an obligation. He
trusted every one. A proud boast of his was that neither
white man nor red man had ever betrayed his trust. His cowboys took advantage of him, his neighbors imposed upon
him, but none were there who did not make good their debts
of service or stock. Belllounds was one of the great pioneers
of the frontier days to whom the West owed its settlement;
and he was finer than most, because he proved that the Indians, if not robbed or driven, would respond to friendliness.

Belllounds was not seen at his customary tasks on the day
he expected his son. He walked in the fields and around the
corrals; he often paced up and down the porch, scanning
the horizon below, where the road from Kremmling showed
white down the valley; and part of the time he stayed indoors.

It so happened that early in the afternoon he came out
in time to see a buckboard, drawn by dust-and-lather-stained
horses, pull into the yard. And then he saw his son. Some
of the cowboys came running. There were greetings to the
driver, who appeared well known to them.

Jack Belllounds did not look at them. He threw a bag out

of the buckboard and then clambered down slowly, to go
toward the porch.

"Wal, Jack—my son—I'm sure glad you're back home,"
said the old rancher, striding forward. His voice was deep and
full, singularly rich. But that was the only sign of feeling he
showed.

"Howdy—dad!" replied the son, not heartily, as he put
out his hand to his father's.

Jack Belllounds's form was tall, with a promise of his father's bulk. But he did not walk erect; he slouched a little. His
face was pale, showing he had not of late been used to sun
and wind. Any stranger would have seen the resemblance of
boy to man; would have granted the handsome boldness, but
denied the strength. The lower part of Jack Belllounds's face
was weak.

The constraint of this meeting was manifest mostly in
the manner of the son. He looked ashamed, almost sullen.
But if he had been under the influence of liquor at Kremmling, as reported the day before, he had entirely recovered.

"Come on in," said the rancher.

When they got into the big living-room, and Belllounds
had closed the doors, the son threw down his baggage and
faced his father aggressively.

"Do they all know where I've been?" he asked, bitterly.
Broken pride and shame flamed in his face.

"Nobody knows. The secret's been kept," replied Belllounds.

Amaze and relief transformed the young man. "Aw, now,
I'm—glad—" he exclaimed, and he sat down, half covering
his face with shaking hands.

"Jack, we'll start over," said Belllounds, earnestly, and his
big eyes shone with a warm and beautiful light. "Right hyar.
We'll never speak of where you've been these three years.
Never again!"

Jack gazed up, then, with all the sullenness and shadow
gone.

"Father, you were wrong about—doing me good. It's done
me harm. But now, if nobody knows—why, I'll try to forget it."

"Mebbe I blundered," replied Belllounds, pathetically. "Yet, God knows I meant well. You sure were— But thet's enough palaver. . . . You'll go to work as foreman of White Slides. An' if you make a success of it I'll be only too glad to have you boss the ranch. I'm gettin' along in years, son. An' the last year has made me poorer. Hyar's a fine range, but I've less stock this year than last. There's been some rustlin' of cattle, an' a big loss from wolves an' lions an' poison-weed. . . . What d'you say, son?"

"I'll run White Slides," replied Jack, with a wave of his hand. "I hadn't hoped for such a chance. But it's due me. Who's in the outfit I know?"

"Reckon no one, except Wils Moore."

"Is that cowboy here yet? I don't want him."

"Wal, I'll put him to chasin' varmints with the hounds. An' say, son, this outfit is bad. You savvy—it's bad. You can't run that bunch. The only way you can handle them is to get up early an' come back late. Sayin' little, but sawin' wood. Hard work."

Jack Belllounds did not evince any sign of assimilating the seriousness of his father's words.

"I'll show them," he said. "They'll find out who's boss. Oh, I'm aching to get into boots and ride and tear around."

Belllounds stroked his grizzled beard and regarded his son with mingled pride and doubt. Not at this moment, most assuredly, could he get away from the wonderful fact that his only son was home.

"Thet's all right, son. But you've been off the range fer three years. You'll need advice. Now listen. Be gentle with hosses. You used to be mean with a hoss. Some cowboys jam their hosses around an' make 'em pitch an' bite. But it ain't the best way. A hoss has got sense. I've some fine stock, an' don't want it spoiled. An' be easy an' quiet with the boys. It's hard to get help these days. I'm short on hands now. . . . You'd do best, son, to stick to your dad's ways with hosses an' men."

"Dad, I've seen you kick horses an' shoot at men," replied Jack.

"Right, you have. But them was particular bad cases. I'm not advisin' thet way. . . . Son, it's close to my heart—this hope I have thet you'll—"

The full voice quavered and broke. It would indeed have been a hardened youth who could not have felt something of the deep and unutterable affection in the old man. Jack Bell-lounds put an arm around his father's shoulder.

"Dad, I'll make you proud of me yet. Give me a chance. And don't be sore if I can't do wonders right at first."

"Son, you shall have every chance. An' thet reminds me. Do you remember Columbine?"

"I should say so," replied Jack, eagerly. "They spoke of her in Kremmling. Where is she?"

"I reckon somewheres about. Jack, you an' Columbine are to marry."

"Marry! Columbine and me?" he ejaculated.

"Yes. You're my son an' she's my adopted daughter. I won't split my property. An' it's right she had a share. A fine, strong, quiet, pretty lass, Jack, an' she'll make a good wife. I've set my heart on the idee."

"But Columbine always hated me."

"Wal, she was a kid then an' you teased her. Now she's a woman, an' willin' to please me. Jack, you'll not buck ag'in' this deal?"

"That depends," replied Jack. "I'd marry 'most any girl you wanted me to. But if Columbine were to flout me as she used to—why, I'd buck sure enough. . . . Dad, are you sure she knows nothing, suspects nothing of where you—you sent me?"

"Son, I swear she doesn't."

"Do you mean you'd want us to marry soon?"

"Wal, yes, as soon as Collie would think reasonable. Jack, she's shy an' strange, an' deep, too. If you ever win her heart you'll be richer than if you owned all the gold in the Rockies. I'd say go slow. But contrariwise, it'd mebbe be surer to steady you, keep you home, if you married right off."

"Married right off!" echoed Jack, with a laugh. "It's like a story. But wait till I see her."

At that very moment Columbine was sitting on the topmost log of a high corral, deeply interested in the scene before her.

Two cowboys were in the corral with a saddled mustang. One of them carried a canvas sack containing tools and horse-shoes. As he dropped it with a metallic clink the mustang snorted and jumped and rolled the whites of his eyes. He knew what that clink meant.

"Miss Collie, air you-all goin' to sit up thar?" inquired the taller cowboy, a lean, supple, and powerful fellow, with a rough, red-blue face, hard as a rock, and steady, bright eyes.

"I sure am, Jim," she replied, imperturbably.

"But we've gotta hawg-tie him," protested the cowboy.

"Yes, I know. And you're going to be gentle about it."

Jim scratched his sandy head and looked at his comrade, a little gnarled fellow, like the bleached root of a tree. He seemed all legs.

"You hear, you Wyomin' galoot," he said to Jim. "Them shoes goes on Whang right gentle."

Jim grinned, and turned to speak to his mustang. "Whang, the law's laid down an' we wanta see how much hoss sense you hev."

The shaggy mustang did not appear to be favorably impressed by this speech. It was a mighty distrustful look he bent upon the speaker.

"Jim, seein' as how this here job's aboot the last Miss Collie will ever boss us on, we gotta do it without Whang turnin' a hair," drawled the other cowboy.

"Lem, why is this the last job I'll ever boss you boys?" demanded Columbine, quickly.

Jim gazed quizzically at her, and Lem assumed that blank, innocent face Columbine always associated with cowboy deviltry.

"Wal, Miss Collie, we reckon the new boss of White Slides rode in today."

"You mean Jack Belllounds came home," said Columbine. "Well, I'll boss you boys the same as always."

"Thet'd be mighty fine for us, but I'm feared it ain't writ in the fatal history of White Slides," replied Jim.

"Buster Jack will run over the ole man an' marry you," added Lem.

"Oh, so that's your idea," rejoined Columbine, lightly. "Well, if such a thing did come to pass I'd be your boss more than ever."

"I reckon no, Miss Collie, for we'll not be ridin' fer White Slides," said Jim, simply.

Columbine had sensed this very significance long before when the possibility of Buster Jack's return had been rumored. She knew cowboys. As well try to change the rocks of the hills!

"Boys, the day you leave White Slides will be a sad one for me," sighed Columbine.

"Miss Collie, we 'ain't gone yet," put in Lem, with awkward softness. "Jim has long hankered fer Wyomin' an' he jest talks thet way."

Then the cowboys turned to the business in hand. Jim removed the saddle, but left the bridle on. This move, of course, deceived Whang. He had been broken to stand while his bridle hung, and, like a horse that would have been good if given a chance, he obeyed as best he could, shaking in every limb. Jim, apparently to hobble Whang, roped his forelegs together, low down, but suddenly slipped the rope over the knees. Then Whang knew he had been deceived. He snorted fire, let out a scream, and, rearing on his hind legs, he pawed the air savagely. Jim hauled on the rope while Whang screamed and fought with his forefeet high in the air. Then Jim, with a powerful jerk, pulled Whang down and threw him, while Lem, seizing the bridle, hauled him over on his side and sat upon his head. Whereupon Jim slipped the loop off one front hoof and pulled the other leg back across one of the hind ones, where both were secured by a quick hitch. Then the lasso was wound and looped around front and back hoofs together. When this had been done the mustang was rolled over on his other side, his free front hoof lassoed and pulled back to the hind one, where both were secured, as had been the others. This rendered the mustang powerless, and the shoeing proceeded.

Columbine hated to sit by and watch it, but she always

stuck to her post, when opportunity afforded, because she knew the cowboys would not be brutal while she was there.

"Wal, he'll step high tomorrer," said Lem, as he got up from his seat on the head of Whang.

"Ahuh! An', like a mule, he'll be my friend fer twenty years jest to get a chance to kick me," replied Jim.

For Columbine, the most interesting moment of this incident was when the mustang raised his head to look at his legs, in order to see what had been done to them. There was something almost human in that look. It expressed intelligence and fear and fury.

The cowboys released his legs and let him get up. Whang stamped his iron-shod hoofs.

"It was a mean trick, Whang," said Columbine. "If I owned you that'd never be done to you."

"I reckon you can have him fer the askin'," said Jim, as he threw on the saddle. "Nobody but me can ride him. Do you want to try?"

"Not in these clothes," replied Columbine, laughing.

"Wal, Miss Collie, you're shore dressed up fine today, fer some reason or other," said Lem, shaking his head, while he gathered up the tools from the ground.

"Ahuh! An' here comes the reason," exclaimed Jim, in a low, hoarse whisper.

Columbine heard the whisper and at the same instant a sharp footfall on the gravel road. She quickly turned, almost losing her balance. And she recognized Jack Belllounds. The boy Buster Jack she remembered so well was approaching, now a young man, taller, heavier, older, with paler face and bolder look. Columbine had feared this meeting, had prepared herself for it. But all she felt when it came was annoyance at the fact that he had caught her sitting on top of the corral fence, with little regard for dignity. It did not occur to her to jump down. She merely sat straight, smoothed down her skirt, and waited.

Jim led the mustang out of the corral and Lem followed. It looked as if they wanted to avoid the young man, but he prevented that.

"Howdy, boys! I'm Jack Belllounds," he said, rather loftily.

But his manner was nonchalant. He did not offer to shake hands.

Jim mumbled something, and Lem said, "Hod do."

"That's an ornery-looking bronc," went on Belllounds, and he reached with careless hand for the mustang. Whang jerked so hard that he pulled Jim half over.

"Wal, he ain't a bronc, but I reckon he's all the rest," drawled Jim.

Both cowboys seemed slow, careless. They were neither indifferent nor responsive. Columbine saw their keen, steady glances go over Belllounds. Then she took a second and less hasty look at him. He wore high-heeled, fancy-topped boots, tight-fitting trousers of dark material, a heavy belt with silver buckle, and a white, soft shirt, with wide collar, open at the neck. He was bareheaded.

"I'm going to run White Slides," he said to the cowboys. "What're your names?"

Columbine wanted to giggle, which impulse she smothered. The idea of any one asking Jim his name! She had never been able to find out.

"My handle is Lemuel Archibawld Billings," replied Lem, blandly. The middle name was an addition no one had ever heard.

Belllounds then directed his glance and steps toward the girl. The cowboys dropped their heads and shuffled on their way.

"There's only one girl on the ranch," said Belllounds, "so you must be Columbine."

"Yes. And you're Jack," she replied, and slipped off the fence. "I'm glad to welcome you home."

She offered her hand, and he held it until she extricated it. There was genuine surprise and pleasure in his expression.

"Well, I'd never have known you," he said, surveying her from head to foot. "It's funny. I had the clearest picture of you in mind. But you're not at all like I imagined. The Columbine I remember was thin, white-faced, and all eyes."

"It's been a long time. Seven years," she replied. "But I knew you. You're older, taller, bigger, but the same Buster Jack."

"I hope not," he said, frankly condemning that former self. "Dad needs me. He wants me to take charge here—to be a man. I'm back now. It's good to be home. I never was worth much. Lord! I hope I don't disappoint him again."

"I hope so, too," she murmured. To hear him talk frankly, seriously, like this counteracted the unfavorable impression she had received. He seemed earnest. He looked down at the ground, where he was pushing little pebbles with the toe of his boot. She had a good opportunity to study his face, and availed herself of it. He did look like his father, with his big, handsome head, and his blue eyes, bolder perhaps from their prominence than from any direct gaze or fire. His face was pale, and shadowed by worry or discontent. It seemed as though a repressed character showed there. His mouth and chin were undisciplined. Columbine could not imagine that she despised anything she saw in the features of this young man. Yet there was something about him that held her aloof. She had made up her mind to do her part unselfishly. She would find the best in him, like him for it, be strong to endure and to help. Yet she had no power to control her vague and strange perceptions. Why was it that she could not feel in him what she liked in Jim Montana or Lem or Wilson Moore?

"This was my second long stay away from home," said Belllounds. "The first was when I went to school in Kansas City. I liked that. I was sorry when they turned me out—sent me home. . . . But the last three years were hell."

His face worked, and a shade of dark blood rippled over it.

"Did you work?" queried Columbine.

"Work! It was worse than work. . . . Sure I worked," he replied.

Columbine's sharp glance sought his hands. They looked as soft and unscarred as her own. What kind of work had he done, if he told the truth?

"Well, if you work hard for dad, learn to handle the cowboys, and never take up those old bad habits—"

"You mean drink and cards? I swear I'd forgotten them for three years—until yesterday. I reckon I've the better of them."

"Then you'll make dad and me happy. You'll be happy, too."

Columbine thrilled at the touch of fineness coming out in him. There was good in him, whatever the mad, wild pranks of his boyhood.

"Dad wants us to marry," he said, suddenly, with shyness and a strange, amused smile. "Isn't that funny? You and me —who used to fight like cat and dog! Do you remember the time I pushed you into the old mudhole? And you lay in wait for me, behind the house, to hit me with a rotten cabbage?"

"Yes, I remember," replied Columbine, dreamily. "It seems so long ago."

"And the time you ate my pie, and how I got even by tearing off your little dress, so you had to run home almost without a stitch on?"

"Guess I've forgotten that," replied Columbine, with a blush. "I must have been very little then."

"You were a little devil. . . . Do you remember the fight I had with Moore—about you?"

She did not answer, for she disliked the fleeting expression that crossed his face. He remembered too well.

"I'll settle that score with Moore," he went on. "Besides, I won't have him on the ranch."

"Dad needs good hands," she said, with her eyes on the gray sage slopes. Mention of Wilson Moore augmented the aloofness in her. An annoyance pricked along her veins.

"Before we get any farther I'd like to know something. Has Moore ever made love to you?"

Columbine felt that prickling augment to a hot, sharp wave of blood. Why was she at the mercy of strange, quick, unfamiliar sensations? Why did she hesitate over that natural query from Jack Belllounds?

"No. He never has," she replied, presently.

"That's damn queer. You used to like him better than anybody else. You sure hated me. . . . Columbine, have you outgrown that?"

"Yes, of course," she answered. "But I hardly hated you."

"Dad said you were willing to marry me. Is that so?"

Columbine dropped her head. His question, kindly put,

did not affront her, for it had been expected. But his actual
presence, the meaning of his words, stirred in her an unutterable spirit of protest. She had already in her will con-
sented to the demand of the old man; she was learning now,
however, that she could not force her flesh to consent to a
surrender it did not desire.

"Yes, I'm willing," she replied, bravely.

"Soon?" he flashed, with an eager difference in his voice.

"If I had my way it'd not be—too soon," she faltered. Her
downcast eyes had seen the stride he had made closer to her,
and she wanted to run.

"Why? Dad thinks it'd be good for me," went on Belllounds, now, with strong, self-centered thought. "It'd give
me responsibility. I reckon I need it. Why not soon?"

"Wouldn't it be better to wait awhile?" she asked. "We
do not know each other—let alone care—"

"Columbine, I've fallen in love with you," he declared,
hotly.

"Oh, how could you!" cried Columbine, incredulously.

"Why, I always was moony over you—when we were kids,"
he said. "And now to meet you grown up like this—so pretty
and sweet—such a—a healthy, blooming girl. . . . And dad's
word that you'd be my wife soon—*mine*—why, I just went
off my head at sight of you."

Columbine looked up at him and was reminded of how, as
a boy, he had always taken a quick, passionate longing for
things he must and would have. And his father had not denied
him. It might really be that Jack had suddenly fallen in love
with her.

"Would you want to take me without my—my love?" she
asked, very low. "I don't love you now. I might some time, if
you were good—if you made dad happy—if you conquered—"

"Take you! I'd take you if you—if you hated me," he replied, now in the grip of passion.

"I'll tell dad how I feel," she said, faintly, "and—and marry
you when he says."

He kissed her, would have embraced her had she not put
him back.

"Don't! Some—some one will see."

"Columbine, we're engaged," he asserted, with a laugh of possession. "Say, you needn't look so white and scared. I won't eat you. But I'd like to. . . . Oh, you're a sweet girl! Here I was hating to come home. And look at my luck!"

Then with a sudden change, that seemed significant of his character, he lost his ardor, dropped the half-bold, half-masterful air, and showed the softer side.

"Collie, I never was any good," he said. "But I want to be better. I'll prove it. I'll make a clean breast of everything. I won't marry you with any secret between us. You might find out afterward and hate me. . . . Do you have any idea where I've been these last three years?"

"No," answered Columbine.

"I'll tell you right now. But you must promise never to mention it to any one—or throw it up to me—ever."

He spoke hoarsely, and had grown quite white. Suddenly Columbine thought of Wilson Moore! He had known where Jack had spent those years. He had resisted a strong temptation to tell her. That was as noble in him as the implication of Jack's whereabouts had been base.

"Jack, that is big of you," she replied, hurriedly. "I respect you—like you for it. But you needn't tell me. I'd rather you didn't. I'll take the will for the deed."

Belllounds evidently experienced a poignant shock of amaze, of relief, of wonder, of gratitude. In an instant he seemed transformed.

"Collie, if I hadn't loved you before I'd love you now. That was going to be the hardest job I ever had—to tell you my—my story. I meant it. And now I'll not have to feel your shame for me and I'll not feel I'm a cheat or a liar. . . . But I will tell you this—if you love me you'll make a man of me!"

3

THE RANCHER THOUGHT it best to wait till after the round-up before he turned over the foremanship to his son. This was wise, but Jack did not see it that way. He showed that his old, intolerant spirit had, if anything, grown during his absence. Belllounds patiently argued with him, explaining what certainly should have been clear to a young man brought up in Colorado. The fall round-up was the most important time of the year, and during the strenuous drive the appointed foreman should have absolute control. Jack gave in finally with a bad grace.

It was unfortunate that he went directly from his father's presence out to the corrals. Some of the cowboys who had ridden all the day before and stood guard all night had just come in. They were begrimed with dust, weary, and sleepy-eyed.

"This hyar outfit won't see my tracks no more," said one, disgustedly. "I never kicked on doin' two men's work. But when it comes to rustlin' day and night, all the time, I'm agoin' to pass."

"Turn in, boys, and sleep till we get back with the chuck-wagon," said Wilson Moore. "We'll clean up that bunch to-day."

"Ain't you tired, Wils?" queried Bludsoe, a squat, bow-legged cowpuncher who appeared to be crippled or very lame.

"Me? Naw!" grunted Moore, derisively. "Blud, you sure ask fool questions. . . . Why, you —— mahogany-colored, stump-legged, biped of a cowpuncher, I've had three hours' sleep in four nights!"

"What's a biped?" asked Bludsoe, dubiously.

Nobody enlightened him.

"Wils, you-all air the only eddicated cowman I ever loved, but I'm a son-of-a-gun if we ain't agoin' to come to blows some day," declared Bludsoe.

"He shore can sling English," drawled Lem Billings. "I reckon he swallowed a dictionary onct."

"Wal, he can sling a rope, too, an' thet evens up," added Jim Montana.

Just at this moment Jack Belllounds appeared upon the scene. The cowboys took no notice of him. Jim was bandaging a leg of his horse; Bludsoe was wearily gathering up his saddle and trappings; Lem was giving his tired mustang a parting slap that meant much. Moore evidently awaited a fresh mount. A Mexican lad had come in out of the pasture leading several horses, one of which was the mottled white mustang that Moore rode most of the time.

Belllounds lounged forward with interest as Moore whistled, and the mustang showed his pleasure. Manifestly he did not like the Mexican boy and he did like Moore.

"Spottie, it's drag yearlings around for you today," said the cowboy, as he caught the mustang. Spottie tossed his head and stepped high until the bridle was on. When the saddle was thrown and strapped in place the mustang showed to advantage. He was beautiful, but not too graceful or sleek or fine-pointed or prancing to prejudice any cowboy against his qualities for work.

Jack Belllounds admiringly walked all around the mustang, a little too close to please Spottie.

"Moore, he's a fair-to-middling horse," said Belllounds, with the air of judge of horseflesh. "What's his name?"

"Spottie," replied Moore, shortly, as he made ready to mount.

"Hold on, will you!" ordered Jack, peremptorily. "I like this horse. I want to look him over."

When he grasped the bridle-reins out of the cowboy's hand Spottie jumped as if he had been shot at. Belllounds jerked at him and went closer. The mustang reared, snorting, plunging to get loose. Then Jack Belllounds showed the sudden temper for which he was noted. Red stained his pale cheeks.

"Damn you—come down!" he shouted, infuriated at the mustang, and with both hands he gave a powerful lunge. Spottie came down, and stood there, trembling all over, his ears laid back, his eyes showing fright and pain. Blood dripped from his mouth where the bit had cut him.

"I'll teach you to stand," said Belllounds, darkly. "Moore, lend me your spurs. I want to try him out."

"I don't lend my spurs—or my horse, either," replied the cowboy, quietly, with a stride that put him within reach of Spottie.

The other cowboys had dropped their trappings and stood at attention, with intent gaze and mute lips.

"Is he your horse?" demanded Jack, with a quick flush.

"I reckon so," replied Moore, slowly. "No one but me ever rode him."

"Does my father own him or do you own him?"

"Well, if that's the way you figure—he belongs to White Slides," returned the cowboy. "I never bought him. I only raised him from a colt, broke him, and rode him."

"I thought so. Moore, he's mine, and I'm going to ride him now. Lend me spurs, one of you cowpunchers."

Nobody made any motion to comply. There seemed to be a suspense at hand that escaped Belllounds.

"I'll ride him without spurs," he declared, presently, and again he turned to mount the mustang.

"Belllounds, it'd be better for you not to ride him now," said Moore, coolly.

"Why, I'd like to know?" demanded Belllounds, with the temper of one who did not tolerate opposition.

"He's the only horse left for me to ride," answered the cowboy. "We're branding today. Hudson was hurt yesterday. He was foreman, and he appointed me to fill his place. I've got to rope yearlings. Now, if you get up on Spottie you'll excite him. He's high-strung, nervous. That'll be bad for him, as he hates cutting-out and roping."

The reasonableness of this argument was lost upon Belllounds.

"Moore, maybe it'd interest you to know that I'm foreman of White Slides," he asserted, not without loftiness.

His speech manifestly decided something vital for the cowboy.

"Ahuh! . . . I'm sure interested this minute," replied Moore, and then, stepping to the side of the mustang, with swift hands he unbuckled the cinch, and with one sweep he drew saddle and blanket to the ground.

The action surprised Belllounds. He stared. There seemed something boyish in his lack of comprehension. Then his temper flamed.

"What do you mean by that?" he demanded, with a strident note in his voice. "Put that saddle back."

"Not much. It's my saddle. Cost sixty dollars at Kremmling last year. Good old hard-earned saddle! . . . And you can't ride it. Savvy?"

"Yes, I savvy," replied Belllounds, violently. "Now you'll savvy what I say. I'll have you discharged."

"Nope. Too late," said Moore, with cool, easy scorn. "I figured that. And I quit a minute ago—when you showed what little regard you had for a horse."

"You quit! . . . Well, it's damned good riddance. I wouldn't have you in the outfit."

"You couldn't have kept me, Buster Jack."

The epithet must have been an insult to Belllounds. "Don't you dare call me that," he burst out, furiously.

Moore pretended surprise. "Why not? It's your range name. We all get a handle, whether we like it or not. There's Montana and Blud and Lemme Two Bits. They call me Professor. Why should you kick on yours?"

"I won't stand it now. Not from any one—especially not you."

"Ahuh! Well, I'm afraid it'll stick," replied Moore, with sarcasm. "It sure suits you. Don't you bust everything you monkey with? Your old dad will sure be glad to see you bust the round-up today—and I reckon the outfit tomorrow."

"You insolent cowpuncher!" shouted Belllounds, growing beside himself with rage. "If you don't shut up I'll bust your face."

"Shut up! . . . Me? Nope. It can't be did. This is a free country, Buster Jack." There was no denying Moore's cool, stinging repetition of the epithet that had so affronted Bell-lounds.

"I always hated you!" he rasped out, hoarsely. Striking hard at Moore, he missed, but a second effort landed a glancing blow on the cowboy's face.

Moore staggered back, recovered his balance, and, hitting out shortly, he returned the blow. Belllounds fell against the corral fence, which upheld him.

"Buster Jack—you're crazy!" cried the cowboy, his eyes flashing. "Do you think you can lick me—after where you've been these three years?"

Like a maddened boy Belllounds leaped forward, this time his increased violence and wildness of face expressive of malignant rage. He swung his arms at random. Moore avoided his blows and planted a fist squarely on his adversary's snarling mouth. Belllounds fell with a thump. He got up with clumsy haste, but did not rush forward again. His big, prominent eyes held a dark and ugly look. His lower jaw wabbled as he panted for breath and speech at once.

"Moore—I'll kill—you!" he hissed, with glance flying everywhere for a weapon. From ground to cowboys he looked. Bludsoe was the only one packing a gun. Belllounds saw it, and he was so swift in bounding forward that he got a hand on it before Bludsoe could prevent.

"Let go! Give me—that gun! By God! I'll fix him!" yelled Belllounds, as Bludsoe grappled with him.

There was a sharp struggle. Bludsoe wrenched the other's hands free, and, pulling the gun, he essayed to throw it. But Belllounds blocked his action and the gun fell at their feet.

"Grab it!" sang out Bludsoe, ringingly. "Quick, somebody! The damned fool'll kill Wils."

Lem, running in, kicked the gun just as Belllounds reached for it. When it rolled against the fence Jim was there to se-cure it. Lem likewise grappled with the struggling Belllounds.

"Hyar, you Jack Belllounds," said Lem, "couldn't you see Wils wasn't packin' no gun? A-r'arin' like thet! . . . Stop your rantin' or we'll sure handle you rough."

"The old man's comin'," called Jim, warningly.

The rancher appeared. He strode swiftly, ponderously. His gray hair waved. His look was as stern as that of an eagle.

"What the hell's goin' on?" he roared.

The cowboys released Jack. That worthy, sullen and downcast, muttering to himself, stalked for the house.

"Jack, stand your ground," called old Belllounds.

But the son gave no heed. Once he looked back over his shoulder, and his dark glance saw no one save Moore.

"Boss, thar's been a little argyment," explained Jim, as with swift hand he hid Bludsoe's gun. "Nuthin' much."

"Jim, you're a liar," replied the old rancher.

"Aw!" exclaimed Jim, crestfallen.

"What're you hidin'? . . . You've got somethin' there. Gimme thet gun."

Without more ado Jim handed the gun over.

"It's mine, boss," put in Bludsoe.

"Ahuh? Wal, what was Jim hidin' it fer?" demanded Belllounds.

"Why, I jest tossed it to him—when I—sort of j'ined in with the argyment. We was tusslin' some an' I didn't want no gun."

How characteristic of cowboys that they lied to shield Jack Belllounds! But it was futile to attempt to deceive the old rancher. Here was a man who had been forty years dealing with all kinds of men and events.

"Bludsoe, you can't fool me," said old Bill, calmly. He had roared at them, and his eyes still flashed like blue fire, but he was calm and cool. Returning the gun to its owner, he continued: "I reckon you'd spare my feelin's an' lie about some trick of Jack's. Did he bust out?"

"Wal, tolerable like," replied Bludsoe, dryly.

"Ahuh! Tell me, then—an' no lies."

Belllounds's shrewd eyes had rested upon Wilson Moore. The cowboy's face showed the red marks of battle and the white of passion.

"I'm not going to lie, you can bet on that," he declared, forcefully.

"Ahuh! I might hev knowed you an' Jack'd clash," said Belllounds, gruffly. "What happened?"

"He hurt my horse. If it hadn't been for that there'd been no trouble."

A light leaped up in the old man's bold eyes. He was a lover of horses. Many hard words, and blows, too, he had dealt cowboys for being brutal.

"What'd he do?"

"Look at Spottie's mouth."

The rancher's way of approaching a horse was singularly different from his son's, notwithstanding the fact that Spottie knew him and showed no uneasiness. The examination took only a moment.

"Tongue cut bad. Thet's a damn shame. Take thet bridle off. . . . There. If it'd been an ornery hoss, now. . . . Moore, how'd this happen?"

"We just rode in," replied Wilson, hurriedly. "I was saddling Spottie when Jack came up. He took a shine to the mustang and wanted to ride him. When Spottie reared—he's shy with strangers—why, Jack gave a hell of a jerk on the bridle. The bit cut Spottie. . . . Well, that made me mad, but I held in. I objected to Jack riding Spottie. You see, Hudson was hurt yesterday and he appointed me foreman for today. I needed Spottie. But your son couldn't see it, and that made me sore. Jack said the mustang was his—"

"His?" interrupted Belllounds.

"Yes. He claimed Spottie. Well, he wasn't really mine, so I gave in. When I threw off the saddle, which *was* mine, Jack began to roar. He said he was foreman and he'd have me discharged. But I said I'd quit already. We both kept getting sorer and I called him Buster Jack. . . . He hit me first. Then we fought. I reckon I was getting the best of him when he made a dive for Bludsoe's gun. And that's all."

"Boss, as sure as I'm a born cowman," put in Bludsoe, "he'd hev plugged Wils if he'd got my gun. At thet he damn near got it!"

The old man stroked his scant gray beard with his huge, steady hand, apparently not greatly concerned by the disclosure.

"Montana, what do you say?" he queried, as if he held strong store by that quiet cowboy's opinion.

"Wal, boss," replied Jim, reluctantly, "Buster Jack's temper was bad onct, but now it's plumb wuss."

Whereupon Belllounds turned to Moore with a gesture and a look of a man who, in justice to something in himself, had to speak.

"Wils, it's onlucky you clashed with Jack right off," he said. "But thet was to be expected. I reckon Jack was in the wrong. Thet hoss was yours by all a cowboy holds right an' square. Mebbe by law Spottie belonged to White Slides Ranch—to me. But he's yours now, fer I give him to you."

"Much obliged, Belllounds. I sure do appreciate that," replied Moore, warmly. "It's what anybody'd gamble Bill Belllounds would do."

"Ahuh! An' I'd take it as a favor if you'd stay on today an' get thet brandin' done."

"All right, I'll do that for you," replied Moore. "Lem, I guess you won't get your sleep till tonight. Come on."

"Aw!" sighed Lem, as he picked up his bridle.

Late that afternoon Columbine sat upon the porch, watching the sunset. It had been a quiet day for her, mostly indoors. Once only had she seen Jack, and then he was riding by toward the pasture, whirling a lasso round his head. Jack could ride like one born to the range, but he was not an adept in the use of a rope. Nor had Columbine seen the old rancher since breakfast. She had heard his footsteps, however, pacing slowly up and down his room.

She was watching the last rays of the setting sun rimming with gold the ramparts of the mountain eastward, and burning a crown for Old White Slides peak. A distant bawl and bellow of cattle had died away. The branding was over for that fall. How glad she felt! The wind, beginning to grow cold as the sun declined, cooled her hot face. In the solitude of her room Columbine had cried enough that day to scald her cheeks.

Presently, down the lane between the pastures, she saw a cowboy ride into view. Very slowly he came, leading another horse. Columbine recognized Lem a second before she saw that he was leading Pronto. That struck her as strange. An-

other glance showed Pronto to be limping. Apparently he
could just get along, and that was all. Columbine ran out
in dismay, reaching the corral gate before Lem did. At first
she had eyes only for her beloved mustang.

"Oh, Lem—Pronto's hurt!" she cried.

"Wal, I should smile he is," replied Lem.

But Lem was not smiling. And when he wore a serious
face for Columbine something had indeed happened. The
cowboy was the color of dust and so tired that he reeled.

"Lem, he's all bloody!" exclaimed Columbine, as she ran
toward Pronto.

"Hyar, you jest wait," ordered Lem, testily. "Pronto's all
cut up, an' you gotta hustle some linen an' salve."

Columbine flew away to do his bidding, and so quick and
violent was she that when she got back to the corral she was
out of breath. Pronto whinnied as she fell, panting, on her
knees beside Lem, who was examining bloody gashes on the
legs of the mustang.

"Wal, I reckon no great harm did," said Lem, with relief.
"But he shore hed a close shave. Now you help me doctor
him up."

"Yes—I'll help," panted Columbine. "I've done this kind—
of thing often—but never—to Pronto. . . . Oh, I was afraid
—he'd been gored by a steer."

"Wal, he come damn near bein'," replied Lem, grimly. "An'
if it hedn't been fer ridin' you don't see every day, why thet
ornery Texas steer'd hev got him."

"Who was riding? Lem, was it you? Oh, I'll never be able
to do enough for you!"

"Wuss luck, it weren't me," said Lem.

"No? Who, then?"

"Wal, it was Wils, an' he made me swear to tell you nuthin'—leastways about him."

"Wils! Did *he* save Pronto? . . . And didn't want you to tell
me? Lem, something has happened. You're not like yourself."

"Miss Collie, I reckon I'm nigh all in," replied Lem,
wearily. "When I git this bandagin' done I'll fall right off my
hoss."

"But you're on the ground now, Lem," said Columbine, with a nervous laugh. "What happened?"

"Did you hear about the argyment this mawnin'?"

"No. What—who—"

"You can ask Ole Bill aboot thet. The way Pronto was hurt come off like this. Buster Jack rode out to where we was brandin' an' jumped his hoss over a fence into the pasture. He hed a rope an' he got to chasin' some hosses over thar. One was Pronto, an' the son-of-a-gun somehow did get the noose over Pronto's head. But he couldn't hold it, or didn't want to, fer Pronto broke loose an' jumped the fence. This wasn't so bad as far as it went. But one of them bad steers got after Pronto. He run an' sure stepped on the rope, an' fell. The big steer nearly piled on him. Pronto broke some records then. He shore was scared. Howsoever he picked out rough ground an' run plumb into some dead brush. Reckon thar he got cut up. We was all a good ways off. The steer went bawlin' an' plungin' after Pronto. Wils yelled fer a rifle, but nobody hed one. Nor a six-shooter, either. . . . I'm goin' back to packin' a gun. Wal, Wils did some ridin' to git over thar in time to save Pronto."

"Lem, that is not all," said Columbine, earnestly, as the cowboy concluded. Her knowledge of the range told her that Lem had narrated nothing so far which could have been cause for his cold, grim, evasive manner; and her woman's intuition divined a catastrophe.

"Nope. . . . Wils's hoss fell on him."

Lem broke that final news with all a cowboy's bluntness.

"Was he hurt—*Lem!*" cried Columbine.

"Say, Miss Collie," remonstrated Lem, "we're doctorin' up your hoss. You needn't drop everythin' an' grab me like thet. An' you're white as a sheet, too. It ain't nuthin' much fer a cowboy to hev a hoss fall on him."

"Lem Billings, I'll hate you if you don't tell me quick," flashed Columbine, fiercely.

"Ahuh! So thet's how the land lays," replied Lem, shrewdly. "Wal, I'm sorry to tell you thet Wils was bad hurt. Now, not *real* bad! . . . The hoss fell on his leg an' broke it. I cut off his

boot. His foot was all smashed. But thar wasn't any other hurt
—honest! They're takin' him to Kremmlin'."

"Ah!" Columbine's low cry sounded strangely in her ears,
as if some one else had uttered it.

"Buster Jack made two bursts this hyar day," concluded
Lem, reflectively. "Miss Collie, I ain't shore how you're re-
gardin' thet individool, but I'm tellin' you this, fer your own
good. He's bad medicine. He has his old man's temper thet
riles up at nuthin' an' never felt a halter. Wusser'n thet, he's
spoiled an' he acts like a colt thet'd tasted loco. The idee of
his ropin' Pronto right thar near the round-up! Any one
would think he jest come West. Old Bill is no fool. But he
wears blinders when he looks at his son. I'm predictin' bad
days fer White Slides Ranch."

4

◉

ONLY ONE MAN at Meeker appeared to be attracted by the
news that Rancher Bill Belllounds was offering employment.
This was a little cadaverous-looking fellow, apparently neither
young nor old, who said his name was Bent Wade. He had
drifted into Meeker with two poor horses and a pack.

"Whar you from?" asked the innkeeper, observing how
Wade cared for his horses before he thought of himself. The
query had to be repeated.

"Cripple Creek. I was cook for some miners an' I panned
gold between times," was the reply.

"Humph! Thet oughter been a better-payin' job than any
to be hed hereabouts."

"Yes, got big pay there," said Wade, with a sigh.

"What'd you leave fer?"

"We hed a fight over the diggin's an' I was the only one
left. I'll tell you. . . ." Whereupon Wade sat down on a box,

removed his old sombrero, and began to talk. An idler saun-tered over, attracted by something. Then a miner happened by to halt and join the group.

Next, old Kemp, the patriarch of the village, came and listened attentively. Wade seemed to have a strange mag-netism, a magic tongue.

He was small of stature, but wiry and muscular. His gar-ments were old, soiled, worn. When he removed the wide-brimmed sombrero he exposed a remarkable face. It was smooth except for a drooping mustache, and pallid, with drops of sweat standing out on the high, broad forehead; gaunt and hollow-cheeked, with an enormous nose, and cav-ernous eyes set deep under shaggy brows. These features, how-ever, were not so striking in themselves. Long, sloping, almost invisible lines of pain, the shadow of mystery and gloom in the deep-set, dark eyes, a sad harmony between features and expression, these marked the man's face with a record no keen eye could miss.

Wade told a terrible tale of gold and blood and death. It seemed to relieve him. His face changed, and lost what might have been called its tragic light, its driven intensity.

His listeners shook their heads in awe. Hard tales were com-mon in Colorado, but this one was exceptional. Two of the group left without comment. Old Kemp stared with narrow, half-recognizing eyes at the new-comer.

"Wal! Wal!" ejaculated the innkeeper. "It do beat hell what can happen! . . . Stranger, will you put up your hosses an' stay?"

"I'm lookin' for work," replied Wade.

It was then that mention was made of Belllounds sending to Meeker for hands.

"Old Bill Belllounds thet settled Middle Park an' made friends with the Utes," said Wade, as if certain of his facts.

"Yep, you have Bill to rights. Do you know him?"

"I seen him once twenty years ago."

"Ever been to Middle Park? Belllounds owns ranches there," said the innkeeper.

"He ain't livin' in the Park now," interposed Kemp. "He's

at White Slides, I reckon, these last eight or ten years. Thet's over the Gore Range."

"Prospected all through that country," said Wade.

"Wal, it's a fine part of Colorado. Hay an' stock country— too high fer grain. Did you mean you'd been through the Park?"

"Once—long ago," replied Wade, staring with his great, cavernous eyes into space. Some memory of Middle Park haunted him.

"Wal, then, I won't be steerin' you wrong," said the inn- keeper. "I like thet country. Some people don't. An' I say if you can cook or pack or punch cows or 'most anythin' you'll find a bunk with Old Bill. I understand he was needin' a hunter most of all. Lions an' wolves bad! Can you hunt?"

"Hey?" queried Wade, absently, as he inclined his ear. "I'm deaf on one side."

"Are you a good man with dogs an' guns?" shouted his questioner.

"Tolerable," replied Wade.

"Then you're sure of a job."

"I'll go. Much obliged to you."

"Not a-tall. I'm doin' Belllounds a favor. Reckon you'll put up here tonight?"

"I always sleep out. But I'll buy feed an' supplies," replied Wade, as he turned to his horses.

Old Kemp trudged down the road, wagging his gray head as if he was contending with a memory sadly failing him. An hour later when Bent Wade rode out of town he passed Kemp, and hailed him. The old-timer suddenly slapped his leg: "By Golly! I knowed I'd met him before!"

Later, he said with a show of gossipy excitement to his friend the innkeeper, "Thet fellar was Bent Wade!"

"So he told me," returned the other.

"But didn't you never hear of him? *Bent Wade?*"

"Now you tax me, thet name do 'pear familiar. But dash take it, I can't remember. I knowed he was somebody, though. Hope I didn't wish a gun-fighter or outlaw on Old Bill. Who was he, anyhow?"

"They call him Hell-Bent Wade. I seen him in Wyomin',

whar he were a stage-driver. But I never heerd who he was an' what he was till years after. Thet was onct I dropped down into Boulder. Wade was thar, all shot up, bein' nussed by Sam Coles. Sam's dead now. He was a friend of Wade's an' knowed him fer long. Wal, I heerd all thet anybody ever heerd about him, I reckon. Accordin' to Coles this hyar Hell-Bent Wade was a strange, wonderful sort of fellar. He had the most amazin' ways. He could do anythin' under the sun better'n any one else. Bad with guns! He never stayed in one place fer long. He never hunted trouble, but trouble fol-lered him. As I remember Coles, thet was Wade's queer idee —he couldn't shake trouble. No matter whar he went, al-ways thar was hell. Thet's what gave him the name Hell-Bent. . . . An' Coles swore thet Wade was the whitest man he ever knew. Heart of gold, he said. Always savin' some-body, helpin' somebody, givin' his money or time—never thinkin' of himself a-tall. . . . When he began to tell thet story about Cripple Creek then my ole head begun to ache with rememberin'. Fer I'd heerd Bent Wade talk before. Jest the same kind of story he told hyar, only wuss. Lordy! but thet fellar has seen times. An' queerest of all is thet idee he has how hell's on his trail an' everywhere he roams it ketches up with him, an' thar he meets the man who's got to hear his tale!"

Sunset found Bent Wade far up the valley of White River under the shadow of the Flat Top Mountains.

It was beautiful country. Grassy hills, with colored aspen groves, swelled up on his left, and across the brawling stream rose a league-long slope of black spruce, above which the bare red-and-gray walls of the range towered, glorious with the blaze of sinking sun. White patches of snow showed in the sheltered nooks. Wade's gaze rested longest on the colored heights.

By and by the narrow valley opened into a park, at the upper end of which stood a log cabin. A few cattle and horses grazed in an inclosed pasture. The trail led by the cabin. As Wade rode up a bushy-haired man came out of the door, rifle in hand. He might have been going out to hunt, but his scrutiny of Wade was that of a lone settler in a wild land.

"Howdy, stranger!" he said.

"Good evenin'," replied Wade. "Reckon you're Blair an' I'm nigh the headwaters of this river?"

"Yep, a matter of three miles to Trapper's Lake."

"My name's Wade. I'm packin' over to take a job with Bill Belllounds."

"Git down an' come in," returned Blair. "Bill's man stopped with me some time ago."

"Obliged, I'm sure, but I'll be goin' on," responded Wade. "Do you happen to have a hunk of deer meat? Game powerful scarce comin' up this valley."

"Lots of deer an' elk higher up. I chased a bunch of more'n thirty, I reckon, right out of my pasture this mornin'."

Blair crossed to an open shed near by and returned with half a deer haunch, which he tied upon Wade's pack-horse.

"My ole woman's ailin'. Do you happen to hev some terbaccer?"

"I sure do—both smokin' an' chewin', an' I can spare more chewin'. A little goes a long ways with me."

"Wal, gimme some of both, most chewin'," replied Blair, with evident satisfaction.

"You acquainted with Belllounds?" asked Wade, as he handed over the tobacco.

"Wal, yes, everybody knows Bill. You'd never find a whiter boss in these hills."

"Has he any family?"

"Now, I can't say as to thet," replied Blair. "I heerd he lost a wife years ago. Mebbe he married ag'in. But Bill's gittin' along."

"Good day to you, Blair," said Wade, and took up his bridle.

"Good day an' good luck. Take the right-hand trail. Better trot up a bit, if you want to make camp before dark."

Wade soon entered the spruce forest. Then he came to a shallow, roaring river. The horses drank the water, foaming white and amber around their knees, and then with splash and thump they forded it over the slippery rocks. As they cracked out upon the trail a covey of grouse whirred up into the low branches of spruce-trees. They were tame.

"That's somethin' like," said Wade. "First birds I've seen this fall. Reckon I can have stew any day."

He halted his horse and made a move to dismount, but with his eyes on the grouse he hesitated. "Tame as chickens, an' they sure are pretty."

Then he rode on, leading his pack-horse. The trail was not steep, although in places it had washed out, thus hindering a steady trot. As he progressed the forest grew thick and darker, and the fragrance of pine and spruce filled the air. A dreamy roar of water rushing over rocks rang in the traveler's ears. It receded at times, then grew louder. Presently the forest shade ahead lightened and he rode out into a wide space where green moss and flags and flowers surrounded a wonderful spring-hole. Sunset gleams shone through the trees to color the wide, round pool. It was shallow all along the margin, with a deep, large green hole in the middle, where the water boiled up. Trout were feeding on gnats and playing on the surface, and some big ones left wakes behind them as they sped to deeper water. Wade had an appreciative eye for all this beauty, his gaze lingering longest upon the flowers.

"Wild woods is the place for me," he soliloquized, as the cool wind fanned his cheeks and the sweet tang of evergreen tingled his nostrils. "But sure I'm most haunted in these lonely, silent places."

Bent Wade had the look of a haunted man. Perhaps the consciousness he confessed was part of his secret.

Twilight had come when again he rode out into the open. Trapper's Lake lay before him, a beautiful sheet of water, mirroring the black slopes and the fringed spruces and the flat peaks. Over all its gray, twilight-softened surface showed little swirls and boils and splashes where the myriads of trout were rising. The trail led out over open grassy shores, with a few pines straggling down to the lake, and clumps of spruces raising dark blurs against the background of gleaming lake. Wade heard a sharp crack of hoofs on rock, and he knew he had disturbed deer at their drinking; also he heard a ring of horns on the branch of a tree, and was sure an elk was slipping off through the woods. Across the lake he saw a camp-fire and a pale, sharp-pointed object that was a trapper's tent or an Indian's tepee.

Selecting a camp-site for himself, he unsaddled his horse, threw the pack off the other, and, hobbling both animals, he turned them loose. His roll of bedding, roped in canvas tarpaulin, he threw under a spruce-tree. Then he opened his oxhide-covered packs and laid out utensils and bags, little and big. All his movements were methodical, yet swift, accurate, habitual. He was not thinking about what he was doing. It took him some little time to find a suitable log to split for fire-wood, and when he had started a blaze night had fallen, and the light as it grew and brightened played fantastically upon the isolating shadows.

Lid and pot of the little Dutch oven he threw separately upon the sputtering fire, and while they heated he washed his hands, mixed the biscuits, cut slices of meat off the deer haunch, and put water on to boil. He broiled his meat on the hot, red coals, and laid it near on clean pine chips, while he waited for bread to bake and coffee to boil. The smell of wood-smoke and odorous steam from pots and the fragrance of spruce mingled together, keen, sweet, appetizing. Then he ate his simple meal hungrily, with the content of the man who had fared worse.

After he had satisfied himself he washed his utensils and stowed them away, with the bags. Whereupon his movements acquired less dexterity and speed. The rest hour had come. Still, like the long-experienced man in the open, he looked around for more to do, and his gaze fell upon his weapons, lying on his saddle. His rifle was a Henry—shiny and smooth from long service and care. His small gun was a Colt's .45. It had been carried in a saddle holster. Wade rubbed the rifle with his hands, and then with a greasy rag which he took from the sheath. After that he held the rifle to the heat of the fire. A squall of rain had overtaken him that day, wetting his weapons. A subtle and singular difference seemed to show in the way he took up the Colt's. His action was slow, his look reluctant. The small gun was not merely a thing of steel and powder and ball. He dried it and rubbed it with care, but not with love, and then he stowed it away.

Next Wade unrolled his bed under the spruce, with one end of the tarpaulin resting on the soft mat of needles. On top of that came the two woolly sheepskins, which he used to lie upon, then his blankets, and over all the other end of the tarpaulin.

This ended his tasks for the day. He lighted his pipe and composed himself beside the camp-fire to smoke and rest awhile before going to bed. The silence of the wilderness enfolded lake and shore; yet presently it came to be a silence accentuated by near and distant sounds, faint, wild, lonely—the low hum of falling water, the splash of tiny waves on the shore, the song of insects, and the dismal hoot of owls.

"Bill Belllounds—an' he needs a hunter," soliloquized Bent Wade, with gloomy, penetrating eyes, seeing far through the red embers. "That will suit me an' change my luck, likely. Livin' in the woods, away from people—I could stick to a job like that. . . . But if this White Slides is close to the old trail I'll never stay."

He sighed, and a darker shadow, not from flickering fire, overspread his cadaverous face. Eighteen years ago he had driven the woman he loved away from him, out into the world with her baby girl. Never had he rested beside a camp-fire that that old agony did not recur! Jealous fool! Too late he had discovered his fatal blunder; and then had begun a search over Colorado, ending not a hundred miles across the wild mountains from where he brooded that lonely hour—a search ended by news of the massacre of a wagon-train by Indians.

That was Bent Wade's secret.

And no earthly sufferings could have been crueler than his agony and remorse, as through the long years he wandered on and on. The very good that he tried to do seemed to foment evil. The wisdom that grew out of his suffering opened pitfalls for his wandering feet. The wildness of men and the passion of women somehow waited with incredible fatality for that hour when chance led him into their lives. He had toiled, he had given, he had fought, he had sacrificed, he had killed, he had endured for the human nature which in his savage youth he had betrayed. Yet out of his supreme and endless striving to undo, to make reparation, to give his life, to find God, had come, it seemed to Wade in his abasement, only a driving torment.

But though his thought and emotion fluctuated, varying, wandering, his memory held a fixed and changeless picture of a woman, fair and sweet, with eyes of nameless blue, and face as white as a flower.

"Baby would have been—let's see—'most nineteen years old now—if she'd lived," he said. "A big girl, I reckon, like her mother. . . . Strange how, as I grow older, I remember better!"

The night wind moaned through the spruces; dark clouds scudded across the sky, blotting out the bright stars; a steady, low roar of water came from the outlet of the lake. The camp-fire flickered and burned out, so that no sparks blew into the blackness, and the red embers glowed and paled and crackled. Wade at length got up and made ready for bed. He threw back tarpaulin and blankets, and laid his rifle alongside where he could cover it. His coat served for a pillow and he put the Colt's gun under that; then pulling off his boots, he slipped into bed, dressed as he was, and, like all men in the open, at once fell asleep.

For Wade, and for countless men like him, who for many years had roamed the West, this sleeping alone in wild places held both charm and peril. But the fascination of it was only a vague realization, and the danger was laughed at.

Over Bent Wade's quiet form the shadows played, the spruce boughs waved, the piny needles rustled down, the wind moaned louder as the night advanced. By and by the horses rested from their grazing; the insects ceased to hum; and the continuous roar of water dominated the solitude. If wild animals passed Wade's camp they gave it a wide berth.

Sunrise found Wade on the trail, climbing high up above the lake, making for the pass over the range. He walked, lead-ing his horses up a zigzag trail that bore the tracks of recent travelers. Although this country was sparsely settled, yet there were men always riding from camp to camp or from one valley town to another. Wade never tarried on a well-trodden trail.

As he climbed higher the spruce-trees grew smaller, no longer forming a green aisle before him, and at length they became dwarfed and stunted, and at last failed altogether. Soon he was above timber-line and out upon a flat-topped mountain range, where in both directions the land rolled and dipped, free of tree or shrub, colorful with grass and flowers. The elevation exceeded eleven thousand feet. A whipping wind swept across the plain-land. The sun was pale-bright in the east, slowly being obscured by gray clouds. Snow began to fall, first in scudding, scanty flakes, but increasing until the air was full of a great, fleecy swirl. Wade rode along the rim of a mountain wall, watching a beautiful snow-storm falling into the brown gulf beneath him. Once as he headed round a break he caught sight of mountain-sheep cuddled under a protecting shelf. The snow-squall blew away, like a receding wall, leaving grass and flowers wet. As the dark clouds parted, the sun shone warmer out of the blue. Gray peaks, with patches of white, stood up above their black-timbered slopes.

Wade soon crossed the flat-topped pass over the range and faced a descent, rocky and bare at first, but yielding gradually to the encroachment of green. He left the cold winds and bleak trails above him. In an hour, when he was half down the slope, the forest had become warm and dry, fragrant and still. At length he rode out upon the brow of a last wooded bench above a grassy valley, where a bright, winding stream gleamed in the sun. While the horses rested Wade looked about him. Nature never tired him. If he had any peace it emanated from the silent places, the solemn hills, the flowers and animals of the wild and lonely land.

A few straggling pines shaded this last low hill above the valley. Grass grew luxuriantly there in the open, but not under the trees, where the brown needle-mats jealously obstructed the green. Clusters of columbines waved their graceful, sweet, pale-blue flowers that Wade felt a joy in seeing. He loved flowers—columbines, the glory of Colorado, came first, and next the many-hued purple asters, and then the flaunting spikes of paint-brush, and after them the nameless and numberless wild flowers that decked the mountain meadows and colored the grass of the aspen groves and peeped out of the edge of snow-fields.

"Strange how it seems good to live—when I look at a columbine—or watch a beaver at his work—or listen to the bugle of an elk!" mused Bent Wade. He wondered why, with all his life behind him, he could still find comfort in these things.

Then he rode on his way. The grassy valley, with its winding stream, slowly descended and widened, and left foothill and mountain far behind. Far across a wide plain rose another range, black and bold against the blue. In the afternoon Wade reached Elgeria, a small hamlet, but important by reason of its being on the main stage line, and because here miners and cattlemen bought supplies. It had one street, so wide it appeared to be a square, on which faced a line of bold board houses with high, flat fronts. Wade rode to the inn where the stagecoaches made headquarters. It suited him to feed and rest his horses there, and partake of a meal himself, before resuming his journey.

The proprietor was a stout, pleasant-faced little woman, loquacious and amiable, glad to see a stranger for his own sake rather than from considerations of possible profit. Though Wade had never before visited Elgeria, he soon knew all about the town, and the miners up in the hills, and the only happenings of moment—the arrival and departure of stages.

"Prosperous place," remarked Wade. "I saw that. An' it ought to be growin'."

"Not so prosperous fer me as it uster be," replied the lady. "We did well when my husband was alive, before our competitor come to town. He runs a hotel where miners can drink an' gamble. I don't. . . . But I reckon I've no cause to complain. I live."

"Who runs the other hotel?"

"Man named Smith. Reckon thet's not his real name. I've had people here who—but it ain't no matter."

"Men change their names," replied Wade.

"Stranger, air you packin' through or goin' to stay?"

"On my way to White Slides Ranch, where I'm goin' to work for Belllounds. Do you know him?"

"Know Bill Belllounds? Me? Wal, he's the best friend I ever had when I was at Kremmlin'. I lived there several years. My husband had stock there. In fact, Bill started us in the cattle business. But we got out of there an' come here, where Bob died, an' I've been stuck ever since."

"Everybody has a good word for Belllounds," observed Wade.

"You'll never hear a bad one," replied the woman, with cheerful warmth. "Bill never had but one fault, an' people loved him fer thet."

"What was it?"

"He's got a wild boy thet he thinks the sun rises an' sets in. Buster Jack, they call him. He used to come here often. But Bill sent him away somewhere. The boy was spoiled. I saw his mother years ago—she's dead this long time—an' she was no wife fer Bill Belllounds. Jack took after her. An' Bill was thet woman's slave. When she died all his big heart went to the son, an' thet accounts. Jack will never be any good."

Wade thoughtfully nodded his head, as if he understood, and was pondering other possibilities.

"Is he the only child?"

"There's a girl, but she's not Bill's kin. He adopted her when she was a baby. An' Jack's mother hated this child—jealous, we used to think, because it might grow up an' get some of Bill's money."

"What's the girl's name?" asked Wade.

"Columbine. She was over here last summer with Old Bill. They stayed with me. It was then Bill had hard words with Smith across the street. Bill was resentin' somethin' Smith put in my way. Wal, the lass's the prettiest I ever seen in Colorado, an' as good as she's pretty. Old Bill hinted to me he'd likely make a match between her an' his son Jack. An' I ups an' told him, if Jack hadn't turned over a new leaf when he comes home, thet such a marriage would be tough on Columbine. Whew! but Old Bill was mad. He jest can't stand a word ag'in' thet Buster Jack."

"Columbine Belllounds," mused Wade. "Queer name."

"Oh, I've knowed three girls named Columbine. Don't you know the flower? It's common in these parts. Very delicate, like a sago lily, only paler."

"Were you livin' in Kremmlin' when Belllounds adopted the girl?" asked Wade.

"Laws no!" was the reply. "Thet was long before I come to Middle Park. But I heerd all about it. The baby was found by gold-diggers up in the mountains. Must have got lost from a wagon-train thet Indians set on soon after—so the miners said. Anyway, Old Bill took the baby an' raised her as his own."

"How old is she now?" queried Wade, with a singular change in his tone.

"Columbine's around nineteen."

Bent Wade lowered his head a little, hiding his features under the old, battered, wide-brimmed hat. The amiable innkeeper did not see the tremor that passed over him, nor the slight stiffening that followed, nor the gray pallor of his face. She went on talking until some one called her.

Wade went outdoors, and with bent head walked down the street, across a little river, out into green pasture-land. He struggled with an amazing possibility. Columbine Belllounds might be his own daughter. His heart leaped with joy. But the joy was short-lived. No such hope in this world for Bent Wade! This coincidence, however, left him with a strange, prophetic sense in his soul of a tragedy coming to White Slides Ranch. Wade possessed some power of divination, some strange gift to pierce the veil of the future. But he could not exercise this power at will; it came involuntarily, like a messenger of trouble in the dark night. Moreover, he had never yet been able to draw away from the fascination of this knowledge. It lured him on. Always his decision had been to go on, to meet this boding circumstance, or to remain and meet it, in the hope that he might take some one's burden upon his shoulders. He sensed it now, in the keen, poignant clairvoyance of the moment—the tangle of life that he was about to enter. Old Bill Belllounds, big and fine, victim of love for a wayward son; Buster Jack, the waster, the tearerdown, the destroyer, the wild youth at a wild time; Columbine, the girl of unknown birth, good and loyal, subject to a condition sure to ruin her. Wade's strange mind revolved a hundred outcomes to this conflict of characters, but not one of them was the one that was written. That remained dark. Never had he received so strong a call out of the unknown, nor had he ever felt such intense curiosity. Hope had long been dead in him, except the one that he might atone in some way for the wrong he had done his wife. So the pangs of emotion that recurred, in spite of reason and bitterness, were not recognized by him as lingering hopes. Wade denied the human in him, but he thrilled at the thought of meeting Columbine Belllounds. There was something here beyond all his comprehension.

"It *might*—be true!" he whispered. "I'll know when I see her."

Then he walked back toward the inn. On the way he looked into the barroom of the hotel run by Smith. It was a hard-looking place, half full of idle men, whose faces were as open pages to Bent Wade. Curiosity did not wholly control the impulse that made him wait at the door till he could have a look at the man Smith. Somewhere, at some time, Wade had met most of the veterans of western Colorado. So much he had traveled! But the impulse that held him was answered and explained when Smith came in—a burly man, with an ugly scar marring one eye. Bent Wade recognized Smith. He recognized the scar. For that scar was his own mark, dealt to this man, whose name was not Smith, and who had been as evil as he looked, and whose nomadic life was not due to remorse or love of travel.

Wade passed on without being seen. This recognition meant less to him than it would have ten years ago, as he was not now the kind of man who hunted old enemies for revenge or who went to great lengths to keep out of their way. Men there were in Colorado who would shoot at him on sight. There had been more than one that had shot to his cost.

That night Wade camped in the foothills east of Elgeria, and upon the following day, at sunrise, his horses were breaking the frosty grass and ferns of the timbered range. This he crossed, rode down into a valley where a lonely cabin nestled, and followed an old, blazed trail that wound up the course of a brook. The water was of a color that made rock and sand and moss seem like gold. He saw no signs or tracks of game. A gray jay now and then screeched his approach to unseen denizens of the woods. The stream babbled past him over mossy ledges, under the dark shade of clumps of spruces, and it grew smaller as he progressed toward its source. At length it was lost in a swale of high, rank grass, and the blazed trail led on through heavy pine woods. At noon he reached the crest of the divide, and, halting upon an open, rocky eminence, he gazed down over a green and black forest, slow-descending to a great irregular park that was his destination for the night.

Wade needed meat, and to that end, as he went on, he kept a sharp lookout for deer, especially after he espied fresh tracks crossing the trail. Slipping along ahead of his horses, that followed him almost too closely to permit of his noiseless approach to game, he hunted all the way down to the great open park without getting a shot.

This park was miles across and miles long, covered with tall, waving grass, and it had straggling arms that led off into the surrounding belt of timber. It sloped gently toward the center, where a round, green acreage of grass gave promise of water. Wade rode toward this, keeping somewhat to the right, as he wanted to camp at the edge of the woods. Soon he rode out beyond one of the projecting peninsulas of forest to find the park spreading wider in that direction. He saw horses grazing with elk, and far down at the notch, where evidently the park had outlet in a narrow valley, he espied the black, hump-shaped, shaggy forms of buffalo. They bobbed off out of sight. Then the elk saw or scented him, and they trotted away, the antlered bulls ahead of the cows. Wade wondered if the horses were wild. They showed great interest, but no fear. Beyond them was a rising piece of ground, covered with pine, and it appeared to stand aloft from the forest on the far side as well as upon that by which he was approaching. Riding a mile or so farther he ascertained that this bit of wooded ground resembled an island in a lake. Presently he saw smoke arising above the treetops.

A tiny brook welled out of the green center of the park and meandered around to pass near the island of pines. Wade saw unmistakable signs of prospecting along this brook, and farther down, where he crossed it, he found tracks made that day.

The elevated plot of ground appeared to be several acres in extent, covered with small-sized pines, and at the far edge there was a little log cabin. Wade expected to surprise a lone prospector at his evening meal. As he rode up a dog ran out of the cabin, barking furiously. A man, dressed in fringed buckskin, followed. He was tall, and had long, iron-gray hair over his shoulders. His bronzed and weather-beaten face was a mass of fine wrinkles where the grizzled hair did not hide them, and his shining, red countenance proclaimed an honest, fearless spirit.

"Howdy, stranger!" he called, as Wade halted several rods distant. His greeting was not welcome, but it was civil. His keen scrutiny, however, attested to more than his speech.

"Evenin', friend," replied Wade. "Might I throw my pack here?"

"Sure. Get down," answered the other. "I calkilate I never seen you in these diggin's."

"No. I'm Bent Wade, an' on my way to White Slides to work for Belllounds."

"Glad to meet you. I'm new hereabouts, myself, but I know Belllounds. My name's Lewis. I was jest cookin' grub. An' it'll burn, too, if I don't rustle. Turn your hosses loose an' come in."

Wade presented himself with something more than his usual methodical action. He smelled buffalo steak, and he was hungry. The cabin had been built years ago, and was a ramshackle shelter at best. The stone fireplace, however, appeared well preserved. A bed of red coals glowed and cracked upon the hearth.

"Reckon I sure smelled buffalo meat," observed Wade, with much satisfaction. "It's long since I chewed a hunk of that."

"All ready. Now pitch in. . . . Yes, thar's some buffalo left in here. Not hunted much. Thar's lots of elk an' herds of deer. After a little snow you'd think a drove of sheep had been trackin' around. An' some bear."

Wade did not waste many words until he had enjoyed that meal. Later, while he helped his host, he recurred to the subject of game.

"If there's so many deer then there's lions an' wolves."

"You bet. I see tracks every day. Had a shot at a lofer not long ago. Missed him. But I reckon thar's more varmints over in the Troublesome country back of White Slides."

"Troublesome! Do they call it that?" asked Wade, with a queer smile.

"Sure. An' it *is* troublesome. Belllounds has been tryin' to hire a hunter. Offered me big wages to kill off the wolves an' lions."

"That's the job I'm goin' to take."

"Good!" exclaimed Lewis. "I'm sure glad. Belllounds is a nice fellar. I felt sort of cheap till I told him I wasn't really a hunter. You see, I'm prospectin' up here, an' pretendin' to be a hunter."

"What do you make that bluff for?" queried Wade. "You couldn't fool any one who'd ever prospected for gold. I saw your signs out here."

"Wal, you've sharp eyes, thet's all. Wade, I've some on-desirable neighbors over here. I'd just as lief they didn't see me diggin' gold. Lately I've had a hunch they're rustlin' cattle. Anyways, they've sold cattle in Kremmlin' thet came from over around Elgeria."

"Wherever there's cattle there's sure to be some stealin'," observed Wade.

"Wal, you needn't say anythin' to Belllounds, because mebbe I'm wrong. An' if I found out I was right I'd go down to White Slides an' tell it myself. Belllounds done me some favors."

"How far to White Slides?" asked Wade, with a puff on his pipe.

"Roundabout trail, an' rough, but you'll make it in one day, easy. Beautiful country. Open, big peaks an' ranges, with valleys an' lakes. Never seen such grass!"

"Did you ever see Belllounds's son?"

"No. Didn't know he hed one. But I seen his gal the fust

day I was thar. She was nice to me. I went thar to be fixed
up a bit. Nearly chopped my hand off. The gal—Columbine, she's called—doctored me up. Fact is, I owe considerable to thet White Slides Ranch. There's a cowboy, Wils somethin', who rode up here with some medicine fer me—some
they didn't have when I was thar. You'll like thet boy. I seen
he was sweet on the gal an' I sure couldn't blame him."

Bent Wade removed his pipe and let out a strange laugh,
significant with its little note of grim confirmation.

"What's funny about thet?" demanded Lewis, rather surprised.

"I was only laughin'," replied Wade. "What you said about
the cowboy bein' sweet on the girl popped into my head before you told it. Well, boys will be boys. I was young once
an' had my day."

Lewis grunted as he bent over to lift a red coal to light
his pipe, and as he raised his head he gave Wade a glance of
sympathetic curiosity.

"Wal, I hope I'll see more of you," he said, as his guest
rose, evidently to go.

"Reckon you will, as I'll be chasin' hounds all over. An' I
want a look at them neighbors you spoke of that might be
rustlers. . . . I'll turn in now. Good night."

5

◉

BENT WADE RODE out of the forest to look down upon the
White Slides country at the hour when it was most beautiful.

"Never seen the beat of that!" he exclaimed, as he halted.

The hour was sunset, with the golden rays and shadows
streaking ahead of him down the rolling sage hills, all rosy
and gray with rich, strange softness. Groves of aspens stood
isolated from one another—here crowning a hill with blazing

yellow, and there fringing the brow of another with gleaming gold, and lower down reflecting the sunlight with brilliant red and purple. The valley seemed filled with a delicate haze, almost like smoke. White Slides Ranch was hidden from sight, as it lay in the bottomland. The gray old peak towered proud and aloof, clear-cut and sunset-flushed against the blue. The eastern slope of the valley was a vast sweep of sage and hill and grassy bench and aspen bench, on fire with the colors of autumn made molten by the last flashing of the sun. Great black slopes of forest gave sharp contrast, and led up to the red-walled ramparts of the mountain range.

Wade watched the scene until the fire faded, the golden shafts paled and died, the rosy glow on sage changed to cold steel gray. Then he rode out upon the foothills. The trail led up and down slopes of sage. Grass grew thicker as he descended. Once he startled a great flock of prairie-chickens, or sage-hens, large gray birds, lumbering, swift fliers, that whirred up, and soon plumped down again into the sage. Twilight found him on a last long slope of the foothills, facing the pasture-land of the valley, with the ranch still five miles distant, now showing misty and dim in the gathering shadows.

Wade made camp where a brook ran near an aspen thicket. He had no desire to hurry to meet events at White Slides Ranch, although he longed to see this girl that belonged to Belllounds. Night settled down over the quiet foothills. A pack of roving coyotes visited Wade, and sat in a half-circle in the shadows back of the camp-fire. They howled and barked. Nevertheless sleep visited Wade's tired eyelids the moment he lay down and closed them.

Next morning, rather late, Wade rode down to White Slides Ranch. It looked to him like the property of a rich rancher who held to the old and proven customs of his generation. The corrals were new, but their style was old. Wade reflected that it would be hard for rustlers or horse-thieves to steal out of those corrals. A long lane led from the pasture-land, following the brook that ran through the corrals and by the back door of the rambling, comfortable-looking cabin. A cowboy was leading horses across a wide square between the main ranch-house and a cluster of cabins and sheds. He saw the visitor and waited.

"Mornin'," said Wade, as he rode up.

"Hod do," replied the cowboy.

Then these two eyed each other, not curiously nor suspiciously, but with that steady, measuring gaze common to Western men.

"My name's Wade," said the traveler. "Come from Meeker way. I'm lookin' for a job with Belllounds."

"I'm Lem Billings," replied the other. "Ridin' fer White Slides fer years. Reckon the boss'll be glad to take you on."

"Is he around?"

"Sure. I jest seen him," replied Billings, as he haltered his horses to a post. "I reckon I ought to give you a hunch."

"I'd take that as a favor."

"Wal, we're short of hands," said the cowboy. "Jest got the round-up over. Hudson was hurt an' Wils Moore got crippled. Then the boss's son has been put on as foreman. Three of the boys quit. Couldn't stand him. This hyar son of Belllounds is a son-of-a-gun! Me an' pards of mine, Montana an' Bludsoe, are stickin' on—wal, fer reasons thet ain't egzactly love fer the boss. But Old Bill's the best of bosses. . . . Now the hunch is—thet if you git on hyar you'll hev to do two or three men's work."

"Much obliged," replied Wade. "I don't shy at that."

"Wal, git down an' come in," added Billings, heartily.

He led the way across the square, around the corner of the ranch-house, and up on a long porch, where the arrangement of chairs and blankets attested to the hand of a woman. The first door was open, and from it issued voices; first a shrill, petulant boy's complaint, and then a man's deep, slow, patient reply.

Lem Billings knocked on the door-jamb.

"Wal, what's wanted?" called Belllounds.

"Boss, thar's a man wantin' to see you," replied Lem.

Heavy steps approached the doorway and it was filled with the large figure of the rancher. Wade remembered Belllounds and saw only a gray difference in years.

"Good mornin', Lem, an' good mornin' to you, stranger,"

was the rancher's greeting, his bold, blue glance, honest and frank and keen, with all his long experience of men, taking Wade in with one flash.

Lem discreetly walked to the end of the porch as another figure, that of the son who resembled the father, filled the doorway, with eyes less kind, bent upon the visitor.

"My name's Wade. I'm over from Meeker way, hopin' to find a job with you," said Wade.

"Glad to meet you," replied Belllounds, extending his huge hand to shake Wade's. "I need you, sure bad. What's your special brand of work?"

"I reckon any kind."

"Set down, stranger," replied Belllounds, pulling up a chair. He seated himself on a bench and leaned against the log wall. "Now, when a boy comes an' says he can do anythin', why I jest haw! haw! at him. But you're a man, Wade, an' one as has been there. Now I'm hard put fer hands. Jest speak out now fer yourself. No one else can speak fer you, thet's sure. An' this is bizness."

"Any work with stock, from punchin' steers to doctorin' horses," replied Wade, quietly. "Am fair carpenter an' mason. Good packer. Know farmin'. Can milk cows an' make butter. I've been cook in many outfits. Read an' write an' not bad at figures. Can do work on saddles an' harness, an'—"

"Hold on!" yelled Belllounds, with a hearty laugh. "I ain't imposin' on no man, no matter how I need help. You're sure a jack of all range trades. An' I wish you was a hunter."

"I was comin' to that. You didn't give me time."

"Say, do you know hounds?" queried Belllounds, eagerly.

"Yes. Was raised where everybody had packs. I'm from Kentucky. An' I've run hounds off an' on for years. I'll tell you—"

Belllounds interrupted Wade.

"By all that's lucky! An' last, can you handle guns? We 'ain't had a good shot on this range fer Lord knows how long. I used to hit plumb center with a rifle. My eyes are pore now. An' my son can't hit a flock of haystacks. An' the cow-punchers are 'most as bad. Sometimes right hyar where you could hit elk with a club we're out of fresh meat."

"Yes, I can handle guns," replied Wade, with a quiet smile and a lowering of his head. "Reckon you didn't catch my name."

"Wal—no, I didn't," slowly replied Belllounds, and his pause, with the keener look he bestowed upon Wade, told how the latter's query had struck home.

"Wade—Bent Wade," said Wade, with quiet distinctness.

"*Not Hell-Bent Wade!*" ejaculated Belllounds.

"The same. . . . I ain't proud of the handle, but I never sail under false colors."

"Wal, I'll be damned!" went on the rancher. "Wade, I've heerd of you fer years. Some bad, but most good, an' I reckon I'm jest as glad to meet you as if you'd been somebody else."

"You'll give me the job?"

"I should smile."

"I'm thankin' you. Reckon I was some worried. Jobs are hard for me to get an' harder to keep."

"Thet's not onnatural, considerin' the hell which's said to camp on your trail," replied Belllounds, dryly. "Wade, I can't say I take a hell of a lot of stock in such talk. Fifty years I've been west of the Missouri. I know the West an' I know men. Talk flies from camp to ranch, from diggin's to town, an' always some one adds a little more. Now I trust my judgment an' I trust men. No one ever betrayed me yet."

"I'm that way, too," replied Wade. "But it doesn't pay, an' yet I still kept on bein' that way. . . . Belllounds, my name's as bad as good all over western Colorado. But as man to man I tell you—I never did a low-down trick in my life. . . . Never but once."

"An' what was thet?" queried the rancher, gruffly.

"I killed a man who was innocent," replied Wade, with quivering lips, "an'—an' drove the woman I loved to her death."

"Aw! we all make mistakes some time in our lives," said Belllounds, hurriedly. "I made 'most as big a one as yours—so help me God! . . ."

"I'll tell you—" interrupted Wade.

"You needn't tell me anythin'," said Belllounds, interrupting in his turn. "But at thet some time I'd like to hear about the Lascelles outfit over on the Gunnison. I knowed Lascelles. An' a pardner of mine down in Middle Park came back from the Gunnison with the dog-gonedest story I ever heerd. Thet was five years ago this summer. Of course I knowed your name long before, but this time I heerd it powerful strong. You got in thet mix-up to your neck. . . . Wal, what consarns me now is this. Is there any sense in the talk thet wherever you land there's hell to pay?"

"Belllounds, there's no sense in it, but a lot of truth," confessed Wade, gloomily.

"Ahuh! . . . Wal, Hell-Bent Wade, I'll take a chance on you," boomed the rancher's deep voice, rich with the intent of his big heart. "I've gambled all my life. An' the best friends I ever made were men I'd helped. . . . What wages do you ask?"

"I'll take what you offer."

"I'm payin' the boys forty a month, but thet's not enough fer you."

"Yes, that'll do."

"Good, it's settled," concluded Belllounds, rising. Then he saw his son standing inside the door. "Say, Jack, shake hands with Bent Wade, hunter an' all-around man. Wade, this's my boy. I've jest put him on as foreman of the outfit, an' while I'm at it I'll say thet you'll take orders from me an' not from him."

Wade looked up into the face of Jack Belllounds, returned his brief greeting, and shook his limp hand. The contact sent a strange chill over Wade. Young Belllounds's face was marred by a bruise and shaded by a sullen light.

"Get Billin's to take you out to thet new cabin an' sheds I jest had put up," said the rancher. "You'll bunk in the cabin. . . . Aw, I know. Men like you sleep in the open. But you can't do thet under Old White Slides in winter. Not much! Make yourself to home, an' I'll walk out after a bit an' we'll look over the dog outfit. When you see thet outfit you'll holler fer help."

Wade bowed his thanks, and, putting on his sombrero, he turned away. As he did so he caught a sound of light, quick footsteps on the far end of the porch.

"Hello, you-all!" cried a girl's voice, with melody in it that vibrated piercingly upon Wade's sensitive ears.

"Mornin', Columbine," replied the rancher.

Bent Wade's heart leaped up. This girlish voice rang upon the chord of memory. Wade had not the strength to look at her then. It was not that he could not bear to look, but that he could not bear the disillusion sure to follow his first glimpse of this adopted daughter of Belllounds. Sweet to delude himself! Ah! the years were bearing sterner upon his head! The old dreams persisted, sadder now for the fact that from long use they had become half-realities! Wade shuffled slowly across the green square to where the cowboy waited for him. His eyes were dim, and a sickness attended the sinking of his heart.

"Wade, I ain't a bettin' fellar, but I'll bet Old Bill took you up," vouchsafed Billings, with interest.

"Glad to say he did," replied Wade. "You're to show me the new cabin where I'm to bunk."

"Come along," said Lem, leading off. "Air you agoin' to handle stock or chase coyotes?"

"My job's huntin'."

"Wal, it may be thet from sunup to sundown, but between-times you'll be sure busy otherwise, I opine," went on Lem. "Did you meet the boss's son?"

"Yes, he was there. An' Belllounds made it plain I was to take orders from him an' not from his son."

"Thet'll make your job a million times easier," declared Lem, as if to make up for former hasty pessimism. He led the way past some log cabins, and sheds with dirt roofs, and low, flat-topped barns, out across another brook where willow-trees were turning yellow. Then the new cabin came into view. It was small, with one door and one window, and a porch across the front. It stood on a small elevation, near the swift brook, and overlooking the ranch-house perhaps a quarter of a mile below. Above it, and across the brook, had been built a high fence constructed of aspen poles laced closely together. The sounds therefrom proclaimed this stockade to be the dog-pen.

Lem helped Wade unpack and carry his outfit into the cabin. It contained one room, the corner of which was filled with blocks and slabs of pine, evidently left there after the construction of the cabin, and meant for fire-wood. The ample size of the stone fireplace attested to the severity of the winters.

"Real sawed boards on the floor!" exclaimed Lem, meaning to impress the new-comer. "I call this a plumb good bunk."

"Much too good for me," replied Wade.

"Wal, I'll look after your hosses," said Lem. "I reckon you'll fix up your bunk. Take my hunch an' ask Miss Collie to find you some furniture an' sich like. She's Old Bill's daughter, an' she makes up fer——fer——wal, fer a lot we hev to stand. I'll fetch the boys over later."

"Do you smoke?" asked Wade. "I've somethin' fine I fetched up from Leadville."

"Smoke! Me? I'll give you a hoss right now for a cigar. I git one onct a year, mebbe."

"Here's a box I've been packin' for long," replied Wade, as he handed it up to Billings. "They're Spanish, all right. Too rich for my blood!"

A box of gold could not have made that cowboy's eyes shine any brighter.

"*Whoop-ee!*" he yelled. "Why, man, you're like the fairy in the kid's story! Won't I make the outfit wild? Aw, I forgot. Thar's only Jim an' Blud left. Wal, I'll divvy with them. Sure, Wade, you hit me right. I was dyin' fer a real smoke. An' I reckon what's mine is yours."

Then he strode out of the cabin, whistling a merry cowboy tune.

Wade was left sitting in the middle of the room on his roll of bedding, and for a long time he remained there motionless, with his head bent, his worn hands idly clasped. A heavy footfall outside aroused him from his meditation.

"Hey, Wade!" called the cheery voice of Belllounds. Then the rancher appeared at the door. "How's this bunk suit you?"

"Much too fine for an old-timer like me," replied Wade.

"Old-timer! Say, you're young yet. Look at me. Sixty-eight

last birthday! Wal, every dog has his day. . . . What're you needin' to fix this bunk comfortable like?"

"Reckon I don't need much."

"Wal, you've beddin' an' cook outfit. Go get a table, an' a chair an' a bench from thet first cabin. The boys thet had it are gone. Somethin' with a back to it, a rockin'-chair, if there's one. You'll find tools, an' boxes, an' stuff in the workshop, if you want to make a cupboard or anythin'."

"How about a lookin'-glass?" asked Wade. "I had a piece, but I broke it."

"Haw! Haw! Mebbe we can rustle thet, too. My girl's good on helpin' the boys fix up. Woman-like, you know. An' she'll fetch you some decorations on her own hook. Now let's take a look at the hounds."

Belllounds led the way out toward the crude dog-corral, and the way he leaped the brook bore witness to the fact that he was still vigorous and spry. The door of the pen was made of boards hung on wire. As Belllounds opened it there came a pattering rush of many padded feet, and a chorus of barks and whines. Wade's surprised gaze took in forty or fifty dogs, mostly hounds, browns and blacks and yellows, all sizes—a motley, mangy, hungry pack, if he had ever seen one.

"I swore I'd buy every hound fetched to me, till I'd cleaned up the varmints around White Slides. An' sure I was imposed on," explained the rancher.

"Some good-lookin' hounds in the bunch," replied Wade. "An' there's hardly too many. I'll train two packs, so I can rest one when the other's huntin'."

"Wal, I'll be dog-goned!" ejaculated Belllounds, with relief. "I sure thought you'd roar. All this rabble to take care of!"

"No trouble after I've got acquainted," said Wade. "Have they been hunted any?"

"Some of the boys took out a bunch. But they split on deer tracks an' elk tracks an' Lord knows what all. Never put up a lion! Then again Billings took some out after a pack of coyotes, an' gol darn me if the coyotes didn't lick the hounds. An' wuss! Jack, my son, got it into his head thet he was a hunter. The other mornin' he found a fresh lion track back of the corral. An' he ups an' puts the whole pack of hounds on the trail. I had a good many more hounds in the pack than you see now. Wal, anyway, it was great to hear the noise thet pack made. Jack lost every blamed hound of them. Thet night an' next day an' the followin' they straggled in. But twenty some never did come back."

Wade laughed. "They may come yet. I reckon, though, they've gone home where they came from. Are any of these hounds recommended?"

"Every consarned one of them," declared Belllounds.

"That's funny. But I guess it's natural. Do you know for sure whether you bought any good dogs?"

"Yes, I gave fifty dollars for two hounds. Got them of a friend in Middle Park whose pack killed off the lions there. They're good dogs, trained on lion, wolf, an' bear."

"Pick 'em out," said Wade.

With a throng of canines crowding and fawning round him, and snapping at one another, it was difficult for the rancher to draw the two particular ones apart so they could be looked over. At length he succeeded, and Wade drove back the rest of the pack.

"The big fellar's Sampson an' the other's Jim," said Belllounds.

Sampson was a huge hound, gray and yellow, with mottled black marks, very long ears, and big, solemn eyes. Jim, a good-sized dog, but small in comparison with the other, was black all over, except around the nose and eyes. Jim had many scars. He was old, yet not past a vigorous age, and he seemed a quiet, dignified, wise hound, quite out of his element in that mongrel pack.

"If they're as good as they look we're lucky," said Wade, as he tied the ends of his rope round their necks. "Now are there any more you know are good?"

"Denver, come hyar!" yelled Belllounds. A white, yellow-spotted hound came wagging his tail. "I'll swear by Denver. An' there's one more—Kane. He's half bloodhound, a queer, wicked kind of dog. He keeps to himself. . . . Kane! Come hyar!"

Belllounds tramped around the corral, and finally found the hound in question, asleep in a dusty hole. Kane was the only beautiful dog in the lot. If half of him was blood-hound the other half was shepherd, for his black and brown hair was inclined to curl, and his head had the fine thorough-bred contour of the shepherd. His ears, long and drooping and thin, betrayed the hound in him. Kane showed no dis-position to be friendly. His dark eyes, sad and mournful, burned with the fires of doubt.

Wade haltered Kane, Jim, and Sampson, which act almost precipitated a fight, and led them out of the corral. Denver, friendly and glad, followed at the rancher's heels.

"I'll keep them with me an' make lead dogs out of them," said Wade. "Belllounds, that bunch hasn't had enough to eat. They're half starved."

"Wal, thet's worried me more'n you'll guess," declared Bell-lounds, with irritation. "What do a lot of cowpunchin' fellars know about dogs? Why, they nearly ate Bludsoe up. He wouldn't feed 'em. An' Wils, who seemed good with dogs, was taken off bad hurt the other day. Lem's been tryin' to rustle feed fer them. Now we'll give back the dogs you don't want to keep, an' thet way thin out the pack."

"Yes, we won't need 'em all. An' I reckon I'll take the worry of this dog-pack off your mind."

"Thet's your job, Wade. My orders are fer you to kill off the varmints. Lions, wolves, coyotes. An' every fall some ole silvertip gits bad, an' now an' then other bears. Whatever you need in the way of supplies jest ask fer. We send regu-lar to Kremmlin'. You can hunt fer two months yet, barrin' an onusual early winter. . . . I'm askin' you—if my son tramps on your toes—I'd take it as a favor fer you to be patient. He's only a boy yet, an' coltish."

Wade divined that was a favor difficult for Belllounds to ask. The old rancher, dominant and forceful and self-suffi-cient all his days, had begun to feel an encroachment of opposition beyond his control. If he but realized it, the favor he asked of Wade was an appeal.

"Belllounds, I get along with everybody," Wade assured him. "An' maybe I can help your son. Before I'd reached here I'd heard he was wild, an' so I'm prepared."

"If you'd do thet—wal, I'd never forgit it," replied the

rancher, slowly. "Jack's been away fer three years. Only got back a week or so ago. I calkilated he'd be sobered, steadied, by—thet—thet work I put him to. But I'm not sure. He's changed. When he gits his own way he's all I could ask. But thet way he wants ain't always what it ought to be. An' so thar's been clashes. But Jack's a fine young man. An' he'll outgrow his temper an' crazy notions. Work'll do it."

"Boys will be boys," replied Wade, philosophically. "I've not forgotten when I was a boy."

"Neither hev I. Wal, I'll be goin', Wade. I reckon Columbine will be up to call on you. Bein' the only woman-folk in my house, she sort of runs it. An' she's sure interested in thet pack of hounds."

Belllounds trudged away, his fine old head erect, his gray hair shining in the sun.

Wade sat down upon the step of his cabin, pondering over the rancher's remarks about his son. Recalling the young man's physiognomy, Wade began to feel that it was familiar to him. He had seen Jack Belllounds before. Wade never made mistakes in faces, though he often had a task to recall names. And he began to go over the recent past, recalling all that he could remember of Meeker, and Cripple Creek, where he had worked for several months, and so on, until he had gone back as far as his last trip to Denver.

"Must have been there," mused Wade, thoughtfully, and he tried to recall all the faces he had seen. This was impossible, of course, yet he remembered many. Then he visualized the places in Denver that for one reason or another had struck him particularly. Suddenly into one of these flashed the pale, sullen, bold face of Jack Belllounds.

"It was *there!*" he exclaimed, incredulously. "Well! . . . If thet's not the strangest yet! Could I be mistaken? No. I saw him. . . . Belllounds must have known it—must have let him stay there. . . . Maybe put him there! He's just the kind of a man to go to extremes to reform his son."

Singular as was this circumstance, Wade dwelt only momentarily on it. He dismissed it with the conviction that it was another strange happening in the string of events that had turned his steps toward White Slides Ranch. Wade's mind stirred to the probability of an early sight of Columbine Bell-lounds. He would welcome it, both as interesting and pleasurable, and surely as a relief. The sooner a meeting with her was over the better. His life had been one long succession of shocks, so that it seemed nothing the future held could thrill him, amaze him, torment him. And yet how well he knew that his heart was only the more responsive for all it had withstood! Perhaps here at White Slides he might meet with an experience dwarfing all others. It was possible; it was in the nature of events. And though he repudiated such a possibility, he fortified himself against a subtle divination that he might at last have reached the end of his long trail, where anything might happen.

Three of the hounds lay down at Wade's feet. Kane, the bloodhound, stood watching this new master, after the manner of a dog who was a judge of men. He sniffed at Wade. He grew a little less surly.

Wade's gaze, however, was on the path that led down along the border of the brook to disappear in the willows. Above this clump of yellowing trees could be seen the ranch-house. A girl with fair hair stepped off the porch. She appeared to be carrying something in her arms, and shortly disappeared behind the willows. Wade saw her and surmised that she was coming to his cabin. He did not expect any more or think any more. His faculties condensed to the objective one of sight.

The girl, when she reappeared, was perhaps a hundred yards distant. Wade bent on her one keen, clear glance. Then his brain and his blood beat wildly. He saw a slender girl in riding-costume, lithe and strong, with the free step of one used to the open. It was this form, this step that struck Wade. "My—God! how like Lucy!" he whispered, and he tried to pierce the distance to see her face. It gleamed in the sunshine. Her fair hair waved in the wind. She was coming, but so slowly! All of Wade that was physical and emotional seemed to wait—clamped. The moment was age-long, with nothing beyond it. While she was still at a distance her face became distinct. And Wade sustained a terrible shock. . . . Then, as one in a dream, as in a blur of strained peering into a maze, he saw the face of his sweetheart, his wife, the Lucy of his early manhood. It moved him out of the past. Closer! Pang on pang quivered in his heart. Was this only a nightmare? Or had he at last gone mad! This girl raised her head. She was looking—she saw him. Terror mounted upon Wade's consciousness.

"That's Lucy's face!" he gasped. "So help—me, God! . . . It's for this—I wandered here! She's my flesh an' blood—my Lucy's child—my own!"

Fear and presentiment and blank amaze and stricken consciousness left him in the lightning-flash of divination that was recognition as well. A shuddering cataclysm enveloped him, a passion so stupendous that it almost brought oblivion.

The three hounds leaped up with barks and wagging tails. They welcomed this visitor. Kane lost still more of his canine aloofness.

Wade's breast heaved. The blue sky, the gray hills, the green willows, all blurred in his sight, that seemed to hold clear only the face floating closer.

"I'm Columbine Bellllounds," said a voice.

It stilled the storm in Wade. It was real. It was a voice of twenty years ago. The burden on his breast lifted. Then flashed the spirit, the old self-control of a man whose life had held many terrible moments.

"Mornin', miss. I'm glad to meet you," he replied, and there was no break, no tone unnatural in his greeting.

So they gazed at each other, she with that instinctive look peculiar to women in its intuitive powers, but common to all persons who had lived far from crowds and to whom a newcomer was an event. Wade's gaze, intense and all-embracing, found that face now closer in resemblance to the imagined Lucy's—a pretty face, rather than beautiful, but strong and sweet—its striking qualities being a colorless fairness of skin that yet held a rose and golden tint, and the eyes of a rare and exquisite shade of blue.

"Oh! Are you feeling ill?" she asked. "You look so—so pale."

"No. I'm only tuckered out," replied Wade, easily, as he wiped the clammy drops from his brow. "It was a long ride to get here."

"I'm the lady of the house," she said, with a smile. "I'm glad to welcome you to White Slides, and hope you'll like it."

"Well, Miss Columbine, I reckon I will," he replied, returning the smile. "Now if I was younger I'd like it powerful much."

She laughed at that. "Men are all alike, young or old."

"Don't ever think so," said Wade, earnestly.

"No? I guess you're right about that. I've fetched you up some things for your cabin. May I peep in?"

"Come in," replied Wade, rising. "You must excuse my manners. It's long indeed since I had a lady caller."

She went in, and Wade, standing on the threshold, saw her survey the room with a woman's sweeping glance.

"I told dad to put some—"

"Miss, your dad told me to go get them, an' I've not done it yet. But I will presently."

"Very well. I'll leave these things and come back later," she replied, depositing a bundle upon the floor. "You won't mind if I try to—to make you a little comfortable. It's dreadful the way outdoor men live when they do get indoors."

"I reckon I'll be slow in lettin' you see what a good housekeeper I am," he replied. "Because then, maybe, I'll see more of you."

"Weren't you a sad flatterer in your day?" she queried, archly.

Her intonation, the tilt of her head, gave Wade such a pang that he could not answer. And to hide his momentary restraint he turned back to the hounds. Then she came out upon the porch.

"I love hounds," she said, patting Denver, which caress immediately made Jim and Sampson jealous. "I've gotten on pretty well with these, but that Kane won't make up. Isn't he splendid? But he's afraid—no, not afraid of me, but he doesn't like me."

"It's mistrust. He's been hurt. I reckon he'll get over that after a while."

"You don't beat dogs?" she asked, eagerly.

"No, miss. That's not the way to get on with hounds or horses."

Her glance was a blue flash of pleasure.

"How glad that makes me! Why, I quit coming here to see and feed the dogs because somebody was always kicking them around."

Wade handed the rope to her. "You hold them, so when I come out with some meat they won't pile over me." He went inside, took all that was left of the deer haunch out of his pack, and, picking up his knife, returned to the porch. The hounds saw the meat and yelped. They pulled on the rope.

"You hounds behave," ordered Wade, as he sat down on the step and began to cut the meat. "Jim, you're the oldest an' hungriest. Here. . . . Now you, Sampson. Here!" . . . The big hound snapped at the meat. Whereupon Wade slapped him. "Are you a pup or a wolf that you grab for it? Here." Sampson was slower to act, but he snapped again. Whereupon Wade hit him again, with open hand, not with violence or rancor, but a blow that meant Sampson must obey.

Next time the hound did not snap. Denver had to be cuffed several times before he showed deference to this new master. But the bloodhound Kane refused to take any meat out of Wade's hand. He growled and showed his teeth, and sniffed hungrily.

"Kane will have to be handled carefully," observed Wade. "He'd bite pretty quick."

"But he's so splendid," said the girl. "I don't like to think he's mean. You'll be good to him—try to win him?"

"I'll do my best with him."

"Dad's full of glee that he has a real hunter at White Slides at last. Now I'm glad, and sorry, too. I hate to think of little calves being torn and killed by lions and wolves. And it's dreadful to know bears eat grown-up cattle. But I love the mourn of a wolf and the yelp of a coyote. I can't help hoping you don't kill them all—quite."

"It's not likely, miss," he replied. "I'll be pretty sure to clean out the lions an' drive off the bears. But the wolf family can't be exterminated. No animal so cunnin' as a wolf! . . . I'll tell you. . . . Some years ago I went to cook on a ranch north of Denver, on the edge of the plains. An' right off I began to hear stories about a big lobo—a wolf that was an old residenter. He'd been known for long, an' he got meaner an' wiser as he was hunted. His specialty got to be yearlings, an' the ranchers all over rose up in arms against him. They hired all the old hunters an' trappers in the country to kill him. No good! Old Lobo went right on pullin' down yearlings. Every night he'd get one or more. An' he was so cute an' so swift that he'd work on different ranches on different nights. Finally he killed eleven yearlings for my boss on one night. Eleven! Think of that. An' then I said to my boss, 'I reckon you'd better let me go kill that gray butcher.' An' my boss laughed at me. But he let me go. He'd have tried anythin'. I took a hunk of meat, a blanket, my gun, an' a pair of snow-shoes, an' I set out on old Lobo's tracks. . . . An', Miss Columbine, I *walked* old Lobo to death in the snow!"

"Why, how wonderful!" exclaimed the girl, breathless and glowing with interest. "Oh, it seems a pity such a splendid brute should be killed. Wild animals are cruel. I wish it were different."

"Life is cruel, miss, an' I echo your wish," replied Wade, sadly.

"You have had great experiences. Dad said to me, 'Collie, here at last is a man who can tell you enough stories!' . . . But I don't believe you ever could."

"You like stories?" asked Wade, curiously.

"Love them. All kinds, but I like adventure best. *I* should have been a boy. Isn't it strange, I can't hurt anything myself or bear to see even a steer slaughtered? But you can't tell too bloody and terrible stories for me. Except I hate Indian stories. The very thought of Indians makes me shudder. . . . Some day I'll tell you a story."

Wade could not find his tongue readily.

"I must go now," she continued, and moved off the porch. Then she hesitated, and turned with a smile that was wistful and impulsive. "I—I believe we'll be good friends."

"Miss Columbine, we sure will, if I can live up to my part," replied Wade.

Her smile deepened, even while her gaze grew unconsciously penetrating. Wade felt how subtly they were drawn to each other. But she had no inkling of that.

"It takes two to make a bargain," she replied, seriously. "I've my part. Good-by."

Wade watched her lithe stride, and as she drew away the

restraint he had put upon himself loosened. When she disappeared his feeling burst all bounds. Dragging the dogs inside, he closed the door. Then, like one broken and spent, he fell face against the wall, with the hoarsely whispered words, "I'm thankin' God!"

6

◉

SEPTEMBER'S GLORY OF GOLD and red and purple began to fade with the autumnal equinox. It rained enough to soak the frost-bitten leaves, and then the mountain winds sent them flying and fluttering and scurrying to carpet the dells and spot the pools in the brooks and color the trails. When the weather cleared and the sun rose bright again many of the aspen thickets were leafless and bare, and the willows showed stark against the gray sage hills, and the vines had lost their fire. Hills and valleys had sobered with subtle change that left them none the less beautiful.

A mile or more down the road from White Slides, in a protected nook, nestled two cabins belonging to a cattleman named Andrews, who had formerly worked for Belllounds and had recently gone into the stock business for himself. He had a rather young wife, and several children, and a brother who rode for him. These people were the only neighbors of Belllounds for some ten miles on the road toward Kremmling.

Columbine liked Mrs. Andrews and often rode or walked down there for a little visit and a chat with her friend and a romp with the children.

Toward the end of September Columbine found herself combating a strong desire to go down to the Andrews ranch and try to learn some news about Wilson Moore. If anything had been heard at White Slides it certainly had not been told her. Jack Belllounds had ridden to Kremmling and back in one day, but Columbine would have endured much before asking him for information.

She did, however, inquire of the freighter who hauled Belllounds's supplies, and the answer she got was awkwardly evasive. That nettled Columbine. Also it raised a suspicion which she strove to subdue. Finally it seemed apparent that Wilson Moore's name was not to be mentioned to her.

First, in her growing resentment, she had an impulse to go to her new friend, the hunter Wade, and confide in him not only her longing to learn about Wilson, but also other matters that were growing daily more burdensome. How strange for her to feel that in some way Jack Belllounds had come between her and the old man she loved and called father! Columbine had not divined that until lately. She felt it now in the fact that she no longer sought the rancher as she used to, and he had apparently avoided her. But then, Columbine reflected, she might be entirely wrong, for when Belllounds did meet her at meal-times, or anywhere, he seemed just as affectionate as of old. Still he was not the same man. A chill, an atmosphere of shadow, had pervaded the once wholesome ranch. And so, feeling not yet well enough acquainted with Wade to confide so intimately in him, she stifled her impulses and resolved to make some effort herself to find out what she wanted to know.

As luck would have it, when she started out to walk down to the Andrews ranch she encountered Jack Belllounds.

"Where are you going?" he inquired, inquisitively.

"I'm going to see Mrs. Andrews," she replied.

"No, you're not!" he declared, quickly, with a flash.

Columbine felt a queer sensation deep within her, a hot little gathering that seemed foreign to her physical being, and ready to burst out. Of late it had stirred in her at words or acts of Jack Belllounds. She gazed steadily at him, and he returned her look with interest. What he was thinking she had no idea of, but for herself it was a recurrence and an emphasis of the fact that she seemed growing farther away from this young man she had to marry. The weeks since his arrival had been the most worrisome she could remember.

"I *am* going," she replied, slowly.

"No!" he replied, violently. "I won't have you running off down there to—to gossip with that Andrews woman."

"Oh, *you* won't?" inquired Columbine, very quietly. How little he understood her!

"That's what I said."

"You're not my boss yet, Mister Jack Belllounds," she flashed, her spirit rising. He could irritate her as no one else.

"I soon will be. And what's a matter of a week or a month?" he went on, calming down a little.

"I've promised, yes," she said, feeling her face blanch, "and I keep my promises. . . . But I didn't say when. If you talk like that to me it might be a good many weeks—or—or months before I name the day."

"*Columbine!*" he cried, as she turned away. There was genuine distress in his voice. Columbine felt again an assurance that had troubled her. No matter how she was reacting to this new relation, it seemed a fearful truth that Jack was really falling in love with her. This time she did not soften.

"I'll call dad to *make* you stay home," he burst out again, his temper rising.

Columbine wheeled as on a pivot.

"If you do you've got less sense than I thought."

Passion claimed him then.

"I know why you're going. It's to see that club-footed cow-boy Moore! . . . Don't let me catch you with him!"

Columbine turned her back upon Belllounds and swung away, every pulse in her throbbing and smarting. She hurried on into the road. She wanted to run, not to get out of sight or hearing, but to fly from something, she knew not what.

"Oh! it's more than his temper!" she cried, hot tears in her eyes. "He's mean—*mean*—MEAN! What's the use of me denying that—any more—just because I love dad? . . . My life will be wretched. . . . It *is* wretched!"

Her anger did not last long, nor did her resentment. She reproached herself for the tart replies that had inflamed Jack. Never again would she forget herself!

"But he—he makes me furious," she cried, in sudden excuse for herself. "What did he say? 'That club-footed cow-boy Moore'! . . . Oh, that was vile. He's heard, then, that poor Wilson has a bad foot, perhaps permanently crippled. . . . If it's true . . . But why should he yell that he knew I wanted to see Wilson? . . . I did *not!* I *do* not. . . . Oh, but I do, I do!"

And then Columbine was to learn straightway that she would forget herself again, that she had forgotten, and that a sadder, stranger truth was dawning upon her—she was discovering another Columbine within herself, a wilful, passionate, different creature who would no longer be denied.

Almost before Columbine realized that she had started upon the visit she was within sight of the Andrews ranch. So swiftly had she walked! It behooved her to hide such excitement as had dominated her. And to that end she slowed her pace, trying to put her mind on other matters.

The children saw her first and rushed upon her, so that when she reached the cabin door she could not well have been otherwise than rosy and smiling. Mrs. Andrews, ruddy and strong, looked the pioneer rancher's hard-working wife. Her face brightened at the advent of Columbine, and showed a little surprise and curiosity as well.

"Laws, but it's good to see you, Columbine," was her greeting. "You 'ain't been here for a long spell."

"I've been coming, but just put it off," replied Columbine.

And so, after the manner of women neighbors, they began to talk of the fall round-up, and the near approach of winter with its loneliness, and the children, all of which naturally led to more personal and interesting topics.

"An' is it so, Columbine, that you're to marry Jack Bell-lounds?" asked Mrs. Andrews, presently.

"Yes, I guess it is," replied Columbine, smiling.

"Humph! I'm no relative of yours or even a particular, close friend, but I'd like to say—"

"Please don't," interposed Columbine.

"All right, my girl. I guess it's better I don't say anythin'. It's a pity, though, unless you love this Buster Jack. An' you never used to do that, I'll swan."

"No, I don't love Jack—yet—as I ought to love a husband. But I'll try, and if—if I—I never do—still, it's my duty to marry him."

"Some woman ought to talk to Bill Belllounds," declared

Mrs. Andrews with a grimness that boded ill for the old rancher.

"Did you know we had a new man up at the ranch?" asked Columbine, changing the subject.

"You mean the hunter, Hell-Bent Wade?"

"Yes. But I hate that ridiculous name," said Columbine.

"It's queer, like lots of names men get in these parts. An' it'll stick. Wade's been here twice; once as he was passin' with the hounds, an' the other night. I like him, Columbine. He's true-blue, for all his strange name. My men-folks took to him like ducks to water."

"I'm glad. I took to him almost like that," rejoined Columbine. "He has the saddest face I ever saw."

"Sad? Wal, yes. That man has seen a good deal of what they tacked on to his name. I laughed when I seen him first. Little lame fellar, crooked-legged an' ragged, with thet awful homely face! But I forgot how he looked next time he came."

"That's just it. He's not much to look at, but you forget his homeliness right off," replied Columbine, warmly. "You feel something behind all his—his looks."

"Wal, you an' me are women, an' we feel different," replied Mrs. Andrews. "Now my men-folks take much store on what Wade can *do*. He fixed up Tom's gun, that's been out of whack for a year. He made our clock run ag'in, an' run better than ever. Then he saved our cow from that poison-weed. An' Tom gave her up to die."

"The boys up home were telling me Mr. Wade had saved some of our cattle. Dad was delighted. You know he's lost a good many head of stock from this poison-weed. I saw so many dead steers on my last ride up the mountain. It's too bad our new man didn't get here sooner to save them. I asked him how he did it, and he said he was a doctor."

"A cow-doctor," laughed Mrs. Andrews. "Wal, that's a new one on me. Accordin' to Tom, this here Wade, when he seen our sick cow, said she'd eat poison-weed—larkspur, I think he called it—an' then when she drank water it formed a gas in her stomach an' she swelled up turrible. Wade jest stuck his knife in her side a little an' let the gas out, and she got well."

"Ughh! . . . What cruel doctoring! But if it saves the cattle, then it's good."

"It'll save them if they can be got to right off," replied Mrs. Andrews.

"Speaking of doctors," went on Columbine, striving to make her query casual, "do you know whether or not Wilson Moore had his foot treated by a doctor at Kremmling?"

"He did not," answered Mrs. Andrews. "Wasn't no doctor there. They'd had to send to Denver, an', as Wils couldn't take that trip or wait so long, why, Mrs. Plummer fixed up his foot. She made a good job of it, too, as I can testify."

"Oh, I'm—very thankful!" murmured Columbine. "He'll not be crippled or—or club-footed, then?"

"I reckon not. You can see for yourself. For Wils's here. He was drove up night before last an' is stayin' with my brother-in-law—in the other cabin there."

Mrs. Andrews launched all this swiftly, with evident pleasure, but with more of woman's subtle motive. Her eyes were bent with shrewd kindness upon the younger woman.

"Here!" exclaimed Columbine, with a start, and for an instant she was at the mercy of conflicting surprise and joy and alarm. Alternately she flushed and paled.

"Sure he's here," replied Mrs. Andrews, now looking out of the door. "He ought to be in sight somewheres. He's walkin' with a crutch."

"Crutch!" cried Columbine, in dismay.

"Yes, crutch, an' he made it himself. . . . I don't see him nowheres. Mebbe he went in when he see you comin'. For he's powerful sensitive about that crutch."

"Then—if he's so—so sensitive, perhaps I'd better go," said Columbine, struggling with embarrassment and discomfiture. What if she happened to meet him! Would he imagine her purpose in coming there? Her heart began to beat unwontedly.

"Suit yourself, lass," replied Mrs. Andrews, kindly. "I know you and Wils quarreled, for he told me. An' it's a pity. . . . Wal, if you must go, I hope you'll come again before the snow flies. Good-by."

Columbine bade her a hurried good-by and ventured forth with misgivings. And almost around the corner of the second cabin, which she had to pass, and before she had time to recover her composure, she saw Wilson Moore, hobbling along on a crutch, holding a bandaged foot off the ground. He had seen her; he was hurrying to avoid a meeting, or to get behind the corrals there before she observed him.

"Wilson!" she called, involuntarily. The instant the name left her lips she regretted it. But too late! The cowboy halted, slowly turned.

Then Columbine walked swiftly up to him, suddenly as brave as she had been fearful. Sight of him had changed her.

"Wilson Moore, you meant to avoid me," she said, with reproach.

"Howdy, Columbine!" he drawled, ignoring her words.

"Oh, I was so sorry you were hurt!" she burst out. "And now I'm so glad—you're—you're . . . Wilson, you're thin and pale—you've suffered!"

"It pulled me down a bit," he replied.

Columbine had never before seen his face anything except bronzed and lean and healthy, but now it bore testimony to pain and strain and patient endurance. He looked older. Something in the fine, dark, hazel eyes hurt her deeply.

"You never sent me word," she went on, reproachfully. "No one would tell me anything. The boys said they didn't know. Dad was angry when I asked him. I'd never have asked Jack. And the freighter who drove up—he lied to me. So I came down here today purposely to ask news of you, but I never dreamed you were here. . . . Now I'm glad I came."

What a singular, darkly kind, yet strange glance he gave her!

"That was like you, Columbine," he said. "I knew you'd feel badly about my accident. But how could I send word to you?"

"You saved—Pronto," she returned, with a strong tremor in her voice. "I can't thank you enough."

"That was a funny thing. Pronto went out of his head. I hope he's all right."

"He's almost well. It took some time to pick all the splinters out of him. He'll be all right soon—none the worse for that—that cowboy trick of Mister Jack Belllounds."

Columbine finished bitterly. Moore turned his thoughtful gaze away from her.

"I hope Old Bill is well," he remarked, lamely.

"Have you told your folks of your accident?" asked Columbine, ignoring his remark.

"No."

"Oh, Wilson, you ought to have sent for them, or have written at least."

"Me? To go crying for them when I got in trouble? I couldn't see it that way."

"Wilson, you'll be going—home—soon—to Denver—won't you?" she faltered.

"No," he replied, shortly.

"But what will you do? Surely you can't work—not so soon?"

"Columbine, I'll never—be able to ride again—like I used to," he said, tragically. "I'll ride, yes, but never the old way."

"Oh!" Columbine's tone, and the exquisite softness and tenderness with which she placed a hand on the rude crutch, would have been enlightening to any one but these two absorbed in themselves. "I can't bear to believe that."

"I'm afraid it's true. Bad smash, Columbine! I just missed being club-footed."

"You should have care. You should have . . . Wilson, do you intend to stay here with the Andrews?"

"Not much. They have troubles of their own. Columbine, I'm going to homestead one hundred and sixty acres."

"Homestead!" she exclaimed, in amaze. "Where?"

"Up there under Old White Slides. I've long intended to. You know that pretty little valley under the red bluff. There's a fine spring. You've been there with me. There by the old cabin built by prospectors?"

"Yes, I know. It's a pretty place—fine valley, but Wils, you can't *live* there," she expostulated.

"Why not, I'd like to know?"

"That little cubby-hole! It's only a tiny one-room cabin, roof all gone, chinks open, chimney crumbling. . . . Wilson, you don't mean to tell me you want to live there alone?"

"Sure. What'd you think?" he replied, with sarcasm. "Ex-

pect me to *marry* some girl? Well, I wouldn't, even if any
one would have a cripple."

"Who—who will take care of you?" she asked, blushing
furiously.

"I'll take care of myself," he declared. "Good Lord! Columbine, I'm not an invalid yet. I've got a few friends who'll
help me fix up the cabin. And that reminds me. There's a lot
of my stuff up in the bunk-house at White Slides. I'm going
to drive up soon to haul it away."

"Wilson Moore, do you mean it?" she asked, with grave
wonder. "Are you going to homestead near White Slides
Ranch—and *live* there—when—"

She could not finish. An overwhelming disaster, for which
she had no name, seemed to be impending.

"Yes, I am," he replied. "Funny how things turn out, isn't
it?"

"It's very—very funny," she said, dazedly, and she turned
slowly away without another word.

"Good-by, Columbine," he called out after her, with fare-
well, indeed, in his voice.

All the way home Columbine was occupied with feelings
that swayed her to the exclusion of rational consideration of
the increasing perplexity of her situation. And to make matters worse, when she arrived at the ranch it was to meet Jack
Belllounds with a face as black as a thunder-cloud.

"The old man wants to see you," he announced, with an
accent that recalled his threat of a few hours back.

"Does he?" queried Columbine, loftily. "From the courteous
way you speak I imagine it's important."

Belllounds did not deign to reply to this. He sat on the
porch, where evidently he had awaited her return, and he
looked anything but happy.

"Where is dad?" continued Columbine.

Jack motioned toward the second door, beyond which he
sat, the one that opened into the room the rancher used as
a kind of office and storeroom. As Columbine walked by
Jack he grasped her skirt.

"Columbine! you're angry?" he said, appealingly.

"I reckon I am," replied Columbine.

"Don't go in to dad when you're that way," implored Jack. "He's angry, too—and—and—it'll only make matters worse."

From long experience Columbine could divine when Jack had done something in the interest of self and then had awakened to possible consequences. She pulled away from him without replying, and knocked on the office door.

"Come in," called the rancher.

Columbine went in. "Hello, dad! Do you want me?"

Belllounds sat at an old table, bending over a soiled ledger, with a stubby pencil in his huge hand. When he looked up Columbine gave a little start.

"Where've you been?" he asked, gruffly.

"I've been calling on Mrs. Andrews," replied Columbine.

"Did you go thar to see her?"

"Why—certainly!" answered Columbine, with a slow break in her speech.

"You didn't go to meet Wilson Moore?"

"No."

"An' I reckon you'll say you hadn't heerd he was there?"

"I had not," flashed Columbine.

"Wal, *did* you see him?"

"Yes, sir, I did, but quite by accident."

"Ahuh! Columbine, are you lyin' to me?"

The hot blood flooded to Columbine's cheeks, as if she had been struck a blow.

"*Dad!*" she cried, in hurt amaze.

Belllounds seemed thick, imponderable, as if something had forced a crisis in him and his brain was deeply involved. The habitual, cool, easy, bold, and frank attitude in the meeting of all situations seemed to have been encroached upon by a break, a bewilderment, a lessening of confidence.

"Wal, are you lyin'?" he repeated, either blind to or unaware of her distress.

"I could not—lie to you," she faltered, "even—if—I wanted to."

The heavy, shadowed gaze of his big eyes was bent upon her as if she had become a new and perplexing problem.

"But you seen Moore?"

"Yes—sir." Columbine's spirit rose.

"An' talked with him?"

"Of course."

"Lass, I ain't likin' thet, an' I ain't likin' the way you look an' speak."

"I am sorry. I can't help either."

"What'd this cowboy say to you?"

"We talked mostly about his injured foot."

"An' what else?" went on Belllounds, his voice rising.

"About—what he meant to do now."

"Ahuh! An' thet's homesteadin' the Sage Creek Valley?"

"Yes, sir."

"Did you want him to do thet?"

"I! Indeed I didn't."

"Columbine, not so long ago you told me this fellar wasn't sweet on you. An' do you still say that to me—are you still insistin' he ain't in love with you?"

"He never said so—I never believed it . . . and now I'm sure—he isn't!"

"Ahuh! Wal, thet same day you was jest as sure you didn't care anythin' particular fer him. Are you thet sure now?"

"No!" whispered Columbine, very low. She trembled with a suggestion of unknown forces. Not to save a new and growing pride would she evade any question from this man upon whom she had no claim, to whom she owed her life and her bringing up. But something cold formed in her.

Belllounds, self-centered and serious as he strangely was, seemed to check his probing, either from fear of hearing more from her or from an awakening of former kindness. But her reply was a shock to him, and, throwing down his pencil with the gesture of a man upon whom decision was forced, he rose to tower over her.

"You've been like a daughter to me. I've done all I knowed how fer you. I've lived up to the best of my lights. An' I've loved you," he said, sonorously and pathetically. "You know what my hopes are—fer the boy—an' fer you. . . . We needn't waste any more talk. From this minnit you're free to do as you like. Whatever you do won't make any change in my carin' fer you. . . . But you gotta decide. Will you marry Jack or not?"

"I promised you—I would. I'll keep my word," replied Columbine, steadily.

"So far so good," went on the rancher. "I'm respectin' you fer what you say. . . . An' now, *when* will you marry him?"

The little room drifted around in Columbine's vague, blank sight. All seemed to be drifting. She had no solid anchor.

"Any—day you say—the sooner the—better," she whispered.

"Wal, lass, I'm thankin' you," he replied, with voice that sounded afar to her. "An' I swear, if I didn't believe it's best fer Jack an' you, why I'd never let you marry. . . . So we'll set the day. October first! Thet's the day you was fetched to me a baby—more'n seventeen years ago."

"October—first—then, dad," she said, brokenly, and she kissed him as if in token of what she knew she owed him. Then she went out, closing the door behind her.

Jack, upon seeing her, hastily got up, with more than concern in his pale face.

"Columbine!" he cried, hoarsely. "How you look! . . . Tell me. What happened? Girl, don't tell me you've—you've—"

"Jack Belllounds," interrupted Columbine, in tragic amaze at this truth about to issue from her lips, "I've promised to marry you—on October first."

He let out a shout of boyish exultation and suddenly clasped her in his arms. But there was nothing boyish in the way he handled her, in the almost savage evidence of possession. "Collie, I'm mad about you," he began, ardently. "You never let me tell you. And I've grown worse and worse. Today I—when I saw you going down there—where that Wilson Moore is—I got terribly jealous. I was sick. I'd been glad to kill him! . . . It made me see how I loved you. Oh, I didn't know. But now . . . Oh, I'm mad for you!" He crushed her to him, unmindful of her struggles; his face and neck were red; his eyes on fire. And he began trying to kiss her mouth, but failed, as she struggled desperately. His kisses fell upon cheek and ear and hair.

"Let me—go!" panted Columbine. "You've no—no— Oh, you might have waited." Breaking from him, she fled, and got inside her room with the door almost closed, when his foot intercepted it.

Belllounds was half laughing in his exultation, half furious at her escape, and altogether beside himself.

"No," she replied, so violently that it appeared to awake him to the fact that there was some one besides himself to consider.

"Aw!" He heaved a deep sigh. "All right. I won't try to get in. Only listen. . . . Collie, don't mind my—my way of showing you how I felt. Fact is, I went plumb off my head. Is that any wonder, you—you darling—when I've been so scared you'd never have me? Collie, I've felt that you were the one thing in the world I wanted most and would never get. But now. . . . October first! Listen. I promise you I'll not drink any more—nor gamble—nor nag dad for money. I don't like his way of running the ranch, but I'll do it, as long as he lives. I'll even try to tolerate that club-footed cowboy's brass in homesteading a ranch right under my nose. I'll—I'll do anything you ask of me."

"Then—please—go away!" cried Columbine, with a sob.

When he was gone Columbine barred the door and threw herself upon her bed to shut out the light and to give vent to her surcharged emotions. She wept like a girl whose youth was ending; and after the paroxysm had passed, leaving her weak and strangely changed, she tried to reason out what had happened to her. Over and over again she named the appeal of the rancher, the sense of her duty, the decision she had reached, and the disgust and terror inspired in her by Jack Belllounds's reception of her promise. These were facts of the day and they had made of her a palpitating, unhappy creature, who nevertheless had been brave to face the rancher and confess that which she had scarce confessed to herself. But now she trembled and cringed on the verge of a catastrophe that withheld its whole truth.

"I begin to see now," she whispered, after the thought had come and gone and returned to change again. "If Wilson had—cared for me I—I might have—cared, too. . . . But I do—care—something. I couldn't lie to dad. Only I'm not sure—how much. I never dreamed of—of *loving* him, or any one. It's so strange. All at once I feel old. And I can't understand these—these feelings that shake me."

So Columbine brooded over the trouble that had come to her, never regretting her promise to the old rancher, but growing keener in the realization of a complexity in her nature that sooner or later would separate the life of her duty from the life of her desire. She seemed all alone, and when this feeling possessed her a strange reminder of the hunter Wade flashed up. She stifled another impulse to confide in him. Wade had the softness of a woman, and his face was a record of the trials and travails through which he had come unhardened, unembittered. Yet how could she tell her troubles to him? A stranger, a rough man of the wilds, whose name had preceded him, notorious and deadly, with that vital tang of the West in its meaning! Nevertheless, Wade drew her, and she thought of him until the recurring memory of Jack Belllounds's rude clasp again crept over her with an augmenting disgust and fear. Must she submit to that? Had she promised that? And then Columbine felt the dawning of realities.

7

◉

COLUMBINE WAS AWAKENED in the gray dawn by the barking of coyotes. She dreaded the daylight thus heralded. Never before in her life had she hated the rising of the sun. Resolutely she put the past behind her and faced the future, believing now that with the great decision made she needed only to keep her mind off what might have been, and to attend to her duty.

At breakfast she found the rancher in better spirits than he had been for weeks. He informed her that Jack had ridden off early for Kremmling, there to make arrangements for the wedding on October first.

"Jack's out of his head," said Belllounds. "Wal, thet comes only onct in a man's life. I remember . . . Jack's goin' to drive you to Kremmlin' an' ther take stage fer Denver. I allow you'd better put in your best licks on fixin' up an' packin' the clothes you'll need. Women-folk naturally want to look smart on weddin'-trips."

"Dad!" exclaimed Columbine, in dismay. "I never thought of clothes. And I don't want to leave White Slides."

"But, lass, you're goin' to be married!" expostulated Belllounds.

"Didn't it occur to Jack to take me to Kremmling? I can't make new dresses out of old ones."

"Wal, I reckon neither of us thought of thet. But you can buy what you like in Denver."

Columbine resigned herself. After all, what did it matter to her? The vague, haunting dreams of girlhood would never come true. So she went to her wardrobe and laid out all her wearing apparel. Taking stock of it this way caused her further dismay, for she had nothing fit to wear in which either to be married or to take a trip to Denver. There appeared to be nothing to do but take the rancher's advice, and Columbine set about refurbishing her meager wardrobe. She sewed all day.

What with self-control and work and the passing of hours, Columbine began to make some approach to tranquillity. In her simplicity she even began to hope that being good and steadfast and dutiful would earn her a little meed of happiness. Some haunting doubt of this flashed over her mind like a swift shadow of a black wing, but she dispelled that as she had dispelled the fear and disgust which often rose up in her mind.

To Columbine's surprise and to the rancher's concern the prospective bridegroom did not return from Kremmling on the second day. When night came Belllounds reluctantly gave up looking for him.

Jack's non-appearance suited Columbine, and she would have been glad to be let alone until October first, which date now seemed appallingly close. On the afternoon of Jack's third day of absence from the ranch Columbine rode out for some needed exercise. Pronto not being available, she rode another mustang and one that kept her busy. On the way back to the ranch she avoided the customary trail which led by the cabins of Wade and the cowboys. Columbine had not seen one of her friends since the unfortunate visit to the Andrews ranch. She particularly shrank from meeting Wade, which feeling was in strange contrast to her former impulses.

As she rode around the house she encountered Wilson Moore seated in a light wagon. Her mustang reared, almost unseating her. But she handled him roughly, being suddenly surprised and angry at this unexpected meeting with the cowboy.

"Howdy, Columbine!" greeted Wilson, as she brought the mustang to his feet. "You're sure learning to handle a horse —since I left this here ranch. Wonder who's teaching you! I never could get you to rake even a bronc!"

The cowboy had drawled out his admiring speech, half amused and half satiric.

"I'm—mad!" declared Columbine. "That's why."

"What're you mad at?" queried Wilson.

She did not reply, but kept on gazing steadily at him. Moore still looked pale and drawn, but he had improved since last she saw him.

"Aren't you going to speak to a fellow?" he went on.

"How are you, Wils?" she asked.

"Pretty good for a club-footed has-been cowpuncher."

"I wish you wouldn't call yourself such names," rejoined Columbine, peevishly. "You're not a club-foot. I hate that word!"

"Me, too. Well, joking aside, I'm better. My foot is fine. Now, if I don't hurt it again I'll sure never be a club-foot."

"You must be careful," she said, earnestly.

"Sure. But it's hard for me to be idle. Think of me lying still all day with nothing to do but read! That's what knocked me out. I wouldn't have minded the pain if I could have gotten about. . . . Columbine, I've moved in!"

"What! Moved in?" she queried, blankly.

"Sure. I'm in my cabin on the hill. It's plumb great. Tom Andrews and Bert and your hunter Wade fixed up the cabin for me. That Wade is sure a good fellow. And say! what he can do with his hands! He's been kind to me. Took an interest in me, and between you and me he sort of cheered me up."

"Cheered you up! Wils, were you unhappy?" she asked, directly.

"Well, rather. What'd you expect of a cowboy who'd crippled himself—and lost his girl?"

Columbine felt the smart of tingling blood in her face, and she looked from Wilson to the wagon. It contained saddles, blankets, and other cowboy accoutrements for which he had evidently come.

"That's a double misfortune," she replied, evenly. "It's too bad both came at once. It seems to me if I were a cowboy and—and felt so toward a girl, I'd have let her know."

"This girl I mean knew, all right," he said, nodding his head.

"She didn't—she didn't!" cried Columbine.

"How do *you* know?" he queried, with feigned surprise. He was bent upon torturing her.

"You meant me. I'm the girl you lost!"

"Yes, you are—God help me!" replied Moore, with genuine emotion.

"But you—you never told me—you never told me," faltered Columbine, in distress.

"Never told you what? That you were my girl?"

"No—no. But that you—you cared—"

"Columbine Bellounds, I told you—let you see—in every way under the sun," he flashed at her.

"Let me see—what?" faltered Columbine, feeling as if the world were about to end.

"That I loved you."

"Oh! . . . Wilson!" whispered Columbine, wildly.

"Yes—loved you. Could you have been so innocent—so blind you never knew? I can't believe it."

"But I never dreamed you—you—" She broke off dazedly, overwhelmed by a tragic, glorious truth.

"Collie! . . . Would it have made any difference?"

"Oh, all the difference in the world!" she wailed.

"What difference?" he asked, passionately.

Columbine gazed wide-eyed and helpless at the young man. She did not know how to tell him what all the difference in the world really was.

Suddenly Wilson turned away from her to listen. Then she heard rapid beating of hoofs on the road.

"That's Buster Jack," said the cowboy. "Just my luck! There wasn't any one here when I arrived. Reckon I oughtn't have stayed. Columbine, you look pretty much upset."

"What do I care how I look!" she exclaimed, with a sharp resentment attending this abupt and painful break in her agitation.

Next moment Jack Belllounds galloped a foam-lashed horse into the courtyard and hauled up short with a recklessness he was noted for. He swung down hard and violently cast the reins from him.

"Ahuh! I gambled on just this," he declared, harshly.

Columbine's heart sank. His gaze was fixed on her face, with its telltale evidences of agitation.

"What've you been crying about?" he demanded.

"I haven't been," she retorted.

His bold and glaring eyes, hot with sudden temper, passed slowly from her to the cowboy. Columbine became aware then that Jack was under the influence of liquor. His heated red face grew darker with a sneering contempt.

"Where's dad?" he asked, wheeling toward her.

"I don't know. He's not here," replied Columbine, dismounting. The leap of thought and blood to Jack's face gave her a further sinking of the heart. The situation unnerved her.

Wilson Moore had grown a shade paler. He gathered up his reins, ready to drive off.

"Belllounds, I came up after my things I'd left in the bunk," he said, coolly. "Happened to meet Columbine and stopped to chat a minute."

"That's what *you* say," sneered Belllounds. "You were making love to Columbine. I saw that in her face. You know it— and she knows it—and I know it. . . . You're a liar!"

"Belllounds, I reckon I am," replied Moore, turning white. "I did tell Columbine what I thought she knew—what I ought to have told long ago."

"Ahuh! Well, I don't want to hear it. But I'm going to search that wagon."

"What!" ejaculated the cowboy, dropping his reins as if they stung him.

"You just hold on till I see what you've got in there," went on Belllounds, and he reached over into the wagon and pulled at a saddle.

"Say, do you mean anything? . . . This stuff's mine, every strap of it. Take your hands off."

Belllounds leaned on the wagon and looked up with insolent, dark intent.

"Moore, I wouldn't trust you. I think you'd steal anything you got your hands on."

Columbine uttered a passionate little cry of shame and protest.

"Jack, how dare you!"

"You shut up! Go in the house!" he ordered.

"You insult me," she replied, in bitter humiliation.

"Will you go in?" he shouted.

"No, I won't."

"All right, look on, then. I'd just as lief have you." Then he turned to the cowboy. "Moore, show up that wagon-load of stuff unless you want me to throw it out in the road."

"Belllounds, you know I can't do that," replied Moore, coldly. "And I'll give you a hunch. You'd better shut up yourself and let me drive on. . . . If not for her sake, then for your own."

Belllounds grasped the reins, and with a sudden jerk pulled them out of the cowboy's hands.

"You damn club-foot! Your gift of gab doesn't go with me," yelled Belllounds, as he swung up on the hub of the wheel. But it was manifest that his desire to search the wagon was only a pretense, for while he pulled at this and that his evil gaze was on the cowboy, keen to meet any move that might give excuse for violence. Moore evidently read this, for, gazing at Columbine, he shook his head, as if to acquaint her with a situation impossible to help.

"Columbine, please hand me up the reins," he said. "I'm lame, you know. Then I'll be going."

Columbine stepped forward to comply, when Belllounds, leaping down from the wheel, pushed her back with masterful hand. Opposition to him was like waving a red flag in the face of a bull. Columbine recoiled from his look as well as touch.

"You keep out of this or I'll teach you who's boss here," he said, stridently.

"You're going too far!" burst out Columbine.

Meanwhile Wilson had laboriously climbed down out of the wagon, and, utilizing his crutch, he hobbled to where Belllounds had thrown the reins, and stooped to pick them up. Belllounds shoved Columbine farther back, and then he leaped to confront the cowboy.

"I've got you now, Moore," he said, hoarse and low. Stripped of all pretense, he showed the ungovernable nature of his temper. His face grew corded and black. The hand he thrust out shook like a leaf. "You smooth-tongued liar! I'm on to your game. I know you'd put her against me. I know you'd try to win her—less than a week before her wedding-day. . . . But it's not for that I'm going to beat hell out of you! It's because I hate you! Ever since I can remember my father held *you* up to me! And he sent me to—to— he sent me away because of you. By God! that's why I hate you!"

All that was primitive and violent and base came out with strange frankness in Belllounds's tirade. Only when calm could his mind be capable of hidden calculation. The devil that was in him now seemed rampant.

"Belllounds, you're mighty brave to stack up this way against a one-legged man," declared the cowboy, with biting sarcasm.

"If you had two club-feet I'd only be the gladder," yelled Belllounds, and, swinging his arm, he slapped Moore so that it nearly toppled him over. Only the injured foot, coming down hard, saved him.

When Columbine saw that, and then how Wilson winced and grew deathly pale, she uttered a low cry, and she seemed suddenly rooted to the spot, weak, terrified at what was now inevitable, and growing sick and cold and faint.

"It's a damn lucky thing for you I'm not packing a gun," said Moore, grimly. "But you knew—or you'd never hit me— you coward."

"I'll make you swallow that," snarled Belllounds, and this time he swung his fist, aiming a heavy blow at Moore.

Then the cowboy whirled aloft the heavy crutch. "If you hit at me again I'll let out what little brains you've got. God knows that's little enough! . . . Belllounds, I'm going to call you to your face—before this girl your bat-eyed old man means to give you. You're not drunk. You're only ugly— mean. You've got a chance now to lick me because I'm crip-

pled. And you're going to make the most of it. Why, you
cur, I could come near licking you with only one leg. But
if you touch me again I'll brain you! . . . You never were
any good. You're no good now. You never will be anything
but Buster Jack—half dotty, selfish as hell, bull-headed and
mean! . . . And that's the last word I'll ever waste on you."

"I'll kill you!" bawled Belllounds, black with fury.

Moore wielded the crutch menacingly, but as he was not
steady on his feet he was at the disadvantage his adversary
had calculated upon. Belllounds ran around the cowboy,
and suddenly plunged in to grapple with him. The crutch
descended, but to little purpose. Belllounds's heavy onslaught
threw Moore to the ground. Before he could rise Belllounds
pounced upon him.

Columbine saw all this dazedly. As Wilson fell she closed
her eyes, fighting a faintness that almost overcame her. She
heard wrestling, threshing sounds, and sodden thumps, and a
scattering of gravel. These noises seemed at first distant,
then grew closer. As she gazed again with keener percep-
tion, Moore's horse plunged away from the fiercely struggling
forms that had rolled almost under his feet. During the en-
suing moments it was an equal battle so far as Columbine
could tell. Repelled, yet fascinated, she watched. They beat
each other, grappled and rolled over, first one on top, then the
other. But the advantage of being uppermost presently was
Belllounds's. Moore was weakening. That became noticeable
more and more after each time he had wrestled and rolled
about. Then Belllounds, getting this position, lay with his
weight upon Moore, holding him down, and at the same time
kicking with all his might. He was aiming to disable the cowboy by kicking the injured foot. And he was succeeding.
Moore let out a strangled cry, and struggled desperately. But
he was held and weighted down. Belllounds raised up now
and, looking backward, he deliberately and furiously kicked
Moore's bandaged foot; once, twice, again and again, until
the straining form under him grew limp. Columbine, slowly
freezing with horror, saw all this. She could not move. She
could not scream. She wanted to rush in and drag Jack off
of Wilson, to hurt him, to kill him, but her muscles were par-
alyzed. In her agony she could not even look away. Bell-

lounds got up astride his prostrate adversary and began to beat him brutally, swinging heavy, sodden blows. His face then was terrible to see. He meant murder.

Columbine heard approaching voices and the thumping of hasty feet. That unclamped her cloven tongue. Wildly she screamed. Old Bill Belllounds appeared, striding off the porch. And the hunter Wade came running down the path.

"Dad! he's killing Wilson!" cried Columbine.

"Hyar, you devil!" roared the rancher.

Jack Belllounds got up. Panting, disheveled, with hair ruffled and face distorted, he was not a pleasant sight for even the father. Moore lay unconscious, with ghastly, bloody features, and his bandaged foot showed great splotches of red.

"My Gawd, son!" gasped Old Bill. "You didn't pick on this hyar crippled boy?"

The evidence was plain, in Moore's quiet, pathetic form, in the panting, purple-faced son. Jack Belllounds did not answer. He was in the grip of a passion that had at last been wholly unleashed and was still unsatisfied. Yet a malignant and exultant gratification showed in his face.

"That—evens us—up, Moore," he panted, and stalked away.

By this time Wade reached the cowboy and knelt beside him. Columbine came running to fall on her knees. The old rancher seemed stricken.

"Oh— Oh! it was terrible—" cried Columbine. "Oh—he's so white—and the blood—"

"Now, lass, that's no way for a woman," said Wade, and there was something in his kind tone, in his look, in his presence, that calmed Columbine. "I'll look after Moore. You go get some water an' a towel."

Columbine rose to totter into the house. She saw a red stain on the hand she had laid upon the cowboy's face, and with a strange, hot, bursting sensation, strong and thrilling, she put that red place to her lips. Running out with the things required by Wade, she was in time to hear the rancher say, "Looks hurt bad, to me."

"Yes, I reckon," replied Wade.

While Columbine held Moore's head upon her lap the hunter bathed the bloody face. It was battered and bruised and cut, and in some places, as fast as Wade washed away the red, it welled out again.

Columbine watched that quiet face, while her heart throbbed and swelled with emotions wholly beyond her control and understanding. When at last Wilson opened his eyes, fluttering at first, and then wide, she felt a surge that shook her whole body. He smiled wanly at her, and at Wade, and then his gaze lifted to Belllounds.

"I guess—he licked me," he said, in weak voice. "He kept kicking my sore foot—till I fainted. But he licked me—all right."

"Wils, mebbe he did lick you," replied the old rancher, brokenly, "but I reckon he's damn little to be proud of—lickin' a crippled man—thet way."

"Boss, Jack'd been drinking," said Moore, weakly. "And he sure had—some excuse for going off his head. He caught me—talking sweet to Columbine . . . and then—I called him all the names—I could lay my tongue to."

"Ahuh!" The old man seemed at a loss for words, and presently he turned away, sagging in the shoulders, and plodded into the house.

The cowboy, supported by Wade on one side, with Columbine on the other, was helped to an upright position, and with considerable difficulty was gotten into the wagon. He tried to sit up, but made a sorry showing of it.

"I'll drive him home an' look after him," said Wade. "Now, Miss Collie, you're upset, which ain't no wonder. But now you brace. It might have been worse. Just you go to your room till you're sure of yourself again."

Moore smiled another wan smile at her. "I'm sorry," he said.

"What for? Me?" she asked.

"I mean I'm sorry I was so infernal unlucky—running into you—and bringing all this distress—to you. It was my fault. If I'd only kept—my mouth shut!"

"You need not be sorry you met me," she said, with her eyes straight upon his. "I'm glad. . . . But oh! if your foot is badly hurt I'll never—never—"

"Don't say it," interrupted Wilson.

"Lass, you're bent on doin' somethin'," said Wade, in his gentle voice.

"Bent?" she echoed, with something deep and rich in her voice. "Yes, I'm bent—*bent* like your name—to speak my mind!"

Then she ran toward the house and up on the porch, to enter the living-room with heaving breast and flashing eyes. Manifestly the rancher was berating his son. The former gaped at sight of her and the latter shrank.

"Jack Belllounds," she cried, "you're not half a man. . . . You're a coward and a brute!"

One tense moment she stood there, lightning scorn and passion in her gaze, and then she rushed out, impetuously, as she had come.

8

◉

COLUMBINE DID NOT leave her room any more that day. What she suffered there she did not want any one to know. What it cost her to conquer herself again she had only a faint conception of. She did conquer, however, and that night made up the sleep she had lost the night before.

Strangely enough, she did not feel afraid to face the rancher and his son. Recent happenings had not only changed her, but had seemed to give her strength. When she presented herself at the breakfast-table Jack was absent. The old rancher greeted her with more than usual solicitude.

"Jack's sick," he remarked, presently.

"Indeed," replied Columbine.

"Yes. He said it was the drinkin' he's not accustomed to. Wal, I reckon it was what you called him. He didn't take much store on what I called him, which was wuss. . . . I tell you, lass, Jack's set his heart so hard on you thet it's turrible."

"Queer way he has of showing the—the affections of his heart," replied Columbine, shortly.

"Thet was the drink," remonstrated the old man, pathetic and earnest in his motive to smooth over the quarrel.

"But he promised me he would not drink any more."

Belllounds shook his gray old head sadly.

"Ahuh! Jack fires up an' promises anythin'. He means it at the time. But the next hankerin' thet comes over him wipes out the promise. I know. . . . But he's had good excuse fer this break. The boys in town began celebratin' fer October first. Great wonder Jack didn't come home clean drunk."

"Dad, you're as good as gold," said Columbine, softening. How could she feel hard toward him?

"Collie, then you're not agoin' back on the ole man?"

"No."

"I was afeared you'd change your mind about marryin' Jack."

"When I promised I meant it. I didn't make it on conditions."

"But, lass, promises can be broke," he said, with the sonorous roll in his voice.

"I never yet broke one of mine."

"Wal, I hev. Not often, mebbe, but I hev. . . . An', lass, it's reasonable. Thar's times when a man jest can't live up to what he swore by. An' fer a girl—why, I can see how easy she'd change an' grow overnight. It's only fair fer me to say that no matter what you think you owe me you couldn't be blamed now fer dislikin' Jack."

"Dad, if by marrying Jack I can help him to be a better son to you, and more of a man, I'll be glad," she replied.

"Lass, I'm beginnin' to see how big an' fine you are," replied Belllounds, with strong feeling. "An' it's worryin' me. . . . My neighbors hev always accused me of seein' only my son. Only Buster Jack! I was blind an' deaf as to him! . . . Wal, I'm not so damn blind as I used to be. The scales are droppin' off my ole eyes. . . . But I've got one hope left as far as Jack's concerned. Thet's marryin' him to you. An' I'm stickin' to it."

"So will I stick to it, dad," she replied. "I'll go through with October first!"

Columbine broke off, vouchsafing no more, and soon left the breakfast-table, to take up the work she had laid out to do. And she accomplished it, though many times her hands dropped idle and her eyes peered out of her window at the drab slides of the old mountain.

Later, when she went out to ride, she saw the cowboy Lem working in the blacksmith shop.

"Wal, Miss Collie, air you-all still hangin' round this hyar ranch?" he asked, with welcoming smile.

"Lem, I'm almost ashamed now to face my good friends, I've neglected them so long," she replied.

"Aw, now, what're friends fer but to go to? . . . You're lookin' pale, I reckon. More like thet thar flower I see so much on the hills."

"Lem, I want to ride Pronto. Do you think he's all right, now?"

"I reckon some movin' round will do Pronto good. He's eatin' his haid off."

The cowboy went with her to the pasture gate and whistled Pronto up. The mustang came trotting, evidently none the worse for his injuries, and eager to resume the old climbs with his mistress. Lem saddled him, paying particular attention to the cinch.

"Reckon we'd better not cinch him tight," said Lem. "You jest be careful an' remember your saddle's loose."

"All right, Lem," replied Columbine, as she mounted. "Where are the boys this morning?"

"Blud an' Jim air repairin' fence up the crick."

"And where's Ben?"

"Ben? Oh, you mean Wade. Wal, I 'ain't seen him since yestidday. He was skinnin' a lion then, over hyar on the ridge. Thet was in the mawnin'. I reckon he's around, fer I seen some of the hounds."

"Then, Lem—you haven't heard about the fight yesterday between Jack and Wilson Moore?"

Lem straightened up quickly. "Nope, I 'ain't heerd a word."

"Well, they fought, all right," said Columbine, hurriedly. "I saw it. I was the only one there. Wilson was badly used up before dad and Ben got there. Ben drove off with him."

"But, Miss Collie, how'd it come off? I seen Wils the other day. Was up to his homestead. An' the boy jest manages to rustle round on a crutch. He couldn't fight."

"That was just it. Jack saw his opportunity, and he forced Wilson to fight—accused him of stealing. Wils tried to avoid trouble. Then Jack jumped him. Wilson fought and held his own until Jack began to kick his injured foot. Then Wilson fainted and—and Jack beat him."

Lem dropped his head, evidently to hide his expression. "Wal, dog-gone me!" he ejaculated. "Thet's too bad."

Columbine left the cowboy and rode up the lane toward Wade's cabin. She did not analyze her deliberate desire to tell the truth about that fight, but she would have liked to proclaim it to the whole range and to the world. Once clear of the house she felt free, unburdened, and to talk seemed to relieve some congestion of her thoughts.

The hounds heralded Columbine's approach with a deep and booming chorus. Sampson and Jim lay upon the porch, unleashed. The other hounds were chained separately in the aspen grove a few rods distant. Sampson thumped the boards with his big tail, but he did not get up, which laziness attested to the fact that there had been a lion chase the day before and he was weary and stiff. If Wade had been at home he would have come out to see what had occasioned the clamor. As Columbine rode by she saw another fresh lion-pelt pegged upon the wall of the cabin.

She followed the brook. It had cleared since the rains and was shining and sparkling in the rough, swift places, and limpid and green in the eddies. She passed the dam made by the solitary beaver that inhabited the valley. Freshly cut willows showed how the beaver was preparing for the long winter ahead. Columbine remembered then how greatly pleased Wade had been to learn about this old beaver; and more than once Wade had talked about trapping some younger beavers and bringing them there to make company for the old fellow.

The trail led across the brook at a wide, shallow place, where the splashing made by Pronto sent the trout scurrying for deeper water. Columbine kept to the trail, knowing that it led up into Sage Valley, where Wilson Moore had taken up the homestead property. Fresh horse tracks told her that Wade had ridden along there some time earlier. Pronto shied at the whirring of sage-hens. Presently Columbine ascertained they were flushed by the hound Kane, that had broken loose and followed her. He had done so before, and the fact had not displeased her.

"Kane! Kane! come here!" she called. He came readily, but halted a rod or so away, and made an attempt at wagging his tail, a function evidently somewhat difficult for him. When she resumed trotting he followed her.

Old White Slides had lost all but the drabs and dull yellows and greens, and of course those pale, light slopes that had given the mountain its name. Sage Valley was only one of the valleys at its base. It opened out half a mile wide, dominated by the looming peak, and bordered on the far side by an aspen-thicketed slope. The brook babbled along under the edge of this thicket. Cattle and horses grazed here and there on the rich, grassy levels. Columbine was surprised to see so many cattle and wondered to whom they belonged. All of Belllounds's stock had been driven lower down for the winter. There among the several horses that whistled at her approach she espied the white mustang Belllounds had given to Moore. It thrilled her to see him. And next, she suffered a pang to think that perhaps his owner might never ride him again. But Columbine held her emotions in abeyance.

The cabin stood high upon a level terrace, with clusters of aspens behind it, and was sheltered from winter blasts by a gray cliff, picturesque and crumbling, with its face overgrown by creeping vines and colorful shrubs. Wilson Moore could not have chosen a more secluded and beautiful valley for his homesteading adventure. The little gray cabin, with smoke curling from the stone chimney, had lost its look of dilapidation and disuse, yet there was nothing new that Columbine could see. The last quarter of the ascent of the slope, and the few rods across the level terrace, seemed extraordinarily long to Columbine. As she dismounted and tied Pronto her heart was beating and her breath was coming fast.

The door of the cabin was open. Kane trotted past the hesitating Columbine and went in.

"You son-of-a-hound-dog!" came to Columbine's listening ears in Wade's well-known voice. "I'll have to beat you—sure as you're born."

"I heard a horse," came in a lower voice, that was Wilson's.

"Darn me if I'm not gettin' deafer every day," was the reply.

Then Wade appeared in the doorway.

"It's nobody but Miss Collie," he announced, as he made way for her to enter.

"Good morning!" said Columbine, in a voice that had more than cheerfulness in it.

"Collie! . . . Did you come to see me?"

She heard this incredulous query just an instant before she saw Wilson at the far end of the room, lying under the light of a window. The inside of the cabin seemed vague and unfamiliar.

"I surely did," she replied, advancing. "How are you?"

"Oh, I'm all right. Tickled to death, right now. . . . Only, I hate to have you see this battered mug of mine."

"You needn't—care," said Columbine, unsteadily. And indeed, in that first glance she did not see him clearly. A mist blurred her sight and there was a lump in her throat. Then, to recover herself, she looked around the cabin.

"Well—Wils Moore—if this isn't fine!" she ejaculated, in amaze and delight. Columbine sustained an absolute surprise. A magic hand had transformed the interior of that rude old prospector's abode. A carpenter and a mason and a decorator had been wonderfully at work. From one end to the other Columbine gazed; from the big window under which Wilson lay on a blanketed couch to the open fireplace where Wade grinned she looked and looked, and then up to the clean, aspen-poled roof and down to the floor, carpeted with deer hides. The chinks between the logs of the walls were plastered with red clay; the dust and dirt were gone; the place smelled like sage and wood-smoke and fragrant, frying meat. Indeed, there were a glowing bed of embers and a steaming kettle and a smoking pot; and the way the smoke and steam curled up into the gray old chimney attested to its splendid draught. In each corner hung a deer-head, from the antlers of which depended accoutrements of a cowboy—spurs, ropes, belts, scarfs, guns. One corner contained a cupboard, ceiling high, with new, clean doors of wood, neatly made; and next to it stood a table, just as new. On the blank wall beyond that were pegs holding saddles, bridles, blankets, clothes.

"He did it—all this inside," burst out Moore, delighted with her delight. "Quicker than a flash! Collie, isn't this great? I don't mind being down on my back. . . . And he says they call him Hell-Bent Wade. I call him Heaven-Sent Wade!"

When Columbine turned to the hunter, bursting with her pleasure and gratitude, he suddenly dropped the forked stick he used as a lift, and she saw his hand shake when he stooped to recover it. How strangely that struck her!

"Ben, it's perfectly possible that you've been sent by Heaven," she remarked, with a humor which still held gravity in it.

"Me! A good angel? That'd be a new job for Bent Wade," he replied, with a queer laugh. "But I reckon I'd try to live up to it."

There were small sprigs of golden aspen leaves and crimson oak leaves on the wall above the foot of Wilson's bed. Beneath them, on pegs, hung a rifle. And on the window-sill stood a glass jar containing columbines. They were fresh. They had just been picked. They waved gently in the breeze, sweetly white and blue, strangely significant to the girl.

Moore laughed defiantly.

"Wade thought to fetch these flowers in," he explained. "They're his favorites as well as mine. It won't be long now till the frost kills them . . . and I want to be happy while I may!"

Again Columbine felt that deep surge within her, beyond her control, beyond her understanding, but now gathering and swelling, soon to be reckoned with. She did not look at Wilson's face then. Her downcast gaze saw that his right hand was bandaged, and she touched it with an unconscious tenderness.

"Your hand! Why is it all wrapped up?"

The cowboy laughed with grim humor.

"Have you seen Jack this morning?"

"No," she replied, shortly.

"Well, if you had, you'd know what happened to my fist."

"Did you hurt it on him?" she asked, with a queer little shudder that was not unpleasant.

"Collie, I busted that fist on his handsome face."

"Oh, it was dreadful!" she murmured. "Wilson, he meant to kill you."

"Sure. And I'd cheerfully have killed him."

"You two must never meet again," she went on.

"I hope to Heaven we never do," replied Moore, with a dark earnestness that meant more than his actual words.

"Wilson, will you avoid him—for my sake?" implored Columbine, unconsciously clasping the bandaged hand.

"I will. I'll take the back trails. I'll sneak like a coyote. I'll hide and I'll watch. . . . But, Columbine Belllounds, if he ever corners me again—"

"Why, you'll leave him to Hell-Bent Wade," interrupted the hunter, and he looked up from where he knelt, fixing those great, inscrutable eyes upon the cowboy. Columbine saw something beyond his face, deeper than the gloom, a passion and a spirit that drew her like a magnet. "An' now, Miss Collie," he went on, "I reckon you'll want to wait on our invalid. He's got to be fed."

"I surely will," replied Columbine, gladly, and she sat down on the edge of the bed. "Ben, you fetch that box and put his dinner on it."

While Wade complied, Columbine, shyly aware of her nearness to the cowboy, sought to keep up conversation.

"Couldn't you help yourself with your left hand?" she inquired.

"That one's worse," he answered, taking it from under the blanket, where it had been concealed.

"Oh!" cried Columbine, in dismay.

"Broke two bones in this one," said Wilson, with animation. "Say, Collie, our friend Wade is a doctor, too. Never saw his beat!"

"And a cook, too, for here's your dinner. You must sit up," ordered Columbine.

"Fold that blanket and help me up on it," replied Moore.

How strange and disturbing for Columbine to bend over him, to slip her arms under him and lift him! It recalled a long-forgotten motherliness of her doll-playing days. And her face flushed hot.

"Can't you move?" she asked, suddenly becoming aware of how dead a weight the cowboy appeared.

"Not—very much," he replied. Drops of sweat appeared on his bruised brow. It must have hurt him to move.

"You said your foot was all right."

"It is," he returned. "It's still on my leg, as I know darned well."

"Oh!" exclaimed Columbine, dubiously. Without further comment she began to feed him.

"It's worth getting licked to have this treat," he said.

"Nonsense!" she rejoined.

"I'd stand it again—to have you come here and feed me. . . . But not from *him*."

"Wilson, I never knew you to be facetious before. Here, take this."

Apparently he did not see her outstretched hand.

"Collie, you've changed. You're older. You're a woman, now—and the prettiest—"

"Are you going to eat?" demanded Columbine.

"Huh!" exclaimed the cowboy, blankly. "Eat? Oh yes, sure. I'm powerful hungry. And maybe Heaven-Sent Wade can't cook!"

But Columbine had trouble in feeding him. What with his helplessness, and his propensity to watch her face instead of her hands, and her own mounting sensations of a sweet, natural joy and fitness in her proximity to him, she was hard put to it to show some dexterity as a nurse. And all the time she was aware of Wade, with his quiet, forceful presence, hovering near. Could he not see her hands trembling? And would he not think that weakness strange? Then driftingly came the thought that she would not shrink from Wade's reading her mind. Perhaps even now he understood her better than she understood herself.

"I can't—eat any more," declared Moore, at last.

"You've done very well for an invalid," observed Columbine. Then, changing the subject, she asked, "Wilson, you're going to stay here—winter here, dad would call it?"

"Yes."

"Are those your cattle down in the valley?"

"Sure. I've got near a hundred head. I saved my money and bought cattle."

"That's a good start for you. I'm glad. But who's going to take care of you and your stock until you can work again?"

"Why, my friend there, Heaven-Sent Wade," replied Moore, indicating the little man busy with the utensils on the table, and apparently hearing nothing.

"Can I fetch you anything to eat—or read?" she inquired.

"Fetch yourself," he replied, softly.

"But, boy, how could I fetch you anything without fetching myself?"

"Sure, that's right. Then fetch me some jam and a book —tomorrow. Will you?"

"I surely will"

"That's a promise. I know your promises of old."

"Then good-by till tomorrow. I must go. I hope you'll be better."

"I'll stay sick in bed till you stop coming."

Columbine left rather precipitously, and when she got outdoors it seemed that the hills had never been so softly, dreamily gray, nor their loneliness so sweet, nor the sky so richly and deeply blue. As she untied Pronto the hunter came out with Kane at his heels.

"Miss Collie, if you'll go easy I'll ketch my horse an' ride down with you," he said.

She mounted, and walked Pronto out to the trail, and slowly faced the gradual descent. It was really higher up there than she had surmised. And the view was beautiful. The gray, rolling foothills, so exquisitely colored at that hour, and the black-fringed ranges, one above the other, and the distant peaks, sunset-flushed across the purple, all rose open and clear to her sight, so wildly and splendidly expressive of the Colorado she loved.

At the foot of the slope Wade joined her.

"Lass, I'm askin' you not to tell Belllounds that I'm carin' for Wils," he said, in his gentle, persuasive way.

"I won't. But why not tell dad? He wouldn't mind. He'd do that sort of thing himself."

"Reckon he would. But this deal's out of the ordinary. An' Wils's not in as good shape as he thinks. I'm not takin' any chances. I don't want to lose my job, an' I don't want to be hindered from attendin' to this boy."

They had ridden as far as the first aspen grove when Wade concluded this remark. Columbine halted her horse, causing her companion to do likewise. Her former misgivings were augmented by the intelligence of Wade's sad, lined face.

"Ben, tell me," she whispered, with a hand going to his arm.

"Miss Collie, I'm a sort of doctor in my way. I studied some medicine an' surgery. An' I know. I wouldn't tell you this if it wasn't that I've got to rely on you to help me."

"I will—but go on—tell me," interposed Columbine, trying to fortify herself.

"Wils's foot is all messed up. Buster Jack kicked it all out of shape. An' it's a hundred times worse than ever. I'm afraid of blood-poisonin' an' gangrene. You know gangrene is a dyin' an' rottin' of the flesh. . . . I told the boy straight out that he'd better let me cut his foot off. An' he swore he'd keep his foot or die! . . . Well, if gangrene does set in we can't save his leg, an' maybe not his life."

"Oh, it can't be as bad as all that!" cried Columbine. "Oh, I knew—I knew there was something. . . . Ben, you mean even at best now—he'll be a—" She broke off, unable to finish.

"Miss Collie, in any case Wils'll never ride again—not like a cowboy."

That for Columbine seemed the worst and the last straw. Hot tears blinded her, hot blood gushed over her, hot heartbeats throbbed in her throat.

"Poor boy! That'll—ruin him," she cried. "He loved—a horse. He loved to ride. He was the—best rider of them all. And now he's ruined! He'll be lame—a cripple—clubfooted! . . . All because of that Jack Belllounds! The brute—the coward! I hate him! Oh, I *hate* him! . . . And I've got to marry him—on October first! Oh, God pity me!"

Blindly Columbine reeled out of her saddle and slowly dropped to the grass, where she burst into a violent storm of sobs and tears. It shook her every fiber. It was hopeless, terrible grief. The dry grass received her flood of tears and her incoherent words.

Wade dismounted and, kneeling beside her, placed a gentle hand upon her heaving shoulder, but he spoke no word. By and by, when the storm had begun to subside, he raised her head.

"Lass, nothin' is ever so bad as it seems," he said, softly. "Come, sit up. Let me talk to you."

"Oh, Ben, something terrible *has* happened," she cried. "It's in *me!* I don't know what it is. But it'll kill me."

"I know," he replied, as her head fell upon his shoulder. "Miss Collie, I'm an old fellow that's had everythin' happen to him, an' I'm livin' yet, tryin' to help people along. No one dies so easy. Why, you're a fine, strong girl—an' somethin' tells me you was made for happiness. I know how things turn out. Listen—"

"But, Ben—you don't know—about me," she sobbed. "I've told you—I—hate Jack Belllounds. But I've—got to marry him! . . . His father raised me—from a baby. He brought me up. I owe him—my life. . . . I've no relation—no mother —no father! No one loves me—for myself!"

"Nobody loves you!" echoed Wade, with an exquisite tone of repudiation. "Strange how people fool themselves! Lass, you're huggin' your troubles too hard. An' you're wrong. Why, everybody loves you! Lem an' Jim—why you just brighten the hard world they live in. An' that poor, hot-headed Jack— he loves you as well as he can love anythin'. An' the old man —no daughter could be loved more. . . . An' I—I love you, lass, just like—as if you—might have been my own. I'm goin' to be the friend—the brother you need. An' I reckon I can come somewheres near bein' a mother, if you'll let me."

Something, some subtle power or charm, stole over Columbine, assuaging her terrible sense of loss, of grief. There was tenderness in this man's hands, in his voice, and through them throbbed strong and passionate life and spirit.

"Do you really love me—*love* me?" she whispered, somehow comforted, somehow feeling that what he offered was what she had missed as a child. "And you want to be all that for me?"

"Yes, lass, an' I reckon you'd better try me."

"Oh, how good you are! I felt that—the very first time I was with you. I've wanted to come to you—to tell you my troubles. I love dad and he loves me, but he doesn't understand. Dad is wrapped up in his son. I've had no one. I never had any one."

"You have some one now," returned Wade, with a rich, deep mellowness in his voice that soothed Columbine and made her wonder. "An' because I've been through so much I can tell you what'll help you. . . . Lass, if a woman isn't big an' brave, how will a man ever be? There's more in women than in men. Life has given you a hard knock, placin' you here —no real parents—an' makin' you responsible to a man whose only fault is blinded love for his son. Well, you've got to meet it, face it, with what a woman has more of than any man. Courage! Suppose you do hate this Buster Jack. Suppose you do love this poor, crippled Wilson Moore. . . . Lass, don't look like that! Don't deny. You do love that boy. . . . Well, it's hell. But you can never tell what'll happen when you're honest and square. If you feel it your duty to pay your debt to the old man you call dad—to pay it by marryin' his son, why do it, an' be a woman. There's nothin' as great as a woman can be. There's happiness that comes in strange, unheard-of ways. There's more in this life than what you want most. *You* didn't place yourself in this fix. So if you meet it with courage an' faithfulness to yourself, why, it'll not turn out as you dread. . . . Some day, if you ever think you're broken-hearted, I'll tell you my story. An' then you'll not think your lot so hard. For I've had a broken heart an' ruined life, an' yet I've lived on an' on, findin' happiness I never dreamed would come, fightin' or workin'. An' how I found the world beautiful, an' how I love the flowers an' hills an' wild things so well—that, just that would be enough to live for! . . . An' think, lass, of what a wonderful happiness will come to me in showin' all this to you. That'll be the crownin' glory. An' if it's that much to me, then you be sure there's nothin' on earth I won't do for you."

Columbine lifted her tear-stained face with a light of inspiration.

"Oh, Wilson was right!" she murmured. "You are Heaven-sent! And I'm going to love you!"

9

◉

A NEW SPIRIT, or a liberation of her own, had fired Columbine, and was now burning within her, unquenchable and unutterable. Some divine spark had penetrated into that mysterious depth of her, to inflame and to illumine, so that when she arose from this hour of calamity she felt that to the tenderness and sorrow and fidelity in her soul had been added the lightning flash of passion.

"Oh, Ben—shall I be able to hold on to this?" she cried, flinging wide her arms, as if to embrace the winds of heaven.

"This what, lass?" he asked.

"This—this *woman!*" she answered, passionately, with her hands sweeping back to press her breast.

"No woman who wakes ever goes back to a girl again," he said, sadly.

"I wanted to die—and now I want to live—to fight. . . . Ben, you've uplifted me. I was little, weak, miserable. . . . But in my dreams, or in some state I can't remember or understand, I've waited for your very words. I was ready. It's as if I knew you in some other world, before I was born on this earth; and when you spoke to me here, so wonderfully —as my mother might have spoken—my heart leaped up in recognition of you and your call to my womanhood! . . . Oh, how strange and beautiful!"

"Miss Collie," he replied, slowly, as he bent to his saddle-straps, "you're young, an' you've no understandin' of what's strange an' terrible in life. An' beautiful, too, as you say. . . . Who knows? Maybe in some former state I was somethin' to you. I believe in that. Reckon I can't say how or what. Maybe we were flowers or birds. I've a weakness for that idea."

"Birds! I like the thought, too," replied Columbine. "I love most birds. But there are hawks, crows, buzzards!"

"I reckon. Lass, there's got to be balance in nature. If it weren't for the ugly an' the evil, we wouldn't know the beautiful an' good. . . . An' now let's ride home. It's gettin' late."

"Ben, ought I not go back to Wilson right now?" she asked, slowly.

"What for?"

"To tell him—something—and why I can't come tomorrow, or ever afterward," she replied, low and tremulously.

Wade pondered over her words. It seemed to Columbine that her sharpened faculties sensed something of hostility, of opposition in him.

"Reckon tomorrow would be better," he said, presently. "Wilson's had enough excitement for one day."

"Then I'll go tomorrow," she returned.

In the gathering, cold twilight they rode down the trail in silence.

"Good night, lass," said Wade, as he reached his cabin. "An' remember you're not alone any more."

"Good night, my friend," she replied, and rode on.

Columbine encountered Jim Montana at the corrals, and it was not too dark for her to see his foam-lashed horse. Jim appeared non-committal, almost surly. But Columbine guessed that he had ridden to Kremmling and back in one day, on some order of Jack's.

"Miss Collie, I'll tend to Pronto," he offered. "An' yore supper'll be waitin'."

A bright fire blazed on the living-room hearth. The rancher was reading by its light.

"Hello, rosy-cheeks!" greeted the rancher, with unusual amiability. "Been ridin' ag'in' the wind, hey? Wal, if you ain't pretty, then my eyes are pore!"

"It's cold, dad," she replied, "and the wind stings. But I didn't ride fast nor far. . . . I've been up to see Wilson Moore."

"Ahuh! Wal, how's the boy?" asked Belllounds, gruffly.

"He said he was all right, but—but I guess that's not so," responded Columbine.

"Any friends lookin' after him?"

"Oh yes—he must have friends—the Andrewses and others. I'm glad to say his cabin is comfortable. He'll be looked after."

"Wal, I'm glad to hear thet. I'll send Lem or Wade up thar an' see if we can do anythin' fer the boy."

"Dad—that's just like you," replied Columbine, with her hand seeking his broad shoulder.

"Ahuh! Say, Collie, hyar's letters from 'most everybody in Kremmlin' wantin' to be invited up fer October first. How about askin' 'em?"

"The more the merrier," replied Columbine.

"Wal, I reckon I'll not ask anybody."

"Why not, dad?"

"No one can gamble on thet son of mine, even on his weddin'-day," replied Belllounds, gloomily.

"Dad, what'd Jack do today?"

"I'm not sayin' he did anythin'," answered the rancher.

"Dad, you can gamble on me."

"Wal, I should smile," he said, putting his big arm around her. "I wish you was Jack an' Jack was you."

At that moment the young man spoken of slouched into the room, with his head bandaged, and took a seat at the supper-table.

"Wal, Collie, let's go an' get it," said the rancher, cheerily. "I can always eat, anyhow."

"I'm hungry as a bear," rejoined Columbine, as she took her seat, which was opposite Jack.

"Where've you been?" he asked, curiously.

"Why, good evening, Jack! Did you finally notice me? . . . I've been riding Pronto, the first time since he was hurt. Had a lovely ride—up through Sage Valley."

Jack glowered at her with the one unbandaged eye, and growled something under his breath, and then began to stab meat and potatoes with his fork.

"What's the matter, Jack? Aren't you well?" asked Columbine, with a solicitude just a little too sweet to be genuine.

"Yes, I'm well," snapped Jack.

"But you look sick. That is, what I can see of your face looks sick. Your mouth droops at the corners. You're very pale—and red in spots. And your one eye glows with unearthly woe, as if you were not long for this world!"

The amazing nature of this speech, coming from the girl who had always been so sweet and quiet and backward, was attested to by the consternation of Jack and the mirth of his father.

"Are you making fun of me?" demanded Jack.

"Why, Jack! Do you think I would make fun of you? I only wanted to say how queer you look. . . . Are you going to be married with one eye?"

Jack collapsed at that, and the old man, after a long stare of open-mouthed wonder, broke out: "Haw! Haw! Haw! . . . By golly! lass—I'd never believed thet was in you. . . . Jack, be game an' take your medicine. . . . An' both of you forgive an' forget. Thar'll be quarrels enough, mebbe, without rakin' over the past."

When alone again Columbine reverted to a mood vastly removed from her apparent levity with the rancher and his son. A grave and inward-searching thought possessed her, and it had to do with the uplift, the spiritual advance, the rise above mere personal welfare, that had strangely come to her through Bent Wade. From their first meeting he had possessed a singular attraction for her that now, in the light of the meaning of his life, seemed to Columbine to be the man's nobility and wisdom, arising out of his travail, out of the terrible years that had left their record upon his face.

And so Columbine strove to bind forever in her soul the spirit which had arisen in her, interpreting from Wade's rude words of philosophy that which she needed for her own light and strength.

She appreciated her duty toward the man who had been a father to her. Whatever he asked that would she do. And as for the son she must live with the rest of her life, her duty there was to be a good wife, to bear with his faults, to strive always to help him by kindness, patience, loyalty, and such affection as was possible to her. Hate had to be reckoned with, and hate, she knew, had no place in a good woman's heart. It must be expelled, if that were humanly possible. All this was hard, would grow harder, but she accepted it, and knew her mind.

Her soul was her own, unchangeable through any adversity. She could be with that alone always, aloof from the petty cares and troubles common to people. Wade's words had thrilled her with their secret, with their limitless hope of an unknown world of thought and feeling. Happiness, in the ordinary sense, might never be hers. Alas for her dreams! But there had been given her a glimpse of something higher than pleasure and contentment. Dreams were but dreams. But she could still dream of what had been, of what might have been, of the beauty and mystery of life, of something in nature that called sweetly and irresistibly to her. Who could rob her of the rolling, gray, velvety hills, and the purple peaks and the black ranges, among which she had been found a waif, a little lost creature, born like a columbine under the spruces?

Love, sudden-dawning, inexplicable love, was her secret, still tremulously new, and perilous in its sweetness. That only did she fear to realize and to face, because it was an unknown factor, a threatening flame. Her sudden knowledge of it seemed inextricably merged with the mounting, strong, and steadfast stream of her spirit.

"I'll go to him. I'll tell him," she murmured. "He shall have *that!* . . . Then I must bid him—good-by—forever!"

To tell Wilson would be sweet; to leave him would be bitter. Vague possibilities haunted her. What might come of the telling? How dark loomed the bitterness! She could not know what hid in either of these acts until they were fulfilled. And the hours became long, and sleep far off, and the quietness of the house a torment, and the melancholy wail of coyotes a reminder of happy girlhood, never to return.

When next day the long-deferred hour came Columbine selected a horse that she could run, and she rode up the winding valley swift as the wind. But at the aspen grove, where Wade's keen, gentle voice had given her secret life, she suffered a reaction that made her halt and ascend the slope very slowly and with many stops.

Sight of Wade's horse haltered near the cabin relieved Columbine somewhat of a gathering might of emotion. The hunter would be inside and so she would not be compelled at once to confess her secret. This expectancy gave impetus to her lagging steps. Before she reached the open door she called out.

"Collie, you're late," answered Wilson, with both joy and reproach, as she entered. The cowboy lay upon his bed, and he was alone in the room.

"Oh! . . . Where is Ben?" exclaimed Columbine.

"He was here. He cooked my dinner. We waited, but you never came. The dinner got cold. I made sure you'd backed out—weren't coming at all—and I couldn't eat. . . . Wade said he knew you'd come. He went off with the hounds, some-where . . . and oh, Collie, it's all right now!"

Columbine walked to his bedside and looked down upon him with a feeling as if some giant hand was tugging at her heart. He looked better. The swelling and redness of his face were less marked. And at that moment no pain shadowed his eyes. They were soft, dark, eloquent. If Columbine had not come with her avowed resolution and desire to unburden her heart she would have found that look in his eyes a des-perately hard one to resist. Had it ever shone there before? Blind she had been.

"You're better," she said, happily.

"Sure—*now*. But I had a bad night. Didn't sleep till near daylight. Wade found me asleep. . . . Collie, it's good of you to come. You look so—so wonderful! I never saw your face glow like that. And your eyes—oh!"

"You think I'm pretty, then?" she asked, dreamily, not occupied at all with that thought.

He uttered a contemptuous laugh.

"Come closer," he said, reaching for her with a clumsy bandaged hand.

Down upon her knees Columbine fell. Both hands flew to cover her face. And as she swayed forward she shook vio-lently, and there escaped her lips a little, muffled sound.

"Why—Collie!" cried Moore, astounded. "Good Heavens! Don't cry! I—I didn't mean anything. I only wanted to feel you—touch your hand."

"Here," she answered, blindly holding out her hand, grop-

ing for his till she found it. Her other was still pressed to
her eyes. One moment longer would Columbine keep her
secret—hide her eyes—revel in the unutterable joy and sadness of this crisis that could come to a woman only once.

"What in the world?" ejaculated the cowboy, now bewil-
dered. But he possessed himself of the trembling hand offered.
"Collie, you act so strange. . . . You're *not* crying! . . . Am
I only locoed, or flighty, or what? Dear, look at me."

Columbine swept her hand from her eyes with a gesture of
utter surrender.

"Wilson, I'm ashamed—and sad—and gloriously happy,"
she said, with swift breathlessness.

"Why?" he asked.

"Because of—of something I have to tell you," she whispered.

"What is that?"

She bent over him.

"Can't you guess?"

He turned pale, and his eyes burned with intense fire.

"I won't guess . . . I daren't guess."

"It's something that's been true for years—forever, it
seems—something I never dreamed of till last night," she
went on, softly.

"Collie!" he cried. "Don't torture me!"

"Do you remember long ago—when we quarreled so
dreadfully—because you kissed me?" she asked.

"Do you think I could kiss *you*—and live to forget?"

"I love you!" she whispered, shyly, feeling the hot blood
burn her.

That whisper transformed Wilson Moore. His arm flashed
round her neck and pulled her face down to his, and, holding
her in a close embrace, he kissed her lips and cheeks and wet
eyes, and then again her lips, passionately and tenderly.

Then he pressed her head down upon his breast.

"My God! I can't believe! Say it again!" he cried, hoarsely.

Columbine buried her flaming face in the blanket covering
him, and her hands clutched it tightly. The wildness of his
joy, the strange strength and power of his kisses, utterly
changed her. Upon his breast she lay, without desire to lift

her face. All seemed different, wilder, as she responded to his appeal: "Yes, I love you! Oh, I love—love—love you!"

"Dearest! . . . Lift your face. . . . It's true now. I know. It's proved. But let me look at you."

Columbine lifted herself as best she could. But she was blinded by tears and choked with utterance that would not come, and in the grip of a shuddering emotion that was realization of loss in a moment when she learned the supreme and imperious sweetness of love.

"Kiss me, Columbine," he demanded.

Through blurred eyes she saw his face, white and rapt, and she bent to it, meeting his lips with her first kiss, which was her last.

"Again, Collie—again!" he begged.

"No—no more," she whispered, very low, and encircling his neck with her arms she hid her face and held him convulsively, and stifled the sobs that shook her.

Then Moore was silent, holding her with his free hand, breathing hard, and slowly quieting down. Columbine felt then that he knew that there was something terribly wrong, and that perhaps he dared not voice his fear. At any rate, he silently held her, waiting. That silent wait grew unendurable for Columbine. She wanted to prolong this moment that was to be all she could ever surrender. But she dared not do so, for she knew if he ever kissed her again her duty to Belllounds would vanish like mist in the sun.

To release her hold upon him seemed like a tearing of her heartstrings. She sat up, she wiped the tears from her eyes, she rose to her feet, all the time striving for strength to face him again.

A loud voice, ringing from the cliffs outside, startled Columbine. It came from Wade calling the hounds. He had returned, and the fact stirred her.

"I'm to marry Jack Belllounds on October first."

The cowboy raised himself up as far as he was able. It was agonizing for Columbine to watch the changing and whitening of his face!

"No—no!" he gasped.

"Yes, it's true," she replied, hopelessly.

"*No!*" he exclaimed, hoarsely.

"But, Wilson, I tell you yes. I came to tell you. It's true—oh, it's true!"

"But, girl, you said you love me," he declared, transfixing her with dark, accusing eyes.

"That's just as terribly true."

He softened a little, and something of terror and horror took the place of anger.

Just then Wade entered the cabin with his soft tread, hesitated, and then came to Columbine's side. She could not unrivet her gaze from Moore to look at her friend, but she reached out with trembling hand to him. Wade clasped it in a horny palm.

Wilson fought for self-control in vain.

"Collie, if you love me, how can you marry Jack Belllounds?" he demanded.

"I must."

"Why must you?"

"I owe my life and my bringing up to his father. He wants me to do it. His heart is set upon my helping Jack to become a man. . . . Dad loves me, and I love him. I must stand by him. I must repay him. It is my duty."

"You've a duty to yourself—as a woman!" he rejoined, passionately. "Belllounds is wrapped up in his son. He's blind to the shame of such a marriage. But you're not."

"Shame?" faltered Columbine.

"Yes. The shame of marrying one man when you love another. You can't love two men. . . . You'll give yourself. You'll be his *wife!* Do you understand what that means?"

"I—I think—I do," replied Columbine, faintly. Where had vanished all her wonderful spirit? This fire-eyed boy was breaking her heart with his reproach.

"But you'll bear his children," cried Wilson. "Mother of —them—when you love me! . . . Didn't you think of that?"

"Oh no—I never did—I never did!" wailed Columbine.

"Then you'll think before it's too late?" he implored, wildly. "Dearest Collie, think! You won't ruin yourself! You won't! Say you won't!"

"But— Oh, Wilson, what *can* I say? I've got to marry him."

"Collie, I'll kill him before he gets you."

"You mustn't talk so. If you fought again—if anything terrible happened, it'd kill me."

"You'd be better off!" he flashed, white as a sheet.

Columbine leaned against Wade for support. She was fast weakening in strength, although her spirit held. She knew what was inevitable. But Wilson's agony was rending her.

"Listen," began the cowboy again. "It's your life—your happiness—your soul. . . . Belllounds is crazy over that spoiled boy. He thinks the sun rises and sets in him. . . . But Jack Belllounds is no good on this earth! . . . Collie dearest, don't think that's my jealousy. I am horribly jealous. But I know him. He's not worth *you!* No man is—and he the least. He'll break your heart, drag you down, ruin your health—kill you, as sure as you stand there. I want you to know I could prove to you what he is. But don't make me. Trust me, Collie. Believe me."

"Wilson, I do believe you," cried Columbine. "But it doesn't make any difference. It only makes my duty harder."

"He'll treat you like he treats a horse or a dog. He'll beat you—"

"He never will! If he ever lays a hand on me—"

"If not that, he'll tire of you. Jack Belllounds never stuck to anything in his life, and never will. It's not in him. He wants what he can't have. If he gets it, then right off he doesn't want it. Oh, I've know him since he was a kid. . . . Columbine, you've a mistaken sense of duty. No girl need sacrifice her all because some man found her a lost baby and gave her a home. A woman owes more to herself than to any one."

"Oh, that's true, Wilson. I've thought it all. . . . But you're unjust—hard. You make no allowance for—for some possible good in every one. Dad swears I can reform Jack. Maybe I can. I'll pray for it."

"Reform Jack Belllounds! How can you save a bad egg? That damned coward! Didn't he prove to you what he was when he jumped on me and kicked my broken foot till I fainted? . . . What do you want?"

"Don't say any more—please," cried Columbine. "Oh, I'm so sorry. . . . I oughtn't have come. . . . Ben, take me home."

"But, Collie, I love you," frantically urged Wilson. "And he—he may love you—but he's—Collie—he's been—"

Here Moore seemed to bite his tongue, to hold back speech, to fight something terrible and desperate and cowardly in himself.

Columbine heard only his impassioned declaration of love, and to that she vibrated.

"You speak as if this was one-sided," she burst out, as once more the gush of hot blood surged over her. "You don't love me any more than I love you. Not as much, for I'm a woman! . . . I love with all my heart and soul!"

Moore fell back upon the bed, spent and overcome.

"Wade, my friend, for God's sake do something," he whispered, appealing to the hunter as if in a last hope. "Tell Collie what it'll mean for her to marry Belllounds. If that doesn't change her, then tell her what it'll mean to me. I'll never go home. I'll never leave here. If she hadn't told me she loved me then, I might have stood anything. But now I can't. It'll kill me, Wade."

"Boy, you're talkin' flighty again," replied Wade. "This mornin' when I come you were dreamin' an' talkin'—clean out of your head. . . . Well, now, you an' Collie listen. You're right an' she's right. I reckon I never run across a deal with two people fixed just like you. But that doesn't hinder me from feelin' the same about it as I'd feel about somethin' I was used to."

He paused, and, gently releasing Columbine, he went to Moore, and retied his loosened bandage, and spread out the disarranged blankets. Then he sat down on the edge of the bed and bent over a little, running a roughened hand through the scant hair that had begun to silver upon his head. Presently he looked up, and from that sallow face, with its lines and furrows, and from the deep, inscrutable eyes, there fell a light which, however sad and wise in its infinite understanding of pain and strife, was still ruthless and unquenchable in its hope.

"Wade, for God's sake save Columbine!" importuned Wilson.

"Oh, if you only could!" cried Columbine, impelled beyond her power to resist by that prayer.

"Lass, you stand by your convictions," he said, impressively. "An' Moore, you be a man an' don't make it so hard for her. Neither of you can do anythin'. . . . Now there's old Belllounds—he'll never change. He might r'ar up for this or that, but he'll never change his cherished hopes for his son. . . . But Jack might change! Lookin' back over all the years I remember many boys like this Buster Jack, an' I remember how in the nature of their doin's they just hanged themselves. I've a queer foresight about people whose trouble I've made my own. It's somethin' that never fails. When their trouble's goin' to turn out bad then I feel a terrible yearnin' to tell the story of Hell-Bent Wade. That foresight of trouble gave me my name. . . . But it's not operatin' here. . . . An' so, my young friends, you can believe me when I say somethin' will happen. As far as October first is concerned, or any time near, Collie isn't goin' to marry Jack Belllounds."

10

◉

ONE DAY WADE remarked to Belllounds: "You can never tell what a dog is until you know him. Dogs are like men. Some of 'em look good, but they're really bad. An' that works the other way round. If a dog's born to run wild an' be a sheep-killer, that's what he'll be. I've known dogs that loved men as no humans could have loved them. It doesn't make any difference to a dog if his master is a worthless scamp."

"Wal, I reckon most of them hounds I bought had no-good masters, judgin' from the way they act," replied the rancher.

"I'm developin' a first-rate pack," said Wade. "Jim hasn't any faults exceptin' he doesn't bay enough. Sampson's not as true-nosed as Jim, but he'll follow Jim, an' he has a deep, heavy bay you can hear for miles. So that makes up for Jim's one fault. These two hounds hang together, an' with them I'm developin' others. Denver will split off of bear or lion tracks when he jumps a deer. I reckon he's not young enough to be cured of that. Some of the younger hounds are comin' on fine. But there's two dogs in that bunch that beat me all hollow."

"Which ones?" asked Belllounds.

"There's that bloodhound, Kane," replied the hunter. "He's sure a queer dog. I can't win him. He minds me now because I licked him, an' once good an' hard when he bit me. . . . But he doesn't cotton to me worth a damn. He's gettin' fond of Miss Columbine, an' I believe might make a good watch-dog for her. Where'd he come from, Belllounds?"

"Wal, if I don't disremember he was born in a prairie-schooner, comin' across the plains. His mother was a full-blood, an' come from Louisiana."

"That accounts for an instinct I see croppin' out in Kane," rejoined Wade. "He likes to trail a man. I've caught him doin' it. An' he doesn't take to huntin' lions or bear. Why, the other day, when the hounds treed a lion an' went howlin' wild, Kane came up, an' he looked disgusted an' went off by himself. He hunts by himself, anyhow. First off I thought he might be a sheep-killer. But I reckon not. He can trail men, an' that's about all the good he is. His mother must have been a slave-hunter, an' Kane inherits that trailin' instinct."

"Ahuh! Wal, train him on trailin' men, then. I've seen times when a dog like thet'd come handy. An' if he takes to Collie an' you approve of him, let her have him. She's been coaxin' me fer a dog."

"That isn't a bad idea. Miss Collie walks and rides alone a good deal, an' she never packs a gun."

"Funny about thet," said Belllounds. "Collie is game in most ways, but she'd never kill anythin'. . . . Wade, you ain't thinkin' she ought to stop them lonesome walks an' rides?"

"No, sure not, so long as she doesn't go too far away."

"Ahuh! Wal, supposin' she rode up out of the valley, west on the Black Range?"

"That won't do, Belllounds," replied Wade, seriously. "But Miss Collie's not goin' to, for I've cautioned her. Fact is I've run across some hard-lookin' men between here an' Buffalo Park. They're not hunters or prospectors or cattlemen or travelers."

"Wal, you don't say!" rejoined Belllounds. "Now, Wade, are you connectin' up them strangers with the stock I missed on this last round-up?"

"Reckon I can't go as far as that," returned Wade. "But I didn't like their looks."

"Thet comin' from you, Wade, is like the findin's of a jury. . . . It's gettin' along toward October. Snow'll be flyin' soon. You don't reckon them strangers will winter in the woods?"

"No, I don't. Neither does Lewis. You recollect him?"

"Yes, thet prospector who hangs out around Buffalo Park, lookin' fer gold. He's been hyar. Good fellar, but crazy on gold."

"I've met Lewis several times, one place and another. I lost the hounds day before yesterday. They treed a lion an' Lewis heard the racket, an' he stayed with them till I come up. Then he told me some interestin' news. You see he's been worryin' about this gang thet's rangin' around Buffalo Park, an' he's tried to get a line on them. Somebody took a shot at him in the woods. He couldn't swear it was one of that outfit, but he could swear he wasn't near shot by accident. Now Lewis says these men pack to an' fro from Elgeria, an' he has a hunch they're in cahoots with Smith, who runs a place there. You know Smith?"

"No, I don't, an' haven't any wish to," declared Belllounds, shortly. "He always looked shady to me. An' he's not been square with friends of mine in Elgeria. But no one ever proved him crooked, whatever was thought. Fer my part, I never missed a guess in my life. Men don't have scars on their face like his fer nothin'."

"Boss, I'm confidin' what I want kept under your hat," said Wade, quietly. "I knew Smith. He's as bad as the West makes them. I gave him that scar. . . . An' when he sees me he's goin' for his gun."

"Wal, I'll be darned! Doesn't surprise me. It's a small world. . . . Wade, I'll keep my mouth shut, sure. But what's your game?"

"Lewis an' I will find out if there is any connection between Smith an' this gang of strangers—an' the occasional loss of a few head of stock."

"Ahuh! Wal, you have my good will, you bet. . . . Sure thar's been some rustlin' of cattle. Not enough to make any rancher holler, an' I reckon there never will be any more of thet in Colorado. Still, if we get the drop on some outfit we sure ought to corral them."

"Boss, I'm tellin' you—"

"Wade, you ain't agoin' to start thet tellin' hell-bent happenin's to come hyar at White Slides?" interrupted Belllounds, plaintively.

"No, I reckon I've no hunch like that now," responded Wade, seriously. "But I was about to say that if Smith is in on any rustlin' of cattle he'll be hard to catch, an' if he's caught there'll be shootin' to pay. He's cunnin' an' has had long experience. It's not likely he'd work openly, as he did years ago. If he's stealin' stock or buyin' an' sellin' stock that some one steals for him, it's only on a small scale, an' it'll be hard to trace."

"Wal, he might be deep," said Belllounds, reflectively. "But men like thet, no matter how deep or cunnin' they are, always come to a bad end. Jest works out natural. . . . Had you any grudge ag'in' Smith?"

"What I give him was for somebody else, an' was sure little enough. He's got the grudge against me."

"Ahuh! Wal, then, don't you go huntin' fer trouble. Try an' make White Slides one place thet'll disprove your name. All the same, don't shy at sight of anythin' suspicious round the ranch."

The old man plodded thoughtfully away, leaving the hunter likewise in a brown study.

"He's gettin' a hunch that I'll tell him of some shadow hoverin' black over White Slides," soliloquized Wade. "Maybe —maybe so. But I don't see any yet. . . . Strange how a man will say what he didn't start out to say. Now, I started to tell him about that amazin' dog Fox."

Fox was the great dog of the whole pack, and he had been absolutely overlooked, which fact Wade regarded with contempt for himself. Discovery of this particular dog came about by accident. Somewhere in the big corral there was a hole where the smaller dogs could escape, but Wade had been unable to find it. For that matter the corral was full of holes, not any of which, however, it appeared to Wade, would permit anything except a squirrel to pass in and out.

One day when the hunter, very much exasperated, was prowling around and around inside the corral, searching for this mysterious vent, a rather small dog, with short gray and brown woolly hair, and shaggy brows half hiding big, bright eyes, came up wagging his stump of a tail.

"Well, what do you know about it?" demanded Wade. Of course he had noticed this particular dog, but to no purpose. On this occasion the dog repeated so unmistakably former overtures of friendship that Wade gave him close scrutiny. He was neither young nor comely nor thoroughbred, but there was something in his intelligent eyes that struck the hunter significantly. "Say, maybe I overlooked somethin'? But there's been a heap of dogs round here an' you're no great shucks for looks. Now, if you're talkin' to me come an' find that hole."

Whereupon Wade began another search around the corral. It covered nearly an acre of ground, and in some places the fence-poles had been sunk near rocks. More than once Wade got down upon his hands and knees to see if he could find the hole. The dog went with him, watching with knowing eyes that the hunter imagined actually laughed at him. But they were glad eyes, which began to make an appeal. Presently, when Wade came to a rough place, the dog slipped under a shelving rock, and thence through a half-concealed hole in the fence; and immediately came back through to wag his stump of a tail and look as if the finding of that hole was easy enough.

"You old fox," declared Wade, very much pleased, as he patted the dog. "You found it for me, didn't you? Good dog! Now I'll fix that hole, an' then you can come to the cabin with me. An' your name's Fox."

That was how Fox introduced himself to Wade, and found his opportunity. The fact that he was not a hound had operated against his being taken out hunting, and therefore little or no attention had been paid him. Very shortly Fox showed himself to be a dog of superior intelligence. The hunter had lived much with dogs and had come to learn that the longer he lived with them the more there was to marvel at and love.

Fox insisted so strongly on being taken out to hunt with the hounds that Wade, vowing not to be surprised at anything, let him go. It happened to be a particularly hard day on hounds because of old tracks and cross-tracks and difficult ground. Fox worked out a labyrinthine trail that Sampson gave up and Jim failed on. This delighted Wade, and that night he tried to find out from Andrews, who sold the dog to Belllounds, something about Fox. All the information obtainable was that Andrews suspected the fellow from whom he had gotten Fox had stolen him. Belllounds had never noticed him at all. Wade kept the possibilities of Fox to himself and reserved his judgment, and every day gave the dog another chance to show what he knew.

Long before the end of that week Wade loved Fox and decided that he was a wonderful animal. Fox liked to hunt, but it did not matter what he hunted. That depended upon the pleasure of his master. He would find hobbled horses that were hiding out and standing still to escape detection. He would trail cattle. He would tree squirrels and point grouse. Invariably he suited his mood to the kind of game he hunted. If put on an elk track, or that of deer, he would follow it, keeping well within sight of the hunter, and never uttering a single bark or yelp; and without any particular eagerness he would stick until he had found the game or until he was called off. Bear and cat tracks, however, roused the savage instinct in him, and transformed him. He yelped at every jump on a trail, and whenever his yelp became piercing and continuous Wade well knew the quarry was in sight. He fought bear like a wise old dog that knew when to rush in with a snap and when to keep away. When lions or wildcats were treed Fox lost much of his ferocity and interest. Then the matter of that particular quarry was ended. His most valuable characteristic, however, was his ability to stick on the track upon which he was put. Wade believed if he put Fox on the trail of a rabbit, and if a bear or lion were to cross that trail ahead of him, Fox would stick to the rabbit. Even more remarkable was it that Fox would not steal a piece of meat and that he would fight the other dogs for being thieves.

Fox and Kane, it seemed to the hunter in his reflective foreshadowing of events at White Slides, were destined to play most important parts.

Upon a certain morning, several days before October first —which date rankled in the mind of Wade—he left Moore's cabin, leading a pack-horse. The hounds he had left behind at the ranch, but Fox accompanied him.

"Wade, I want some elk steak," old Belllounds had said the day before. "Nothin' like a good rump steak! I was raised on elk meat. Now hyar, more'n a week ago I told you I wanted some. There's elk all round. I heerd a bull whistle at sunup to-day. Made me wish I was young ag'in! . . . You go pack in an elk."

"I haven't run across any bulls lately," Wade had replied, but he did not mention that he had avoided such a circumstance. The fact was Wade admired and loved the elk above all horned wild animals. So strange was his attitude toward elk that he had gone meat-hungry many a time with these great stags bugling near his camp.

As he climbed the yellow, grassy mountain-side, working round above the valley, his mind was not centered on the task at hand, but on Wilson Moore, who had come to rely on him with the unconscious tenacity of a son whose faith in his father was unshakable. The crippled cowboy kept his hope, kept his cheerful, grateful spirit, obeyed and suffered with a patience that was fine. There had been no improvement in his injured foot. Wade worried about that much more than Moore. The thing that mostly occupied the cowboy was the near approach of October first, with its terrible possibility for him. He did not talk about it, except when fever made him irrational, but it was plain to Wade how he prayed and hoped and waited in silence. Strange how he trusted Wade to avert catastrophe of Columbine's marriage! Yet such trust seemed familiar to Wade, as he reflected over past years. Had he not wanted such trust—had he not invited it?

For twenty years no happiness had come to Wade in any sense comparable to that now secretly his, as he lived near Columbine Belllounds, divining more and more each day how truly she was his own flesh and the image of the girl he had loved and married and wronged. Columbine was his daughter. He saw himself in her. And Columbine, from being strongly attracted to him and trusting in him and relying upon him, had come to love him. That was the most beautiful and terrible fact of his life—beautiful because it brought back the past, her babyhood, and his barren years, and gave him this sudden change, where he lived transported with the sense and the joy of his possession. It was terrible because she was unhappy, because she was chained to duty and honor, because ruin faced her, and lastly because Wade began to have the vague, gloomy intimations of distant tragedy. Far off, like a cloud on the horizon, but there! Long ago he had learned the uselessness of fighting his morbid visitations. But he clung to hope, to faith in life, to the victory of the virtuous, to the defeat of evil. A thousand proofs had strengthened him in that clinging.

There were personal dread and poignant pain for Wade in Columbine Belllounds's situation. After all, he had only his subtle and intuitive assurance that matters would turn out well for her in the end. To trust that now, when the shadow began to creep over his own daughter, seemed unwise—a juggling with chance.

"I'm beginnin' to feel that I couldn't let her marry that Buster Jack," soliloquized Wade, as he rode along the grassy trail. "Fust off, seein' how strong was her sense of duty an' loyalty, I wasn't so set against it. But somethin's growin' in me. Her love for that crippled boy, now, an' his for her! Lord! they're so young an' life must be so hot an' love so sweet! I reckon that's why I couldn't let her marry Jack. . . . But, on the other hand, there's the old man's faith in his son, an' there's Collie's faith in herself an' in life. Now I believe in that. An' the years have proved to me there's hope for the worst of men. . . . I haven't even had a talk with this Buster Jack. I don't know him, except by hearsay. An' I'm sure prejudiced, which's no wonder, considerin' where I saw him in Denver. . . . I reckon, before I go any farther, I'd better meet this Belllounds boy an' see what's in him."

It was characteristic of Wade that this soliloquy abruptly ended his thoughtful considerations for the time being. This was owing to the fact that he rested upon a decision, and also because it was time he began to attend to the object of his climb.

Bench after bench he had ascended, and the higher he got the denser and more numerous became the aspen thickets and the more luxuriant the grass. Presently the long black slope of spruce confronted him, with its edge like a dark wall. He entered the fragrant forest, where not a twig stirred nor a sound pervaded the silence. Upon the soft, matted earth the hoofs of the horses made no impression and scarcely a perceptible thud.

Wade headed to the left, avoiding rough, rocky defiles of weathered cliff and wind-fallen trees, and aimed to find easy going up to the summit of the mountain bluff far above. This was new forest to him, consisting of moderate-sized spruce-trees growing so closely together that he had to go carefully to keep from snapping dead twigs. Fox trotted on in the lead, now and then pausing to look up at his master, as if for instructions.

A brightening of the dark-green gloom ahead showed the hunter that he was approaching a large glade or open patch, where the sunlight fell strongly. It turned out to be a swale, or swampy place, some few acres in extent, and directly at the foot of a last steep, wooded slope. Here Fox put his nose into the air and halted.

"What're you scentin', Fox, old boy?" asked Wade, with low voice, as he peered ahead. The wind was in the wrong direction for him to approach close to game without being detected. Fox wagged his stumpy tail and looked up with knowing eyes. Wade proceeded cautiously. The swamp was a rank growth of long, weedy grasses and ferns, with here and there a green-mossed bog half hidden and a number of dwarf oak-trees. Wade's horse sank up to his knees in the mire. On the other side showed fresh tracks along the wet margin of the swale.

"It's elk, all right," said Wade, as he dismounted. "Heard us comin'. Now, Fox, stick your nose in that track. An' go slow."

With rifle ready Wade began the ascent of the slope on foot, leading his horse. An old elk trail showed a fresh track. Fox accommodated his pace to that of the toiling hunter. The

ascent was steep and led up through dense forest. At inter-
vals, when Wade halted to catch his breath and listen, he
heard faint snapping of dead branches far above. At length
he reached the top of the mountain, to find a wide, open
space, with heavy forest in front, and a bare, ghastly, burned-
over district to his right. Fox growled, and appeared about to
dash forward. Then, in an opening through the forest, Wade
espied a large bull elk, standing at gaze, evidently watching
him. He was a gray old bull, with broken antlers. Wade made
no move to shoot, and presently the elk walked out of sight.

"Too old an' tough, Fox," explained the hunter to the
anxious dog. But perhaps that was not all Wade's motive in
sparing him.

Once more mounted, Wade turned his attention to the
burned district. It was a dreary, hideous splotch, a black-
ened slash in the green cover of the mountain. It sloped down
into a wide hollow and up another bare slope. The ground
was littered with bleached logs, trees that had been killed
first by fire and then felled by wind. Here and there a lofty,
spectral trunk still withstood the blasts. Across the hollow
sloped a considerable area where all trees were dead and
still standing—a melancholy sight. Beyond, and far around
and down to the left, opened up a slope of spruce and bare
ridge, where a few cedars showed dark, and then came black,
spear-tipped forest again, leading the eye to the magnificent
panorama of endless range on range, purple in the distance.

Wade found patches of grass where beds had been recently
occupied.

"Mountain-sheep, by cracky!" exclaimed the hunter. "An'
fresh tracks, too! . . . Now I wonder if it wouldn't do to kill
a sheep an' tell Belllounds I couldn't find any elk."

The hunter had no qualms about killing mountain-sheep,
but he loved the lordly stags and would have lied to spare
them. He rode on, with keen gaze shifting everywhere to
catch a movement of something in this wilderness before him.
If there was any living animal in sight it did not move. Wade
crossed the hollow, wended a circuitous route through the
upstanding forest of dead timber, and entered a thick woods
that skirted the rim of the mountain. Presently he came out
upon the open rim, from which the depths of green and

gray yawned mightily. Far across, Old White Slides loomed
up, higher now, with a dignity and majesty unheralded from
below.

Wade found fresh sheep tracks in the yellow clay of the
rim, small as little deer tracks, showing that they had just
been made by ewes and lambs. Not a ram track in the
group!

"Well, that lets me out," said Wade, as he peered under
the bluff for sight of the sheep. They had gone over the
steep rim as if they had wings. "Beats hell how sheep can
go down without fallin'! An' how they can hide!"

He knew they were near at hand and he wasted time
peering to spy them out. Nevertheless, he could not locate
them. Fox waited impatiently for the word to let him prove
how easily he could rout them out, but this permission was
not forthcoming.

"We're huntin' elk, you Jack-of-all-dogs," reprovingly spoke
the hunter to Fox.

So they went on around the rim, and after a couple of
miles of travel came to the forest, and then open heads of
hollows that widened and deepened down. Here was excel-
lent pasture and cover for elk. Wade left the rim to ride
down these slow-descending half-open ridges, where cedars
grew and jack-pines stood in clumps, and little grassy-bor-
dered brooks babbled between. He saw tracks where a big
buck deer had crossed ahead of him, and then he flushed a
covey of grouse that scared the horses, and then he saw
where a bear had pulled a rotten log to pieces. Fox did not
show any interest in these things.

By and by Wade descended to the junction of these hollows, where three tiny brooklets united to form a stream of
pure, swift, clear water, perhaps a foot deep and several
yards wide.

"I reckon this's the head of the Troublesome," said Wade.
"Whoever named this brook had no sense. . . . Yet here, at
its source, it's gatherin' trouble for itself. That's the way of
youth."

The grass grew thickly and luxuriantly and showed signs
of recent grazing. Elk had been along the brook that morn-

ing. There were many tracks, like cow tracks, only smaller, deeper, and more oval; and there were beds where elk had lain, and torn-up places where bulls had plowed and stamped with heavy hoofs.

Fox trailed the herd to higher ground, where evidently they had entered the woods. Here Wade tied his horses, and, whispering to Fox, he proceeded stealthily through this strip of spruce. He came out to an open point, taking care, however, to keep well screened, from which he had a glimpse of a parklike hollow, grassy and watered. Working round to better vantage, he soon espied what had made Fox stand so stiff and bristling. A herd of elk were trooping up the opposite slope, scarcely a hundred yards distant. They had heard or scented him, but did not appear alarmed. They halted to look back. The hunter's quick estimate credited nearly two dozen to the herd, mostly cows. A magnificent bull, with wide-spreading antlers, and black head and shoulders and gray hind quarters, stalked out from the herd, and stood an instant, head aloft, splendidly significant of the wild. Then he trotted into the woods, his antlers noiselessly spreading the green. Others trotted off likewise. Wade raised his rifle and looked through the sight at the bull, and let him pass. Then he saw another over his rifle, and another. Reluctant and forced, he at last aimed and pulled trigger. The heavy Henry boomed out in the stillness. Fox dashed down with eager barks. When the smoke cleared away Wade saw the opposite slope bare except for one fallen elk.

Then he returned to his horses, and brought them back to where Fox perched beside the dead quarry.

"Well, Fox, that stag'll never bugle any more of a sunrise," said Wade. "Strange how we're made so we have to eat meat! I'd 'a' liked it otherwise."

He cut up the elk, and packed all the meat the horse could carry, and hung the best of what was left out of the reach of coyotes. Mounting once more, he ascended to the rim and found a slope leading down to the west. Over the basin country below he had hunted several days. This way back to the ranch was longer, he calculated, but less arduous for man and beast. His pack-horse would have hard enough going in any event. From time to time Wade halted to rest the burdened pack-animal. At length he came to a trail he had himself made, which he now proceeded to follow. It led out of the basin, through burned and boggy ground and down upon the forest slope, thence to the grassy and aspened uplands. One aspen grove, where he had rested before, faced the west, and, for reasons hard to guess, had suffered little from frost. All the leaves were intact, some still green, but most of them a glorious gold against the blue. It was a large grove, sloping gently, carpeted with yellow grass and such a profusion of purple asters as Wade had never seen in his flower-loving life. Here he dismounted and sat against an aspen-tree. His horses ruthlessly cropped the purple blossoms.

Nature in her strong prodigality had outdone herself here. Pale white the aspen-trees shone, and above was the fluttering, quivering canopy of gold tinged with green, and below clustered the asters, thick as stars in the sky, waving, nodding, swaying gracefully to each little autumn breeze, lilac-hued and lavender and pale violet, and all the shades of exquisite purple.

Wade lingered, his senses predominating. This was one of those moments that colored his lonely wanderings. Only to see was enough. He would have shut out the encroaching thoughts of self, of others, of life, had that been wholly possible. But here, after the first few moments of exquisite riot of his senses, where fragrance of grass and blossom filled the air, and blaze of gold canopied the purple, he began to think how beautiful the earth was, how Nature hid her rarest gifts for those who loved her most, how good it was to live, if only for these blessings. And sadness crept into his meditations because all this beauty was ephemeral, all the gold would soon be gone, and the asters, so pale and pure and purple, would soon be like the glory of a dream that had passed.

Yet still followed the saving thought that frost and winter must again yield to sun, and spring, summer, autumn would return with the flowers of their season, in that perennial birth so gracious and promising. The aspen leaves would quiver and slowly gild, the grass would wave in the wind, the asters would bloom, lifting star-pale faces to the sky. Next autumn, and every year, and forever, as long as the sun warmed the earth!

It was only man who would not always return to the haunts he loved.

11

◉

WHEN BENT WADE desired opportunities they seemed to gravitate to him.

Upon riding into the yard of White Slides Ranch he espied Jack Belllounds sitting in idle, moping posture on the porch. Something in his dejected appearance roused Wade's pity. No one else was in sight, so the hunter took advantage of the moment.

"Hey, Belllounds, will you give me a lift with this meat?" called Wade.

"Sure," replied Jack, readily enough, and he got up.

Wade led the pack-horse to the door of the store-cabin, which stood back of the kitchen and was joined to it by a roof. There, with Jack's assistance, he unloaded the meat and hung it up on pegs. This done, Wade set to work with knife in hand.

"I reckon a little trimmin' will improve the looks of this carcass," observed Wade.

"Wade, we never had any one round except dad who could cut up a steer or elk," said Jack. "But you've got him beat."

"I'm pretty handy at most things."

"Handy! . . . I wish I could do just one thing as well as you. I can ride, but that's all. No one ever taught me anything."

"You're a young fellow yet, an' you've time, if you only take kindly to learnin'. I was past your age when I learned most I know."

The hunter's voice and his look, and that fascination which

subtly hid in his presence, for the first time seemed to find the response of interest in young Belllounds.

"I can't stick, dad says, and he swears at me," replied Belllounds. "But I'll bet I could learn from you."

"Reckon you could. Why can't you stick to anythin'?"

"I don't know. I've been as enthusiastic over work as over riding mustangs. To ride came natural, but in work, when I do it wrong, then I hate it."

"Ahuh! That's too bad. You oughtn't to hate work. Hard work makes for what I reckon you like in a man, but don't understand. As I look back over my life—an' let me say, young fellar, it's been a tough one—what I remember most an' feel best over are the hardest jobs I ever did, an' those that cost the most sweat an' blood."

As Wade warmed to his subject, hoping to sow a good seed in Belllounds's mind, he saw that he was wasting his earnestness. Belllounds did not keep to the train of thought. His mind wandered, and now he was examining Wade's rifle.

"Old Henry forty-four," he said. "Dad has one. Also an old needle-gun. Say, can I go hunting with you?"

"Glad to have you. How do you handle a rifle?"

"I used to shoot pretty well before I went to Denver," he replied. "Haven't tried since I've been home. . . . Suppose you let me take a shot at that post?" And from where he stood in the door he pointed to a big hitching-post near the corral gate.

The corral contained horses, and in the pasture beyond were cattle, any of which might be endangered by such a shot. Wade saw that the young man was in earnest, that he wanted to respond to the suggestion in his mind. Consequences of any kind did not awaken after the suggestion.

"Sure. Go ahead. Shoot low, now, a little below where you want to hit," said Wade.

Belllounds took aim and fired. A thundering report shook the cabin. Dust and splinters flew from the post.

"I hit it!" he exclaimed, in delight. "I was sure I wouldn't, because I aimed 'way under."

"Reckon you did. It was a good shot."

Then a door slammed and Old Bill Belllounds appeared,

his hair upstanding, his look and gait proclaiming him on the rampage.

"Jack! What'n hell are you doin'?" he roared, and he stamped up to the door to see his son standing there with the rifle in his hands. "By Heaven! If it ain't one thing it's another!"

"Boss, don't jump over the traces," said Wade. "I'll allow if I'd known the gun would let out a bellar like that I'd not have told Jack to shoot. Reckon it's because we're under the open roof that it made the racket. I'm wantin' to clean the gun while it's hot."

"Ahuh! Wal, I was scared fust, harkin' back to Indian days, an' then I was mad because I figgered Jack was up to mischief. . . . Did you fetch in the meat?"

"You bet. An' I'd like a piece for myself," replied Wade.

"Help yourself, man. An' say, come down an' eat with us fer supper."

"Much obliged, boss. I sure will."

Then the old rancher trudged back to the house.

"Wade, it was bully of you!" exclaimed Jack, gratefully. "You see how quick dad's ready to jump me? I'll bet he thought I'd picked a shooting-scrape with one of the cowboys."

"Well, he's gettin' old an' testy," replied Wade. "You ought to humor him. He'll not be here always."

Belllounds answered to that suggestion with a shadowing of eyes and look of realization, affection, remorse. Feelings seemed to have a quick rise and play in him, but were not lasting. Wade casually studied him, weighing his impressions, holding them in abeyance for a sum of judgment.

"Belllounds, has anybody told you about Wils Moore bein' bad hurt?" abruptly asked the hunter.

"He is, is he?" replied Jack, and to his voice and face came sudden change. "How bad?"

"I reckon he'll be a cripple for life," answered Wade, seriously, and now he stopped in his work to peer at Belllounds. The next moment might be critical for that young man.

"Club-footed! . . . He won't lord it over the cowboys any more—or ride that white mustang!" The softer, weaker expression of his face, that which gave him some title to good looks, changed to an ugliness hard for Wade to define, since it was neither glee, nor joy, nor gratification over his rival's misfortune. It was rush of blood to eyes and skin, a heated change that somehow to Wade suggested an anxious, selfish hunger. Belllounds lacked something, that seemed certain. But it remained to be proved how deserving he was of Wade's pity.

"Belllounds, it was a dirty trick—your jumpin' Moore," declared Wade, with deliberation.

"The hell you say!" Belllounds flared up, with scarlet in his face, with sneer of amaze, with promise of bursting rage. He slammed down the gun.

"Yes, the hell I say," returned the hunter. "They call me Hell-Bent Wade!"

"Are you friends with Moore?" asked Belllounds, beginning to shake.

"Yes, I'm that with every one. I'd like to be friends with you."

"I don't want you. And I'm giving you notice—you won't last long at White Slides."

"Neither will you!"

Belllounds turned dead white, not apparently from fury or fear, but from a shock that had its birth within the deep, mysterious, emotional reachings of his mind. He was utterly astounded, as if confronting a vague, terrible premonition of the future. Wade's swift words, like the ring of bells, had not been menacing, but prophetic.

"Young fellar, you need to be talked to, so if you've got any sense at all it'll get a wedge in your brain," went on Wade. "I'm a stranger here. But I happen to be a man who sees through things, an' I see how your dad handles you wrong. You don't know who I am an' you don't care. But if you'll listen you'll learn what might help you. . . . No boy can answer to all his wild impulses without ruinin' himself. It's not natural. There are other people—people who have wills an' desires, same as you have. You've got to live with people. Here's your dad an' Miss Columbine, an' the cowboys, an' me, an' all the ranchers, so down to Kremmlin' an' other places. These are the people you've got to live with. You can't go on as you've begun, without ruinin' yourself an' your dad an' the—the girl. . . . It's never too late to begin to be better. I know that. But it gets too late, sometimes, to save the happiness of others. Now I see where you're headin' as clear as if I had pictures of the future. I've got a gift that way. . . . An', Belllounds, you'll not last. Unless you begin to control your temper, to forget yourself, to kill your wild impulses, to be kind, to learn what love is—you'll never last! . . . In the very nature of things, one comin' after another, like your fights with Moore, an' your scarin' of Pronto, an' your drinkin' at Kremmlin', an' just now your r'arin' at me—it's in the very nature of life that goin' on so you'll sooner or later meet with hell! You've got to change, Belllounds. No half-way, spoiled-boy changin', but the straight right-about-face of a man! . . . It means you must see you're no good an' have a change of heart. Men have revolutions like that. I was no good. I did worse than you'll ever do, because you're not big enough to be really bad, an' yet I've turned out worth livin'. . . . There, I'm through, an' I'm offerin' to be your friend an' to help you."

Belllounds stood with arms spread outside the door, still astounded, still pale; but as the long admonition and appeal ended he exploded stridently. "Who the hell are *you?* . . . If I hadn't been so surprised—if I'd had a chance to get a word in—I'd shut your trap! Are you a preacher masquerading here as hunter? Let me tell you, I won't be talked to like that—not by any man. Keep your advice an' friendship to yourself."

"You don't want me, then?"

"No," Belllounds snapped.

"Reckon you don't need either advice or friend, hey?"

"No, you owl-eyed, soft-voiced fool!" yelled Belllounds.

It was then Wade felt a singular and familiar sensation, a cold, creeping thing, physical and elemental, that had not visited him since he had been at White Slides.

"I reckoned so," he said, with low and gloomy voice, and he knew, if Belllounds did not know, that he was not acquiescing with the other's harsh epithet, but only greeting the advent of something in himself.

Belllounds shrugged his burly shoulders and slouched away. Wade finished his dressing of the meat. Then he rode up to

spend an hour with Moore. When he returned to his cabin
he proceeded to change his hunter garb for the best he owned.
It was a proof of his unusual preoccupation that he did this
before he fed the hounds. It was sunset when he left his
cabin. Montana Jim and Lem hailed as he went by. Wade
paused to listen to their good-natured raillery.

"See hyar, Bent, this ain't Sunday," said Lem.

"You're spruced up powerful fine. What's it fer?" added
Montana.

"Boss asked me down to supper."

"Wal, you lucky son-of-a-gun! An' hyar we've no invite,"
returned Lem. "Say, Wade, I heerd Buster Jack roarin' at you.
I was ridin' in by the storehouse. . . . 'Who the hell are you?'
was what collared my attention, an' I had to laugh. An' I
listened to all he said. So you was offerin' him advice an'
friendship?"

"I reckon."

"Wal, all I say is thet you was wastin' yore breath," declared Lem. "You're a queer fellar, Wade."

"Queer? Aw, Lem, he ain't queer," said Montana. "He's
jest white. Wade, I feel the same as you. I'd like to do somethin' fer thet locoed Buster Jack."

"Montana, you're the locoed one," rejoined Lem. "Buster
Jack knows what he's doin'. He can play a slicker hand of
poker than you."

"Wal, mebbe. Wade, do you play poker?"

"I'd hate to take your money," replied Wade.

"You needn't be so all-fired kind about thet. Come over
tonight an' take some of it. Buster Jack invited himself up to
our bunk. He's itchin' fer cards. So we says shore. Blud's
goin' to sit in. Now you come an' make it five-handed."

"Wouldn't young Belllounds object to me?"

"What? Buster Jack shy at gamblin' with you? Not much.
He's a born gambler. He'd bet with his grandmother an' he'd
cheat the coppers off a dead nigger's eyes."

"Slick with cards, eh?" inquired Wade.

"Naw, Jack's not slick. But he tries to be. An' we jest go
him one slicker."

"Wouldn't Old Bill object to this card-playin'?"

"He'd be ory-eyed. But, by Golly! we're not leadin' Jack

astray. An' we ain't hankerin' to play with him. All the same a little game is welcome enough."

"I'll come over," replied Wade, and thoughtfully turned away.

When he presented himself at the ranch-house it was Columbine who let him in. She was prettily dressed, in a way he had never seen her before, and his heart throbbed. Her smile, her voice added to her nameless charm, that seemed to come from the past. Her look was eager and longing, as if his presence might bring something welcome to her.

Then the rancher stalked in. "Hullo, Wade! Supper's 'most ready. What's this trouble you had with Jack? He says he won't eat with you."

"I was offerin' him advice," replied Wade.

"What on?"

"Reckon on general principles."

"Humph! Wal, he told me you harangued him till you was black in the face, an'——"

"Jack had it wrong. He got black in the face," interrupted Wade.

"Did you say he was a spoiled boy an' thet he was no good an' was headin' plumb fer hell?"

"That was a little of what I said," returned Wade, gently.

"Ahuh! How'd thet come about?" queried Belllounds, gruffly. A slight stiffening and darkening overcast his face.

Wade then recalled and recounted the remarks that had passed between him and Jack; and he did not think he missed them very far. He had a great curiosity to see how Belllounds would take them, and especially the young man's scornful rejection of a sincerely offered friendship. All the time Wade was talking he was aware of Columbine watching him, and when he finished it was sweet to look at her.

"Wade, wasn't you takin' a lot on yourself?" queried the rancher, plainly displeased.

"Reckon I was. But my conscience is beholden to no man. If Jack had met me half-way that would have been better for him. An' for me, because I get good out of helpin' any one."

His reply silenced Belllounds. No more was said before supper was announced, and then the rancher seemed taciturn. Columbine did the serving, and most all of the talking. Wade felt strangely at ease. Some subtle difference was at work in him, transforming him, but the moment had not yet come for him to question himself. He enjoyed the supper. And when he ventured to look up at Columbine, to see her strong, capable hands and her warm, blue glance, glad for his presence, sweetly expressive of their common secret and darker with a shadow of meaning beyond her power to guess, then Wade felt havoc within him, the strife and pain and joy of the truth he never could reveal. For he could never reveal his identity to her without betraying his baseness to her mother. Otherwise, to hear her call him father would have been earning that happiness with a lie. Besides, she loved Belllounds as her father, and were this trouble of the present removed she would grow still closer to the old man in his declining days. Wade accepted the inevitable. She must never know. If she might love him it must be as the stranger who came to her gates, it must be through the mysterious affinity between them and through the service he meant to render.

Wade did not linger after the meal was ended despite the fact that Bellounds recovered his cordiality. It was dark when he went out. Columbine followed him, talking cheerfully. Once outside she squeezed his hand and whispered, "How's Wilson?"

The hunter nodded his reply, and, pausing at the porch step, he pressed her hand to make his assurance stronger. His reward was instant. In the bright starlight she stood white and eloquent, staring down at him with dark, wide eyes.

Presently she whispered: "Oh, my friend! It wants only three days till October first!"

"Lass, it might be a thousand years for all you need worry," he replied, his voice low and full. Then it seemed, as she flung up her arms, that she was about to embrace him. But her gesture was an appeal to the stars, to Heaven above, for something she did not speak.

Wade bade her good night and went his way.

The cowboys and the rancher's son were about to engage in a game of poker when Wade entered the dimly lighted, smoke-hazed room. Montana Jim was sticking tallow candles in the middle of a rude table; Lem was searching his clothes, manifestly for money; Bludsoe shuffled a greasy deck of cards, and Jack Belllounds was filling his pipe before a fire of blazing logs on the hearth.

"Dog-gone it! I hed more money'n thet," complained Lem. "Jim, you rode to Kremmlin' last. Did you take my money?"

"Wal, come to think of it, I reckon I did," replied Jim, in surprise at the recollection.

"An' whar's it now?"

"Pard, I 'ain't no idee. I reckon it's still in Kremmlin'. But I'll pay you back."

"I should smile you will. Pony up now."

"Bent Wade, did you come over calkilated to git skinned?" queried Bludsoe.

"Boys, I was playin' poker tolerable well in Missouri when you all was nursin'," replied Wade, imperturbably.

"I heerd he was a card-sharp," said Jim. "Wal, grab a box or a chair to set on an' let's start. Come along, Jack; you don't look as keen to play as usual."

Belllounds stood with his back to the fire and his manner did not compare favorably with that of the genial cowboys.

"I prefer to play four-handed," he said.

This declaration caused a little check in the conversation and put an end to the amiability. The cowboys looked at one another, not embarrassed, but just a little taken aback, as if they had forgotten something that they should have remembered.

"You object to my playin'?" asked Wade, quietly.

"I certainly do," replied Belllounds.

"Why, may I ask?"

"For all I know, what Montana said about you may be true," returned Belllounds, insolently.

Such a remark flung in the face of a Westerner was an insult. The cowboys suddenly grew stiff, with steady eyes on Wade. He, however, did not change in the slightest.

"I might be a card-sharp at that," he replied, coolly. "You fellows play without me. I'm not carin' about poker any more. I'll look on."

Thus he carried over the moment that might have been dangerous. Lem gaped at him; Montana kicked a box forward to sit upon, and his action was expressive; Bludsoe slammed the cards down on the table and favored Wade with a comprehending look. Belllounds pulled a chair up to the table.

"What'll we make the limit?" asked Jim.

"Two bits," replied Lem, quickly.

Then began an argument. Belllounds was for a dollar limit. The cowboys objected.

"Why, Jack, if the ole man got on to us playin' a dollar limit he'd fire the outfit," protested Bludsoe.

This reasonable objection in no wise influenced the old man's son. He overruled the good arguments, and then hinted at the cowboys' lack of nerve. The fun faded out of their faces. Lem, in fact, grew red.

"Wal, if we're agoin' to *gamble*, thet's different," he said, with a cold ring in his voice, as he straddled a box and sat down. "Wade, lemme some money."

Wade slipped his hand into his pocket and drew forth a goodly handful of gold, which he handed to the cowboy. Not improbably, if this large amount had been shown earlier, before the change in the sentiment, Lem would have looked aghast and begged for mercy. As it was, he accepted it as if he were accustomed to borrowing that much every day. Belllounds had rendered futile the easy-going, friendly advances of the cowboys, as he had made it impossible to play a jolly little game for fun.

The game began, with Wade standing up, looking on. These boys did not know what a vast store of poker knowledge lay back of Wade's inscrutable eyes. As a boy he had learned the intricacies of poker in the country where it orginated; and as a man he had played it with piles of yellow coins and guns on the table. His eagerness to look on here, as far as the cowboys were concerned, was mere pretense. In Belllounds's case, however, he had a profound interest. Rumors had drifted to him from time to time, since his advent at White Slides, regarding Belllounds's weakness for gambling. It might have been cowboy gossip. Wade held that there was nothing in the West as well calculated to test a boy, to prove his real character, as a game of poker.

Belllounds was a feverish better, an exultant winner, a

poor loser. His understanding of the game was rudimentary. With him, the strong feeling beginning to be manifested to Wade was not the fun of matching wits and luck with his antagonists, nor a desire to accumulate money—for his reck-lessness disproved that—but the liberation of the gambling passion. Wade recognized that when he met it. And Jack Bell-lounds was not in any sense big. He was selfish and grasp-ing in the numberless little ways common to the game, and positive about his own rights, while doubtful of the claims of others. His cheating was clumsy and crude. He held out cards, hiding them in his palm; he shuffled the deck so he left aces at the bottom, and these he would slip off to him-self, and he was so blind that he could not detect his fellow-player in tricks as transparent as his own. Wade was amazed and disgusted. The pity he had felt for Belllounds shifted to the old father, who believed in his son with stubborn and unquenchable faith.

"Haven't you got something to drink?" Jack asked of his companions.

"Nope. Whar'd we git it?" replied Jim.

Belllounds evidently forgot, for presently he repeated the query. The cowboys shook their heads. Wade knew they were lying, for they did have liquor in the cabin. It occurred to him, then, to offer to go to his own cabin for some, just to see what this young man would say. But he refrained.

The luck went against Belllounds and so did the gambling. He was not a lamb among wolves, by any means, but the fleecing he got suggested that. According to Wade he was get-ting what he deserved. No cowboys, even such good-natured and fine fellows as these, could be expected to be subjects for Belllounds's cupidity. And they won all he had.

"I'll borrow," he said, with feverish impatience. His face was pale, clammy, yet heated, especially round the swollen bruises; his eyes stood out, bold, dark, rolling and glaring, full of sullen fire. But more than anything else his mouth be-trayed the weakling, the born gambler, the self-centered, spoiled, intolerant youth. It was here his bad blood showed.

"Wal, I ain't lendin' money," replied Lem, as he assorted his winnings. "Wade, here's what you staked me, an' much obliged."

"I'm out, an' I can't lend you any," said Jim.

Bludsoe had a good share of the profits of that quick game, but he made no move to lend any of it. Belllounds glared impatiently at them.

"Hell! you took my money. I'll have satisfaction," he broke out, almost shouting.

"We won it, didn't we?" rejoined Lem, cool and easy. "An' you can have all the satisfaction you want, right now or any time."

Wade held out a handful of money to Belllounds.

"Here," he said, with his deep eyes gleaming in the dim room. Wade had made a gamble with himself, and it was that Belllounds would not even hesitate to take money.

"Come on, you stingy cowpunchers," he called out, snatching the money from Wade. His action then, violent and vivid as it was, did not reveal any more than his face.

But the cowboys showed amaze, and something more. They fell straightway to gambling, sharper and fiercer than before, actuated now by the flaming spirit of this son of Belllounds. Luck, misleading and alluring, favored Jack for a while, transforming him until he was radiant, boastful, exultant. Then it changed, as did his expression. His face grew dark.

"I tell you I want drink," he suddenly demanded. "I know damn well you cowpunchers have some here, for I smelled it when I came in."

"Jack, we drank the last drop," replied Jim, who seemed less stiff than his two bunk-mates.

"I've some very old rye," interposed Wade, looking at Jim, but apparently addressing all. "Fine stuff, but awful strong an' hot! . . . Makes a fellow's blood dance."

"Go get it!" Belllounds's utterance was thick and full, as if he had something in his mouth.

Wade looked down into the heated face, into the burning eyes; and through the darkness of passion that brooked no interference with its fruition he saw this youth's stark and naked soul. Wade had seen into the depths of many such abysses.

"See hyar, Wade," broke in Jim, with his quiet force, "never mind fetchin' thet red-hot rye tonight. Some other time, mebbe, when Jack wants more satisfaction. Reckon we've got a drop or so left."

"All right, boys," replied Wade, "I'll be sayin' good night."

He left them playing and strode out to return to his cabin. The night was still, cold, starlit, and black in the shadows. A lonesome coyote barked, to be answered by a wakeful hound. Wade halted at his porch, and lingered there a moment, peering up at the gray old peak, bare and star-crowned.

"I'm sorry for the old man," muttered the hunter, "but I'd see Jack Belllounds in hell before I'd let Columbine marry him."

October first was a holiday at White Slides Ranch. It happened to be a glorious autumn day, with the sunlight streaming gold and amber over the grassy slopes. Far off the purple ranges loomed hauntingly.

Wade had come down from Wilson Moore's cabin, his ears ringing with the crippled boy's words of poignant fear.

Fox favored his master with unusually knowing gaze. There was not going to be any lion-chasing or elk-hunting this day. Something was in the wind. And Fox, as a privileged dog, manifested his interest and wonder.

Before noon a buckboard with team of sweating horses halted in the yard of the ranch-house. Besides the driver it contained two women whom Belllounds greeted as relatives, and a stranger, a pale man whose dark garb proclaimed him a minister.

"Come right in, folks," welcomed Belllounds, with hearty excitement.

It was Wade who showed the driver where to put the horses. Strangely, not a cowboy was in sight, an omission of duty the rancher had noted. Wade might have informed him where they were.

The door of the big living-room stood open, and from it came the sound of laughter and voices. Wade, who had returned to his seat on the end of the porch, listened to them, while his keen gaze seemed fixed down the lane toward the cabins. How intent must he have been not to hear Columbine's step behind him!

"Good morning, Ben," she said.

Wade wheeled as if internal violence had ordered his movement.

"Lass, good mornin'," he replied. "You sure look sweet this October first—like the flower for which you're named."

"My friend, it *is* October first—my marriage day!" murmured Columbine.

Wade felt her intensity, and he thrilled to the brave, sweet resignation of her face. Hope and faith were unquenchable in her, yet she had fortified herself to the wreck of dreams and love.

"I'd seen you before now, but I had some job with Wils, persuadin' him that we'd not have to offer you congratulations yet awhile," replied Wade, in his slow, gentle voice.

"*Oh!*" breathed Columbine.

Wade saw her full breast swell and the leaping blood wave over her pale face. She bent to him to see his eyes. And for Wade, when she peered with straining heart and soul, all at once to become transfigured, that instant was a sweet and all-fulfilling reward for his years of pain.

"You drive me mad!" she whispered.

The heavy tread of the rancher, like the last of successive steps of fate in Wade's tragic expectancy, sounded on the porch.

"Wal, lass, hyar you are," he said, with a gladness deep in his voice. "Now, whar's the boy?"

"Dad—I've not—seen Jack since breakfast," replied Columbine, tremulously.

"Sort of a laggard in love on his weddin'-day," rejoined the rancher. His gladness and forgetfulness were as big as his heart. "Wade, have you seen Jack?"

"No—I haven't," replied the hunter, with slow, long-drawn utterance. "But—I see—him now."

Wade pointed to the figure of Jack Belllounds approaching from the direction of the cabins. He was not walking straight.

Old man Belllounds shot out his gray head like a striking eagle.

"What the hell?" he muttered, as if bewildered at this strange, uneven gait of his son. "Wade, what's the matter with Jack?"

Wade did not reply. That moment had its sorrow for him as

well as understanding of the wonder expressed by Columbine's cold little hand trembling in his.

The rancher suddenly recoiled.

"So help me Gawd—he's drunk!" he gasped, in a distress that unmanned him.

Then the parson and the invited relatives came out upon the porch, with gay voices and laughter that suddenly stilled when old Belllounds cried, brokenly: "Lass—go—in—the house."

But Columbine did not move, and Wade felt her shaking as she leaned against him.

The bridegroom approached. Drunk indeed he was; not hilariously, as one who celebrated his good fortune, but sullenly, tragically, hideously drunk.

Old Belllounds leaped off the porch. His gray hair stood up like the mane of a lion. Like a giant's were his strides. With a lunge he met his reeling son, swinging a huge fist into the sodden red face. Limply Jack fell to the ground.

"Lay there, you damned prodigal!" he roared, terrible in his rage. "You disgrace me—an' you disgrace the girl who's been a daughter to me! . . . If you ever have another weddin'-day it'll not be me who sets it!"

12

◉

NOVEMBER WAS WELL advanced before there came indications that winter was near at hand.

One morning, when Wade rode up to Moore's cabin, the whole world seemed obscured in a dense gray fog, through which he could not see a rod ahead of him. Later, as he left, the fog had lifted shoulder-high to the mountains, and was breaking to let the blue sky show. Another morning it was worse, and apparently thicker and grayer. As Wade climbed the trail up toward the mountain-basin, where he hunted most these days, he expected the fog to lift. But it did not. The trail under the hoofs of the horse was scarcely perceptible to him, and he seemed lost in a dense, gray, soundless obscurity.

Suddenly Wade emerged from out the fog into brilliant sunshine. In amaze he halted. This phenomenon was new to him. He was high up on the mountain-side, the summit of which rose clear-cut and bold into the sky. Below him spread what resembled a white sea. It was an immense cloud-bank, filling all the valleys as if with creamy foam or snow, soft, thick, motionless, contrasting vividly with the blue sky above. Old White Slides stood out, gray and bleak and brilliant, as if it were an island rock in a rolling sea of fleece. Far across this strange, level cloud-floor rose the black line of the range. Wade watched the scene with a kind of rapture. He was alone on the heights. There was not a sound. The winds were stilled. But there seemed a mighty being awake all around him, in the presence of which Wade felt how little were his sorrows and hopes.

Another day brought dull-gray scudding clouds, and gusts of wind and squalls of rain, and a wailing through the bare aspens. It grew colder and bleaker and darker. Rain changed to sleet and sleet to snow. That night brought winter.

Next morning, when Wade plodded up to Moore's cabin, it was through two feet of snow. A beautiful glistening white mantle covered valley and slope and mountain, transforming all into a world too dazzlingly brilliant for the unprotected gaze of man.

When Wade pushed open the door of the cabin and entered he awakened the cowboy.

"Mornin', Wils," drawled Wade, as he slapped the snow from boots and legs. "Summer has gone, winter has come, an' the flowers lay in their graves! How are you, boy?"

Moore had grown paler and thinner during his long confinement in bed. A weary shade shone in his face and a shadow of pain in his eyes. But the spirit of his smile was the same as always.

"Hello, Bent, old pard!" replied Moore. "I guess I'm fine. Nearly froze last night. Didn't sleep much."

"Well, I was worried about that," said the hunter. "We've got to arrange things somehow."

"I heard it snowing. Gee! how the wind howled! And I'm snowed in?"

"Sure are. Two feet on a level. It's good I snaked down a lot of fire-wood. Now I'll set to work an' cut it up an' stack it round the cabin. Reckon I'd better sleep up here with you, Wils."

"Won't Old Bill make a kick?"

"Let him kick. But I reckon he doesn't need to know any-thin' about it. It is cold in here. Well, I'll soon warm it up. . . . Here's some letters Lem got at Kremmlin' the other day. You read while I rustle some grub for you."

Moore scanned the addresses on the several envelopes and sighed.

"From home! I hate to read them."

"Why?" queried Wade.

"Oh, because when I wrote I didn't tell them I was hurt. I feel like a liar."

"It's just as well, Wils, because you swear you'll not go home."

"Me? I should smile not. . . . Bent—I—I—hoped Collie might answer the note you took her from me."

"Not yet. Wils, give the lass time."

"Time? Heavens! it's three weeks and more."

"Go ahead an' read your letters or I'll knock you on the head with one of these chunks," ordered Wade, mildly.

The hunter soon had the room warm and cheerful, with steaming breakfast on the red-hot coals. Presently, when he made ready to serve Moore, he was surprised to find the boy crying over one of the letters.

"Wils, what's the trouble?" he asked.

"Oh, nothing. I—I—just feel bad, that's all," replied Moore.

"Ahuh! So it seems. Well, tell me about it?"

"Pard, my father—has forgiven me."

"The old son-of-a-gun! Good! What for? You never told me you'd done anythin'."

"I know—but I did—do a lot. I was sixteen then. We quarreled. And I ran off up here to punch cows. But after a while I wrote home to mother and my sister. Since then they've tried to coax me to come home. This letter's from the old man himself. Gee! . . . Well, he says he's had to knuckle. That he's ready to forgive me. But I must come home and take charge of his ranch. Isn't that great? . . . Only I can't go. And I couldn't—I couldn't ever ride a horse again—if I did go."

"Who says you couldn't?" queried Wade. "*I* never said so. I only said you'd never be a bronco-bustin' cowboy again. Well, suppose you're not? You'll be able to ride a little, if I can save that leg. . . . Boy, your letter is damn good news. I'm sure glad. That will make Collie happy."

The cowboy had a better appetite that morning, which fact mitigated somewhat the burden of Wade's worry. There was burden enough, however, and Wade had set this day to make important decisions about Moore's injured foot. He had dreaded to remove the last dressing because conditions at that time had been unimproved. He had done all he could to ward off the threatened gangrene.

"Wils, I'm goin' to look at your foot an' tell you things," declared Wade, when the dreaded time could be put off no longer.

"Go ahead. . . . And, pard, if you say my leg has to be cut off—why just pass me my gun!"

The cowboy's voice was gay and bantering, but his eyes were alight with a spirit that frightened the hunter.

"Ahuh! . . . I know how you feel. But, boy, I'd rather live with one leg an' be loved by Collie Belllounds than have nine legs for some other lass."

Wilson Moore groaned his helplessness.

"Damn you, Bent Wade! You always say what kills me! . . . Of course I would!"

"Well, lie quiet now, an' let me look at this poor, messed-up foot."

Wade's deft fingers did not work with the usual precision and speed natural to them. But at last Moore's injured member lay bare, discolored and misshapen. The first glance made the hunter quicker in his movements, closer in his scrutiny. Then he yelled his joy.

"Boy, it's better! No sign of gangrene! We'll save your leg!"

"Pard, I never feared I'd lose that. All I've feared was that I'd be club-footed. . . . Let me look," replied the cowboy, and he raised himself on his elbow. Wade lifted the unsightly foot.

"My God, it's crooked!" cried Moore, passionately. "Wade, it's healed. It'll stay that way always! I can't move it! . . . Oh, but Buster Jack's ruined me!"

The hunter pushed him back with gentle hands. "Wils, it might have been worse."

"But I never gave up hope," replied Moore, in poignant grief. "I couldn't. But now! . . . How can you look at that—that club-foot, and not swear?"

"Well, well, boy, cussin' won't do any good. Now lay still an' let me work. You've had lots of good news this mornin'. So I think you can stand to hear a little bad news."

"What! Bad news?" queried Moore, with a start.

"I reckon. Now listen. . . . The reason Collie hasn't answered your note is because she's been sick in bed for three weeks."

"Oh no!" exclaimed the cowboy, in amaze and distress.

"Yes, an' I'm her doctor," replied Wade, with pride. "First off they had Mrs. Andrews. An' Collie kept askin' for me. She was out of her head, you know. An' soon as I took charge she got better."

"Heavens! Collie ill and you never told me!" cried Moore. "I can't believe it. She's so healthy and strong. What ailed her, Bent?"

"Well, Mrs. Andrews said it was nervous breakdown. An' Old Bill was afraid of consumption. An' Jack Bellounds swore she was only shammin'."

The cowboy cursed violently.

"Here—I won't tell you any more if you're goin' to cuss that way an' jerk around," protested Wade.

"I—I'll shut up," appealed Moore.

"Well, that puddin'-head Jack is more'n you called him, if you care to hear my opinion. . . . Now, Wils, the fact is that none of them know what ails Collie. But I know. She'd been under a high strain leadin' up to October first. An' the way that weddin'-day turned out—with Old Bill layin' Jack cold, an' with no marriage at all—why, Collie had a shock. An' after that she seemed pale an' tired all the time an' she didn't eat right. Well, when Buster Jack got over that awful punch he'd got from the old man he made up to Collie harder than ever. She didn't tell me then, but I saw it. An' she couldn't avoid him, except by stayin' in her room, which she did a good deal. Then Jack showed a streak of bein' decent. He surprised everybody, even Collie. He delighted Old Bill. But he didn't pull the wool over my eyes. He was like a boy spoilin' for a new toy, an' he got crazy over Collie. He's sure terribly in love with her, an' for days he behaved himself in a way calculated to make up for his drinkin' too much. It shows he can behave himself when he wants to. I mean he can control his temper an' impulse. Anyway, he made himself so good that Old Bill changed his mind, after what he swore that day, an' set another day for the weddin'. Right off, then, Collie goes down on her back. . . . They didn't send for me very soon. But when I did get to see her, an' felt the way she grabbed me—as if she was drownin'—then I knew what ailed her. It was love."

"Love!" gasped Moore, breathlessly.

"Sure. Jest love for a dog-gone lucky cowboy named Wils Moore! . . . Her heart was breakin', an' she'd have died but for me! Don't imagine, Wils, that people can't die of broken hearts. They do. I know. Well, all Collie needed was me, an' I cured her ravin' and made her eat, an' now she's comin' along fine."

"Wade, I've believed in Heaven since you came down to White Slides," burst out Moore, with shining eyes. "But tell me—what did you tell her?"

"Well, my particular medicine first off was to whisper in her ear that she'd never have to marry Jack Belllounds. An' after that I gave her daily doses of talk about you."

"Pard! She loves me—still?" he whispered.

"Wils, hers is the kind that grows stronger with time. I know."

Moore strained in his intensity of emotion, and he clenched his fists and gritted his teeth.

"Oh God! this's hard on me!" he cried. "I'm a man. I love that girl more than life. And to know she's suffering for love of me—for fear of that marriage being forced upon her—to know that while I lie here a helpless cripple—it's almost unbearable."

"Boy, you've got to mend now. We've the best of hope now—for you—for her—for everythin'."

"Wade, I think I love you, too," said the cowboy. "You're saving me from madness. Somehow I have faith in you—to do whatever you want. But how could you tell Collie she'd never have to marry Buster Jack?"

"Because I know she never will," replied Wade, with his slow, gentle smile.

"You *know* that?"

"Sure."

"How on earth can you prevent it? Belllounds will never give up planning that marriage for his son. Jack will nag Collie till she can't call her soul her own. Between them they will wear her down. My friend, *how* can you prevent it?"

"Wils, fact is, I haven't reckoned out how I'm goin' to save Collie. But that's no matter. Sufficient unto the day is the evil thereof. I will do it. You can gamble on me, Wils. You must use that hope an' faith to help you get well. For we mustn't forget that you're in more danger than Collie."

"I *will* gamble on you—my life—my very soul," replied Moore, fervently. "By Heaven! I'll be the man I might have been. I'll rise out of despair. I'll even reconcile myself to being a cripple."

"An', Wils, will you rise above hate?" asked Wade, softly.

"Hate! Hate of whom?"

"Jack Belllounds."

The cowboy stared, and his lean, pale face contracted.

"Pard, you wouldn't—you couldn't expect me to—to forgive him?"

"No. I reckon not. But you needn't hate him. I don't. An' I reckon I've some reason, more than you could guess. . . . Wils, hate is a poison in the blood. It's worse for him who feels it than for him against whom it rages. I know. . . . Well, if you put thought of Jack out of your mind—quit broodin' over what he did to you—an' realize that he's not to blame, you'll overcome your hate. For the son of Old Bill is to be pitied. Yes, Jack Belllounds needs pity. He was ruined before he was born. He never should have been born. An' I want you to understand that, an' stop hatin' him. Will you try?"

"Wade, you're afraid I'll kill him?" whispered Moore.

"Sure. That's it. I'm afraid you might. An' consider how hard that would be for Columbine. She an' Jack were raised sister an' brother, almost. It would be hard on her. You see, Collie has a strange an' powerful sense of duty to Old Bill. If you killed Jack it would likely kill the old man, an' Collie would suffer all her life. You couldn't cure her of that. You want her to be happy."

"I do—I do. Wade, I swear I'll never kill Buster Jack. And for Collie's sake I'll try not to hate him."

"Well, that's fine. I'm sure glad to hear you promise that. Now I'll go out an' chop some wood. We mustn't let the fire go out any more."

"Pard, I'll write another note—a letter to Collie. Hand me the blank-book there. And my pencil. . . . And don't hurry with the wood."

Wade went outdoors with his two-bladed ax and shovel. The wood-pile was a great mound of snow. He cleaned a wide space and a path to the side of the cabin. Working in snow was not unpleasant for him. He liked the cleanness, the whiteness, the absolute purity of new-fallen snow. The air was crisp and nipping, the frost crackled under his feet, the smoke from his pipe seemed no thicker than the steam from his breath, the ax rang on the hard aspens. Wade swung this implement like a born woodsman. The chips flew and the dead wood smelled sweet. Some logs he chopped into three-foot pieces; others he chopped and split. When he tired a little of swinging the ax he carried the cut pieces to the cabin and stacked them near the door. Now and then he would halt a moment to gaze away across the whitened slopes and rolling hills. The sense of his physical power matched something within, and his heart warmed with more than the vigorous exercise.

When he had worked thus for about two hours and had stacked a pile of wood almost as large as the cabin he considered it sufficient for the day. So he went indoors. Moore was so busily and earnestly writing that he did not hear Wade come in. His face wore an eloquent glow.

"Say, Wils, are you writin' a book?" he inquired.

"Hello! Sure I am. But I'm 'most done now. . . . If Columbine doesn't answer *this* . . ."

"By the way, I'll have two letters to give her, then—for I never gave her the first one," replied Wade.

"You son-of-a-gun!"

"Well, hurry along, boy. I'll be goin' now. Here's a pole I've fetched in. You keep it there, where you can reach it, an' when the fire needs more wood you roll one of these logs on. I'll be up tonight before dark, an' if I don't fetch you a letter it'll be because I can't persuade Collie to write."

"Pard, if you bring me a letter I'll obey you—I'll lie still—I'll sleep—I'll stand anything."

"Ahuh! Then I'll fetch one," replied Wade, as he took the little book and deposited it in this pocket. "Good-by, now, an' think of your good news that come with the snow."

"Good-by, Heaven-Sent Hell-Bent Wade!" called Moore. "It's no joke of a name any more. It's a fact."

Wade plodded down through the deep snow, stepping in his old tracks, and as he toiled on his thoughts were deep and comforting. He was thinking that if he had his life to live over again he would begin at once to find happiness in other people's happiness. Upon arriving at his cabin he set to work cleaning a path to the dog corral. The snow had drifted there and he had no easy task. It was well that he had built an inclosed house for the hounds to winter in. Such a heavy snow as this one would put an end to hunting for the time being. The ranch had ample supply of deer, bear, and elk meat, all solidly frozen this morning, that would surely keep well until used. Wade reflected that his tasks round the ranch would be feeding hounds and stock, chopping wood, and doing such chores as came along in winter-time. The pack of hounds, which he had thinned out to a smaller number, would be a care on his hands. Kane had become a much-prized possession of Columbine's and lived at the house, where he had things his own way, and always greeted Wade with a look of disdain and distrust. Kane would never forgive the hand that had hurt him. Sampson and Jim and Fox, of course, shared Wade's cabin, and vociferously announced his return.

Early in the afternoon Wade went down to the ranch-house. The snow was not so deep there, having blown considerably in the open places. Some one was pounding iron in the blacksmith shop; horses were cavorting in the corrals; cattle were bawling round the hay-ricks in the barn-yard.

The hunter knocked on Columbine's door.

"Come in," she called.

Wade entered, to find her alone. She was sitting up in bed, propped up with pillows, and she wore a warm, woolly jacket or dressing-gown. Her paleness was now marked, and the shadows under her eyes made them appear large and mournful.

"Ben Wade, you don't care for me any more!" she exclaimed, reproachfully.

"Why not, lass?" he asked.

"You were so long in coming," she replied, now with petulance. "I guess now I don't want you at all."

"Ahuh! That's the reward of people who worry an' work for others. Well, then, I reckon I'll go back an' not give you what I brought."

He made a pretense of leaving, and he put a hand to his pocket as if to insure the safety of some article. Columbine blushed. She held out her hands. She was repentant of her words and curious as to his.

"Why, Ben Wade, I count the minutes before you come," she said. "What'd you bring me?"

"Who's been in here?" he asked, going forward. "That's a poor fire. I'll have to fix it."

"Mrs. Andrews just left. It was good of her to drive up. She came in the sled, she said. Oh, Ben, it's winter. There was snow on my bed when I woke up. I think I am better today. Jack hasn't been in here yet!"

At this Wade laughed, and Columbine followed suit.

"Well, you look a little sassy today, which I take is a good sign," said Wade. "I've got some news that will come near to makin' you well."

"Oh, tell it quick!" she cried.

"Wils won't lose his leg. It's gettin' well. An' there was a letter from his father, forgivin' him for somethin' he never told me."

"My prayers were answered!" whispered Columbine, and she closed her eyes tight.

"An' his father wants him to come home to run the ranch," went on Wade.

"Oh!" Her eyes popped open with sudden fright. "But he can't—he won't go?"

"I reckon not. He wouldn't if he could. But some day he will, an' take you home with him."

Columbine covered her face with her hands, and was silent a moment.

"Such prophecies! They—they—" She could not conclude.

"Ahuh! I know. The strange fact is, lass, that they all come true. I wish I had all happy ones, instead of them black, croakin' ones that come like ravens. . . . Well, you're better today?"

"Yes. Oh yes. Ben, what have you got for me?"

"You're in an awful hurry. I want to talk to you, an' if I show what I've got then there will be no talkin'. You say Jack hasn't been in today?"

"Not yet, thank goodness."

"How about Old Bill?"

"Ben, you never call him my dad. I wish you would. When you *don't* it always reminds me that he's really *not* my dad."

"Ahuh! Well, well!" replied Wade, with his head bowed. "It is just queer I can never remember. . . . An' how was he today?"

"For a wonder he didn't mention poor me. He was full of talk about going to Kremmling. Means to take Jack along. Do you know, Ben, dad can't fool me. He's afraid to leave Jack here alone with me. So dad talked a lot about selling stock an' buying supplies, and how he needed Jack to go, and so forth. I'm mighty glad he means to take him. But my! won't Jack be sore."

"I reckon. It's time he broke out."

"And now, dear Ben—what have you got for me? I know it's from Wilson," she coaxed.

"Lass, would you give much for a little note from Wils?" asked Wade, teasingly.

"Would I? When I've been hoping and praying for just that!"

"Well, if you'd give so much for a note, how much would you give me for a whole bookful that took Wils two hours to write?"

"Ben! Oh, I'd—I'd give—" she cried, wild with delight. "I'd *kiss* you!"

"You mean it?" he queried, waving the book aloft.

"Mean it? Come here!"

There was fun in this for Wade, but also a deep and beautiful emotion that quivered through him. Bending over her, he placed the little book in her hand. He did not see clearly, then, as she pulled him lower and kissed him on the cheek, generously, with sweet, frank gratitude and affection.

Moments strong and all-satisfying had been multiplying for Bent Wade of late. But this one magnified all. As he sat back upon the chair he seemed a little husky of voice.

"Well, well, an' so you kissed ugly old Bent Wade?"

"Yes, and I've wanted to do it before," she retorted. The dark excitement in her eyes, the flush of her pale cheeks, made her beautiful then.

"Lass, now you read your letter an' answer it. You can tear out the pages. I'll sit here an' be makin' out to be readin' aloud out of this book here, if any one happens in sudden-like!"

"Oh, how you think of everything!"

The hunter sat beside her pretending to be occupied with the book he had taken from the table when really he was stealing glances at her face. Indeed, she was more than pretty then. Illness and pain had enhanced the sweetness of her expression. As she read on it was manifest that she had forgotten the hunter's presence. She grew pink, rosy, scarlet, radiant. And Wade thrilled with her as she thrilled, loved her more and more as she loved. Moore must have written words of enchantment. Wade's hungry heart suffered a pang of jealousy, but would not harbor it. He read in her perusal of that letter what no other dreamed of, not even the girl herself; and it was certitude of tragic and brief life for her if she could not live for Wilson Moore. Those moments of watching her were unutterably precious to Wade. He saw how some divine guidance had directed his footsteps to this home. How many years had it taken him to get there? Columbine read and read and reread—a girl with her first love-letter. And for Wade, with his keen eyes that seemed to see the senses and the soul, there shone something infinite through her rapture. Never until that unguarded moment had he divined her innocence, nor had any conception been given him of the exquisite torture of her maiden fears or the havoc of love fighting for itself. He learned then much of the mystery and meaning of a woman's heart.

13

◉

"DEAR WILSON,—THE note and letter from you have taken my breath away. I couldn't tell—I wouldn't dare tell, how they made me feel.

"Your good news fills me with joy. And when Ben told me you wouldn't lose your leg—that you would get well—then my eyes filled and my heart choked me, and I thanked God, who'd answered my prayers. After all the heartache and dread, it's so wonderful to find things not so terrible as they seemed. Oh, I am thankful! You have only to take care of yourself now, to lie patiently and wait, and obey Ben, and soon the time will have flown by and you will be well again. Maybe, after all, your foot will not be so bad. Maybe you can ride again, if not so wonderfully as before, then well enough to ride on your father's range and look after his stock. For, Wilson dear, you'll have to go home. It's your duty. Your father must be getting old now. He needs you. He has forgiven you—you bad boy! And you are very lucky. It almost kills me to think of your leaving White Slides. But that is selfish. I'm going to learn to be like Ben Wade. He never thinks of himself.

"Rest assured, Wilson, that I will never marry Jack Bell-lounds. It seems years since that awful October first. I gave my word then, and I would have lived up to it. But I've changed. I'm older. I see things differently. I love dad as well. I feel as sorry for Jack Bellounds. I still think I might help him. I still believe in my duty to his father. But I can't marry him. It would be a sin. I have no right to marry a man whom I do not love. When it comes to thought of his touching me, then I hate him. Duty toward dad is one thing, and I hold it high, but that is not reason enough for a woman to give herself. Some duty to myself is higher than that. It's hard for me to tell you—for me to understand. Love of you has opened my eyes. Still I don't think it's love of you that makes me selfish. I'm true to something in me that I never knew before. I could marry Jack, loving you, and utterly sacrifice myself, if it were right. But it would be wrong. I never realized this until you kissed me. Since then the thought of anything that approaches personal relations—any hint of intimacy with Jack—fills me with disgust.

"So I'm not engaged to Jack Bellounds, and I'm never going to be. There will be trouble here. I feel it. I see it coming. Dad keeps at me persistently. He grows older. I don't think he's failing, but then there's a loss of memory, and an almost childish obsession in regard to the marriage he has set his heart on. Then his passion for Jack seems greater as he learns little by little that Jack is not all he might be. Wilson, I give you my word; I believe if dad ever really sees Jack as I see him or you see him, then something dreadful will happen. In spite of everything dad still believes in Jack. It's beautiful and terrible. That's one reason why I've wanted to help Jack. Well, it's not to be. Every day, every hour, Jack Bellounds grows farther from me. He and his father will try to persuade me to consent to this marriage. They may even try to force me. But in that way I'll be as hard and as cold as Old White Slides. No! Never! For the rest, I'll do my duty to dad. I'll stick to him. I could not engage myself to you, no matter how much I love you. And that's more every minute! . . . So don't mention taking me to your home—don't ask me again. Please, Wilson; your asking shook my very soul! Oh, how sweet that would be—your wife! . . . But if dad turns me away—I don't think he would. Yet he's so strange and like iron for all concerning Jack. If ever he turned me out I'd have no home. I'm a waif, you know. Then—then, Wil-

son . . . Oh, it's horrible to be in the position I'm in. I won't
say any more. You'll understand, dear.

"It's your love that awoke me, and it's Ben Wade who has
saved me. Wilson, I love him almost as I do dad, only strangely. Do you know I believe he had something to do with Jack
getting drunk that awful October first. I don't mean Ben
would stoop to get Jack drunk. But he might have cunningly
put that opportunity in Jack's way. Drink is Jack's weakness, as gambling is his passion. Well, I know that the liquor
was some fine old stuff which Ben gave to the cowboys. And
it's significant now how Jack avoids Ben. He hates him. He's
afraid of him. He's jealous because Ben is so much with
me. I've heard Jack rave to dad about this. But dad is just to
others, if he can't be to his son.

"And so I want you to know that it's Ben Wade who has
saved me. Since I've been sick I've learned more of Ben.
He's like a woman. He understands. I never have to tell
him anything. You, Wilson, were sometimes stupid or stubborn (forgive me) about little things that girls feel but can't
explain. Ben knows. I tell you this because I want you to
understand how and why I love him. I think I love him
most for his goodness to you. Dear boy, if I hadn't loved you
before Ben Wade came I'd have fallen in love with you since,
just listening to his talk of you. But this will make you conceited. So I'll go on about Ben. He's our friend. Why, Wilson,
that sweetness, softness, gentleness about him, the heart that
makes him love us, that must be only the woman in him.
I don't know what a mother would feel like, but I do know
that I seem strangely happier since I've confessed my troubles
to this man. It was Lem who told me how Ben offered to be
a friend to Jack. And Jack flouted him. I've a queer notion
that the moment Jack did this he turned his back on a better
life.

"To repeat, then, Ben Wade is our friend, and to me
something more than I've tried to explain. Maybe telling you
this will make you think more of him and listen to his advice. I hope so. Did any boy and girl ever before so need
a friend? I need that something he instils in me. If I lost it
I'd be miserable. And, Wilson, I'm such a coward. I'm so
weak. I have such sinkings and burnings and tossings. Oh,

I'm only a woman! But I'll die fighting. That is what Ben
Wade instils into me. While there was life this strange little
man would never give up hope. He makes me feel that he
knows more than he tells. Through him I shall get the strength
to live up to my convictions, to be true to myself, to be faith-
ful to you.

"With love,

"COLUMBINE."

"December 3d.

"DEAREST COLLIE,—Your last was only a note, and I
told Wade if he didn't fetch more than a note next time
there would be trouble round this bunk-house. And then he
brought your letter!

"I'm feeling exuberant (I think it's that) today. First
time I've been up. Collie, I'm able to get up! WHOOPEE! I
walk with a crutch, and don't dare put my foot down. Not
that it hurts, but that my boss would have a fit! I'm glad
you've stopped heaping praise upon our friend Bent because
now I can get over my jealousy and be half decent. He's
the whitest man I ever knew.

"Now listen, Collie. I've had ideas lately. I've begun to eat
and get stronger and to feel good. The pain is gone. And to
think I swore to Wade I'd forgive Jack Belllounds and never
hate him—or kill him! . . . There, that's letting the cat out of
the bag, and it's done now. But no matter. The truth is,
though, that I never could stop hating Jack while the pain
lasted. Now I could shake hands with him and smile at him.

"Well, as I said, I've ideas. They're great. Grab hold of
the pommel now so you won't get thrown! I'm going to
pitch! . . . When I get well—able to ride and go about,
which Bent says will be in the spring—I'll send for my father
to come to White Slides. He'll come. Then I'll tell him everything, and if Bent and I can't win him to our side then *you*
can. Father never could resist you. When he has fallen in
love with you, which won't take long, then we'll go to Old
Bill Belllounds and lay the case before him. Are you still
in the saddle, Collie?

"Well, if you are, be sure to get a better hold, for I'm
going to run some next. Bent Wade approved of my plan. He

says Belllounds can be brought to reason. He says he can *make* him see the ruin for everybody were you forced to marry Jack. Strange, Collie, how Wade included himself with you, me, Jack, and the old man, in the foreshadowed ruin! Wade is as deep as the cañon there. Sometimes when he's thoughtful he gives me a creepy feeling. At others, when he comes out with one of his easy, cool assurances that we are all right—that we will get each other—why, then something grim takes possession of me. I believe him, I'm happy, but there crosses my mind a fleeting realization—not of what our friend is now, but what he has been. And it disturbs me, chills me. I don't understand it. For, Collie, though I understand your feeling of what he is, I don't understand mine. You see, I'm a man. I've been a cowboy for ten years and more. I've seen some hard experiences and worked with a good many rough boys and men. Cowboys, Indians, Mexicans, miners, prospectors, ranchers, hunters—some of whom were bad medicine. So I've come to see men as you couldn't see them. And Ben Wade has been everything a man could be. He seems all men in one. And despite all his kindness and goodness and hopefulness, there is the sense I have of something deadly and terrible and inevitable in him.

"It makes my heart almost stop beating to know I have this man on my side. Because I sense in him the man element, the physical—oh, I can't put it in words, but I mean something great in him that can't be beaten. What he says *must* come true! . . . And so I've already begun to dream and to think of you as my wife. If you ever are—no! *when* you are, then I will owe it to Bent Wade. No man ever owed another for so precious a gift. But, Collie, I can't help a little vague dread—of what, I don't know, unless it's a sense of the possibilities of Hell-Bent Wade. . . . Dearest, I don't want to worry you or frighten you, and I can't follow out my own gloomy fancies. Don't you mind too much what I think. Only you must realize that Wade is the greatest factor in our hopes of the future. My faith in him is so unshakable that it's foolish. Next to you I love him best. He seems even dearer to me than my own people. He has made me look at life differently. Likewise he has inspired you. But you, dearest Columbine, are only a sensitive, delicate girl, a frail and tender thing like the columbine flowers of the hills. And for your own sake you must not be blind to what Wade is capable of. If you keep on loving him and idealizing him, blind to what has made him great, that is, blind to the tragic side of him, then if he did something terrible here for you and for me the shock would be bad for you. Lord knows I have no suspicions of Wade. I have no clear ideas at all. But I do know that for you he would not stop at anything. He loves you as much as I do, only differently. Such power a pale, sweet-faced girl has over the lives of men!

"Good-by for this time.

"Faithfully,
"WILSON."

"*January 10th.*

"DEAR WILSON,—In every letter I tell you I'm better! Why, pretty soon there'll be nothing left to say about my health. I've been up and around now for days, but only lately have I begun to gain. Since Jack has been away I'm getting fat. I eat, and that's one reason I suppose. Then I move around more.

"You ask me to tell you all I do. Goodness! I couldn't and I wouldn't. You are getting mighty bossy since you're able to hobble around, as you call it. But you can't boss *me!* However, I'll be nice and tell you a little. I don't work very much. I've helped dad with his accounts, all so hopelessly muddled since he let Jack keep the books. I read a good deal. Your letters are worn out! Then, when it snows, I sit by the window and watch. I love to see the snowflakes fall, so fleecy and white and soft! But I don't like the snowy world after the storm has passed. I shiver and hug the fire. I must have Indian in me. On moonlit nights to look out at Old White Slides, so cold and icy and grand, and over the white hills and ranges, makes me shudder. I don't know why. It's all beautiful. But it seems to me like death. . . . Well, I sit idly a lot and think of you and how terribly big my love has grown, and . . . but that's all about that!

"As you know, Jack has been gone since before New Year's Day. He said he was going to Kremmling. But dad heard he went to Elgeria. Well, I didn't tell you that dad and Jack quarreled over money. Jack kept up his good behavior for so long that I actually believed he'd changed for the better. He kept at me, not so much on the marriage question, but to love him. Wilson, he nearly drove me frantic with his love-making. Finally I got mad and I pitched into him. Oh, I convinced him! Then he came back to his own self again. Like a flash he was Buster Jack once more. 'You can go to hell!' he yelled at me. And such a look! . . . Well, he went out, and that's when he quarreled with dad. It was about money. I couldn't help but hear some of it. I don't know whether or not dad gave Jack money, but I think he didn't. Anyway, Jack went.

"Dad was all right for a few days. Really, he seemed nicer and kinder for Jack's absence. Then all at once he sank into the glooms. I couldn't cheer him up. When Ben Wade came in after supper dad always got him to tell some of those terrible stories. You know what perfectly terrible stories Ben can tell. Well, dad had to hear the worst ones. And poor me, I didn't want to listen, but I couldn't resist. Ben *can* tell stories. And oh, what he's lived through!

"I got the idea it wasn't Jack's absence so much that made dad sit by the hour before the fire, staring at the coals, sigh-ing, and looking so God-forsaken. My heart just aches for dad. He broods and broods. He'll break out some day, and then I don't want to be here. There doesn't seem to be any idea when Jack will come home. He might never come. But Ben says he will. He says Jack hates work and that he couldn't be gambler enough or wicked enough to support himself without working. Can't you hear Ben Wade say that? 'I'll tell you,' he begins, and then comes a prophecy of trouble or evil. And, on the other hand, think how he used to say: 'Wait! Don't give up! Nothin' is ever so bad as it seems at first! Be true to what your heart says is right! It's never too late! Love is the only good in life! Love each other and wait and trust! It'll all come right in the end!' . . . And, Wilson, I'm bound to confess that both his sense of calamity and his hope of good seem infallible. Ben Wade is supernatural. Some-times, just for a moment, I dare to let myself believe in what he says—that our dream will come true and I'll be yours. Then oh! oh! oh! joy and stars and bells and heaven!

I—I . . . But what *am* I writing? Wilson Moore, this is quite enough for today. Take care you don't believe I'm so—so *very* much in love.

> "Ever,
>> "COLUMBINE."

>> *"February —.*

"DEAREST COLLIE,—I don't know the date, but spring's coming. Today I kicked Bent Wade with my once sore foot. It didn't hurt me, but hurt Wade's feelings. He says there'll be no holding me soon. I should say not. I'll eat you up. I'm as hungry as the mountain-lion that's been prowling round my cabin of nights. He's sure starved. Wade tracked him to a hole in the cliff.

"Collie, I can get around first rate. Don't need my crutch any more. I can make a fire and cook a meal. Wade doesn't think so, but I do. He says if I want to hold your affection, not to let you eat anything I cook. I can rustle around, too. Haven't been far yet. My stock has wintered fairly well. This valley is sheltered, you know. Snow hasn't been too deep. Then I bought hay from Andrews. I'm hoping for spring now, and the good old sunshine on the gray sage hills. And summer, with its columbines! Wade has gone back to his own cabin to sleep. I miss him. But I'm glad to have the nights alone once more. I've got a future to plan! Read that over, Collie.

"Today, when Wade came with your letter, he asked me, sort of queer, 'Say, Wils, do you know how many letters I've fetched you from Collie?' I said, 'Lord, no, I don't, but they're a lot.' Then he said there were just forty-seven letters. Forty-seven! I couldn't believe it, and told him he was crazy. I never had such good fortune. Well, he made me count them, and, dog-gone it, he was right. Forty-seven wonderful love-letters from the sweetest girl on earth! But think of Wade remembering every one! It beats me. He's beyond understanding.

"So Jack Belllounds still stays away from White Slides. Collie, I'm sure sorry for his father. What it would be to have a son like Buster Jack! My God! But for your sake I go around yelling and singing like a locoed Indian. Pretty soon spring will come. Then, you wild-flower of the hills, you girl with the sweet mouth and the sad eyes—then I'm coming after you! And all the king's horses and all the king's men can never take you away from me again!

                              "Your faithful

                                        "WILSON."

                                        "*March 19th.*

"DEAREST WILSON,—Your last letters have been read and reread, and kept under my pillow, and have been both my help and my weakness during these trying days since Jack's return.

"It has not been that I was afraid to write—though, Heaven knows, if this letter should fall into the hands of dad it would mean trouble for me, and if Jack read it—I *am* afraid to think of that! I just have not had the heart to write you. But all the time I knew I must write and that I would. Only, now, what to say tortures me. I am certain that confiding in you relieves me. That's why I've told you so much. But of late I find it harder to tell what I know about Jack Belllounds. I'm in a queer state of mind, Wilson dear. And you'll wonder, and you'll be sorry to know I haven't seen much of Ben lately —that is, not to talk to. It seems I can't *bear* his faith in me, his hope, his love—when lately matters have driven me into torturing doubt.

"But lest you might misunderstand, I'm going to try to tell you something of what is on my mind, and I want you to read it to Ben. He has been hurt by my strange reluctance to be with him.

"Jack came home on the night of March second. You'll remember that day, so gloomy and dark and dreary. It snowed and sleeted and rained. I remember how the rain roared on the roof. It roared so loud we didn't hear the horse. But we heard heavy boots on the porch outside the living-room, and the swish of a slicker thrown to the floor. There was a bright fire. Dad looked up with a wild joy. All of a sudden he changed. He blazed. He recognized the heavy tread of his son. If I ever pitied and loved him it was then. I thought of the return of the Prodigal Son! . . . There came a knock on the door. Then dad recovered. He threw it open wide. The streaming light fell upon Jack Belllounds, indeed, but not as I knew him. He entered. It was the first time I ever saw Jack look in the least like a man. He was pale, haggard, much older, sullen, and bold. He strode in with a 'Howdy, folks,' and threw his wet hat on the floor, and walked to the fire. His boots were soaked with water and mud. His clothes began to steam.

"When I looked at dad I was surprised. He seemed cool and bright, with the self-contained force usual for him when something critical is about to happen.

" 'Ahuh! So you come back,' he said.

" 'Yes, I'm home,' replied Jack.

" 'Wal, it took you quite a spell to get hyar.'

" 'Do you want me to stay?'

"This question from Jack seemed to stump dad. He stared. Jack had appeared suddenly, and his manner was different from that with which he used to face dad. He had something up his sleeve, as the cowboys say. He wore an air of defiance and indifference.

" 'I reckon I do,' replied dad, deliberately. 'What do you mean by askin' me that?'

" 'I'm of age, long ago. You can't make me stay home. I can do as I like.'

" 'Ahuh! I reckon you think you can. But not hyar at White Slides. If you ever expect to get this property you'll not do as you like.'

" 'To hell with that. I don't care whether I ever get it or not.'

"Dad's face went as white as a sheet. He seemed shocked. After a moment he told me I'd better go to my room. I was about to go when Jack said: 'No, let her stay. She'd best hear now what I've got to say. It concerns her.'

" 'So ho! Then you've got a heap to say?' exclaimed dad, queerly. 'All right, you have your say first.'

"Jack then began to talk in a level and monotonous voice, so unlike him that I sat there amazed. He told how, early in the winter, before he left the ranch, he had found out that he was honestly in love with me. That it had changed him— made him see he had never been any good—and inflamed him with the resolve to be better. He had tried. He had suc-

ceeded. For six weeks he had been all that could have been
asked of any young man. I am bound to confess that he
was! . . . Well, he went on to say how he had fought it out
with himself until he absolutely *knew* he could control
himself. The courage and inspiration had come from his
love for me. That was the only good thing he'd ever felt. He
wanted dad and he wanted me to understand absolutely, without any doubt, that he had found a way to hold on to his
good intentions and good feelings. And that was for *me!* . . .
I was struck all a-tremble at the truth. It was true! Well, then
he forced me to a decision. Forced me, without ever hinting
of this change, this possibility in him. I had told him I
couldn't love him. Never! Then he said I could go to hell
and he gave up. Failing to get money from dad he stole it,
without compunction and without regret. He had gone to
Kremmling, then to Elgeria.

"'I let myself go,' he said, without shame, 'and I drank
and gambled. When I was drunk I didn't remember Collie.
But when I was sober I did. And she haunted me. That grew
worse all the time. So I drank to forget her. . . . The money
lasted a great deal longer than I expected. But that was because I won as much as I lost, until lately. Then I borrowed
a good deal from those men I gambled with, but mostly
from ranchers who knew my father would be responsible. . . .
I had a shooting-scrape with a man named Elbert, in Smith's
place at Elgeria. We quarreled over cards. He cheated. And
when I hit him he drew on me. But he missed. Then I shot
him. . . . He lived three days—and died. That sobered me.
And once more there came to me truth of what I might have
been. I went back to Kremmling. And I tried myself out again.
I worked awhile for Judson, who was the rancher I had
borrowed most from. At night I went into town and to the
saloons, where I met my gambling cronies. I put myself in
the atmosphere of drink and cards. And I resisted both. I
could make myself indifferent to both. As soon as I was sure
of myself I decided to come home. And here I am.'

"This long speech of Jack's had a terrible effect upon me. I
was stunned and sick. But if it did that to me *what* did it do
to dad? Heaven knows, I can't tell you. Dad gave a lurch,

and a great heave, as if at the removal of a rope that had all but strangled him.

" 'Ahuh-huh!' he groaned. 'An' now you're hyar—what's thet mean?'

" 'It means that it's not yet too late,' replied Jack. 'Don't misunderstand me. I'm not repenting with that side of me which is bad. But I've sobered up. I've had a shock. I see my ruin. I still love you, dad, despite—the cruel thing you did to me. I'm your son and I'd like to make up to you for all my shortcomings. And so help me Heaven! I can do that, and will do it, if Collie will marry me. Not only marry me—that'd not be enough—but love me—I'm crazy for her love. It's terrible.'

" 'You spoiled weaklin'!' thundered dad. 'How'n hell can I believe you?'

" 'Because I know it,' declared Jack, standing right up to his father, white and unflinching.

"Then dad broke out in such a rage that I sat there scared so stiff I could not move. My heart beat thick and heavy. Dad got livid of face, his hair stood up, his eyes rolled. He called Jack every name I ever heard any one call him, and then a thousand more. Then he cursed him. Such dreadful curses! Oh, how sad and terrible to hear dad!

" 'Right you are!' cried Jack, bitter and hard and ringing of voice. 'Right, by God! But am I all to blame? Did I bring myself here on this earth? . . . There's something wrong in me that's not all my fault. . . . You can't shame me or scare me or hurt me. I could fling in your face those damned three years of hell you sent me to! But what's the use for you to roar at me or for me to reproach you? I'm ruined unless you give me Collie—make her love me. That will save me. And I want it for your sake and hers—not for my own. Even if I do love her madly I'm not wanting her for that. I'm no good. I'm not fit to touch her. . . . I've just come to tell you the truth. I feel for Collie—I'd do for Collie—as you did for my mother! Can't you understand? I'm your son. I've some of you in me. And I've found out what it is. Do you and Collie want to take me at my word?'

"I think it took dad longer to read something strange and convincing in Jack than it took me. Anyway, dad got the stunning consciousness that Jack *knew* by some divine or intuitive power that his reformation was inevitable, if I loved him. Never have I had such a distressing and terrible moment as that revelation brought to me! I felt the truth. I could save Jack Belllounds. No woman is ever fooled at such critical moments of life. Ben Wade once said that I could have reformed Jack were it possible to love him. Now the truth of that came home to me, and somehow it was overwhelming.

"Dad received this truth—and it was beyond me to realize what it meant to him. He must have seen all his earlier hopes fulfilled, his pride vindicated, his shame forgotten, his love rewarded. Yet he must have seen all that, as would a man leaning with one foot over a bottomless abyss. He looked transfigured, yet conscious of terrible peril. His great heart seemed to leap to meet this last opportunity, with all forgiveness, with all gratitude; but his will yielded with a final and irrevocable resolve. A resolve dark and sinister!

"He raised his huge fists higher and higher, and all his body lifted and strained, towering and trembling, while his face was that of a righteous and angry god.

" 'My son, I take your word!' he rolled out, his voice filling the room and reverberating through the house. 'I give you Collie! . . . She will be yours! . . . But, by the love I bore your mother—I swear—if you ever steal again—I'll kill you!'

"I can't say any more—

"COLUMBINE."

14

◉

SPRING CAME EARLY that year at White Slides Ranch. The snow melted off the valleys, and the wild flowers peeped from the greening grass while yet the mountain domes were white. The long stone slides were glistening wet, and the brooks ran full-banked, noisy and turbulent and roily.

Soft and fresh of color the gray old sage slopes came out from under their winter mantle; the bleached tufts of grass waved in the wind and showed tiny blades of green at the roots; the aspens and oaks, and the vines on fences and cliffs, and the round-clumped, brook-bordering willows took on a hue of spring.

The mustangs and colts in the pastures snorted and ran and kicked and cavorted; and on the hillsides the cows began to climb higher, searching for the tender greens, bawling for the new-born calves. Eagles shrieked the release of the snow-bound peaks, and the elks bugled their piercing calls. The grouse-cocks spread their gorgeous brown plumage in parade before their twittering mates, and the jays screeched in the woods, and the sage-hens sailed along the bosom of the gray slopes.

Black bears, and browns, and grizzlies came out of their winter's sleep, and left huge, muddy tracks on the trails; the timber wolves at dusk mourned their hungry calls for life, for meat, for the wildness that was passing; the coyotes yelped at sunset, joyous and sharp and impudent.

But winter yielded reluctantly its hold on the mountains. The black, scudding clouds, and the squalls of rain and sleet and snow, whitening and melting and vanishing, and the cold, clear nights, with crackling frost, all retarded the work of the warming sun. The day came, however, when the greens held their own with the grays; and this was the assurance of nature that spring could not be denied, and that summer would follow.

Bent Wade was hiding in the willows along the trail that followed one of the brooks. Of late, on several mornings, he had skulked like an Indian under cover, watching for some one. On this morning, when Columbine Belllounds came riding along, he stepped out into the trail in front of her.

"Oh, Ben! you startled me!" she exclaimed, as she held hard on the frightened horse.

"Good mornin', Collie," replied Wade. "I'm sorry to scare you, but I'm particular anxious to see you. An' considerin' how you avoid me these days, I had to waylay you in regular road-agent style."

Wade gazed up searchingly at her. It had been some time since he had been given the privilege and pleasure of seeing her close at hand. He needed only one look at her to confirm his fears. The pale, sweet, resolute face told him much.

"Well, now you've waylaid me, what do you want?" she queried, deliberately.

"I'm goin' to take you to see Wils Moore," replied Wade, watching her closely.

"No!" she cried, with the red staining her temples.

"Collie, see here. Did I ever oppose anythin' you wanted to do?"

"Not—yet," she said.

"I reckon you expect me to?"

She did not answer that. Her eyes drooped, and she nervously twisted the bridle reins.

"Do you doubt my—my good intentions toward you—my love for you?" he asked, in gentle and husky voice.

"Oh, Ben! No! No! It's that I'm afraid of your love for me! I can't bear—what I have to bear—if I see you, if I listen to you."

"Then you've weakened? You're no proud, high-strung, thoroughbred girl any more? You're showin' yellow?"

"Ben Wade, I deny that," she answered, spiritedly, with an uplift of her head. "It's not weakness, but strength I've found."

"Ahuh! Well, I reckon I understand. Collie, listen. Wils let me read your last letter to him."

"I expected that. I think I told him to. Anyway, I wanted you to know—what—what ailed me."

"Lass, it was a fine, brave letter—written by a girl facin' an upheaval of conscience an' soul. But in your own trouble you forget the effect that letter might have on Wils Moore."

"Ben! . . . I—I've lain awake at night— Oh, was he hurt?"

"Collie, I reckon if you don't see Wils he'll kill himself or kill Buster Jack," replied Wade, gravely.

"I'll see—him!" she faltered. "But oh, Ben—you don't mean that Wilson would be so base—so cowardly?"

"Collie, you're a child. You don't realize the depths to which a man can sink. Wils has had a long, hard pull this winter. My nursin' an' your letters have saved his life. He's well, now, but that long, dark spell of mind left its shadow on him. He's morbid."

"What does he—want to see me—for?" asked Columbine, tremulously. There were tears in her eyes. "It'll only cause more pain—make matters worse."

"Reckon I don't agree with you. Wils just wants an' needs to *see* you. Why, he appreciated your position. I've heard him cry like a woman over it an' our helplessness. What ails him is lovesickness, the awful feelin' which comes to a man who believes he has lost his sweetheart's love."

"Poor boy! So he imagines I don't love him any more? Good Heavens! How stupid men are! . . . I'll see him, Ben. Take me to him."

For answer, Wade grasped the bridle of her horse and, turning him, took a course leading away behind the hill that lay between them and the ranch-house. The trail was narrow and brushy, making it necessary for him to walk ahead of the horse. So the hunter did not speak to her or look at her for some time. He plodded on with his eyes downcast. Something tugged at Wade's mind, an old, familiar, beckoning thing, vague and mysterious and black, a presage of catastrophe. But it was only an opening wedge into his mind. It had not entered. Gravity and unhappiness occupied him. His senses, nevertheless, were alert. He heard the low roar of the flooded brook, the whir of rising grouse ahead, the hoofs of deer on stones, the song of spring birds. He had an eye also for the wan wild flowers in the shaded corners. Presently he led the horse out of the willows into the open and up a low-swelling, long slope of fragrant sage. Here he dropped back to Columbine's side and put his hand upon the pommel of her saddle. It was not long until her own hand softly fell upon his and clasped it. Wade thrilled under the warm touch. How well he knew her heart! When she ceased to love any one to whom she had given her love then she would have ceased to breathe.

"Lass, this isn't the first mornin' I've waited for you," he said, presently. "An' when I had to go back to Wils without you—well, it was hard."

"Then he wants to see me—so badly?" she asked.

"Reckon you've not thought much about him or me lately," said Wade.

"No. I've tried to put you out of my mind. I've had so much to think of—why, even the sleepless nights have flown!"

"Are you goin' to confide in me—as you used to?"

"Ben, there's nothing to confide. I'm just where I left off in that letter to Wilson. And the more I think the more muddled I get."

Wade greeted this reply with a long silence. It was enough to feel her hand upon his and to have the glad comfort and charm of her presence once more. He seemed to have grown older lately. The fragrant breath of the sage slopes came to him as something precious he must feel and love more. A haunting transience mocked him from these rolling gray hills. Old White Slides loomed gray and dark up into the blue, grim and stern reminder of age and of fleeting time. There was a cloud on Wade's horizon.

"Wils is waitin' down there," said Wade, pointing to a grove of aspens below. "Reckon it's pretty close to the house, an' a trail runs along there. But Wils can't ride very well yet, an' this appeared to be the best place."

"Ben, I don't care if dad or Jack know I've met Wilson. I'll tell them," said Columbine.

"Ahuh! Well, if I were you I wouldn't," he replied.

They went down the slope and entered the grove. It was an open, pretty spot, with grass and wild flowers, and old, bleached logs, half sunny and half shady under the newborn, fluttering aspen leaves. Wade saw Moore sitting on his horse. And it struck the hunter significantly that the cowboy should be mounted when an hour back he had left him sitting disconsolately on a log. Moore wanted Columbine to see him first, after all these months of fear and dread, mounted upon his horse. Wade heard Columbine's glad little cry, but he did not turn to look at her then. But when they reached the spot where Moore stood Wade could not resist the desire to see the meeting between the lovers.

Columbine, being a woman, and therefore capable of hiding agitation, except in moments of stress, met that trying situation with more apparent composure than the cowboy. Moore's long, piercing gaze took the rose out of Columbine's cheeks.

"Oh, Wilson! I'm so happy to see you on your horse again!"

she exclaimed. "It's too good to be true. I've prayed for that more than anything else. Can you get up into your saddle like you used to? Can you ride well again? . . . Let me see your foot."

Moore held out a bulky foot. He wore a shoe, and it was slashed.

"I can't wear a boot," he explained.

"Oh, I see!" exclaimed Columbine, slowly, with her glad smile fading. "You can't put that—that foot in a stirrup, can you?"

"No."

"But—it—it will—you'll be able to wear a boot soon," she implored.

"Never again, Collie," he said, sadly.

And then Wade perceived that, like a flash, the old spirit leaped up in Columbine. It was all he wanted to see.

"Now, folks," he said, "I reckon two's company an' three's a crowd. I'll go off a little ways an' keep watch."

"Ben, you stay here," replied Columbine, hurriedly.

"Why, Collie? Are you afraid—or ashamed to be with me alone?" asked Moore, bitterly.

Columbine's eyes flashed. It was seldom they lost their sweet tranquillity. But now they had depth and fire.

"No, Wilson, I'm neither afraid nor ashamed to be with you alone," she declared. "But I can be as natural—as much myself with Ben here as I could be alone. Why can't you be? If dad and Jack heard of our meeting the fact of Ben's presence might make it look different to them. And why should I heap trouble upon my shoulders?"

"I beg pardon, Collie," said the cowboy. "I've just been afraid of—of things."

"My horse is restless," returned Columbine. "Let's get off and talk."

So they dismounted. It warmed Wade's gloomy heart to see the woman-look in Columbine's eyes as she watched the cowboy get off and walk. For a crippled man he did very well. But that moment was fraught with meaning for Wade. These unfortunate lovers, brave and fine in their suffering, did not realize the peril they invited by proximity. But Wade knew.

He pitied them, he thrilled for them, he lived their torture with them.

"Tell me—everything," said Columbine, impulsively.

Moore, with dragging step, approached an aspen log that lay off the ground, propped by the stump, and here he leaned for support. Columbine laid her gloves on the log.

"There's nothing to tell that you don't know," replied Moore. "I wrote you all there was to write, except"—here he dropped his head—"except that the last three weeks have been hell."

"They've not been exactly heaven for me," replied Columbine, with a little laugh that gave Wade a twinge.

Then the lovers began to talk about spring coming, about horses and cattle, and feed, about commonplace ranch matters not interesting to them, but which seemed to make conversation and hide their true thoughts. Wade listened, and it seemed to him that he could read their hearts.

"Lass, an' you, Wils—you're wastin' time an' gettin' nowhere," interposed Wade. "Now let me go, so's you'll be alone."

"You stay right there," ordered Moore.

"Why, Ben, I'm ashamed to say that I actually forgot you were here," said Columbine.

"Then I'll remind you," rejoined the hunter. "Collie, tell us about Old Bill an' Jack."

"Tell you? What?"

"Well, I've seen changes in both. So has Wils, though Wils hasn't seen as much as he's heard from Lem an' Montana an' the Andrews boys."

"Oh! . . ." Columbine choked a little over her exclamation of understanding. "Dad has gotten a new lease on life, I guess. He's happy, like a boy sometimes, an' good as gold. . . . It's all because of the change in Jack. That is remarkable. I've not been able to believe my own eyes. Since that night Jack came home and had the—the understanding with dad he has been another person. He has left me alone. He treats me with deference, but not a familiar word or look. He's kind. He offers the little civilities that occur, you know. But he never intrudes upon me. Not one word of the past! It is as if he would earn my respect, and have that or nothing. . . . Then he works as he never worked before—on dad's books, in the shop, out on the range. He seems obsessed with some thought all the time. He talks little. All the old petulance, obstinacy, selfishness, and especially his sudden, queer impulses, and bull-headed tenacity—all gone! He has suffered physical distress, because he never was used to hard work. And more, he's suffered terribly for the want of liquor. I've heard him say to dad: 'It's hell—this burning thirst. I never knew I had it. I'll stand it, if it kills me. . . . But wouldn't it be easier on me to take a drink now and then, at these bad times?' . . . And dad said: 'No, son. Break off fer keeps! This taperin' off is no good way to stop drinkin'. Stand the burnin'. An' when it's gone you'll be all the gladder an' I'll be all the prouder.' . . . I have not forgotten all Jack's former failings, but I am forgetting them, little by little. For dad's sake I'm overjoyed. For Jack's I am glad. I'm convinced now that he's had his lesson—that he's sowed his wild oats—that he has become a man."

Moore listened eagerly, and when she had concluded he thoughtfully bent his head and began to cut little chips out of the log with his knife.

"Collie, I've heard a good deal of the change in Jack," he said, earnestly. "Honest Injun, I'm glad—glad for his father's sake, for his own, and for yours. The boys think Jack's locoed. But his reformation is not strange to me. If I were no good—just like he was—well, I could change as greatly for—for you."

Columbine hastily averted her face. Wade's keen eyes, apparently hidden under his old hat, saw how wet her lashes were, how her lips trembled.

"Wilson, you think then—you believe Jack will last—will stick to his new ways?" she queried, hurriedly.

"Yes, I do," he replied, nodding.

"How good of you! Oh! Wilson, it's like you to be noble —splendid. When you might have—when it'd have been so natural for you to doubt—to scorn him!"

"Collie, I'm honest about that. And now you be just as honest. Do you think Jack will stand to his colors? Never drink—never gamble—never fly off the handle again?"

"Yes, I honestly believe that—providing he gets—providing I—"

Her voice trailed off faintly.

Moore wheeled to address the hunter.

"Pard, what do you think? Tell me now. Tell us. It will help me, and Collie, too. I've asked you before, but you wouldn't— Tell us now, do you believe Buster Jack will live up to his new ideals?"

Wade had long parried that question, because the time to answer it had not come till this moment.

"No," he replied, gently.

Columbine uttered a little cry.

"Why not?" demanded Moore, his face darkening.

"Reckon there are reasons that you young folks wouldn't think of, an' couldn't know."

"Wade, it's not like you to be hopeless for any man," said Moore.

"Yes, I reckon it is, sometimes," replied Wade, wagging his head solemnly. "Young folks, I'm grantin' all you say as to Jack's reformation, except that it's permanent. I'm grantin' he's sincere—that he's not playin' a part—that his vicious instincts are smothered under a noble impulse to be what he ought to be. It's no trick. Buster Jack has all but done the impossible."

"Then why isn't his sincerity and good work to be permanent?" asked Moore, impatiently, and his gesture was violent.

"Wils, his change is not moral force. It's passion."

The cowboy paled. Columbine stood silent, with intent eyes upon the hunter. Neither of them seemed to understand him well enough to make reply.

"Love can work marvels in any man," went on Wade. "But love can't change the fiber of a man's heart. A man is born so an' so. He loves an' hates an' feels accordin' to the nature. It'd be accordin' to nature for Jack Belllounds to stay reformed if his love for Collie lasted. An' that's the point. It can't last. Not in a man of his stripe."

"Why not?" demanded Moore.

"Because Jack's love will never be returned—satisfied. It takes a man of different caliber to love a woman who'll never love him. Jack's obsessed by passion now. He'd per-

form miracles. But that's not possible. The miracle necessary here would be for him to change his moral force, his
blood, the habits of his mind. That's beyond his power."

Columbine flung out an appealing hand.

"Ben, I could pretend to love him—I might *make* myself
love him, if that would give him the power."

"Lass, don't delude yourself. You can't do that," replied
Wade.

"How do you know what I can do?" she queried, struggling with her helplessness.

"Why, child, I know you better than you know yourself."

"Wilson, he's right, he's right!" she cried. "That's why it's
so terrible for me now. He knows my very heart. He reads
my soul. . . . I can *never* love Jack Bellounds. Nor *ever*
pretend love!"

"Collie, if Ben knows you so well, you ought to listen to
him, as you used to," said Moore, touching her hand with
infinite sympathy.

Wade watched them. His pity and affection did not obstruct
the ruthless expression of his opinions or the direction of his
intentions.

"Lass, an' you, Wils, listen," he said, with all his gentleness.
"It's bad enough without you makin' it worse. Don't blind
yourselves. That's the hell with so many people in trouble.
It's hard to see clear when you're sufferin' and fightin'.
But *I* see clear. . . . Now with just a word I could fetch this
new Jack Bellounds back to his Buster Jack tricks!"

"Oh, Ben! No! No! No!" cried Columbine, in a distress
that showed how his force dominated her.

Moore's face turned as white as ashes.

Wade divined then that Moore was aware of what he himself knew about Jack Bellounds. And to his love for Moore
was added an infinite respect.

"I won't unless Collie forces me to," he said, significantly.

This was the critical moment, and suddenly Wade answered
to it without restraint. He leaped up, startling Columbine.

"Wils, you call me pard, don't you? I reckon you never
knew me. Why, the game's 'most played out, an' I haven't
showed my hand! . . . I'd see Jack Bellounds in hell before
I'd let him have Collie. An' if she carried out her strange an'

lofty idea of duty—an' married him right this afternoon
—I could an' I would part them before night!"

He ended that speech in a voice neither had ever heard
him use before. And the look of him must have been in harmony with it. Columbine, wide-eyed and gasping, seemed
struck to the heart. Moore's white face showed awe and fear
and irresponsible primitive joy. Wade turned away from
them, the better to control the passion that had mastered
him. And it did not subside in an instant. He paced to and
fro, his head bowed. Presently, when he faced around, it was
to see what he had expected to see.

Columbine was clasped in Moore's arms.

"Collie, you didn't—you haven't—promised to marry him
—again!"

"No, oh—no! I haven't! I was only—only trying to—to
make up my mind. Wilson, don't look at me so terribly!"

"You'll not agree again? You'll not set another day?" demanded Moore, passionately. He strained her to him, yet
held her so he could see her face, thus dominating her with
both strength and will. His face was corded now, and darkly
flushed. His jaw quivered. "You'll never marry Jack Belllounds! You'll not let sudden impulse—sudden persuasion or
force change you? Promise! Swear you'll never marry him.
Swear!"

"Oh, Wilson, I promise—I swear!" she cried. "Never! I'm
yours. It would be a sin. I've been mad to—to blind myself."

"You love me! You love me!" he cried, in a sudden trans-
port.

"Oh, yes, yes! I do."

"Say it then! Say it—so I'll never doubt—never suffer
again!"

"I love you, Wilson! I—I love you—unutterably," she whispered. "I love you—so—I'm broken-hearted now. I'll never
live without you. I'll die—I love you so!"

"You—you flower—you angel!" he whispered in return.
"You woman! You precious creature! I've been crazed at
loss of you!"

Wade paced out of earshot, and this time he remained away
for a considerable time. He lived again moments of his own

past, unforgettable and sad. When at length he returned toward the young couple they were sitting apart, composed once more, talking earnestly. As he neared them Columbine rose to greet him with wonderful eyes, in which reproach blended with affection.

"Ben, so this is what you've done!" she exclaimed.

"Lass, I'm only a humble instrument, an' I believe God guides me right," replied the hunter.

"I love you more, it seems, for what you make me suffer," she said, and she kissed him with a serious sweetness. "I'm only a leaf in the storm. But—let what will come. . . . Take me home."

They said good-by to Wilson, who sat with head bowed upon his hands. His voice trembled as he answered them. Wade found the trail while Columbine mounted. As they went slowly down the gentle slope, stepping over the numerous logs fallen across the way, Wade caught out of the tail of his eye a moving object along the outer edge of the aspen grove above them. It was the figure of a man, skulking behind the trees. He disappeared. Wade casually remarked to Columbine that now she could spur the pony and hurry on home. But Columbine refused. When they got a little farther on, out of sight of Moore and somewhat around to the left, Wade espied the man again. He carried a rifle. Wade grew somewhat perturbed.

"Collie, you run on home," he said, sharply.

"Why? You've complained of not seeing me. Now that I want to be with you . . . Ben, you see some one!"

Columbine's keen faculties evidently sensed the change in Wade, and the direction of his uneasy glance convinced her.

"Oh, there's a man! . . . Ben, it is—yes, it's Jack," she exclaimed, excitedly.

"Reckon you'd have it better if you say Buster Jack," replied Wade. with his tragic smile.

"Ah!" whispered Columbine, as she gazed up at the aspen slope, with eyes lighting to battle.

"Run home, Collie, an' leave him to me," said Wade.

"Ben, you mean he—he saw us up there in the grove? Saw me in Wilson's arms—saw me kissing him?"

"Sure as you're born, Collie. He watched us. He saw all

your love-makin'. I can tell that by the way he walks. It's Buster Jack again! Alas for the new an' noble Jack! I told you, Collie. Now you run on an' leave him to me."

Wade became aware that she turned at his last words and regarded him attentively. But his gaze was riveted on the striding form of Belllounds.

"Leave him to you? For what reason, my friend?" she asked.

"Buster Jack's on the rampage. Can't you see that? He'll insult you. He'll—"

"I will not go," interrupted Columbine, and, halting her pony, she deliberately dismounted.

Wade grew concerned with the appearance of young Belllounds, and it was with a melancholy reminder of the infallibility of his presentiments. As he and Columbine halted in the trail, Belllounds's hurried stride lengthened until he almost ran. He carried the rifle forward in a most significant manner. Black as a thunder-cloud was his face. Alas for the dignity and pain and resolve that had only recently showed there!

Belllounds reached them. He was frothing at the mouth. He cocked the rifle and thrust it toward Wade, holding low down.

"You—meddling sneak! If you open your trap I'll bore you!" he shouted, almost incoherently.

Wade knew when danger of life loomed imminent. He fixed his glance upon the glaring eyes of Belllounds.

"Jack, seein' I'm not packin' a gun, it'd look sorta natural, along with your other tricks, if you bored me."

His gentle voice, his cool mien, his satire, were as giant's arms to drag Belllounds back from murder. The rifle was raised, the hammer reset, the butt lowered to the ground, while Belllounds, snarling and choking, fought for speech.

"I'll get even—with you," he said, huskily. "I'm on to your game now. I'll fix you later. But—I'll do you harm now if you mix in with this!"

Then he wheeled to Columbine, and as if he had just recognized her, a change that was pitiful and shocking convulsed his face. He leaned toward her, pointing with shaking, accusing hand.

"I saw you—up there. I watched—you," he panted.

Columbine faced him, white and mute.

"It was you—wasn't it?" he yelled.

"Yes, of course it was."

She might have struck him, for the way he flinched.

"What was that—a trick—a game—a play all fixed up for my benefit?"

"I don't understand you," she replied.

"Bah! You—you white-faced cat! . . . I saw you! Saw you in Moore's arms! Saw him hug you—kiss you! . . . Then—I saw—you put up your arms—round his neck—kiss him—kiss him—kiss him! . . . I saw all that—didn't I?"

"You must have, since you say so," she returned, with perfect composure.

"But *did* you?" he almost shrieked, the blood cording and bulging red, as if about to burst the veins of temples and neck.

"Yes, I did," she flashed. There was primitive woman uppermost in her now, and a spirit no man might provoke with impunity.

"*You love him?*" he asked, very low, incredulously, with almost insane eagerness for denial in his query.

Then Wade saw the glory of her—saw her mother again in that proud, fierce uplift of face, that flamed red and then blazed white—saw hate and passion and love in all their primal nakedness.

"Love him? Love Wilson Moore? Yes, you fool! I love him! Yes! *Yes! YES!*"

That voice would have pierced the heart of a wooden image, so Wade thought, as all his strung nerves quivered and thrilled.

Belllounds uttered a low cry of realization, and all his instinctive energy seemed on the verge of collapse. He grew limp, he sagged, he tottered. His sensorial perceptions seemed momentarily blunted.

Wade divined the tragedy, and a pang of great compassion overcame him. Whatever Jack Belllounds was in character, he had inherited his father's power to love, and he was human. Wade felt the death in that stricken soul, and it was the last flash of pity he ever had for Jack Belllounds.

"You—you—" muttered Belllounds, raising a hand that

gathered speed and strength in the action. The moment of a great blow had passed, like a storm-blast through a leafless tree. Now the thousand devils of his nature leaped into ascendancy. "You!—" He could not articulate. Dark and terrible became his energy. It was like a resistless current forced through leaping thought and leaping muscle.

He struck her on the mouth, a cruel blow that would have felled her but for Wade; and then he lunged away, bowed and trembling, yet with fierce, instinctive motion, as if driven to run with the spirit of his rage.

15

◉

WADE NOTICED THAT after her trying experience with him and Wilson and Belllounds Columbine did not ride frequently.

He managed to get a word or two with her whenever he went to the ranch-house, and he needed only look at her to read her sensitive mind. All was well with Columbine, despite her trouble. She remained upheld in spirit, while yet she seemed to brood over an unsolvable problem. She had said, "But—let what will come!"—and she was waiting.

Wade hunted for more than lions and wolves these days. Like an Indian scout who scented peril or heard an unknown step upon his trail, Wade rode the hills, and spent long hours hidden on the lonely slopes, watching with somber, keen eyes. They were eyes that knew what they were looking for. They had marked the strange sight of the son of Bill Belllounds, gliding along that trail where Moore had met Columbine, sneaking and stooping, at last with many a covert glance about, to kneel in the trail and compare the horse tracks there with horseshoes he took from his pocket. That alone made Bent Wade eternally vigilant. He kept his counsel. He worked more swiftly, so that he might have leisure for his peculiar seeking. He spent an hour each night with the cowboys, listening to their recounting of the day and to their homely and shrewd opinions. He haunted the vicinity of the ranch-house at night, watching and listening for that moment which was to aid him in the crisis that was impending. Many a time he had been near when Columbine passed from the living-room to her corner of the house. He had heard her sigh and could almost have touched her.

Buster Jack had suffered a regurgitation of the old driving and insatiate temper, and there was gloom in the house of Belllounds. Trouble clouded the old man's eyes.

May came with the spring round-up. Wade was called to use a rope and brand calves under the order of Jack Bell-lounds, foreman of White Slides. That round-up showed a loss of one hundred head of stock, some branded steers, and year-lings, and many calves, in all a mixed herd. Belllounds re-ceived the amazing news with a roar. He had been ready for something to roar at. The cowboys gave as reasons winter-kill, and lions, and perhaps some head stolen since the thaw. Wade emphatically denied this. Very few cattle had fallen prey to the big cats, and none, so far as he could find, had been frozen or caught in drifts. It was the young foreman who stunned them all. "Rustled," he said, darkly. "There's too many loafers and homesteaders in these hills!" And he stalked out to leave his hearers food for reflection.

Jack Belllounds drank, but no one saw him drunk, and no one could tell where he got the liquor. He rode hard and fast; he drove the cowboys one way while he went another; he had grown shifty, cunning, more intolerant than ever. Some nights he rode to Kremmling, or said he had been there, when next day the cowboys found another spent and broken horse to turn out. On other nights he coaxed and bullied them into playing poker. They won more of his money than they cared to count.

Columbine confided to Wade, with mournful whisper, that Jack paid no attention to her whatever, and that the old rancher attributed this coldness, and Jack's backsliding, to her irresponsiveness and her tardiness in setting the wedding-day that must be set. To this Wade had whispered in reply, "Don't ever forget what I said to you an' Wils that day!"

So Wade upheld Columbine with his subtle dominance, and watched over her, as it were, from afar. No longer was he welcome in the big living-room. Belllounds reacted to his son's influence.

Twice in the early mornings Wade had surprised Jack Belllounds in the blacksmith shop. The meetings were accidental, yet Wade ever remembered how coincidence beckoned him thither and how circumstance magnified strange reflections. There was no reason why Jack should not be tinkering in the blacksmith shop early of a morning. But Wade followed an uncanny guidance. Like his hound Fox, he never split on trails. When opportunity afforded he went into the shop and looked it over with eyes as keen as the nose of his dog. And in the dust of the floor he had discovered little circles with dots in the middle, all uniform in size. Sight of them did not shock him until they recalled vividly the little circles with dots in the earthen floor of Wilson Moore's cabin. Little marks made by the end of Moore's crutch! Wade grinned then like a wolf showing his fangs. And the vitals of a wolf could no more strongly have felt the instinct to rend.

For Wade, the cloud on his horizon spread and darkened, gathered sinister shape of storm, harboring lightning and havoc. It was the cloud in his mind, the foreshadowing of his soul, the prophetic sense of like to like. Where he wandered there the blight fell!

Significant was the fact that Belllounds hired new men. Bludsoe had quit. Montana Jim grew surly these days and packed a gun. Lem Billings had threatened to leave. New and strange hands for Jack Belllounds to direct had a tendency to release a strain and tide things over.

Every time the old rancher saw Wade he rolled his eyes and wagged his head, as if combating superstition with an intelligent sense of justice. Wade knew what troubled Belllounds, and it strengthened the gloomy mood that, like a poison lichen, seemed to be finding root.

Every day Wade visited his friend Wilson Moore, and most of their conversation centered round that which had become a ruling passion for both. But the time came when Wade deviated from his gentleness of speech and leisure of action.

"Bent, you're not like you were," said Moore, once, in surprise at the discovery. "You're losing hope and confidence."

"No. I've only somethin' on my mind."

"What?"

"I reckon I'm not goin' to tell you now."

"You've got *hell* on your mind!" flashed the cowboy, in grim inspiration.

Wade ignored the insinuation and turned the conversation to another subject.

"Wils, you're buyin' stock right along?"

"Sure am. I saved some money, you know. And what's the use to hoard it? I'll buy cheap. In five years I'll have five hundred, maybe a thousand head. Wade, my old dad will be pleased to find out I've made the start I have."

"Well, it's a fine start, I'll allow. Have you picked up any unbranded stock?"

"Sure I have. Say, pard, are you worrying about this two-bit rustler work that's been going on?"

"Wils, it ain't two bits any more. I reckon it's gettin' into the four-bit class."

"I've been careful to have my business transactions all in writing," said Moore. "It makes these fellows sore, because some of them can't write. And they're not used to it. But I'm starting this game in my own way."

"Have you sold any stock?"

"Not yet. But the Andrews boys are driving some thirty-odd head to Kremmling for me to be sold."

"Ahuh! Well, I'll be goin'," Wade replied, and it was significant of his state of mind that he left his young friend sorely puzzled. Not that Wade did not see Moore's anxiety! But the drift of events at White Slides had passed beyond the stage where sympathetic and inspiring hope might serve Wade's purpose. Besides, his mood was gradually changing as these events, like many fibers of a web, gradually closed in toward a culminating knot.

That night Wade lounged with the cowboys and new hands in front of the little storehouse where Belllounds kept supplies for all. He had lounged there before in the expectation of seeing the rancher's son. And this time anticipation was verified. Jack Belllounds swaggered over from the ranch-house.

He met civility and obedience now where formerly he had
earned but ridicule and opposition. So long as he worked
hard himself the cowboys endured. The subtle change in him
seemed of sterner stuff. The talk, as usual, centered round the
stock subjects and the banter and gossip of ranch-hands.
Wade selected an interval when there was a lull in the conversation, and with eyes that burned under the shadow of
his broad-brimmed sombrero he watched the son of Belllounds.

"Say, boys, Wils Moore has begun sellin' cattle," remarked
Wade, casually. "The Andrews brothers are drivin' for him."

"Wal, so Wils's spread-eaglin' into a real rancher!" ejaculated Lem Billings. "Mighty glad to hear it. Thet boy shore
will git rich."

Wade's remark incited no further expressions of interest.
But it was Jack Belllounds's secret mind that Wade wished to
pierce. He saw the leaping of a thought that was neither
interest nor indifference nor contempt, but a creative thing
which lent a fleeting flash to the face, a slight shock to the
body. Then Jack Belllounds bent his head, lounging there for
a little while longer, lost in absorption, and presently he
strolled away.

Whatever that mounting thought of Jack Belllounds's was
it brought instant decision to Wade. He went to the ranch-
house and knocked upon the living-room door. There was a
light within, sending rays out through the windows into the
semi-darkness. Columbine opened the door and admitted
Wade. A bright fire crackled in the hearth. Wade flashed a
reassuring look at Columbine.

"Evenin', Miss Collie. Is your dad in?"

"Oh, it's you, Ben!" she replied, after her start. "Yes, dad's
here."

The old rancher looked up from his reading. "Howdy,
Wade! What can I do fer you?"

"Belllounds, I've cleaned out the cats an' most of the varmints on your range. An' my work, lately, has been all sorts,
not leavin' me any time for little jobs of my own. An' I want
to quit."

"Wade, you've clashed with Jack!" exclaimed the rancher,
jerking erect.

"Nothin' of the kind. Jack an' me haven't had words for a good while. I'm not denyin' we might, an' probably would clash sooner or later. But that's not my reason for quittin'."

Manifestly this put an entirely different complexion upon the matter. Belllounds appeared immensely relieved.

"Wal, all right. I'll pay you at the end of the month. Let's see, thet's not long now. You can lay off tomorrow."

Wade thanked him and waited for further remarks. Columbine had fixed big, questioning eyes upon Wade, which he found hard to endure. Again he tried to flash her a message of reassurance. But Columbine did not lose her look of blank wonder and gravity.

"Ben! Oh, you're not going to leave White Slides?" she asked.

"Reckon I'll hang around yet awhile," he replied.

Belllounds was wagging his head regretfully and ponderingly.

"Wal, I remember the day when no man quit me. Wal, wal!—times change. I'm an old man now. Mebbe, mebbe I'm testy. An' then thar's thet boy!"

With a shrug of his broad shoulders he dismissed what seemed an encroachment of pessimistic thought.

"Wade, you're packin' off, then, on the trail? Always on the go, eh?"

"No, I'm not hurryin' off," replied Wade.

"Wal, might I ask what you're figgerin' on?"

"Sure. I'm considerin' a cattle deal with Moore. He's a pretty keen boy an' his father has big ranchin' interests. I've saved a little money an' I'm no spring chicken any more. Wils has begun to buy an' sell stock, so I reckon I'll go in with him."

"Ahuh!" Belllounds gave a grunt of comprehension. He frowned, and his big eyes set seriously upon the blazing fire. He grasped complications in this information.

"Wal, it's a free country," he said at length, and evidently his personal anxieties were subjected to his sense of justice. "Owin' to the peculiar circumstances hyar at my range, I'd prefer thet Moore an' you began somewhar else. Thet's natural. But you've my good will to start on an' I hope I've yours."

"Belllounds, you've every man's good will," replied Wade. "I hope you won't take offense at my leavin'. You see I'm on Wils Moore's side in—in what you called these peculiar circumstances. He's got nobody else. An' I reckon you can look back an' remember how you've taken sides with some poor devil an' stuck to him. Can't you?"

"Wal, I reckon I can. An' I'm not thinkin' less of you fer speakin' out like thet."

"All right. Now about the dogs. I turn the pack over to you, an' it's a good one. I'd like to buy Fox."

"Buy nothin', man. You can have Fox, an' welcome."

"Much obliged," returned the hunter, as he turned to go. "Fox will sure be help for me. Belllounds, I'm goin' to round up this outfit that's rustlin' your cattle. They're gettin' sort of bold."

"Wade, you'll do thet on your own hook?" asked the rancher, in surprise.

"Sure. I like huntin' men more than other varmints. Then I've a personal interest. You know the hint about homesteaders hereabouts reflects some on Wils Moore."

"Stuff!" exploded the rancher, heartily. "Do you think any cattleman in these hills would believe Wils Moore a rustler?"

"The hunch has been whispered," said Wade. "An' you know how all ranchers say they rustled a little on the start."

"Aw, hell! Thet's different. Every new rancher drives in a few unbranded calves an' keeps them. But stealin' stock— thet's different. An' I'd as soon suspect my own son of rustlin' as Wils Moore."

Belllounds spoke with a sincere and frank ardor of defense for a young man once employed by him and known to be honest. The significance of the comparison he used had not struck him. His was the epitome of a successful rancher, sure in his opinions, speaking proudly and unreflectingly of his own son, and being just to another man.

Wade bowed and backed out of the door. "Sure that's what I'd reckon you'd say, Belllounds. . . . I'll drop in on you if I find any sign in the woods. Good night."

Columbine went with him to the end of the porch, as she

had used to go before the shadow had settled over the lives of the Bellloundses.

"Ben, you're up to something," she whispered, seizing him with hands that shook.

"Sure. But don't you worry," he whispered back.

"Do they hint that Wilson is a rustler?" she asked, intensely.

"Somebody did, Collie."

"How vile! Who? Who?" she demanded, and her face gleamed white.

"Hush, lass! You're all a-tremble," he returned, warily, and he held her hands.

"Ben, they're pressing me hard to set another wedding-day. Dad is angry with me now. Jack has begun again to demand. Oh, I'm afraid of him! He has no respect for me. He catches at me with hands like claws. I have to jerk away. . . . Oh, Ben, Ben! dear friend, what on earth shall I do?"

"Don't give in. Fight Jack! Tell the old man you must have time. Watch your chance when Jack is away an' ride up the Buffalo Park trail an' look for me."

Wade had to release his hands from her clasp and urge her gently back. How pale and tragic her face gleamed!

Wade took his horses, his outfit, and the dog Fox, and made his abode with Wilson Moore. The cowboy hailed Wade's coming with joy and pestered him with endless questions.

From that day Wade haunted the hills above White Slides, early and late, alone with his thoughts, his plans, more and more feeling the suspense of happenings to come. It was on a June day when Jack Belllounds rode to Kremmling that Wade met Columbine on the Buffalo Park trail. She needed to see him, to find comfort and strength. Wade far exceeded his own confidence in his effort to uphold her. Columbine was in a strange state, not of vacillation between two courses, but of a standstill, as if her will had become obstructed and waited for some force to upset the hindrance. She did not inquire as to the welfare of Wilson Moore, and Wade vouchsafed no word of him. But she importuned the hunter to see her every day or no more at all. And Wade answered her appeal and her need by assuring her that he would see her, come what might. So she was to risk more frequent rides.

During the second week of June Wade rode up to visit the prospector, Lewis, and learned that which complicated the matter of the rustlers. Lewis had been suspicious, and active on his own account. According to the best of his evidence and judgment there had been a gang of rough men come of late to Gore Peak, where they presumably were prospecting. This gang was composed of strangers to Lewis. They had ridden to his cabin, bought and borrowed of him, and, during his absence, had stolen from him. He believed they were in hiding, probably being guilty of some depredation in another locality. They gave both Kremmling and Elgeria a wide berth. On the other hand, the Smith gang from Elgeria rode to and fro, like ranchers searching for lost horses. There were only three in this gang, including Smith. Lewis had seen these men driving unbranded stock. And lastly, Lewis casually imparted the information, highly interesting to Wade, that he had seen Jack Belllounds riding through the forest. The prospector did not in the least, however, connect the appearance of the son of Belllounds with the other facts so peculiarly interesting to Wade. Cowboys and hunters rode trails across the range, and though they did so rather infrequently, there was nothing unusual about encountering them.

Wade remained all night with Lewis, and next morning rode six miles along the divide, and then down into a valley, where at length he found a cabin described by the prospector. It was well hidden in the edge of the forest, where a spring gushed from under a low cliff. But for water and horse tracks Wade would not have found it easily. Rifle in hand, and on foot, he slipped around in the woods, as a hunter might have, to stalk drinking deer. There were no smoke, no noise, no horses anywhere round the cabin, and after watching awhile Wade went forward to look at it. It was an old ramshackle hunter's or prospector's cabin, with dirt floor, a crumbling fireplace and chimney, and a bed platform made of boughs. Including the door, it had three apertures, and the two smaller ones, serving as windows, looked as if they had been intended for port-holes as well. The inside of the cabin was large and unusually well lighted, owing to the windows and to the open chinks between the logs. Wade saw a deck of cards lying bent and scattered in one corner, as if a violent hand had flung them against the wall. Strange that Wade's memory returned a vivid picture of Jack Belllounds in just that act of violence! The only other thing around the place which earned scrutiny from Wade was a number of horseshoe tracks outside, with the left front shoe track familiar to him. He examined the clearest imprints very carefully. If they had not been put there by Wilson Moore's white mustang. Spottie, then they had been made by a horse with a strangely similar hoof and shoe. Spottie had a hoof malformed, somewhat in the shape of a triangle, and the iron shoe to fit it always had to be bent, so that the curve was sharp and the ends closer together than those of his other shoes.

Wade rode down to White Slides that day, and at the evening meal he casually asked Moore if he had been riding Spottie of late.

"Sure. What other horse could I ride? Do you think I'm up to trying one of those broncs?" asked Moore, in derision.

"Reckon you haven't been leavin' any tracks up Buffalo Park way?"

The cowboy slammed down his knife. "Say, Wade, are you growing dotty? Good Lord! if I'd ridden that far—if I was able to do it—wouldn't you hear me yell?"

"Reckon so, come to think of it. I just saw a track like Spottie's, made two days ago."

"Well, it wasn't his, you can gamble on that," returned the cowboy.

Wade spent four days hiding in an aspen grove, on top of one of the highest foothills above White Slides Ranch. There he lay at ease, like an Indian, calm and somber, watching the trails below, waiting for what he knew was to come.

On the fifth morning he was at his post at sunrise. A casual remark of one of the new cowboys the night before accounted for the early hour of Wade's reconnoiter. The dawn was fresh and cool, with sweet odor of sage on the air; the jays were squalling their annoyance at this early disturber of their grove; the east was rosy above the black range and soon glowed with gold and then changed to fire. The sun had risen. All the mountain world of black range and gray hill and green valley, with its shining stream, was transformed as if by magic color. Wade sat down with his back to an aspen-tree, his gaze down upon the ranch-house and the corrals. A lazy column of blue smoke curled up toward the sky, to be lost there. The burros were braying, the calves were bawling, the colts were whistling. One of the hounds bayed full and clear.

The scene was pastoral and beautiful. Wade saw it clearly and whole. Peace and plenty, a happy rancher's home, the joy of the dawn and the birth of summer, the rewards of toil—all seemed significant there. But Wade pondered on how pregnant with life that scene was—nature in its simplicity and freedom and hidden cruelty, and the existence of people, blindly hating, loving, sacrificing, mostly serving some noble aim, and yet with baseness among them, the lees with the wine, evil intermixed with good.

By and by the cowboys appeared on their spring mustangs, and in twos and threes they rode off in different directions. But none rode Wade's way. The sun rose higher, and there was warmth in the air. Bees began to hum by Wade, and fluttering moths winged uncertain flight over him.

At the end of another hour Jack Bellounds came out of the house, gazed around him, and then stalked to the barn where he kept his horses. For a little while he was not in sight; then he reappeared, mounted on a white horse, and he rode into the pasture, and across that to the hay-field, and along the edge of this to the slope of the hill. Here he climbed to a small clump of aspens. This grove was not so far from Wilson Moore's cabin; in fact, it marked the boundary-line between the rancher's range and the acres that Moore had acquired. Jack vanished from sight here, but not before Wade had made sure he was dismounting.

"Reckon he kept to that grassy ground for a reason of his own—and plainer to me than any tracks," soliloquized Wade, as he strained his eyes. At length Bellounds came out of the grove, and led his horse round to where Wade knew there was a trail leading to and from Moore's cabin. At this point

Jack mounted and rode west. Contrary to his usual custom, which was to ride hard and fast, he trotted the white horse as a cowboy might have done when going out on a day's work. Wade had to change his position to watch Belllounds, and his somber gaze followed him across the hill, down the slope, along the willow-bordered brook, and so on to the opposite side of the great valley, where Jack began to climb in the direction of Buffalo Park.

After Belllounds had disappeared and had been gone for an hour, Wade went down on the other side of the hill, found his horse where he had left him, in a thicket, and, mounting, he rode around to strike the trail upon which Belllounds had ridden. The imprint of fresh horse tracks showed clear in the soft dust. And the left front track had been made by a shoe crudely triangular in shape, identical with that peculiar to Wilson Moore's horse.

"Ahuh!" muttered Wade, in greeting to what he had expected to see. "Well, Buster Jack, it's a plain trail now—damn your crooked soul!"

The hunter took up that trail, and he followed it into the woods. There he hesitated. Men who left crooked trails frequently ambushed them, and Belllounds had made no effort to conceal his tracks. Indeed, he had chosen the soft, open ground, even after he had left the trail to take to the grassy, wooded benches. There were cattle here, but not as many as on the more open aspen slopes across the valley. After deliberating a moment, Wade decided that he must risk being caught trailing Belllounds. But he would go slowly, trusting to eye and ear, to outwit this strangely acting foreman of White Slides Ranch.

To that end he dismounted and took the trail. Wade had not followed it far before he became convinced that Belllounds had been looking in the thickets for cattle; and he had not climbed another mile through the aspens and spruce before he discovered that Belllounds was driving cattle. Thereafter Wade proceeded more cautiously. If the long grass had not been wet he would have encountered great difficulty in trailing Belllounds. Evidence was clear now that he was hiding the tracks of the cattle by keeping to the grassy levels and slopes which, after the sun had dried them, would not leave a trace.

There were stretches where even the keen-eyed hunter had to work to find the direction taken by Belllounds. But here and there, in other localities, there showed faint signs of cattle and horse tracks.

The morning passed, with Wade slowly climbing to the edge of the black timber. Then, in a hollow where a spring gushed forth, he saw the tracks of a few cattle that had halted to drink, and on top of these the tracks of a horse with a crooked left front shoe. The rider of this horse had dismounted. There was an imprint of a cowboy's boot, and near it little sharp circles with dots in the center.

"Well, I'll be damned!" ejaculated Wade. "I call that mighty cunnin'. Here they are—proofs as plain as writin'—that Wils Moore rustled Old Bill's cattle! . . . Buster Jack, you're not such a fool as I thought. . . . He's made somethin' like the end of Wils's crutch. An' knowin' how Wils uses that every time he gets off his horse, why, the dirty pup carried his instrument with him an' made these tracks!"

Wade left the trail then, and, leading his horse to a covert of spruce, he sat down to rest and think. Was there any reason for following Belllounds farther? It did not seem needful to take the risk of being discovered. The forest above was open. No doubt Belllounds would drive the cattle somewhere and turn them over to his accomplices.

"Buster Jack's outbusted himself this time, sure," soliloquized Wade. "He's double-crossin' his rustler friends, same as he is Moore. For he's goin' to blame this cattle-stealin' onto Wils. An' to do that he's layin' his tracks so he can follow them, or so any good trailer can. It doesn't concern me so much now who're his pards in this deal. Reckon it's Smith an' some of his gang."

Suddenly it dawned upon Wade that Jack Belllounds was stealing cattle from his father. "Whew!" he whistled softly. "Awful hard on the old man! Who's to tell him when all this comes out? Aw, I'd hate to do it. I wouldn't. There's some things even I'd not tell."

Straightway this strange aspect of the case confronted Wade and gripped his soul. He seemed to feel himself changing inwardly, as if a gray, gloomy, sodden hand, as intangible as a ghostly dream, had taken him bodily from himself and was now leading him into shadows, into drear, lonely, dark solitude, where all was cold and bleak; and on and on over naked shingles that marked the world of tragedy. Here he must tell his tale, and as he plodded on his relentless leader forced him to tell his tale anew.

Wade recognized this as his black mood. It was a morbid dominance of the mind. He fought it as he would have fought a devil. And mastery still was his. But his brow was clammy and his heart was leaden when he had wrested that somber, mystic control from his will.

"Reckon I'd do well to take up this trail tomorrow an' see where it leads," he said, and as a gloomy man, burdened with thought, he retraced his way down the long slope, and over the benches, to the grassy slopes and aspen groves, and thus to the sage hills.

It was dark when he reached the cabin, and Moore had supper almost ready.

"Well, old-timer, you look fagged out," called out the cowboy, cheerily. "Throw off your boots, wash up, and come and get it!"

"Pard Wils, I'm not reboundin' as natural as I'd like. I reckon I've lived some years before I got here, an' a lifetime since."

"Wade, you have a queer look, lately," observed Moore, shaking his head solemnly. "Why, I've seen a dying man look just like you—now—round the mouth—but most in the eyes!"

"Maybe the end of the long trail is White Slides Ranch," replied Wade, sadly and dreamily, as if to himself.

"If Collie heard you say that!" exclaimed Moore, in anxious concern.

"Collie an' you will hear me say a lot before long," returned Wade. "But, as it's calculated to make you happy— why, all's well. I'm tired an' hungry."

Wade did not choose to sit round the fire that night, fearing to invite interrogation from his anxious friend, and for that matter from his other inquisitively morbid self.

Next morning, though Wade felt rested, and the sky was blue and full of fleecy clouds, and the melody of birds charmed his ear, and over all the June air seemed thick and beating with the invisible spirit he loved, he sensed the oppression, the nameless something that presaged catastrophe.

Therefore, when he looked out of the door to see Columbine swiftly riding up the trail, her fair hair flying and shining in the sunlight, he merely ejaculated, "Ahuh!"

"What's that?" queried Moore, sharp to catch the inflection.

"Look out," replied Wade, as he began to fill his pipe.

"Heavens! It's Collie! Look at her riding! Uphill, too!"

Wade followed him outdoors. Columbine was not long in arriving at the cabin, and she threw the bridle and swung off in the same motion, landing with a light thud. Then she faced them, pale, resolute, stern, all the sweetness gone to bitter strength—another and a strange Columbine.

"I've not slept a wink!" she said. "And I came as soon as I could get away."

Moore had no word for her, not even a greeting. The look of her had stricken him. It could have only one meaning.

"Mornin', lass," said the hunter, and he took her hand. "I couldn't tell you looked sleepy, for all you said. Let's go into the cabin."

So he led Columbine in, and Moore followed. The girl manifestly was in a high state of agitation, but she was neither trembling nor frightened nor sorrowful. Nor did she betray any lack of an unflinching and indomitable spirit. Wade read the truth of what she imagined was her doom in the white glow of her, in the matured lines of womanhood that had come since yesternight, in the sustained passion of her look.

"Ben! Wilson! The worst has come!" she announced.

Moore could not speak. Wade held Columbine's hand in both of his.

"Worst! Now, Collie, that's a terrible word. I've heard it many times. An' all my life the worst's been comin'. An' it hasn't come yet. You—only twenty years old—talkin' wild—the worst has come! . . . Tell me your trouble now an' I'll tell you where you're wrong."

"Jack's a thief—a cattle-thief!" rang Columbine's voice, high and clear.

"Ahuh! Well, go on," said Wade.

"Jack has taken money from rustlers—*for cattle stolen from his father!*"

Wade felt the lift of her passion, and he vibrated to it.

"Reckon that's no news to me," he replied.

Then she quivered up to a strong and passionate delivery of the thing that had transformed her.

"I'M GOING TO MARRY JACK BELLLOUNDS!"

Wilson Moore leaped toward her with a cry, to be held back by Wade's hand.

"Now, Collie," he soothed, "tell us all about it."

Columbine, still upheld by the strength of her spirit, related how she had ridden out the day before, early in the afternoon, in the hope of meeting Wade. She rode over the sage hills, along the edges of the aspen benches, everywhere that she might expect to meet or see the hunter, but as he did not appear, and as she was greatly desirous of talking with him, she went on up into the woods, following the line of the Buffalo Park trail, though keeping aside from it. She rode very slowly and cautiously, remembering Wade's instructions. In this way she ascended the aspen benches, and the spruce-bordered ridges, and then the first rise of the black forest. Finally she had gone farther than ever before and farther than was wise.

When she was about to turn back she heard the thud of hoofs ahead of her. Pronto shot up his ears. Alarmed and anxious, Columbine swiftly gazed about her. It would not do for her to be seen. Yet, on the other hand, the chances were that the approaching horse carried Wade. It was lucky that she was on Pronto, for he could be trusted to stand still and not neigh. Columbine rode into a thick clump of spruces that had long, shelving branches, reaching down. Here she hid, holding Pronto motionless.

Presently the sound of hoofs denoted the approach of several horses. That augmented Columbine's anxiety. Peering out of her covert, she espied three horsemen trotting along the trail, and one of them was Jack Belllounds. They appeared to be in strong argument, judging from gestures and emphatic movements of their heads. As chance would have it they halted their horses not half a dozen rods from Columbine's place of concealment. The two men with Belllounds were

rough-looking, one of them, evidently a leader, having a dark
face disfigured by a horrible scar.

Naturally they did not talk loud, and Columbine had to
strain her ears to catch anything. But a word distinguished
here and there, and accompanying actions, made transparent the meaning of their presence and argument. The big
man refused to ride any farther. Evidently he had come so far
without realizing it. His importunities were for "more head
of stock." His scorn was for a "measly little bunch not worth
the risk." His anger was for Belllounds's foolhardiness in
"leavin' a trail." Belllounds had little to say, and most of that
was spoken in a tone too low to be heard. His manner seemed
indifferent, even reckless. But he wanted "money." The scar-
faced man's name was "Smith." Then Columbine gathered
from Smith's dogged and forceful gestures, and his words
"no money" and "bigger bunch," that he was unwilling to pay
what had been agreed upon unless Belllounds promised to
bring a larger number of cattle. Here Belllounds roundly
cursed the rustler, and apparently argued that course "next
to impossible." Smith made a sweeping movement with his
arm, pointing south, indicating some place afar, and part of
his speech was "Gore Peak." The little man, companion of
Smith, got into the argument, and, dismounting from his
horse, he made marks upon the smooth earth of the trail.
He was drawing a rude map showing direction and locality.
At length, when Belllounds nodded as if convinced or now
informed, this third member of the party remounted, and
seemed to have no more to say. Belllounds pondered sullenly. He snatched a switch from off a bough overhead and
flicked his boot and stirrup with it, an action that made his
horse restive. Smith leered and spoke derisively, of which
speech Columbine heard, "Aw hell!" and "yellow streak,"
and "no one'd ever," and "son of Bill Belllounds," and "rustlin' stock." Then this scar-faced man drew out a buckskin
bag. Either the contempt or the gold, or both, overbalanced
vacillation in the weak mind of Jack Belllounds, for he
lifted his head, showing his face pale and malignant, and
without trace of shame or compunction he snatched the bag
of gold, shouted a hoarse, "All right, damn you!" and, when

ing the white mustang, he spurred away, quickly disappearing.

The rustlers sat their horses, gazing down the trail, and Smith wagged his dark head doubtfully. Then he spoke quite distinctly, "I ain't a-trustin' thet Belllounds pup!" and his comrade replied, "Boss, we ain't stealin' the stock, so what th' hell!" Then they turned their horses and trotted out of sight and hearing up the timbered slope.

Columbine was so stunned, and so frightened and horrified, that she remained hidden there for a long time before she ventured forth. Then, heading homeward, she skirted the trail and kept to the edge of the forest, making a wide detour over the hills, finally reaching the ranch at sunset. Jack did not appear at the evening meal. His father had one of his spells of depression and seemed not to have noticed her absence. She lay awake all night thinking and praying.

Columbine concluded her narrative there, and, panting from her agitation and hurry, she gazed at the bowed figure of Moore, and then at Wade.

"I *had* to tell you this shameful secret," she began again. "I'm forced. If you do not help me, if something is not done, there'll be a horrible—end to all!"

"We'll help you, but how?" asked Moore, raising a white face.

"I don't know yet. I only *feel*—I only *feel* what may happen, if I don't prevent it. . . . Wilson, you must go home—at least for a while."

"It'll not look right for Wils to leave White Slides now," interposed Wade, positively.

"But why? Oh, I fear—"

"Never mind now, lass. It's a good reason. An' you mustn't fear anythin'. I agree with you—we've got to prevent this—this that's goin' to happen."

"Oh, Ben, my dear friend, we must prevent it—you *must!*"

"Ahuh! . . . So I was figurin'."

"Ben, you must go to Jack an' tell him—show him the peril—frighten him terribly—so that he will not do—do this shameful thing again."

"Lass, I reckon I could scare Jack out of his skin. But what good would that do?"

"It'll stop this—this madness. . . . Then I'll marry him—and keep him safe—after that!"

"Collie, do you think marryin' Buster Jack will stop his bustin' out?"

"Oh, I *know* it will. He had conquered over the evil in him. I saw that. I felt it. He conquered over his baser nature for love of me. Then—when he heard—from my own lips—that I loved Wilson—why, then he fell. He didn't care. He drank again. He let go. He sank. And now he'll ruin us all. Oh, it looks as if he meant it that way! . . . But I can change him. I will marry him. I will love him—or I will *live a lie.* I will make him think I love him!"

Wilson Moore, deadly pale, faced her with flaming eyes.

"Collie, *why?* For God's sake, explain why you will shame your womanhood and ruin me—all for that coward—that thief?"

Columbine broke from Wade and ran to Wilson, as if to clasp him, but something halted her and she stood before him.

"Because dad will kill him!" she cried.

"My God! what are you saying?" exclaimed Moore, incredulously. "Old Bill would roar and rage, but hurt that boy of his—never!"

"Wils, I reckon Collie is right. You haven't got Old Bill figured. I know," interposed Wade, with one of his forceful gestures.

"Wilson, listen, and don't set your heart against me. For I *must* do this thing," pleaded Columbine. "I heard dad swear he'd kill Jack. Oh, I'll never forget! He was terrible! If he ever finds out that Jack stole from his own father—stole cattle like a common rustler, and sold them for gold to gamble and drink with—he will kill him! . . . That's as true as fate. . . . Think how horrible that would be for me! Because I'm to blame here, mostly. I fell in love with *you,* Wilson Moore, otherwise I could have saved Jack already.

"But it's not that I think of myself. Dad has loved me. He has been as a father to me. You know he's not my real father. Oh, if I only had a real one! . . . And I owe him so much. But then it's not because I owe him or because I love him. It's because of his own soul! . . . That splendid, noble old man, who has been so good to every one—who had only one fault, and that love of his son—must he be let go in blinded and insane rage at the failure of his life, the ruin of his son—must he be allowed to kill his own flesh and blood? . . . It would be *murder!* It would damn dad's soul to everlasting torment. No! No! I'll not let that be!"

"Collie—how about—your own soul?" whispered Moore, lifting himself as if about to expend a tremendous breath.

"That doesn't matter," she replied.

"Collie—Collie—" he stammered, but could not go on.

Then it seemed to Wade that they both turned to him unconscious of the inevitableness of his relation to this catastrophe, yet looking to him for the spirit, the guidance that became habitual to them. It brought the warm blood back to Wade's cold heart. It was his great reward. How intensely and implacably did his soul mount to that crisis!

"Collie, I'll never fail you," he said, and his gentle voice was deep and full. "If Jack can be scared into haltin' in his mad ride to hell—then I'll do it. I'm not promisin' so much for him. But I'll swear to you that Old Belllounds's hands will never be stained with his son's blood!"

"Oh, Ben! Ben!" she cried, in passionate gratitude. "I'll love you—bless you all my life!"

"Hush, lass! I'm not one to bless. . . . An' now you must do as I say. Go home an' tell them you'll marry Jack in August. Say August thirteenth."

"So long! Oh, why put it off? Wouldn't it be better—safer, to settle it all—once and forever?"

"No man can tell everythin'. But that's my judgment."

"Why August thirteenth?" she queried, with strange curiosity. "An unlucky date!"

"Well, it just happened to come to my mind—that date," replied Wade, in his slow, soft voice of reminiscence. "I was married on August thirteenth—twenty-one years ago. . . . An', Collie, my wife looked somethin' like you. Isn't that strange, now? It's a little world. . . . An' she's been gone eighteen years!"

"Ben, I never dreamed you ever had a wife," said Columbine, softly, with her hands going to his shoulder. "You must

tell me of her some day. . . . But now—if you want time—if
you think it best—I'll not marry Jack till August thirteenth."

"That'll give me time," replied Wade. "I'm thinkin' Jack
ought to be—reformed, let's call it—before you marry him.
If all you say is true—why we can turn him round. Your
promise will do most. . . . So, then, it's settled?"

"Yes—dear—friends," faltered the girl, tremulously, on the
verge of a breakdown, now that the ordeal was past.

Wilson Moore stood gazing out of the door, his eyes far
away on the gray slopes.

"Queer how things turn out," he said, dreamily. "August
thirteenth! . . . That's about the time the columbines blow on
the hills. . . . And I always meant columbine-time—"

Here he sharply interrupted himself, and the dreamy musing
gave way to passion. "But I mean it yet! I'll—I'll die before
I give up hope of you!"

16

◉

WADE, WATCHING COLUMBINE ride down the slope on her
homeward way, did some of the hardest thinking he had yet
been called upon to do. It was not necessary to acquaint
Wilson Moore with the deeper and more subtle motives that
had begun to actuate him. It would not utterly break the cowboy's spirit to live in suspense. Columbine was safe for the
present. He had insured her against fatality. Time was all
he needed. Possibility of an actual consummation of her marriage to Jack Belllounds did not lodge for an instant in
Wade's consciousness. In Moore's case, however, the present
moment seemed critical. What should he tell Moore—what
should he conceal from him?

"Son, come in here," he called to the cowboy.

"Pard, it looks—bad!" said Moore, brokenly.

Wade looked at the tragic face and cursed under his breath.

"Buck up! It's never as bad as it looks. Anyway, we *know* ow what to expect, an' that's well."

Moore shook his head. "Couldn't you see how like steel Collie was? . . . But I'm on to you, Wade. You think by persuading Collie to put that marriage off that we'll gain time. You're gambling with time. You swear Buster Jack will hang imself. You won't quit fighting this deal."

"Buster Jack has slung the noose over a tree, an' he's bout ready to slip his head into it," replied Wade.

"Bah! . . . You drive me wild," cried Moore, passionately. How can you? Where's all that feeling you seemed to have or me? You nursed me—you saved my leg—and my life. You nust have cared about me. But now—you talk about that olt—that spoiled old man's pet—that damned cur, as if you elieved he'd ruin himself. No such luck! no such hope! . . . Every day things grow worse. Yet the worse they grow the tronger you seem! It's all out of proportion. It's dreams. Wade, I hate to say it, but I'm sure you're not always—just ight in your mind."

"Wils, now ain't that queer?" replied Wade, sadly. "I'm greein' with you."

"Aw!" Moore, shook himself savagely and laid an affecionate and appealing arm on his friend's shoulder. "Forgive ne, pard! . . . It's me who's out of his head. . . . But my eart's broken."

"That's what you think," rejoined Wade, stoutly. "But a nan's heart can't break in a day. I know. . . . An' the God's ruth is Buster Jack will hang himself!"

Moore raised his head sharply, flinging himself back from is friend so as to scrutinize his face. Wade felt the piercing ower of that gaze.

"Wade, what do you mean?"

"Collie told us some interestin' news about Jack, didn't she? Well, she didn't know what I know. Jack Belllounds had aid a cunnin' an' devilish trap to prove you guilty of rustlin' is father's cattle."

"Absurd!" ejaculated Moore, with white lips.

"I'd never given him credit for brains to hatch such a plot," vent on Wade. "Now listen. Not long ago Buster Jack made a emark in front of the whole outfit, includin' his father, that the homesteaders on the range were rustlin' cattle. It fell sort of flat, that remark. But no one could calculate on his infernal cunnin'. I quit workin' for Belllounds that night, an' I've put my time in spyin' on the boy. In my day I've done a good deal of spyin', but I've never run across any one slicker than Buster Jack. To cut it short—he got himself a white-speckled mustang that's a dead ringer for Spottie. He measured the tracks of your horse's left front foot—the bad hoof, you know, an' he made a shoe exactly the same as Spottie wears. Also, he made some kind of a contraption that's like the end of your crutch. These he packs with him. I saw him ride across the pasture to hide his tracks, climb up the sage for the same reason, an' then hide in that grove of aspens over there near the trail you use. Here, you can bet, he changed shoes on the left front foot of his horse. Then he took to the trail, an' he left tracks for a while, an' then he was careful to hide them again. He stole his father's stock an' drove it up over the grassy benches where even you or I couldn't track him next day. But up on top, when it suited him, he left some horse tracks, an' in the mud near a spring-hole he gets off his horse, steppin' with one foot—an' makin' little circles with dots like those made by the end of your crutch. Then 'way over in the woods there's a cabin where he meets his accomplices. Here he leaves the same horse tracks an' crutch tracks. . . . Simple as a b c, Wils, when you see how he did it. But I'll tell you straight—if I hadn't been suspicious of Buster Jack —that trick of his would have made you a rustler!"

"Damn him!" hissed the cowboy, in utter consternation and fury.

"Ahuh! That's my sentiment exactly."

"I swore to Collie I'd never kill him!"

"Sure you did, son. An' you've got to keep that oath. I pin you down to it. You can't break faith with Collie. . . . An' you don't want his bad blood on your hands."

"No! No!" he replied, violently. "Of course I don't. I won't. But God! how sweet it would be to tear out his lying tongue—to—"

"I reckon it would. Only don't talk about that," interrupted Wade, bluntly. "You see, now, don't you, how he's about hanged himself."

"No, pard, I don't. We can't squeal that on him, any more than we can squeal what Collie told us."

"Son, you're young in dealin' with crooked men. You don't get the drift of motives. Buster Jack is not only robbin' his father an' hatchin' a dirty trap for you, but he's double-crossin' the rustlers he's sellin' the cattle to. He's riskin' their necks. He's goin' to find *your* tracks, showin' you dealt with them. Sure, he won't give them away, an' he's figurin' on their gettin' out of it, maybe by leavin' the range, or a shootin'-fray, or some way. The big thing with Jack is that he's goin' to accuse you of rustlin' an' show your tracks to his father. Well, that's a risk he's given the rustlers. It happens that I know this scar-face Smith. We've met before. Now it's easy to see from what Collie heard that Smith is not trustin' Buster Jack. So, all underneath this Jack Belllounds's game, there's forces workin' unbeknown to him, beyond his control, an' sure to ruin him."

"I see. I see. By Heaven! Wade, nothing else but ruin seems possible! . . . But suppose it works out his way! . . . What then? What of Collie?"

"Son, I've not got that far along in my reckonin'," replied Wade.

"But for my sake—think. If Buster Jack gets away with his trick—if he doesn't hang himself by some blunder or fit of temper or spree—what then of Collie?"

Wade could not answer this natural and inevitable query for the reason that he had found it impossible of consideration.

"Sufficient unto the day is the evil thereof," he replied.

"Wade, you've said that before. It helped me. But now I need more than a few words from the Bible. My faith is low. I . . . oh, I tried to pray because Collie told me she had prayed! But what are prayers? We're dealing with a stubborn, iron-willed old man who idolizes his son; we're dealing with a crazy boy, absolutely self-centered, crafty, and vicious, who'll stop at nothing. And, lastly, we're dealing with a girl who's so noble and high-souled that she'll sacrifice her all—her life to pay her debt. If she were really Bill Belllounds's daughter she'd *never* marry Jack, saying, of course, that he was not her brother. . . . Do you know that it will *kill* her, if she marries him?"

"Ahuh! I reckon it would," replied Wade, with his head bowed. Moore roused his gloomy forebodings. He did not care to show this feeling or the effect the cowboy's pleading had upon him.

"Ah! so you admit it? Well, then, what of Collie?"

"*If* she marries him—she'll have to die, I suppose," replied Wade.

Then Wilson Moore leaped at his friend and with ungentle hands lifted him, pushed him erect.

"Damn you, Wade! You're not square with me! You don't tell me all!" he cried, hoarsely.

"Now, Wils, you're set up. I've told you all I know. I swear that."

"But you couldn't stand the thought of Collie dying for that brute! You couldn't! Oh, I know. I can feel some things that are hard to tell. So, you're either out of your head or you've something up your sleeve. It's hard to explain how you affect me. One minute I'm ready to choke you for that damned strangeness—whatever it is. The next minute I feel it—I trust it, myself. . . . Wade, you're not—you *can't* be infallible!"

"I'm only a man, Wils, an' your friend. I reckon you do find me queer. But that's no matter. Now let's look at this deal—each from his own side of the fence. An' each actin' up to his own lights! You do what your conscience dictates, always thinkin' of Collie—not of yourself! An' I'll live up to my principles. Can we do more?"

"No, indeed, Wade, we can't," replied Moore, eloquently.

"Well, then, here's my hand. I've talked too much, I reckon. An' the time for talkin' is past."

In silence Moore gripped the hand held out to him, trying to read Wade's mind, apparently once more uplifted and strengthened by that which he could not divine.

Wade's observations during the following week brought forth the fact that Jack Belllounds was not letting any grass grow under his feet. He endeavored to fulfil his agreement with Smith, and drove a number of cattle by moonlight. These were part of the stock that the rancher had sold to buyers at Kremmling, and which had been collected and held in the big, fenced pasture down the valley next to the Andrews ranch. The loss was not discovered until the cattle had been counted at Kremmling. Then they were credited to loss by straying. In driving a considerable herd of half-wild steers, with an inadequate force of cowboys, it was no unusual thing to lose a number.

Wade, however, was in possession of the facts not later than the day after this midnight steal in the moonlight. He was forced to acknowledge that no one would have believed it possible for Jack Belllounds to perform a feat which might well have been difficult for the best of cowboys. But Jack accomplished it and got back home before daylight. And Wade was bound to admit that circumstantial evidence against Wilson Moore, which, of course, Jack Belllounds would soon present, would be damning and apparently irrefutable.

Waiting for further developments, Wade closely watched the ranch-house, which duty interfered with his attention to the outlying trails. What he did not want to miss was being present when Jack Belllounds accused Wilson Moore of rustling cattle.

So it chanced that Wade was chatting with the cowboys one Sunday afternoon when Jack, accompanied by three strangers, all mounted on dusty, tired horses, rode up to the porch and dismounted.

Lem Billings manifested unusual excitement.

"Montana, ain't thet Sheriff Burley from Kremmlin'?" he queried.

"Shore looks like him. . . . Yep, thet's him. Now, what's doin'?"

The cowboys exchanged curious glances, and then turned to Wade.

"Bent, what do you make of thet?" asked Lem, as he waved his hand toward the house. "Buster Jack ridin' up with Sheriff Burley."

The rancher, Belllounds, who was on the porch, greeted the visitors, and then they all went into the house.

"Boys, it's what I've been lookin' for," replied Wade.

"Shore. Reckon we all have idees. An' if my idee is correct I'm agoin' to git pretty damn sore pronto," declared Lem.

They were all silent for a few moments, meditating over this singular occurrence, and watching the house. Presently Old Bill Belllounds strode out upon the porch, and, walking out into the court, he peered around as if looking for some one. Then he espied the little group of cowboys.

"Hey!" he yelled. "One of you boys ride up an' fetch Wils Moore down hyar!"

"All right, boss," called Lem, in reply, as he got up and gave a hitch to his belt.

The rancher hurried back, head down, as if burdened.

"Wade, I reckon you want to go fetch Wils?" queried Lem.

"If it's all the same to you, I'd rather not," replied Wade.

"By Golly! I don't blame you. Boys, shore'n hell, Burley's after Wils."

"Wal, suppos'n' he is," said Montana. "You can gamble Wils ain't agoin' to run. I'd jest like to see him face thet outfit. Burley's a pretty square fellar. An' he's no fool."

"It's as plain as your nose, Montana, an' thet's shore big enough," returned Lem, with a hard light in his eyes. "Buster Jack's busted out, an' he's figgered Wils in some deal thet's rung in the sheriff. Wal, I'll fetch Wils." And, growling to himself, the cowboy slouched off after his horse.

Wade got up, deliberate and thoughtful, and started away.

"Say, Bent, you're shore goin' to see what's up?" asked Montana, in surprise.

"I'll be around, Jim," replied Wade, and he strolled off to be alone. He wanted to think over this startling procedure of Jack Belllounds's. Wade was astonished. He had expected that an accusation would be made against Moore by Jack, and an exploitation of such proofs as had been craftily prepared, but he had never imagined Jack would be bold enough to carry matters so far. Sheriff Burley was a man of wide experience, keen, practical, shrewd. He was also one of the countless men Wade had rubbed elbows with in the eventful past. It had been Wade's idea that Jack would be satisfied to face his father with the accusation of Moore, and thus cover his tracks. Whatever Old Belllounds might have felt over the loss of a few cattle, he would never have hounded and

arrested a cowboy who had done well by him. Burley, however, was a sheriff, and a conscientious one, and he happened to be particularly set against rustlers.

Here was a complication of circumstances. What would
Jack Bellllounds insist upon? How would Columbine take this
plot against the honor and liberty of Wilson Moore? How
would Moore himself react to it? Wade confessed that he was
helpless to solve these queries, and there seemed to be a
further one, insistent and gathering—what was to be his own
attitude here? That could not be answered, either, because
only a future moment, over which he had no control, and
which must decide events, held that secret. Worry beset Wade,
but he still found himself proof against the insidious gloom
ever hovering near, like his shadow.

He waited near the trail to intercept Billings and Moore
on their way to the ranch-house; and to his surprise they appeared sooner than it would have been reasonable to expect
them. Wade stepped out of the willows and held up his hand.
He did not see anything unusual in Moore's appearance.

"Wils, I reckon we'd do well to talk this over," said Wade.

"Talk what over?" queried the cowboy, sharply.

"Why, Old Bill's sendin' for you, an' the fact of Sheriff
Burley bein' here."

"Talk nothing. Let's see what they want, and then talk.
Pard, you remember the agreement we made not long ago?"

"Sure. But I'm sort of worried, an' maybe—"

"You needn't worry about me. Come on," interrupted
Moore. "I'd like you to be there. And, Lem, fetch the boys."

"I shore will, an' if you need any backin' you'll git it."

When they reached the open Lem turned off toward the
corrals, and Wade walked beside Moore's horse up to the
house.

Bellllounds appeared at the door, evidently having heard
the sound of hoofs.

"Hello, Moore! Get down an' come in," he said, gruffly.

"Bellllounds, if it's all the same to you I'll take mine in the
open," replied the cowboy, coolly.

The rancher looked troubled. He did not have the ease
and force habitual to him in big moments.

"Come out hyar, you men," he called in the door.

Voices, heavy footsteps, the clinking of spurs, preceded the appearance of the three strangers, followed by Jack Bell-lounds. The foremost was a tall man in black, sandy-haired and freckled, with clear gray eyes, and a drooping mustache that did not hide stern lips and rugged chin. He wore a silver star on his vest, packed a gun in a greasy holster worn low down on his right side, and under his left arm he carried a package.

It suited Wade, then, to step forward; and if he expected surprise and pleasure to break across the sheriff's stern face he certainly had not reckoned in vain.

"Wal, I'm a son-of-a-gun!" ejaculated Burley, bending low, with quick movement, to peer at Wade.

"Howdy, Jim. How's tricks?" said Wade, extending his hand, and the smile that came so seldom illumined his sallow face.

"Hell-Bent Wade, as I'm a born sinner!" shouted the sheriff, and his hand leaped out to grasp Wade's and grip it and wring it. His face worked. "My Gawd! I'm glad to see you, old-timer! Wal, you haven't changed at all! . . . Ten years! How time flies! An' it's shore you?"

"Same, Jim, an' powerful glad to meet you," replied Wade.

"Shake hands with Bridges an' Lindsay," said Burley, in-dicating his two comrades. "Stockmen from Grand Lake. . . . Boys, you've heerd me talk about him. Wade an' I was both in the old fight at Blair's ranch on the Gunnison. An' I've shore reason to recollect him! . . . Wade, what're you doin' up in these diggin's?"

"Drifted over last fall, Jim, an' have been huntin' varmints for Belllounds," replied Wade. "Cleaned the range up fair to middlin'. An' since I quit Belllounds I've been hangin' round with my young pard here, Wils Moore, an' interestin' myself in lookin' up cattle tracks."

Burley's back was toward Belllounds and his son, so it was impossible for them to see the sudden little curious light that gleamed in his eyes as he looked hard at Wade, and then at Moore.

"Wils Moore. How d'ye do? I reckon I remember you, though I don't ride up this way much of late years."

The cowboy returned the greeting civilly enough, but with brevity.

Belllounds cleared his throat and stepped forward. His manner showed he had a distasteful business at hand.

"Moore, I sent for you on a serious matter, I'm sorry to say."

"Well, here I am. What is it?" returned the cowboy, with clear, hazel eyes, full of fire, steady on the old rancher's.

"Jack, you know, is foreman of White Slides now. An' he's made a charge against you."

"Then let him face me with it," snapped Moore.

Jack Belllounds came forward, hands in his pockets, self-possessed, even a little swaggering, and his pale face and bold eyes showed the gravity of the situation and his mastery over it.

Wade watched this meeting of the rivals and enemies with an attention powerfully stimulated by the penetrating scrutiny Burley laid upon them. Jack did not speak quickly. He looked hard into the tense face of Moore. Wade detected a vibration of Jack's frame and a gleam of eye that showed him not wholly in control of exultation and revenge. Fear had not struck him yet.

"Well, Buster Jack, what's the charge?" demanded Moore, impatiently.

The old name, sharply flung at Jack by this cowboy, seemed to sting and reveal and inflame. But he restrained himself as with roving glance he searched Moore's person for sight of a weapon. The cowboy was unarmed.

"I accuse you of stealing my father's cattle," declared Jack, in low, husky accents. After he got the speech out he swallowed hard.

Moore's face turned a dead white. For a fleeting instant a red and savage gleam flamed in his steady glance. Then it vanished.

The cowboys, who had come up, moved restlessly. Lem Billings dropped his head, muttering. Montana Jim froze in his tracks.

Moore's dark eyes, scornful and piercing, never moved from Jack's face. It seemed as if the cowboy would never speak again.

"You call me thief! *You?*" at length he exclaimed.

"Yes, I do," replied Belllounds, loudly.

"Before this sheriff and your father you accuse me of stealing cattle?"

"Yes."

"And you accuse me before this man who saved my life,
who *knows* me—before Hell-Bent Wade?" demanded Moore,
as he pointed to the hunter.

Mention of Wade in that significant tone of passion and
wonder was not without effect upon Jack Belllounds.

"What in hell do I care for Wade?" he burst out, with the
old intolerance. "Yes, I accuse you. Thief, rustler! . . . And
for all I know your precious Hell-Bent Wade may be—"

He was interrupted by Burley's quick and authoritative
interference.

"Hyar, young man, I'm allowin' for your natural feelin's,"
he said, dryly, "but I advise you to bite your tongue. I ain't
acquainted with Mister Moore, but I happen to know Wade.
Do you savvy? . . . Wal, then, if you've any more to say to
Moore get it over."

"I've had my say," replied Belllounds, sullenly.

"On what grounds do you accuse me?" demanded Moore.

"I trailed you. I've got my proofs."

Burley stepped off the porch and carefully laid down his
package.

"Moore, will you get off your hoss?" he asked. And when
the cowboy had dismounted and limped aside the sheriff continued, "Is this the hoss you ride most?"

"He's the only one I have."

Burley sat down upon the edge of the porch and, carefully
unwrapping the package, he disclosed some pieces of hard-
baked yellow mud. The smaller ones bore the imprint of a
circle with a dot in the center, very clearly defined. The larger
piece bore the imperfect but reasonably clear track of a curiously shaped horseshoe, somewhat triangular. The sheriff
placed these pieces upon the ground. Then he laid hold of
Moore's crutch, which was carried like a rifle in a sheath
hanging from the saddle, and, drawing it forth, he carefully
studied the round cap on the end. Next he inserted this end
into both the little circles on the pieces of mud. They fitted

perfectly. The cowboys bent over to get a closer view, and Billings was wagging his head. Old Belllounds had an earnest eye for them, also. Burley's next move was to lift the left front foot of Moore's horse and expose the bottom to view. Evidently the white mustang did not like these proceedings, but he behaved himself. The iron shoe on this hoof was somewhat triangular in shape. When Burley held the larger piece of mud, with its imprint, close to the hoof, it was not possible to believe that this iron shoe had not made the triangular-shaped track.

Burley let go of the hoof and laid the pieces of mud down. Slowly the other men straightened up. Some one breathed hard.

"Moore, what do them tracks look like to you?" asked the sheriff.

"They look like mine," replied the cowboy.

"They are yours."

"I'm not denying that."

"I cut them pieces of mud from beside a water-hole over hyar under Gore Peak. We'd trailed the cattle Belllounds lost, an' then we kept on trailin' them, clear to the road that goes over the ridge to Elgeria. . . . Now Bridges an' Lindsay hyar bought stock lately from strange cattlemen who didn't give no clear idee of their range. Jest buyin' an' sellin', they claimed. . . . I reckon the extra hoss tracks we run across at Gore Peak connects up them buyers an' sellers with whoever drove Belllounds's cattle up thar. . . . Have you anythin' more to say?"

"No. Not here," replied Moore, quietly.

"Then I'll have to arrest you an' take you to Kremmlin' fer trial."

"All right. I'll go."

The old rancher seemed genuinely shocked. Red tinged his cheek and a flame flared in his eyes.

"Wils, you done me dirt," he said wrathfully. "An' I always swore by you. . . . Make a clean breast of the whole damn bizness, if you want me to treat you white. You must have been locoed or drunk, to double-cross me thet way. Come on, out with it."

"I've nothing to say," replied Moore.

"You act amazin' strange fer a cowboy I've knowed to lean toward fightin' at the drop of a hat. I tell you, speak out an' I'll do right by you. . . . I ain't forgettin' thet White Slides gave you a hard knock. An' I was young once an' had hot blood."

The old rancher's wrathful pathos stirred the cowboy to a straining-point of his unnatural, almost haughty composure. He seemed about to break into violent utterance. Grief and horror and anger seemed at the back of his trembling lips. The look he gave Belllounds was assuredly a strange one, to come from a cowboy who was supposed to have stolen his former employer's cattle. Whatever he might have replied was cut off by the sudden appearance of Columbine.

"Dad, I heard you!" she cried, as she swept upon them, fearful and wide-eyed. "What has Wilson Moore done—that you'll do right by him?"

"Collie, go back in the house," he ordered.

"No. There's something wrong here," she said, with mounting dread in the swift glance she shot from man to man. "Oh! You're—Sheriff Burley!" she gasped.

"I reckon I am, miss, an' if young Moore's a friend of yours I'm sorry I came," replied Burley.

Wade himself reacted subtly and thrillingly to the presence of the girl. She was alive, keen, strung, growing white, with darkening eyes of blue fire, beginning to grasp intuitively the meaning here.

"My friend! He *was* more than that—not long ago. . . . What has he done? Why are you here?"

"Miss, I'm arrestin' him."

"Oh! . . . For what?"

"Rustlin' your father's cattle."

For a moment Columbine was speechless. Then she burst out, "Oh, there's a terrible mistake!"

"Miss Columbine, I shore hope so," replied Burley, much embarrassed and distressed. Like most men of his kind, he could not bear to hurt a woman. "But it looks bad fer Moore. . . . See hyar! There! Look at the tracks of his hoss— left front foot—shoe all crooked. Thet's his hoss's. He acknowledges thet. An', see hyar. Look at the little circles an dots. . . . I found these 'way over at Gore Peak, with the tracks of the stolen cattle. An' no *other* tracks, Miss Columbine!"

"Who put you on that trail?" she asked, piercingly.

"Jack, hyar. He found it fust, an' rode to Kremmlin' fer me."

"Jack! Jack Belllounds!" she cried, bursting into wild and furious laughter. Like a tigress she leaped at Jack as if to tear him to pieces. "You put the sheriff on that trail! You accuse Wilson Moore of stealing dad's cattle!"

"Yes, and I proved it," replied Jack, hoarsely.

"You! *You* proved it? So that's your revenge? . . . But you're to reckon with me, Jack Belllounds! You villain! You devil! You—" Suddenly she shrank back with a strong shudder. She gasped. Her face grew ghastly white. *"Oh, my God! . . . horrible—unspeakable!"* . . . She covered her face with her hands, and every muscle of her seemed to contract until she was stiff. Then her hands shot out to Moore.

"Wilson Moore, what have *you* to say—to this sheriff—to Jack Belllounds—to *me?*"

Moore bent upon her a gaze that must have pierced her soul, so like it was to a lightning flash of love and meaning and eloquence.

"Collie, they've got the proof. I'll take my medicine. . . . Your dad is good. He'll be easy on me!"

"You lie!" she whispered. "And I will tell why you lie!"

Moore did not show the shame and guilt that should have been natural with his confession. But he showed an agony of distress. His hand sought Wade and dragged at him.

It did not need this mute appeal to tell Wade that in another moment Columbine would have flung the shameful truth into the face of Jack Belllounds. She was rising to that. She was terrible and beautiful to see.

"Collie," said Wade, with that voice he knew had strange power over her, with a clasp of her outflung hand, "no more! This is a man's game. It's not for a woman to judge. Not here! It's Wils's game—an' it's *mine.* I'm his friend. Whatever his trouble or guilt, I take it on my shoulders. An' it will be as if it were not!"

Moaning and wringing her hands, Columbine staggered with the burden of the struggle in her.

"I'm quite—quite mad—or dreaming. Oh, Ben!" she cried.

"Brace up, Collie. It's sure hard. Wils, your friend and playmate so many years—it's hard to believe! We all understand, Collie. Now you go in, an' don't listen to any more or look any more."

He led her down the porch to the door of her room, and as he pushed it open he whispered, "I will save you, Collie, an' Wils, an' the old man you call dad!"

Then he returned to the silent group in the yard.

"Jim, if I answer fer Wils Moore bein' in Kremmlin' the day you say, will you leave him with me?"

"Wal, I shore will, Wade," replied Burley, heartily.

"I object to that," interposed Jack Belllounds, stridently. "He confessed. He's got to go to jail."

"Wal, my hot-tempered young fellar, thar ain't any jail nearer'n Denver. Did you know that?" returned Burley, with his dry, grim humor. "Moore's under arrest. An' he'll be as well off hyar with Wade as with me in Kremmlin', an' a damn sight happier."

The cowboy had mounted, and Wade walked beside him as he started homeward. They had not progressed far when Wade's keen ears caught the words, "Say, Belllounds, I got it figgered thet you an' your son don't savvy this fellar Wade."

"Wal, I reckon not," replied the old rancher.

And his son let out a peal of laughter, bitter and scornful and unsatisfied.

17

◉

GORE PEAK WAS the highest point of the black range that extended for miles westward from Buffalo Park. It was a rounded dome, covered with timber and visible as a landmark from the surrounding country. All along the eastern slope of that range an unbroken forest of spruce and pine spread down to the edge of the valley. This valley narrowed toward its source, which was Buffalo Park. A few well-beaten trails crossed that country, one following Red Brook down to Kremmling; another crossing from the Park to White Slides; and another going over the divide down to Elgeria. The only well-known trail leading to Gore Peak was a branch-off from the valley, and it went round to the south and more accessible side of the mountain.

All that immense slope of timbered ridges, benches, ravines, and swales west of Buffalo Park was exceedingly wild and rough country. Here the buffalo took to cover from hunters, and were safe until they ventured forth into the parks again. Elk and deer and bear made this forest their home.

Bent Wade, hunter now for bigger game than wild beasts of the range, left his horse at Lewis's cabin and penetrated the dense forest alone, like a deer-stalker or an Indian in his movements. Lewis had acted as scout for Wade, and had ridden furiously down to Sage Valley with news of the rustlers. Wade had accompanied him back to Buffalo Park that night, riding in the dark. There were urgent reasons for speed. Jack Belllounds had ridden to Kremmling, and the hunter did not believe he would return by the road he had taken.

Fox, Wade's favorite dog, much to his disgust, was left behind with Lewis. The bloodhound, Kane, accompanied Wade. Kane had been ill-treated and then beaten by Jack Belllounds, and he had left White Slides to take up his home at Moore's cabin. And at last he had seemed to reconcile himself to the hunter, not with love, but without distrust. Kane never forgave; but he recognized his friend and master. Wade carried his rifle and a buckskin pouch containing meat and bread. His belt, heavily studded with shells, contained two guns, both now worn in plain sight, with the one on the right side hanging low. Wade's character seemed to have undergone some remarkable change, yet what he represented then was not unfamiliar.

He headed for the concealed cabin on the edge of the high valley, under the black brow of Gore Peak. It was early morning of a July day, with summer fresh and new to the forest. Along the park edges the birds and squirrels were holding carnival. The grass was crisp and bediamonded with

sparkling frost. Tracks of game showed sharp in the white
patches. Wade paused once, listening. Ah! That most beautiful
of forest melodies for him—the bugle of an elk. Clear, reso-
nant, penetrating, with these qualities held and blended by a
note of wildness, it rang thrillingly through all Wade's being.
The hound listened, but was not interested. He kept close beside the hunter or at his heels, a stealthily stepping, warily
glancing hound, not scenting the four-footed denizens of the
forest. He expected his master to put him on the trail of
men.

The distance from the Park to Gore Peak, as a crow
would have flown, was not great. But Wade progressed slowly;
he kept to the dense parts of the forest; he avoided the open
aisles, the swales, the glades, the high ridges, the rocky ground.
When he came to the Elgeria trail he was not disappointed
to find it smooth, untrodden by any recent travel. Half
a mile farther on through the forest, however, he encountered
tracks of three horses, made early the day before. Still farther on he found cattle and horse tracks, now growing old
and dim. These tracks, pointed toward Elgeria, were like
words of a printed page to Wade.

About noon he climbed a rocky eminence that jutted out
from a slow-descending ridge, and from this vantage-point
he saw down the wavering black and green bosom of the
mountain slope. A narrow valley, almost hidden, gleamed
yellow in the sunlight. At the edge of this valley a faint column of blue smoke curled upward.

"Ahuh!" muttered the hunter, as he looked. The hound
whined and pushed a cool nose into Wade's hand.

Then Wade resumed his noiseless and stealthy course
through the woods. He began a descent, leading off somewhat to the right of the point where the smoke had arisen.
The presence of the rustlers in the cabin was of importance,
yet not so paramount as another possibility. He expected
Jack Belllounds to be with them or meet them there, and that
was the thing he wanted to ascertain. When he got down below the little valley he swung around to the left to cross the
trail that came up from the main valley, some miles still farther down. He found it, and was not surprised to see fresh
horse tracks, made that morning. He recognized those tracks.

ack Belllounds was with the rustlers, come, no doubt, to re-
eive his pay.

Then the change in Wade, and the actions of a trailer of
men, became more singularly manifest. He reverted to some
ormer habit of mind and body. He was as slow as a shadow,
bsolutely silent, and the gaze that roved ahead and all
round must have taken note of every living thing, of every
moving leaf or fern or bough. The hound, with hair curling up
tiff on his back, stayed close to Wade, watching, listening, and
tepping with him. Certainly Wade expected the rustlers to
ave some one of their number doing duty as an outlook. So
e kept uphill, above the cabin, and made his careful way
rough the thicket coverts, which at that place were dense and
matted clumps of jack-pine and spruce. At last he could see
he cabin and the narrow, grassy valley just beyond. To his
elief the horses were unsaddled and grazing. No man was in
ight. But there might be a dog. The hunter, in his slow ad-
ance, used keen and unrelaxing vigilance, and at length he
ecided that if there had been a dog he would have been
ed outside to give an alarm.

Wade had now reached his objective point. He was some
ighty paces from the cabin, in line with an open aisle down
which he could see into the cleared space before the door.
n his left were thick, small spruces, with low-spreading
ranches, and they extended all the way to the cabin on that
de, and in fact screened two walls of it. Wade knew exactly
hat he was going to do. No longer did he hesitate. Laying
own his rifle, he tied the hound to a little spruce, patting
im and whispering for him to stay there and be still.

Then Wade's action in looking to his belt-guns was that
f a man who expected to have recourse to them speedily
nd by whom the necessity was neither regretted nor feared.
tooping low, he entered the thicket of spruces. The soft,
pruce-matted ground, devoid of brush or twig, did not give
orth the slightest sound of step, nor did the brushing of the
ranches against his body. In some cases he had to bend the
oughs. Thus, swiftly and silently, with the gliding steps of an
ndian, he approached the cabin till the brown-barked logs
oomed before him, shutting off the clearer light.

He smelled a mingling of wood and tobacco smoke; he

heard low, deep voices of men; the shuffling and patting of cards; the musical click of gold. Resting on his knees a moment the hunter deliberated. All was exactly as he had expected. Luck favored him. These gamblers would be absorbed in their game. The door of the cabin was just around the corner, and he could glide noiselessly to it or gain it in a few leaps. Either method would serve. But which he must try depended upon the position of the men inside and that of their weapons.

Rising silently, Wade stepped up to the wall and peeped through a chink between the logs. The sunshine steamed through windows and door. Jack Belllounds sat on the ground full in its light, back to the wall. He was in his shirt-sleeves. The gambling fever and the grievous soreness of a loser shone upon his pale face. Smith sat with back to Wade, opposite Belllounds. The other men completed the square. All were close enough together to reach comfortably for the cards and gold before them. Wade's keen eyes took this in at a single glance, and then steadied searchingly for smaller features of the scene. Belllounds had no weapon. Smith's belt and gun lay in the sunlight on the hard, clay floor, out of reach except by violent effort. The other two rustlers both wore their weapons. Wade gave a long scrutiny to the faces of these comrades of Smith, and evidently satisfied himself as to what he had to expect from them.

Wade hesitated; then stooping low, he softly swept aside the intervening boughs of spruce, glided out of the thicket into the open. Two noiseless bounds! Another, and he was inside the door!

"Howdy, rustlers! Don't move!" he called.

The surprise of his appearance, or his voice, or both stunned the four men. Belllounds dropped his cards, and his jaw dropped at the same instant. These were absolutely the only visible movements.

"I'm in talkin' humor, an' the longer you listen the longer you'll have to live," said Wade. "But don't move!"

"We ain't movin'," burst out Smith. "Who're you, an' what d'ye want?"

It was singular that the rustler leader had not had a look at Wade, whose movements had been swift and who now stood directly behind him. Also it was obvious that Smith was sitting very stiff-necked and straight. Not improbably he had encountered such situations before.

"Who're you?" he shouted, hoarsely.

"You ought to know me." The voice was Wade's, gentle, cold, with depth and ring in it.

"I've heerd your voice somewhars—I'll gamble on thet."

"Sure. You ought to recognize my voice, Cap," returned Wade.

The rustler gave a violent start—a start that he controlled instantly.

"Cap! You callin' me thet?"

"Sure. We're old friends—*Cap Folsom!*"

In the silence, then, the rustler's hard breathing could be heard; his neck bulged red; only the eyes of his two comrades moved; Belllounds began to recover somewhat from his consternation. Fear had clamped him also, but not fear of personal harm or peril. His mind had not yet awakened to that.

"You've got me pat! But who're you?" said Folsom, huskily.

Wade kept silent.

"Who'n hell is thet man?" yelled the rustler. It was not a query to his comrades any more than to the four winds. It was a furious questioning of a memory that stirred and haunted, and as well a passionate and fearful denial.

"His name's Wade," put in Belllounds, harshly. "He's the friend of Wils Moore. He's the hunter I told you about—worked for my father last winter."

"Wade? . . . What? *Wade!* You never told me his name. It ain't—it ain't—"

"Yes, it is, Cap," interrupted Wade. "It's the old boy that spoiled your handsome mug—long ago."

"*Hell-Bent Wade!*" gasped Folsom, in terrible accents. He shook all over. An ashen paleness crept into his face. Instinctively his right hand jerked toward his gun; then, as in his former motion, froze in the very act.

"Careful, Cap!" warned Wade. "It'd be a shame not to hear me talk a little. . . . Turn around now an' greet an old pard of the Gunnison days."

Folsom turned as if a resistless, heavy force were revolving his head.

"By Gawd! . . . Wade!" he ejaculated. The tone of his voice, the light in his eyes, must have been a spiritual acceptance of a dreadful and irrefutable fact—perhaps the proximity of death. But he was no coward. Despite the hunter's order, given as he stood there, gun drawn and ready, Folsom wheeled back again, savagely to throw the deck of cards in Belllounds's face. He cursed horribly. . . . "You spoiled brat of a rich rancher! Why'n hell didn't you tell me thet varmint-hunter was Wade?"

"I did tell you," shouted Belllounds, flaming of face.

"You're a liar! You never said Wade—W-a-d-e, right out, so I'd hear it. An' I'd never passed by Hell-Bent Wade."

"Aw, that name made me tired," replied Belllounds, contemptuously.

"Haw! Haw! Haw!" bawled the rustler. "Made you tired, hey? Think you're funny? Wal, if you knowed how many men thet name's made tired—an' tired fer keeps—you'd not think it so damn funny."

"Say, what're you giving me? That Sheriff Burley tried to tell me and dad a lot of rot about this Wade. Why, he's only a little, bow-legged, big-nosed meddler—a man with a woman's voice—a sneaking cook and camp-doctor and cow-milker, and God only knows what else."

"Boy, you're correct. God only knows what else! . . . It's the else you've got to learn. An' I'll gamble you'll learn it. . . . Wade, have you changed or grown old thet you let a pup like this yap such talk?"

"Well, Cap, he's very amusin' just now, an' I want you-all to enjoy him. Because, if you don't force my hand I'm goin' to tell you some interestin' stuff about this Buster Jack. . . . Now, will you be quiet an' listen—an' answer for your pards?"

"Wade, I answer fer no man. But, so far as I've noticed, my pards ain't hankerin' to make any loud noise," Folsom replied, indicating his comrades, with sarcasm.

The red-bearded one, a man of large frame and gaunt face, wicked and wild-looking, spoke out, "Say, Smith, or whatever the hell's yore right handle—is this hyar a game we're playin'?"

"I reckon. An' if you turn a trick you'll be damn lucky," growled Folsom.

The other rustler did not speak. He was small, swarthy-faced, with sloe-black eyes and matted hair, evidently a white man with Mexican blood. Keen, strung, furtive, he kept motionless, awaiting events.

"Buster Jack, these new pards of yours are low-down rustlers, an' one of them's worse, as I could prove," said Wade, "but compared with you they're all gentlemen."

Belllounds leered. But he was losing his bravado. Something began to dawn upon his obtuse consciousness.

"What do I care for you or your gabby talk?" he flashed, sullenly.

"You'll care when I tell these rustlers how you double-crossed them."

Belllounds made a spring, like that of a wolf in a trap; but when half-way up he slipped. The rustler on his right kicked him, and he sprawled down again, back to the wall.

"Buster, look into this!" called Wade, and he leveled the gun that quivered momentarily, like a compass needle, and then crashed fire and smoke. The bullet spat into a log. But it had cut the lob of Belllounds's ear, bringing blood. His face turned a ghastly, livid hue. All in a second terror possessed him—shuddering, primitive terror of death.

Folsom haw-hawed derisively and in crude delight. "Say, Buster Jack, don't get any idee thet my ole pard Wade was shootin' at your head. Aw, no!"

The other rustlers understood then, if Belllounds had not, that the situation was in control of a man not in any sense ordinary.

"Cap, did you know Buster Jack accused my friend, Wils Moore, of stealin' these cattle you're sellin'?" asked Wade, deliberately.

"What cattle did you say?" asked the rustler, as if he had not heard aright.

"The cattle Buster Jack stole from his father an' sold to you."

"Wal, now! Bent Wade at his old tricks! I might have knowed it, once I seen you. . . . Naw, I'd no idee Belllounds blamed thet stealin' on to any one."

"He did."

"Ahuh! Wal, who's this Wils Moore?"

"He's a cowboy, as fine a youngster as ever straddled a horse. Buster Jack hates him. He licked Jack a couple of times an' won the love of a girl that Jack wants."

"Ho! Ho! Quite romantic, I declare. . . . Say, thar's some damn queer notions I'm gettin' about you, Buster Jack."

Belllounds lay propped against the wall, sagging there, laboring of chest, sweating of face. The boldness of brow held, because it was fixed, but that of his eyes had gone; and his mouth and chin showed craven weakness. He stared in dread suspense at Wade.

"Listen. An' all of you sit tight," went on Wade, swiftly. "Jack stole the cattle from his father. He's a thief at heart. But he had a double motive. He left a trail—he left tracks behind. He made a crooked horseshoe, like that Wils Moore's horse wears, an' he put that on his own horse. An' he made a contraption—a little iron ring with a dot in it, an' he left the crooked shoe tracks, an' he left the little ring tracks—"

"By Gawd! I seen them funny tracks!" ejaculated Folsom. "At the water-hole an' right hyar in front of the cabin. I seen them. I knowed Jack made them, somehow, but I didn't think. His white hoss has a crooked left front shoe."

"Yes, he has, when Jack takes off the regular shoe an' nails on the crooked one. . . . Men, I followed those tracks. They lead up here to your cabin. Belllounds made them with a purpose. . . . An' he went to Kremmlin' to get Sheriff Burley. An' he put him wise to the rustlin' of cattle to Elgeria. An' he fetched him up to White Slides to accuse Wils Moore. An' he trailed his own tracks up here, showin' Burley the crooked horse track an' the little circle—that was supposed to be made by the end of Moore's crutch—an' he led Burley with his men right to this cabin an' to the trail where you drove the cattle over the divide. . . . An' then he had Burley dig out some cakes of mud holdin' these tracks, an' they fetched them down to White Slides. Buster Jack blamed the stealin' on to Moore. An' Burley arrested Moore. The trial comes off next week at Kremmlin'."

"Damn me!" exclaimed Folsom, wonderingly. "A man's never too old to learn! I knowed this pup was stealin' from his own father, but I reckoned he was jest a natural-born, honest rustler, with a hunch fer drink an' cards."

"Well, he's double-crossed you, Cap. An' if I hadn't rounded you up your chances would have been good for swingin'."

"Ahuh! Wade, I'd sure preferred them chances of swingin' to your over-kind interferin' in my bizness. Allus interferin', Wade, thet's your weakness! . . . But gimme a gun!"

"I reckon not, Cap."

"Gimme a gun!" roared the rustler. "Lemme sit hyar an' shoot the eyes outen this—lyin' pup of a Belllounds. . . . Wade, put a gun in my hand—a gun with two shells—or only one. You can stand with your gun at my head. . . . Let me kill this skunk!"

For all Belllounds could tell, death was indeed close. No trace of a Belllounds was apparent about him then, and his face was a horrid spectacle for a man to be forced to see. A froth foamed over his hanging lower lip.

"Cap, I ain't trustin' you with a gun just this particular minute," said Wade.

Folsom then bawled his curses to his comrades.

"— — —! Kill him! Throw your guns an' bore him— right in them bulgin' eyes! . . . I'm tellin' you—we've gotta fight, anyhow. We're agoin' to cash right hyar. But kill him first!"

Neither of Folsom's lieutenants yielded to the fierce exhortation of their leader or to their own evilly expressed passions. It was Wade who dominated them. Then ensued a silence fraught with suspense, growing more charged every long instant. The balance here seemed about to be struck.

"Wade, I've been a gambler all my life, an' a damn smart one, if I do say it myself," declared the rustler leader, his voice inharmonious with the facetiousness of his words. "An' I'll make a last bet."

"Go ahead, Cap. What'll you bet?" answered the cold voice, still gentle, but different now in its inflection.

"By Gawd! I'll bet all the gold hyar that Hell-Bent Wade wouldn't shoot any man in the back!"

"You win!"

Slowly and stiffly the rustler rose to his feet. When he

reached his height he deliberately swung his leg to kick Bell-lounds in the face.

"Thar! I'd like to have a reckonin' with you, Buster Jack," he said. "I ain't dealin' the cards hyar. But somethin' tells me thet, shaky as I am in my boots, I'd liefer be in mine than yours."

With that, and expelling a heavy breath, he wrestled around to confront the hunter.

"Wade, I've no hunch to your game, but it's slower'n I recollect you."

"Why, Cap, I was in a talkin' humor," replied Wade.

"Hell! You're up to some dodge. What'd you care fer my learnin' thet pup had double-crossed me? You won't let me kill him."

"I reckon I wanted him to learn what real men thought of him."

"Ahuh! Wal, an' now I've onlightened him, what's the next deal?"

"You'll all go to Kremmlin' with me an' I'll turn you over to Sheriff Burley."

That was the gauntlet thrown down by Wade. It was not unexpected, and acceptance seemed a relief. Folsom's eye-balls became living fire with the desperate gleam of the reckless chances of life. Cutthroat he might have been, but he was brave, and he proved the significance of Wade's attitude.

"Pards, hyar's to luck!" he rang out, hoarsely, and with pantherish quickness he leaped for his gun.

A tense, surcharged instant—then all four men, as if released by some galvanized current of rapidity, flashed into action. Guns boomed in unison. Spurts of red, clouds of smoke, ringing reports, and hoarse cries filled the cabin. Wade had fired as he leaped. There was a thudding patter of lead upon the walls. The hunter flung himself prostrate behind the bough framework that had served as bedstead. It was made of spruce boughs, thick and substantial. Wade had not calculated falsely in estimating it as a bulwark of defense. Pulling his second gun, he peeped from behind the covert.

Smoke was lifting, and drifting out of door and windows. The atmosphere cleared. Belllounds sagged against the wall, pallid, with protruding eyes of horror on the scene before him. The dark-skinned little man lay writhing. All at once a tremor stilled his convulsions. His body relaxed limply. As if by magic his hand loosened on the smoking gun. Folsom was on his knees, reeling and swaying, waving his gun, peering like a drunken man for some lost object. His temple appeared half shot away, a bloody and horrible sight.

"Pards, I got him!" he said, in strange, half-strangled whisper. "I got him! . . . Hell-Bent Wade! My respects! I'll meet you—thar!"

His reeling motion brought his gaze in line with Belllounds. The violence of his start sent drops of blood flying from his gory temple.

"Ahuh! The cards run—my way. Belllounds, hyar's to your —lyin' eyes!"

The gun wavered and trembled and circled. Folsom strained in last terrible effort of will to aim it straight. He fired. The bullet tore hair from Belllounds's head, but missed him. Again the rustler aimed, and the gun wavered and shook. He pulled trigger. The hammer clicked upon an empty chamber. With low and gurgling cry of baffled rage Folsom dropped the gun and sank face forward, slowly stretching out.

The red-bearded rustler had leaped behind the stone chimney that all but hid his body. The position made it difficult for him to shoot because his gun-hand was on the inside, and he had to press his body tight to squeeze it behind the corner of ragged stone. Wade had the advantage. He was lying prone with his right hand round the corner of the framework. An overhang of the bough-ends above protected his head when he peeped out. While he watched for a chance to shoot he loaded his empty gun with his left hand. The rustler strained and writhed his body, twisting his neck, and suddenly darting out his head and arm, he shot. His bullet tore the overhang of boughs above Wade's face. And Wade's answering shot, just a second too late, chipped the stone corner where the rustler's face had flashed out. The bullet, glancing, hummed out of the window. It was a close shave. The rustler let out a hissing, inarticulate cry. He was trapped. In his effort to press in closer he projected his left elbow beyond the corner of the chimney. Wade's quick shot shattered his arm.

There was no asking or offering of quarter here. This was

the old feud of the West—of the vicious and the righteous in strife—both reared in the same stern school. The rustler gave his body such contortion that he was twisted almost clear around, with his right hand over his left shoulder. He punched the muzzle of his gun into a crack between two stones, and he pried to open them. The dry clay cement crumbled, the crack widened. Sighting along the barrel he alined it with the narrow strip of Wade's shoulder that was visible above the framework. Then he shot and hit. Wade shrank flatter and closer, hiding himself to better advantage. The rustler made his great blunder then, for in that moment he might have rushed out and killed his adversary. But, instead, he shot again—another time—a third. And his heavy bullets tore and splintered the boughs dangerously close to the hunter's head. Then came an awkward, almost hopeless task for the rustler, in maintaining his position while reloading his gun. He did it, and his panting attested to the labor and pain it cost him.

So much, in fact, that he let his knee protrude. Wade fired, breaking that knee. The rustler sagged in his tracks, his hip stuck out to afford a target for the remorseless Wade. Still the doomed man did not cry out, though it was evident that he could not now keep his body from sagging into sight of the hunter. Then with a desperate courage worthy of a better cause, and with a spirit great in its defeat, the rustler plunged out from his hiding-place, gun extended. His red beard, his gaunt face, fierce and baleful, his wabbling plunge that was really a fall, made a sight which was terrible. He hopped out of that fall. His gun began to blaze. But it only matched the blazes of Wade's. And the rustler pitched headlong over the framework, falling heavily against the wall beyond.

Then there was silence for a long moment. Wade stirred, as if to look around. Belllounds also stirred, and gulped, as if to breathe. The three prostrate rustlers lay inert, their positions singularly tragic and settled. The smoke again began to lift, to float out of the door and windows. In another moment the big room seemed less hazy.

Wade rose, not without effort, and he had a gun in each hand. Those hands were bloody; there was blood on his

ce, and his left shoulder was red. He approached Bellounds.

Wade was terrible then—terrible with a ruthlessness that
as no pretense. To Belllounds it must have represented
eath—a bloody death which he was not prepared to meet.

"Come out of your trance, you pup rustler!" yelled Wade.

"For God's sake, don't kill me!" implored Belllounds, strick-
a with terror.

"Why not? Look around! My busy day, Buster! . . . An'
r that Cap Folsom it's been ten years comin'. . . . I'm goin'
shoot you in the belly an' watch you get sick to your stom-
h!"

Belllounds, with whisper, and hands, and face, begged for
s life in an abjectness of sheer panic.

"What!" roared the hunter. "Didn't you know I come to
ll you?"

"Yes—yes! I've seen—that. It's awful! . . . I never harmed
u. . . . Don't kill me! Let me live, Wade. I swear to God
—I'll never do it again! . . . For dad's sake—for Collie's
ke—don't kill me!"

"I'm Hell-Bent Wade! . . . You wouldn't listen to them—
hen they wanted to tell you who I am!"

Every word of Wade's drove home to this boy the primal
eaning of sudden death. It inspired him with an unutter-
le fear. That was what clamped his brow in a sweaty band
d upreared his hair and rolled his eyeballs. His magni-
d intelligence, almost ghastly, grasped a hope in Wade's
parent vacillation and in the utterance of the name of Col-
nbine. Intuition, a subtle sense, inspired him to beg in that
me.

"Swear you'll give up Collie!" demanded Wade, bran-
shing his guns with bloody hands.

"Yes—yes! My God, I'll do anything!" moaned Belllounds.

"Swear you'll tell your father you'd had a change of heart.
u'll give Collie up! . . . Let Moore have her!"

"I swear! . . . But if you tell dad—I stole his cattle—he'll
for me!"

"We won't squeal that. I'll save you if you give up the girl.
ce more, Buster Jack—try an' make me believe you'll
uare the deal."

Belllounds had lost his voice. But his mute, fluttering lips were infinite proof of the vow he could not speak. The boyishness, the stunted moral force, replaced the manhood in him then. He was only a factor in the lives of others, protected even from this Nemesis by the greatness of his father's love.

"Get up, an' take my scarf," said Wade, "an' bandage these bullet-holes I got."

18

◉

WADE'S WOUNDS WERE not in any way serious, and with Belllounds's assistance he got to the cabin of Lewis, where weakness from loss of blood made it necessary that he remain. Belllounds went home.

The next day Wade sent Lewis with pack-horse down to the rustlers' cabin, to bury the dead men and fetch back their effects. Lewis returned that night, accompanied by Sheriff Burley and two deputies, who had been busy on their own account. They had followed horse tracks from the water hole under Gore Peak to the scene of the fight, and had arrived to find Lewis there. Burley had appropriated the considerable amount of gold, which he said could be identified by cattlemen who had bought the stolen cattle.

When opportunity afforded Burley took advantage of it to speak to Wade when the others were out of earshot.

"Thar was another man in thet cabin when the fight come off," announced the sheriff. "An' he come up hyar with you."

"Jim, you're locoed," replied Wade.

The sheriff laughed, and his shrewd eyes had a kindly, curious gleam.

"Next you'll be givin' me a hunch thet you're in a fever an' out of your head."

"Jim, I'm not as clear-headed as I might be."

"Wal, tell me or not, jest as you like. I seen his tracks—

ollered them. An' Wade, old pard, I've reckoned long ago har's a nigger in the wood-pile."

"Sure. An' you know me. I'd take it friendly of you to put Moore's trial off fer a while—till I'm able to ride to Kremmn'. Maybe then I can tell you a story."

Burley threw up his hands in genuine apprehension. "Not much! You ain't agoin' to tell *me* no story! . . . But I'll wait n you, an' welcome. Reckon I owe you a good deal on this ustler round-up. Wade, thet must have been a man-sized fight, ven fer you. I picked up twenty-six empty shells. An' the ttle half-breed had one empty shell an' five loaded ones in is gun. You must have got him quick. Hey?"

"Jim, I'm observin' you're a heap more curious than ever, n' you always was an inquisitive cuss," complained Wade. I don't recollect what happened."

"Wal, wal, have it your own way," replied Burley, with ood nature. "Now, Wade, I'll pitch camp hyar in the park onight, an' tomorrer I'll ride down to White Slides on my ay to Kremmlin'. What're you wantin' me to tell Bellunds?"

The hunter pondered a moment.

"Reckon it's just as well that you tell him somethin'. . . . ou can say the rustlers are done for an' that he'll get his tock back. I'd like you to tell him that the rustlers were tore to blame than Wils Moore. Just say that an' nothin' lse about Wils. Don't mention about your suspectin' there as another man around when the fight come off. . . . Tell he cowboys that I'll be down in a few days. An' if you happen to get a chance for a word alone with Miss Collie, just ay I'm not bad hurt an' that all will be well."

"Ahuh!" Burley grunted out the familiar exclamation. He id not say any more then, but he gazed thoughtfully down pon the pale hunter, as if that strange individual were one nfinitely to respect, but never to comprehend.

Wade's wounds healed quickly; nevertheless, it was more han several days before he felt spirit enough to undertake he ride. He had to return to White Slides, but he was reuctant to do so. Memory of Jack Belllounds dragged at him, nd when he drove it away it continually returned. This feel-

ing was almost equivalent to an augmentation of his gloom
foreboding, which ever hovered on the fringe of his cor
sciousness. But one morning he started early, and, riding ver
slowly, with many rests, he reached the Sage Valley cabi
before sunset. Moore saw him coming, yelled his delight an
concern, and almost lifted him off the horse. Wade was to
tired to talk much, but he allowed himself to be fed and p
to bed and worked over.

"Boot's on the other foot now, pard," said Moore, wit
delight at the prospect of returning service. "Say, you're a
shot up! And it's I who'll be nurse!"

"Wils, I'll be around tomorrow," replied the hunter. "Hav
you heard any news from down below?"

"Sure. I've met Lem every night."

Then he related Burley's version of Wade's fight with th
rustlers in the cabin. From the sheriff's lips the story gaine
much. Old Bill Belllounds had received the news in a singula
mood; he offered no encomiums to the victor; contrary t
his usual custom of lauding every achievement of labor o
endurance, he now seemed almost to regret the affray. Jac
Belllounds had returned from Kremmling and he was prese
when Burley brought news of the rustlers. What he though
none of the cowboys vouchsafed to say, but he was drun
the next day, and he lost a handful of gold to them. Nev
had he gambled so recklessly. Indeed, it was as if he hate
the gold he lost. Little had been seen of Columbine, but litt
was sufficient to make the cowboys feel concern.

Wade made scarcely any comment upon this news fro
the ranch; next day, however, he was up, and caring for him
self, and he told Moore about the fight and how he had te
rorized Belllounds and exhorted the promises from him.

"Never in God's world will Buster Jack live up to thos
promises!" cried Moore, with absolute conviction. "I kno
him, Bent. He meant them when he made them. He'd swea
his soul away—then next day he'd lie or forget or betray."

"I'm not believin' that till I know," replied the hunte
gloomily. "But I'm afraid of him. . . . I've known bad men t
change. There's a grain of good in all men—somethin' d
vine. An' it comes out now an' then. Men rise on steppin
stones of their dead selves to higher things! . . . This is Be

ounds's chance for the good in him. If it's not there he will
do as you say. If it is—that scare he had will be the turnin'-
point in his life. I'm hopin', but I'm afraid."

"Bent, you wait and see," said Moore, earnestly. "Heaven
knows I'm not one to lose hope for my fellowmen—hope
for the higher things you've taught me. . . . But human nature
is human nature. Jack *can't* give Collie up, just the same as I
can't. That's self-preservation as well as love."

The day came when Wade walked down to White Slides.
There seemed to be a fever in his blood, which he tried to convince himself was a result of his wounds instead of the condition of his mind. It was Sunday, a day of sunshine and squall,
of azure-blue sky, and great, sailing, purple clouds. The sage
of the hills glistened and there was a sweetness in the air.

The cowboys made much of Wade. But the old rancher,
seeing him from the porch, abruptly went into the house. No
one but Wade noticed this omission of courtesy. Directly, Columbine appeared, waving her hand, and running to meet him.

"Dad saw you. He told me to come out and excuse him. . . .
Oh, Ben, I'm so happy to see you! You don't look hurt at
all. What a fight you had! . . . Oh, I was sick! But let me forget that. . . . How are you? And how's Wils?"

Thus she babbled until out of breath.

"Collie, it's sure good to see you," said Wade, feeling the
old, rich thrill at her presence. "I'm comin' on tolerable well.
I wasn't bad hurt, but I bled a lot. An' I reckon I'm older'n
I was when packin' gun-shot holes was nothin'. Every year
tells. Only a man doesn't know till after. . . . An' how are
you, Collie?"

Her blue eyes clouded, and a tremor changed the expression of her sweet lips.

"I am unhappy, Ben," she said. "But what could we expect? It might be worse. For instance, you might have been
killed. I've much to be thankful for."

"I reckon so. We all have. . . . I fetched a message from
Wils, but I oughtn't tell it."

"Please do," she begged, wistfully.

"Well, Wils says, tell Collie I love her every day more an'
more, an' that my love keeps up my courage an' my belief

in God, an' if she ever marries Jack Belllounds she can come
up to visit my grave among the columbines on the hill."

Strange how Wade experienced comfort in thus torturing
her! She was rosy at the beginning of his speech and white
at its close. "Oh, it's true! it's true!" she whispered. "It'll kill
him, as it will me!"

"Cheer up, Columbine," said Wade. "It's a long time till
August thirteenth. . . . An' now tell me, why did Old Bill run
when he saw me comin'?"

"Ben, I suspect dad has the queerest notion you want to
tell him some awful bloody story about the rustlers."

"Ahuh! Well, not yet. . . . An' how's Jack Belllounds actin'
these days?"

Wade felt the momentousness of that query, but it seemed
her face had been telltale enough, without confirmation of
words.

"My friend, somehow I hate to tell you. You're always so
hopeful, so ready to think good instead of evil. . . . But Jack
has been rough with me, almost brutal. He was drunk once.
Every day he drinks, sometimes a little, sometimes more. But
drink changes him. And it's dragging dad down. Dad doesn't
say so, yet I feel he's afraid of what will come next. . . . Jack
has nagged me to marry him right off. He wanted to the
day he came back from Kremmling. He's eager to leave
White Slides. Dad knows that, also, and it worries him. But of
course I refused."

The presence of Columbine, so vivid and sweet and stir-
ring, and all about her the sunlight, the golden gleam
on the sage hills, and Wade's heart and brain and spirit sustained a subtle transformation. It was as if what had been
beautiful with light had suddenly, strangely darkened. Then
Wade imagined he stood alone in a gloomy house, which
was his own heart, and he was listening to the arrival of a
tragic messenger whose foot sounded heavy on the stairs,
whose hand turned slowly upon the knob, whose gray presence opened the door and crossed the threshold.

"Buster Jack didn't break off with you, Collie?" asked the
hunter.

"Break off with me! . . . No, indeed! Whatever possessed
you to say that?"

"An' he didn't offer to give you up to Wils Moore?"

"Ben, are you crazy?" cried Columbine.

"Collie, listen. I'll tell you." The old urge knocked at Wade's mind. "Buster Jack was in the cabin, gamblin' with the rustlers, when I cornered them. You remember I meant to scare Buster Jack within an inch of his life? Well, I made use of my opportunity. I worked up the rustlers. Then I told Jack I'd give away his secret. He made to jump an' run, I reckon. But he hadn't the nerve. I shot a piece out of his ear, just to begin the fun. An' then I told the rustlers how Jack had double-crossed them. Folsom, the boss rustler, roared like a mad steer. He was wild to kill Jack. He begged for a gun to shoot out Jack's eyes. An' so were the other rustlers burnin' to kill him. Bad outfit. There was a fight, which, I'm bound to confess, was not short an' sweet. There was a lot of shootin'. An' in a cabin gun-shots almost lift the roof. Folsom was on his knees, dyin', wavin' his gun, whisperin' in fiendish glee that he had done for me. When he saw Jack an' remembered he shook so with fury that he scattered blood all over. An' he took long aim at Jack, tryin' to steady his gun. He couldn't, an' he missed, an' then fell over dead with his head on Jack's knees. That left the red-bearded rustler, who had hid behind the chimney. Jack watched the rest of that fight, an' for a youngster it must have been nerve-rackin'. I broke the rustler's arm, an' then his knee, an' then I got him in the hip two more times before he hobbled out to his finish. He'd shot me up considerable, so that when I braced Jack I must have been a hair-raisin' sight. I made Jack believe I meant to murder him. He begged an' cried, an' he got to prayin' for his life for your sake. It was sickenin', but it was what I wanted. So then I made him swear he'd free you an' give you up to Moore."

"Oh! Oh, Ben, how awful!" whispered Columbine, shuddering. "How *could* you tell me such a horrible story?"

"Reckon I wanted you to know how Jack come to make the promises an' what they were."

"Promises! What are promises or oaths to Jack Belllounds?" she cried, in passionate contempt. "You wasted your breath. Coward—liar that he is!"

"Ahuh!" Wade looked straight ahead of him as if he saw

some expected and unpleasant thing far in the distance. Then with irresistible steps, neither swift nor slow, but ponderous, he strode to the porch and mounted the steps.

"Why, Ben, where are you going?" called Columbine, in surprise, as she followed him.

He did not answer. He approached the closed door of the living-room.

"Ben!" cried Columbine, in alarm.

But he had no reply for her—indeed, no thought of her. Without knocking, he opened the door with rude and powerful hand, and, striding in, closed it after him.

Bill Belllounds was standing, back against the great stone chimney, arms folded, a stolid and grim figure, apparently fortified against an intrusion he had expected.

"Wal, what do you want?" he asked, gruffly. He had sensed catastrophe in the first sight of the hunter.

"Belllounds, I reckon I want a hell of a lot," replied Wade. "An' I'm askin' you to see we're not disturbed."

"Bar the door."

Wade dropped the bar in place, and then, removing his sombrero, he wiped his moist brow.

"Do you see an enemy in me?" he asked, curiously.

"Speakin' out fair, Wade, there ain't any reason I can see that you're an enemy to me," replied Belllounds. "But I feel somethin'. It ain't because I'm takin' my son's side. It's more than that. A queer feelin', an' one I never had before. I got it first when you told the story of the Gunnison feud."

"Belllounds, we can't escape our fates. An' it was written long ago I was to tell you a worse an' harder story than that."

"Wal, mebbe I'll listen an' mebbe I won't. I ain't promisin', these days."

"Are you goin' to make Collie marry Jack?" demanded the hunter.

"She's willin'."

"You know that's not true. Collie's willin' to sacrifice love, honor, an' life itself, to square her debt to you."

The old rancher flushed a burning red, and in his eyes flared a spirit of earlier years.

"Wade, you can go too far," he warned. "I'm appreciatin' your good-heartedness. It sort of warms me toward you . . .

But this is my business. You've no call to interfere. You've done that too much already. An' I'm reckonin' Collie would be married to Jack now if it hadn't been for you."

"Ahuh! . . . That's why I'm thankin' God I happened along to White Slides. Belllounds, your big mistake is thinkin' your son is good enough for this girl. An' you're makin' mistakes about me. I've interfered here, an' you may take my word for it I had the right."

"Strange talk, Wade, but I'll make allowances."

"You needn't. I'll back my talk. . . . But, first, I'm askin' you—an' if this talk hurts, I'm sorry—why don't you give some of your love for your no-good Buster Jack to Collie?"

Belllounds clenched his huge fists and glared. Anger leaped within him. He recognized in Wade an outspoken, bitter adversary to his cherished hopes for his son and his stubborn, precious pride.

"By Heaven! Wade, I'll—"

"Belllounds, I can make you swallow that kind of talk," interrupted Wade. "It's man to man now. An' I'm a match for you any day. Savvy? . . . Do you think I'm damn fool enough to come here an' brace you unless I knew that? Talk to me as you'd talk about some other man's son."

"It ain't possible," rejoined the rancher, stridently.

"Then listen to me first. . . . Your son Jack, to say the least, will ruin Collie. Do you see that?"

"By Gawd! I'm afraid so," groaned Belllounds, big in his humiliation. "But it's my one last bet, an' I'm goin' to play it."

"Do you know marryin' him will *kill* her?"

"What! . . . You're overdoin' your fears, Wade. Women don't die so easy."

"Some of them die, an' Collie's one that will, *if* she ever marries Jack."

"*If!* . . . Wal, she's goin' to."

"We don't agree," said Wade, curtly.

"Are you runnin' my family?"

"No. But I'm runnin' a large-sized *if* in this game. You'll admit that presently. . . . Belllounds, you make me mad. You don't meet me man to man. You're not the Bill Belllounds of old. Why, all over this state of Colorado you're known as the whitest of the white. Your name's a byword for all that's square an' big an' splendid. But you're so blinded by your worship of that wild boy that you're another man in all pertainin' to him. I don't want to harp on his shortcomin's. I'm for the girl. She doesn't love him. She can't. She will only drag herself down an' die of a broken heart. . . . Now, I'm askin' you, before it's too late—give up this marriage."

"Wade! I've shot men for less than you've said!" thundered the rancher, beside himself with rage and shame.

"Ahuh! I reckon you have. But not men like me. . . . I tell you, straight to your face, it's a fool deal you're workin'—a damn selfish one—a dirty job, to put on an innocent, sweet girl—an' as sure as you stand there, if you do it, you'll ruin four lives!"

"Four!" exclaimed Belllounds. But any word would have expressed his humiliation.

"I should have said three, leavin' Jack out. I meant Collie's an' yours an' Wils Moore's."

"Moore's is about ruined already, I've a hunch."

"You can get hunches you never dreamed of, Belllounds, old as you are. An' I'll give you one presently. . . . But we drift off. Can't you keep cool?"

"Cool! With you rantin' hell-bent for election? Haw! Haw! . . . Wade, you're locoed. You always struck me queer. . . . An' if you'll excuse me, I'm gettin' tired of this talk. We're as far apart as the poles. An' to save what good feelin's we both have, let's quit."

"You don't love Collie, then?" queried Wade, imperturbably.

"Yes, I do. That's a fool idee of yours. It puts me out of patience."

"Belllounds, you're not her real father."

The rancher gave a start, and he stared as he had stared before, fixedly and perplexedly at Wade.

"No, I'm not."

"If she *were* your real daughter—your own flesh an' blood —an' Jack Belllounds was *my* son, would you let her marry him?"

"Wal, Wade, I reckon I wouldn't."

"Then how can you expect my consent to her marriage with your son?"

"WHAT!" Belllounds lunged over to Wade, leaned down, shaken by overwhelming amaze.

"Collie is my daughter!"

A loud expulsion of breath escaped Belllounds. Lower he leaned, and looked with piercing gaze into the face and eyes that in this moment bore strange resemblance to Columbine.

"So help me Gawd! . . . That's the secret? . . . Hell-Bent Wade! An' you've been on my trail!"

He staggered to his big chair and fell into it. No trace of doubt showed in his face. The revelation had struck home because of its very greatness.

Wade took the chair opposite. His likeness to Columbine had faded now. It had been love, a spirit, a radiance, a glory. It was gone. And Wade's face became the emblem of tragedy.

"Listen, Belllounds. I'll tell you! . . . The ways of God are inscrutable. I've been twenty years tryin' to atone for the wrong I did Collie's mother. I've been a prospector for the trouble of others. I've been a bearer of their burdens. An' if I can save Collie's happiness an' her soul, I reckon I won't be denied the peace of meetin' her mother in the other world. . . . I recognized Collie the moment I laid eyes on her. She favors her mother in looks, an' she has her mother's sensitiveness, her fire an' pride, an' she even has her voice. It's low an' sweet—alto, they used to call it. . . . But I'd recognized Collie as my own if I'd been blind an' deaf. . . . It's over eighteen years ago that we had the trouble. I was no boy, but I was terribly in love with Lucy. An' she loved me with a passion I never learned till too late. We came West from Missouri. She was born in Texas. I had a rovin' disposition an' didn't stick long at any kind of work. But I was lookin' for a ranch. My wife had some money an' I had high hopes. We spent our first year of married life travelin' through Kansas. At Dodge I got tied up for a while. You know, in them days Dodge was about the wildest camp on the plains. My wife's brother run a place there. He wasn't much good. But she thought he was perfect. Strange how blood-relations can't see the truth about their own people! Anyway, her brother Spencer had no use for me, because I could tell how slick he was with the cards an' beat him at his own game. Spencer had a gamblin' pard, a cowboy run out of Texas, one Cap Fol— But no matter about his name. One night they were fleecin' a stranger an' I broke into the game, winnin' all they had. The game ended in a fight, with bloodshed, but nobody killed. That set Spencer an' his pard Cap against me. The stranger was a planter from Louisiana. He'd been an officer in the rebel army. A high-strung, handsome Southerner, fond of wine an' cards an' women. Well, he got to payin' my wife a good deal of attention when I was away, which happened to be often. She never told me. I was jealous those days.

"My little girl you call Columbine was born there durin' a long absence of mine. When I got home Lucy an' the baby were gone. Also the Southerner! . . . Spencer an' his pard Cap, an' others they had in the deal, proved to me, so it seemed, that the little girl was not really mine! . . . An' so I set out on a hunt for my wife an' her lover. I found them. An' I killed him before her eyes. But she was innocent, an' so was he, as came out too late. He'd been, indeed, her friend. She scorned me. She told me how her brother Spencer an' his friends had established guilt of mine that had driven her from me.

"I went back to Dodge to have a little quiet smoke with these men who had ruined me. They were gone. The trail led to Colorado. Nearly a year later I rounded them all up in a big wagon-train post north of Denver. Another brother of my wife's, an' her father, had come West, an' by accident or fate we all met there. We had a family quarrel. My wife would not forgive me—would not speak to me, an' her people backed her up. I made the great mistake to take her father an' other brothers to belong to the same brand as Spencer. In this I wronged them an' her.

"What I did to them, Belllounds, is one story I'll never tell to any man who might live to repeat it. But it drove my wife near crazy. An' it made me Hell-Bent Wade! . . . She ran off from me there, an' I trailed her all over Colorado. An' the end of that trail was not a hundred miles from where we stand now. The last trace I had was of the burnin' of a prairie-schooner by Arapahoes as they were goin' home from a foray on the Utes. . . . The little girl might have toddled off the trail. But I reckon she was hidden or dropped by her mother, or some one fleein' for life. Your men found her in the columbines."

Belllounds drew a long, deep breath.

"What a man never expects always comes true. . . . Wade, the lass is yours. I can see it in the way you look at me. I can feel it. . . . She's been like my own. I've done my best, accordin' to my conscience. An' I've loved her, for all they say I couldn't see aught but Jack. . . . You'll take her away from me?"

"No. Never," was the melancholy reply.

"What! Why not?"

"Because she loves you. . . . I could never reveal myself to Collie. I couldn't win her love with a lie. An' I'd have to lie, to be false as hell. . . . False to her mother an' to Collie an' to all I hold high! I'd have to tell Collie the truth—the wrong I did her mother—the *hell* I visited upon her mother's people. . . . She'd fear me."

"Ahuh! . . . An' you'll never change—I reckon that!" exclaimed Belllounds.

"No. I changed once, eighteen years ago. I can't go back. . . . I can't undo all I hoped was good."

"You think Collie'd fear you?"

"She'd never *love* me as she does you, or as she loves me even now. That is my rock of refuge."

"She'd hate you, Wade."

"I reckon. An' so she must never know."

"Ahuh! . . . Wal, wal, life is a hell of a deal! Wade, if you could live yours over again, knowin' what you know now, an' that you'd love an' suffer the same—would you want to do it?"

"Yes. I love life, with all it brings. I wouldn't have the joy without the pain. But I reckon only men who've come to our years would want it over again."

"Wal, I'm with you thar. I'd take what came. Rain an' sun! . . . But all this you tell, an' the hell you hint at, ain't changin' this hyar deal of Jack's an' Collie's. Not one jot! . . . If she remains my adopted daughter she marries my son. . . . Wade, I'm haltered like the north star in that."

"Belllounds, will you take a day to think it over?" appealed Wade.

"Ahuh! But that won't change me."

"Won't it change you to know that if you force this marriage you'll lose all?"

"All! Ain't that more queer talk?"

"I mean lose all—your son, your adopted daughter—his chance of reformin', her hope of happiness. These ought to be all in life left to you."

"Wal, they are. But I can't see your argument. You're beyond me, Wade. You're holdin' back, like you did with your hell-bent story."

Ponderously, as if the burden and the doom of the world weighed him down, the hunter got up and fronted Belllounds.

"When I'm driven to tell I'll come. . . . But, once more, old man, choose between generosity an' selfishness. Between blood tie an' noble loyalty to your good deed in its beginnin'. . . . Will you give up this marriage for your son—so that Collie can have the man she loves?"

"You mean your young pard an' two-bit of a rustler—Wils Moore?"

"Wils Moore, yes. My friend, an' a man, Belllounds, such as you or I never was."

"No!" thundered the rancher, purple in the face.

With bowed head and dragging step Wade left the room.

By slow degrees of plodding steps, and periods of abstracted lagging, the hunter made his way back to Moore's cabin. At his entrance the cowboy leaped up with a startled cry.

"Oh, Wade! . . . Is Collie dead?" he cried.

Such was the extent of calamity he imagined from the somber face of Wade.

"No. Collie's well."

"Then, man, what on earth's happened?"

"Nothin' yet. . . . But somethin' is goin' on in my mind. . . . Moore, I'd like you to let me alone."

At sunset Wade was pacing the aspen grove on the hill. There was sunlight and shade under the trees, a rosy gold on the sage slopes, a purple-and-violet veil between the black ranges and the sinking sun.

Twilight fell. The stars came out white and clear. Night cloaked the valley with dark shadows and the hills with its obscurity. The blue vault overhead deepened and darkened. The hunter patrolled his beat, and hours were moments to him. He heard the low hum of the insects, the murmur of running water, the rustle of the wind. A coyote cut the keen air with high-keyed, staccato cry. The owls hooted, with dismal and weird plaint, one to the other. Then a wolf mourned. But these sounds only accentuated the loneliness and wildness of the silent night.

Wade listened to them, to the silence. He felt the wildness and loneliness of the place, the breathing of nature; he peered aloft at the velvet blue of the mysterious sky with its deceiving stars. All that had been of help to him through days of trial was now as if it had never been. When he lifted his eyes to the great, dark peak, so bold and clear-cut against the sky, it was not to receive strength again. Nature in its cruelty mocked him. His struggle had to do with the most perfect of nature's works—man.

Wade was now in passionate strife with the encroaching mood that was a mocker of his idealism. Many times during the strange, long martyrdom of his penance had he faced this crisis, only to go down to defeat before elemental instincts. His soul was steeped in gloom, but his intelligence had not yet succumbed to passion. The beauty of Columbine's character and the nobility of Moore's were not illusions to Wade. They were true. These two were of the finest fiber of human nature. They loved. They represented youth and hope —a progress through the ages toward a better race. Wade believed in the good to be, in the future of men. Nevertheless, all that was fine and worthy in Columbine and Moore was to go unrewarded, unfulfilled, because of the selfish pride of an old man and the evil passion of the son. It was a conflict as old as life. Of what avail were Columbine's high sense of duty, Moore's fine manhood, the many victories they had won over the headlong and imperious desires of love? What avail were Wade's good offices, his spiritual teaching, his eternal hope in the order of circumstances working out to good? These beautiful characteristics of virtue were not so strong as the unchangeable passion of Old Belllounds and the vicious depravity of his son. Wade could not imagine himself a god, proving that the wages of sin was death. Yet in his life he had often been an impassive destiny, meting out terrible consequences. Here he was incalculably involved. This was the cumulative end of years of mounting plots, tangled and woven into the web of his pain and his remorse and his ideal. But hope was dying. That was his strife—realization against the morbid clairvoyance of his mind. He could not help Jack Belllounds to be a better man. He could not inspire the old rancher to a forgetfulness of selfish and blinded aims. He could not prove to Moore the truth of the reward that came from unflagging hope and unassailable virtue. He could not save Columbine with his ideals.

The night wore on, and Wade plodded under the rustling aspens. The insects ceased to hum, the owls to hoot, the wolves to mourn. The shadows of the long spruces gradually merged into the darkness of night. Above, infinitely high, burned the pale stars, wise and cold, aloof and indifferent, eyes of other worlds of mystery.

In those night hours something in Wade died, but his idealism, unquenchable and inexplicable, the very soul of the man, saw its justification and fulfilment in the distant future.

The gray of the dawn stole over the eastern range, and before its opaque gloom the blackness of night retreated, until valley and slope and grove were shrouded in spectral light, where all seemed unreal.

And with it the gray-gloomed giant of Wade's mind, the morbid and brooding spell, had gained its long-encroaching ascendancy. He had again found the man to whom he must tell his story. Tragic and irrevocable decree! It was his life that forced him, his crime, his remorse, his agony, his endless striving. How true had been his steps! They had led, by devious and tortuous paths, to the home of his daughter.

Wade crouched under the aspens, accepting this burden as a man being physically loaded with tremendous weights. His shoulders bent to them. His breast was sunken and labored. All his muscles were cramped. His blood flowed sluggishly. His heart beat with slow, muffled throbs in his ears.

There was a creeping cold in his veins, ice in his marrow, and death in his soul. The giant that had been shrouded in gray threw off his cloak, to stand revealed, black and terrible. And it was he who spoke to Wade, in dreadful tones, like knells. Bent Wade—man of misery—who could find no peace on earth—whose presence unknit the tranquil lives of people and poisoned their blood and marked them for doom! Wherever he wandered there followed the curse! Always this had been so. He was the harbinger of catastrophe. He who preached wisdom and claimed to be taught by the flowers, who loved life and hated injustice, who mingled with his kind, ever searching for that one who needed him, he must become the woe and the bane and curse of those he would only serve! Insupportable and pitiful fate! The fiends of the past mocked him, like wicked ghouls, voiceless and dim. The faces of the men he had killed were around him in the gray gloom, pale, drifting visages of distortion, accusing him, claiming him. Likewise, these gleams of faces were specters of his mind, a procession eternal, mournful, and silent, wending their way on and on through the regions of his thought. All were united, all drove him, all put him on the trail of catastrophe. They foreshadowed the future, they inclosed events, they lured him with his endless illusions. He was in the vortex of a vast whirlpool, not of water or of wind, but of life. Alas! he seemed indeed the very current of that whirlpool, a monstrous force, around which evil circled and lurked and conquered. Wade—who had the ill-omened croak of the raven—Wade—who bent his driven steps toward hell!

In the brilliant sunlight of the summer morning Wade bent his resistless steps down toward White Slides Ranch. The pendulum had swung. The hours were propitious. Seemingly, events that already cast their shadows waited for him. He saw Jack Belllounds going out on the fast and furious ride which had become his morning habit.

Columbine intercepted Wade. The shade of woe and tragedy in her face were the same as he had pictured there in his gloomy vigil of the night.

"My friend, I was coming to you. . . . Oh, I can bear no more!"

Her hair was disheveled, her dress disordered, the hands
she tremblingly held out bore discolored marks. Wade led
her into the seclusion of the willow trail.

"Oh, Ben! . . . He fought me—like—a beast!" she panted.

"Collie, you needn't tell me more," said Wade, gently. "Go
up to Wils. Tell him."

"But I must tell you. I can bear—no more. . . . He fought
me—hurt me—and when dad heard us—and came—Jack
lied. . . . Oh, the dog! . . . Ben, his father believed—when
Jack swore he was only mad—only trying to shake me—
for my indifference and scorn. . . . But, my God!—Jack
meant . . ."

"Collie, go up to Wils," interposed the hunter.

"I want to see Wils. I need to—I must. But I'm afraid. . .
Oh, it will make things worse!"

"Go!"

She turned away, actuated by more than her will.

"Collie!" came the call, piercingly and strangely after her.
Bewildered, startled by the wildness of that cry, she wheeled.
But Wade was gone. The shaking of the willows attested to
his hurry.

Old Belllounds braced his huge shoulders against the wall
in the attitude of a man driven to his last stand.

"Ahuh!" he rolled, sonorously. "So hyar you are again! . .
Wal, tell your worst, Hell-Bent Wade, an' let's have an end to
your croakin'."

Belllounds had fortified himself, not with convictions or
with illusions, but with the last desperate courage of a man
true to himself.

"I'll tell you . . ." began the hunter.

And the rancher threw up his hands in a mockery that was
furious, yet with outward shrinking.

"Just now, when Buster Jack fought with Collie, he meant
bad by her!"

"Aw, no! . . . He was jest rude—tryin' to be masterful. . . . An' the lass's like a wild filly. She needs a tamin'
down."

Wade stretched forth a lean and quivering hand that
seemed the symbol of presaged and tragic truth.

"Listen, Belllounds, an' I'll tell you. . . . No use tryin' to atch a rotten egg! There's no good in your son. His good ntentions he paraded for virtues, believin' himself that he'd changed. But a flip of the wind made him Buster Jack again. . . . Collie would sacrifice her life for duty to you—whom she loves as her father. Wils Moore sacrificed his honor or Collie—rather than let you learn the truth. . . . But they all me Hell-Bent Wade, an' *I* will tell you!"

The straining hulk of Belllounds crouched lower, as if to gather impetus for a leap. Both huge hands were outspread is if to ward off attack from an unseen but long-dreaded foe. The great eyes rolled. And underneath the terror and cer-ainty and tragedy of his appearance seemed to surge the resistless and rising swell of a dammed-up, terrible rage.

"I'll tell you . . ." went on the remorseless voice. "I watched your Buster Jack. I watched him gamble an' drink. I trailed him. I found the little circles an' the crooked horse tracks—made to trap Wils Moore. . . . A damned cunnin' rick! . . . Burley suspects a nigger in the wood-pile. Wils Moore knows the truth. He lied for Collie's sake an' yours. He'd have stood the trial—an' gone to jail to save Collie from what she dreaded. . . . Belllounds, your son was in the cab-n gamblin' with the rustlers when I cornered them. . . . I offered to keep Jack's secret if he'd swear to give Collie up. He swore on his knees, beggin' in her name! . . . An' he comes back to bully her, an' worse. . . . Buster Jack! . . . He's the horn in your heart, Belllounds. He's the rustler who stole your cattle! . . . Your pet son—a sneakin' thief!"

19

◉

JACK BELLLOUNDS CAME riding down the valley trail. His horse was in a lather of sweat. Both hair and blood showed on the long spurs this son of a great pioneer used in his pleasure rides. He had never loved a horse.

At a point where the trail met the brook there were thic
willow patches, with open, grassy spots between. As Bell
lounds reached this place a man stepped out of the willow
and laid hold of the bridle. The horse shied and tried t
plunge, but an iron arm held him.

"Get down, Buster," ordered the man.

It was Wade.

Belllounds had given as sharp a start as his horse. He wa
sober, though the heated red tinge of his face gave indica
tion of a recent use of the bottle. That color quickly re
ceded. Events of the last month had left traces of the hard
ening and lowering of Jack Belllounds's nature.

"Wha-at? . . . Let go that bridle!" he ejaculated.

Wade held it fast, while he gazed up into the prominer
eyes, where fear shone and struggled with intolerance an
arrogance and quickening gleams of thought.

"You an' I have somethin' to talk over," said the hunter.

Belllounds shrank from the low, cold, even voice, tha
evidently reminded him of the last time he had heard it.

"No, we haven't," he declared, quickly. He seemed t
gather assurance with his spoken thought, and conscious fea
left him. "Wade, you took advantage of me that day—whe
you made me swear things. I've changed my mind. . . . An
as for that deal with the rustlers, I've got my story. It's a
good as yours. I've been waiting for you to tell my fathe
You've got some reason for not telling him. I've a hunch it
Collie. I'm on to you, and I've got my nerve back. You ca
gamble I—"

He had grown excited when Wade interrupted him.

"Will you get off that horse?"

"No, I won't," replied Belllounds, bluntly.

With swift and powerful lunge Wade pulled Bellloun
down, sliding him shoulders first into the grass. The re
leased horse shied again and moved away. Buster Jack raise
himself upon his elbow, pale with rage and alarm. Wad
kicked him, not with any particular violence.

"Get up!" he ordered.

The kick had brought out the rage in Bellounds at the ex
pense of the amaze and alarm.

"Did you kick *me?*" he shouted.

"Buster, I was only handin' you a bunch of flowers—
me columbines, as your taste runs," replied Wade, con-
mptuously.

"I'll—I'll—" returned Buster Jack, wildly, bursting for
:pression. His hand went to his gun.

"Go ahead, Buster. Throw your gun on me. That'll save
aybe a hell of a lot of talk."

It was then Jack Belllounds's face turned livid. Compre-
:nsion had dawned upon him.

"You—you want me to fight you?" he queried, in hoarse
:cents.

"I reckon that's what I meant."

No affront, no insult, no blow could have affected Buster
.ck as that sudden knowledge.

"Why—why—you're crazy! Me fight you—a gunman,"
: stammered. "No—no. It wouldn't be fair. Not an even
eak! . . . No, I'd have no chance on earth!"

"I'll give you first shot," went on Wade, in his strange, mo-
)tonous voice.

"Bah! You're lying to me," replied Belllounds, with pale
imace. "You just want me to get a gun in my hand—then
)u'll drop me, and claim an even break."

"No. I'm square. You saw me play square with your rustler
.rd. He was a lifelong enemy of mine. An' a gun-fighter to
)ot! . . . Pull your gun an' let drive. I'll take my chances."

Buster Jack's eyes dilated. He gasped huskily. He pulled
s gun, but actually did not have strength or courage
.ough to raise it. His arm shook so that the gun rattled
;ainst his chaps.

"No nerve, hey? Not half a man! . . . Buster Jack, why
)n't you finish game? Make up for your low-down tricks.
t the last try to be worthy of your dad. In his day he was a
:al man. . . . Let him have the consolation that you faced
:ll-Bent Wade an' died in your boots!"

"I—can't—fight you!" panted Belllounds. "I know now! . . .
saw you throw a gun! It wouldn't be fair!"

"But I'll make you fight me," returned Wade, in steely
nes. "I'm givin' you a chance to dig up a little manhood.
skin' you to meet me man to man! Handin' you a little the

best of it to make the odds even! . . . Once more, will you b
game?"

"Wade, I'll not fight—I'm going—" replied Belllounds, an
he moved as if to turn.

"Halt! . . ." Wade leaped at the white Belllounds. "If yo
run I'll break a leg for you—an' then I'll beat your miserabl
brains out! . . . Have you no sense? Can't you recogniz
what's comin'? . . . *I'm goin' to kill you, Buster Jack!*"

"My God!" whispered the other, understanding fully at last

"Here's where you pay for your dirty work. The time come
to every man. You've a choice, not to live—for you'll neve
get away from Hell-Bent Wade—but to rise above yourse!
at last."

"But what for? Why do you want to kill me? I neve
harmed you."

"Columbine is my daughter!" replied the hunter.

"Ah!" breathed Belllounds.

"She loves Wils Moore, who's as white a man as you ar
black."

Across the pallid, convulsed face of Belllounds spread
slow, dull crimson.

"Aha, Buster Jack! I struck home there," flashed Wade, hi
voice rising. "That gives your eyes the ugly look . . . I hat
them lyin', bulgin' eyes of yours. An' when my time come
to shoot I'm goin' to put them both out."

"By Heaven! Wade, you'll have to kill me if you eve
expect that club-foot Moore to get Collie!"

"He'll get her," replied Wade, triumphantly. "Collie's wit
him now. I sent her. I told her to tell Wils how you tried
force her—"

Belllounds began to shake all over. A torture of jealou
hate and deadly terror convulsed him.

"Buster, did you ever think you'd get her kisses—as Wils'
gettin' right now?" queried the hunter. "Good Lord! the cor
ceit of some men! . . . Why, you poor, weak-minded, coward
ly pet of a blinded old man—you conceited ass—you selfis
an' spoiled boy! . . . Collie never had any use for you. A
now she hates you."

"It was you who made her!" yelled Belllounds, foamin
at the mouth.

"Sure," went on the deliberate voice, ringing with scorn. "An' only a little while ago she called you a dog. . . . I reckon she meant a different kind of a dog than the hounds over there. For to say they were like you would be an insult to them. . . . Sure she hates you, an' I'll gamble right now she's got her arms around Wils's neck!"

"—— —— ——!" hissed Belllounds.

"Well, you've got a gun in your hand," went on the taunting voice. "Ahuh! . . . Have it your way. I'm warmin' up now, an' I'd like to tell you . . ."

"Shut up!" interrupted the other, frantically. The blood in him was rising to a fever heat. But fear still clamped him. He could not raise the gun and he seemed in agony.

"Your father knows you're a thief," declared Wade, with remorseless, deliberate intent. "I told him how I watched you—trailed you—an' learned the plot you hatched against Wils Moore. . . . Buster Jack busted himself at last, stealin' his own father's cattle. . . . I've seen some ragin' men in my day, but Old Bill had them beaten. You've disgraced him— broken his heart—embittered the end of his life. . . . An' he'd mean for you what I mean now!"

"He'd never—harm me!" gasped Buster Jack, shuddering.

"He'd kill you—you white-livered pup!" cried Wade, with terrible force. "Kill you before he'd let you go to worse dishonor! . . . An' I'm goin' to save him stainin' his hands."

"I'll kill *you!*" burst out Belllounds, ending in a shriek. But this was not the temper that always produced heedless action in him. It was hate. He could not raise the gun. His intelligence still dominated his will. Yet fury had mitigated his terror.

"You'll be doin' me a service, Buster. . . . But you're mighty slow at startin'. I reckon I'll have to play my last trump to make you fight. Oh, by God! I can tell you! . . . Belllounds, there're dead men callin' me now. Callin' me not to murder you in cold blood! I killed one man once—a man who wouldn't fight—an innocent man! I killed him with my bare hands, an' if I tell you my story—an' how I killed him—an' that I'll do the same for you. . . . You'll save me that, Buster. No man with a gun in his hands could face what he knew. . . . But save me more. Save me the tellin'!"

"No! No! I won't listen!"

"Maybe I won't have to," replied Wade, mournfully. He
paused, breathing heavily. The sober calm was gone.

Belllounds lowered the half-raised gun, instantly answering
to the strange break in Wade's strained dominance.

"Don't tell me—any more! I'll not listen! . . . I won't fight!
Wade, you're crazy! Let me off an' I swear—"

"Buster, I told Collie you were three years in jail!" suddenly interrupted Wade.

A mortal blow dealt Belllounds would not have caused
such a shock of amaze, of torture The secret of the punish-
ment meted out to him by his father! The hideous thing
which, instead of reforming, had ruined him! All of hell was
expressed in his burning eyes.

"Ahuh! . . . I've known it long!" cried Wade, tragically.
"Buster Jack, you're the man who must hear my story. . . .
I'll tell you. . . ."

In the aspen grove up the slope of Sage Valley Columbine
and Wilson were sitting on a log. Whatever had been their
discourse, it had left Moore with head bowed in his hands, and
with Columbine staring with sad eyes that did not see what
they looked at. Columbine's mind then seemed a dull blank.
Suddenly she started.

"Wils!" she cried. "Did you hear—anything?"

"No," he replied, wearily raising his head.

"I thought I heard a shot," said Columbine. "It—it sort of
made me jump. I'm nervous."

Scarcely had she finished speaking when two clear, deep
detonations rang out. Gun-shots!

"There! . . . Oh, Wils! Did you hear?"

"Hear!" whispered Moore. He grew singularly white. "Yes
—yes! . . . Collie—"

"Wils," she interrupted, wildly, as she began to shake. "Just
a little bit ago—I saw Jack riding down the trail!"

"Collie! . . . Those two shots came from Wade's gun! I'd
know it among a thousand! . . . Are you sure you heard a
shot before?"

"Oh, something dreadful has happened! Yes, I'm sure. Perfectly sure. A shot not so loud or heavy."

"My God!" exclaimed Moore, staring aghast at Columbine. "Maybe that's what Wade meant. I never saw through him."

"Tell me. Oh, I don't understand!" wailed Columbine, wringing her hands.

Moore did not explain what he meant. For a crippled man, he made quick time in getting to his horse and mounting.

"Collie, I'll ride down there. I'm afraid something has happened. . . . I never understood him! . . . I forgot he was Hell-Bent Wade! If there's been a—a fight or any trouble—I'll ride back and meet you."

Then he rode down the trail.

Columbine had come without her horse, and she started homeward on foot. Her steps dragged. She knew something dreadful had happened. Her heart beat slowly and painfully; there was an oppression upon her breast; her brain whirled with contending tides of thought. She remembered Wade's face. How blind she had been! It exhausted her to walk, though she went so slowly. There seemed to be a chill and a darkening in the atmosphere, and unreality in the familiar slopes and groves, a strangeness and shadow upon White Slides Valley.

Moore did not return to meet her. His white horse grazed in the pasture opposite the first clump of willows, where Sage Valley merged into the larger valley. Then she saw other horses, among them Lem Billings's bay mustang. Columbine faltered on, when suddenly she recognized the horse Jack had ridden—a sorrel, spent and foam-covered, standing saddled, with bridle down and riderless—then certainty of something awful clamped her with horror. Men's husky voices reached her throbbing ears. Some one was running. Footsteps thudded and died away. Then she saw Lem Billings come out of the willows, look her way, and hurry toward her. His awkward, cowboy gait seemed too slow for his earnestness. Columbine felt the piercing gaze of his eyes as her own became dim.

"Miss Collie, thar's been—turrible fight!" he panted.

"Oh, Lem! . . . I know. It was Ben—and Jack," she cried.

"Shore. Your hunch's correct. An' it couldn't be wuss!"

Columbine tried to see his face, the meaning that must have accompanied his hoarse voice; but she seemed going blind.

"Then—then—" she whispered, reaching out for Lem.

"Hyar, Miss Collie," he said, in great concern, as he took kind and gentle hold of her. "Reckon you'd better wait. Le me take you home."

"Yes. But tell—tell me first," she cried, frantically. She could not bear suspense, and she felt her senses slipping away from her.

"My Gawd! who'd ever have thought such hell would come to White Slides!" exclaimed Lem, with strong emotion. "Miss Collie, I'm powerful sorry fer you. But mebbe it's best so. . . They're both dead! . . . Wade just died with his head on Wils' lap. But Jack never knowed what hit him. He was shot plumb center—both his eyes shot out! . . . Wade was shot low down. . . . Montana an' me agreed thet Jack throwed his gun first an' Wade killed him after bein' mortal shot himself."

Late that afternoon, as Columbine lay upon her bed, the strange stillness of the house was disturbed by a heavy tread It passed out of the living-room and came down the porch toward her door. Then followed a knock.

"Dad!" she called, swiftly rising.

Belllounds entered, leaving the door ajar. The sunligh streamed in.

"Wal, Collie, I see you're bracin' up," he said.

"Oh yes, dad, I'm—I'm all right," she replied, eager to hel or comfort him.

The old rancher seemed different from the man of th past months. The pallor of a great shock, the havoc of spen passion, the agony of terrible hours, showed in his face. Bu Old Bill Belllounds had come into his own again—back t the calm, iron pioneer who had lived all events, over whon storm of years had broken, whose great spirit had accepte this crowning catastrophe as it had all the others, who sav his own life clearly, now that its bitterest lesson was told.

"Are you strong enough to bear another shock, my lass an' bear it now—so to make an end—so tomorrer we ca begin anew?" he asked, with the voice she had not heard fo many a day. It was the voice that told of consideration fo her.

"Yes, dad," she replied, going to him.

"Wal, come with me. I want you to see Wade."

He led her out upon the porch, and thence into the living-room, and from there into the room where lay the two dead men, one on each side. Blankets covered the prone, quiet forms.

Columbine had meant to beg to see Wade once before he was laid away forever. She dreaded the ordeal, yet strangely longed for it. And here she was self-contained, ready for some nameless shock and uplift, which she divined was coming as she had divined the change in Belllounds.

Then he stripped back the blanket, disclosing Wade's face. Columbine thrilled to the core of her heart. Death was there, white and cold and merciless, but as it had released the tragic soul, the instant of deliverance had been stamped on the rugged, cadaverous visage, by a beautiful light; not of peace, nor of joy, nor of grief, but of hope! Hope had been the last emotion of Hell-Bent Wade.

"Collie, listen," said the old rancher, in deep and trembling tones. "When a man's dead, what he's been comes to us with startlin' truth. Wade was the whitest man I ever knew. He had a queer idee—a twist in his mind—an' it was thet his steps were bent toward hell. He imagined thet everywhere he traveled there he fetched hell. But he was wrong. His own trouble led him to the trouble of others. He saw through life. An' he was as big in his hope fer the good as he was terrible in his dealin' with the bad. I never saw his like. . . . He loved you, Collie, better than you ever knew. Better than Jack, or Wils, or me! You know what the Bible says about him who gives his life fer his friend. Wal, Wade was my friend, an' Jack's, only we never could see! . . . An' he was Wils's friend. An' to you he must have been more than words can tell. . . . We all know what child's play it would have been fer Wade to kill Jack without bein' hurt himself. But he wouldn't do it. So he spared me an' Jack, an' I reckon himself. Somehow he made Jack fight an' die like a man. God only knows how he did that. But it saved me from—from hell—an' you an' Wils from misery. . . . Wade could have taken you from me an' Jack. He had only to tell you his secret, an' he wouldn't. He saw how you loved me, as if you were my real child. . . . But, Collie, lass, it was *he* who was your father!"

With bursting heart Columbine fell upon her knees besid
that cold, still form.

Belllounds softly left the room and closed the door behind
him.

20

◉

NATURE WAS PRODIGAL with her colors that autumn. The
frosts came late, so that the leaves did not gradually change
their green. One day, as if by magic, there was gold among
the green, and in another there was purple and red. Then
the hilltops blazed with their crowns of aspen groves; and
the slopes of sage shone mellow gray in the sunlight; and the
vines on the stone fences straggled away in lines of bronze
and the patches of ferns under the cliffs faded fast; and the
great rock slides and black-timbered reaches stood out in
their somber shades.

Columbines bloomed in all the dells among the spruces
beautiful stalks with heavy blossoms, the sweetest and palest
of blue-white flowers. Motionless they lifted their faces to
the light. Out in the aspen groves, where the grass was turning
gold, the columbines blew gracefully in the wind, nodding
and swaying. The most exquisite and finest of these columbines hid in the shaded nooks, star-sweet in the silent gloom
of the woods.

Wade's last few whispered words to Moore had been in
terpreted that the hunter desired to be buried among the
columbines in the aspen grove on the slope above Sage Valley
Here, then, had been made his grave.

One day Belllounds sent Columbine to fetch Moore down
to White Slides. It was a warm, Indian-summer afternoon
and the old rancher sat out on the porch in his shirt-sleeves

His hair was white now, but no other change was visible in him. No restraint attended his greeting to the cowboy.

"Wils, I reckon I'd be glad if you'd take your old job as foreman of White Slides," he said.

"Are you asking me?" queried Moore, eagerly.

"Wal, I reckon so."

"Yes, I'll come," replied the cowboy.

"What'll your dad say?"

"I don't know. That worries me. He's coming to visit me. I heard from him again lately, and he means to take stage for Kremmling soon."

"Wal, that's fine. I'll be glad to see him. . . . Wils, you're goin' to be a big cattleman before you know it. Hey, Collie?"

"If you say so, dad, it'll come true," replied Columbine, with her hand on his shoulder.

"Wils, you'll be runnin' White Slides Ranch before long, unless Collie runs you. Haw! Haw!"

Collie could not reply to this startling announcement from the old rancher, and Moore appeared distressed with embarrassment.

"Wal, I reckon you young folks had better ride down to Kremmlin' an' get married."

This kindly, matter-of-fact suggestion completely stunned the cowboy, and all Columbine could do was to gaze at the rancher.

"Say, I hope I ain't intrudin' my wishes on a young couple that's got over dyin' fer each other," dryly continued Belllounds, with his huge smile.

"Dad!" cried Columbine, and then she threw her arms around him and buried her head on his shoulder.

"Wal, wal, I reckon that answers that," he said, holding her close. "Moore, she's yours, with my blessin' an' all I have. . . . An' you must understand I'm glad things have worked out to your good an' to Collie's happiness. . . . Life's not over fer me yet. But I reckon the storms are past, thank God! . . . We learn as we live. I'd hold it onworthy not to look forward an' to hope. I'm wantin' peace an' quiet now, with grandchildren around me in my old age. . . . So ride along to Kremmlin' an' hurry home."

The evening of the day Columbine came home to White Slides the bride of Wilson Moore she slipped away from the simple festivities in her honor and climbed to the aspen grove on the hill to spend a little while beside the grave of her father.

The afterglow of sunset burned dull gold and rose in the western sky, rendering glorious the veil of purple over the ranges. Down in the lowlands twilight had come, softly gray. The owls were hooting; a coyote barked; from far away floated the mourn of a wolf.

Under the aspens it was silent and lonely and sad. The leaves quivered without any sound of rustling. Columbine's heart was full of a happiness that she longed to express somehow, there beside this lonely grave. It was what she owed the strange man who slept here in the shadows. Grief abided with her, and always there would be an eternal remorse and regret. Yet she had loved him. She had been his, all unconsciously. His life had been terrible, but it had been great. As the hours of quiet thinking had multiplied, Columbine had grown in her divination of Wade's meaning. His had been the spirit of man lighting the dark places; his had been the ruthless hand against all evil, terrible to destroy.

Her father! After all, how closely was she linked to the past! How closely protected, even in the hours of most helpless despair! Thus she understood him. Love was the food of life, and hope was its spirituality, and beauty was its reward to the seeing eye. Wade had lived these great virtues, even while he had earned a tragic name.

"I will live them. I will have faith and hope and love, for I am his daughter," she said. A faint, cool breeze strayed through the aspens, rustling the leaves whisperingly, and the slender columbines, gleaming pale in the twilight, lifted their sweet faces.

MAX BRAND

THE MASTER OF TWO-FISTED WESTERN ADVENTURE

____ **Destry Rides Again** 83660/$2.50

____ **Gunman's Reckoning** 61215/$2.75

____ **Hunted Riders** 41562/$2.50

____ **Iron Trail** 61849/$2.75

____ **The Jackson Trail** 63168/$2.75

____ **The Longhorn Feud** 41559/$2.50

____ **The Man From Mustang** 62725/$2.50

____ **Rawhide Justice** 41589/$2.50

____ **Singing Guns** 41571/$2.25

____ **Stolen Stallion** 41581/$2.50

____ **Trouble Kid** 41582/$2.50

POCKET BOOKS, Department MAX
1230 Avenue of the Americas, New York, N.Y. 10020

Please send me the copies I have checked above. I am enclosing $_____
(Please add 75¢ to cover postage and handling. N.Y.S. and N.Y.C. residents please add appropriate sales tax. Send check or money order—no cash, stamps or CODs, please. Allow six weeks for delivery.) For purchases over $10.00, you may use VISA: card number, expiration date and customer signature must be included.

NAME_____

ADDRESS_____

CITY_____ STATE/ZIP_____

933